RILEY PAIGE
MYSTERY BUNDLE:

ONCE GONE (#1) AND ONCE TAKEN (#2)

BLAKE PIERCE

ONCE GONE

(A RILEY PAIGE MYSTERY—BOOK 1)

BLAKE PIERCE

ISBN: 978-1-64029-335-9

BOOKS BY BLAKE PIERCE

RILEY PAIGE MYSTERY SERIES
ONCE GONE (Book #1)
ONCE TAKEN (Book #2)
ONCE CRAVED (Book #3)
ONCE LURED (Book #4)
ONCE HUNTED (Book #5)
ONCE PINED (Book #6)
ONCE FORSAKEN (Book #7)
ONCE COLD (Book #8)
ONCE STALKED (Book #9)
ONCE LOST (Book #10)
ONCE BURIED (Book #11)
ONCE BOUND (Book #12)

MACKENZIE WHITE MYSTERY SERIES
BEFORE HE KILLS (Book #1)
BEFORE HE SEES (Book #2)
BEFORE HE COVETS (Book #3)
BEFORE HE TAKES (Book #4)
BEFORE HE NEEDS (Book #5)
BEFORE HE FEELS (Book #6)
BEFORE HE SINS (Book #7)
BEFORE HE HUNTS (Book #8)

AVERY BLACK MYSTERY SERIES
CAUSE TO KILL (Book #1)
CAUSE TO RUN (Book #2)
CAUSE TO HIDE (Book #3)
CAUSE TO FEAR (Book #4)
CAUSE TO SAVE (Book #5)
CAUSE TO DREAD (Book #6)

KERI LOCKE MYSTERY SERIES
A TRACE OF DEATH (Book #1)
A TRACE OF MUDER (Book #2)
A TRACE OF VICE (Book #3)
A TRACE OF CRIME (Book #4)
A TRACE OF HOPE (Book #5)

PROLOGUE

A new spasm of pain jolted Reba's head upright. She yanked against the ropes that bound her body, tied around her stomach to a vertical length of pipe that had been bolted to the floor and ceiling in the middle of the small room. Her wrists were tied in front, and her ankles were bound.

She realized she'd been dozing, and she was immediately awash in fear. She knew by now that the man was going to kill her. Little by little, wound by wound. It wasn't her death he was after, and it wasn't sex either. He only wanted her pain.

I've got to stay awake, she thought. *I've got to get out of here. If I fall asleep again, I will die.*

Despite the heat in the room, her naked body felt chilled with sweat. She looked down, writhing, and saw her feet were bare against the hardwood floor. The floor around them was caked with patches of dry blood, sure signs that she wasn't the first person to have been tied here. Her panic deepened.

He had gone somewhere. The room's single door was shut tight, but he would come back. He always did. And then he'd do whatever he could think of to make her scream. The windows were boarded, and she had no idea if it was day or night, the only light from the glare of a bare bulb hanging from the ceiling. Wherever this place was, it seemed that no one else could hear her screams.

She wondered if this room had once been a little girl's bedroom; it was, grotesquely, pink, with curly-cues and fairytale motifs everywhere. Someone—she guessed her captor—had long since trashed the place, breaking and overturning stools and chairs and end tables. The floor was scattered with the dismembered limbs and torsos of children's dolls. Little wigs—doll's wigs, Reba guessed—were nailed like scalps on the walls, most of them elaborately braided, all of them in unnatural, toy-like colors. A battered pink vanity table stood upright next to a wall, its heart-shaped mirror shattered into little pieces. The only other piece of furniture intact was a narrow, single bed with a torn, pink canopy. Her captor sometimes rested there.

The man watched her with dark beady eyes, through his black ski mask. At first she had taken heart in the fact that he always wore that mask. If he didn't want her to see his face, didn't that mean that he didn't plan to kill her, that he might let her go?

But she soon caught on that the mask served a different purpose. She could tell that the face behind it had a receded chin

4

and a sloped forehead, and she was sure the man's features were weak and homely. Although he was strong, he was shorter than she, and probably insecure about it. He wore the mask, she guessed, to seem more terrifying.

She'd given up trying to talk him out of hurting her. At first she had thought she could. She knew, after all, that she was pretty. *Or at least I used to be,* she thought sadly.

Sweat and tears mixed on her bruised face, and she could feel the blood matted into her long blond hair. Her eyes stung: he had made her put in contact lenses, and they made it harder to see.

God knows what I look like now.

She let her head drop.

Die now, she begged herself.

It ought to be easy enough to do. She was certain that others had died here before.

But she couldn't. Just thinking about it made her heart pound harder, her breath heave, straining the rope around her belly. Slowly, as she knew she was facing an imminent death, a new feeling began to arise within her. It wasn't panic or fear this time. It wasn't despair. It was something else.

What do I feel?

Then she realized. It was *rage*. Not against her captor. She'd long since exhausted her rage toward him.

It's me, she thought. *I am doing what he wants. When I scream and cry and sob and plead, I'm doing what he wants.*

Whenever she sipped that cold bland broth he'd feed her through a straw, she was doing what he wanted. Whenever she blubbered pathetically that she was a mother with two children who needed her, she was delighting him to no end.

Her mind cleared with new resolve as she finally stopped writhing. Maybe she needed to try a different tack. She had been struggling so hard against the ropes all these days. Maybe that was the wrong approach. They were like those little bamboo toys—the Chinese finger traps, where you'd put your fingers in each end of the tube, and the harder you pulled, the more stuck your fingers became. Maybe the trick was to relax, deliberately and completely. Maybe that was the way out.

Muscle by muscle, she let her body go slack, feeling every sore, every bruise where her flesh touched the ropes. And slowly, she became aware of where the rope's tension lay.

At last, she found what she needed. There was just a little looseness around her right ankle. But it wouldn't do to tug, at least not yet. No, she had to keep her muscles limber. She wiggled her ankle gently, gently, then more aggressively as the rope loosened.

Finally, to her joy and surprise, her heel popped loose, and she withdrew the whole right foot.

She immediately scanned the floor. Only a foot away, amid the scattered doll parts, lay his hunting knife. He always laughed as he left it there, tantalizingly nearby. The blade, encrusted with blood, twinkled tauntingly in the light.

She swung her free foot toward the knife. It swung high and missed.

She let her body slacken again. She slid downward along the post just a few inches and strained with her foot until the knife was within reach. She clutched the filthy blade between her toes, scraped it across the floor, and lifted it carefully with her foot until its handle rested in the palm of her hand. She clutched the handle tight with numb fingers and twisted it around, slowly sawing at the rope that held her wrists. Time seemed to stop, as she held her breath, hoping, praying she didn't drop it. That he didn't come in.

Finally she heard a snap, and to her shock, her hands were loose. Immediately, heart pounding, she cut the rope around her waist.

Free. She could hardly believe it.

For a moment all she could do was crouch there, hands and feet tingling with the return of full circulation. She poked at the lenses over her eyes, resisting the urge to claw them out. She carefully slid them to one side, pinched them, and pulled them out. Her eyes hurt terribly, and it was a relief to have them gone. As she looked at the two plastic disks lying in the palm of her hand, their color sickened her. The lenses were bright blue, unnatural. She threw them aside.

Heart slamming, Reba pulled herself up and quickly limped to the door. She took hold of the knob but didn't turn it.

What if he's out there?

She had no choice.

Reba turned the knob and tugged at the door, which opened noiselessly. She looked down a long empty hallway, lit only by an arched opening on the right. She crept along, naked, barefoot, and silent, and saw that the arch opened into a dimly lit room. She stopped and stared. It was a simple dining room, with a table and chairs, all completely ordinary, as if a family might soon come home to dinner. Old lace curtains hung over the windows.

A new horror rose up in her throat. The very ordinariness of the place was disturbing in a way that a dungeon wouldn't have been. Through the curtains she could see that it was dark outside.

Her spirits lifted at the thought that darkness would make it easier to slip away.

She turned back to the hallway. It ended in a door—a door that simply had to lead outdoors. She limped and squeezed the cold brass latch. The door swung heavily toward her to reveal the night outside.

She saw a small porch, a yard beyond it. The nighttime sky was moonless and starlit. There was no other light anywhere—no sign of nearby houses. She stepped slowly out onto the porch and down into the yard, which was dry and bare of grass. Cool fresh air flooded her aching lungs.

Mixed with her panic, she felt elated. The joy of freedom.

Reba took her first step, preparing to run—when suddenly she felt the hard grip of a hand on her wrist.

Then came the familiar, ugly laugh.

The last thing she felt was a hard object—maybe metal—impacting her head, and then she was spinning into the very depths of blackness.

CHAPTER ONE

At least the stench hasn't kicked in, Special Agent Bill Jeffreys thought.

Still leaning over the body, he couldn't help but detect the first traces of it. It mingled with the fresh scent of pine and the clean mist rising from the creek—a body smell that he ought to have been long since used to. But he never was.

The woman's naked body had been carefully arranged on a large boulder at the edge of the creek. She was sitting up, leaning against another boulder, legs straight and splayed, hands at her sides. An odd crook in the right arm, he could see, suggested a broken bone. The wavy hair was obviously a wig, mangy, with clashing hues of blond. A pink smile was lipsticked over her mouth.

The murder weapon was still tight around her neck; she'd been strangled with a pink ribbon. An artificial red rose lay on the rock in front of her, at her feet.

Bill gently tried to lift the left hand. It didn't budge.

"She's still in rigor mortis," Bill told Agent Spelbren, crouching on the other side of the body. "Hasn't been dead more than twenty-four hours."

"What's with her eyes?" Spelbren asked.

"Stitched wide open with black thread," he answered, without bothering to look closely.

Spelbren stared at him in disbelief.

"Check for yourself," Bill said.

Spelbren peered at the eyes.

"Jesus," he murmured quietly. Bill noticed that he didn't recoil with disgust. Bill appreciated that. He'd worked with other field agents—some of them even seasoned veterans like Spelbren—who would be puking their guts up by now.

Bill had never worked with him before. Spelbren had been called in for this case from a Virginia field office. It had been Spelbren's idea to bring in somebody from the Behavioral Analysis Unit in Quantico. That was why Bill was here.

Smart move, Bill thought.

Bill could see that Spelbren was younger than him by a few years, but even so, he had a weathered, lived-in look that he rather liked.

"She's wearing contacts," Spelbren noted.

Bill took a closer look. He was right. An eerie, artificial blue that made him look away. It was cool here down by the creek late in the morning, but even so, the eyes were flattening in their sockets. It was going to be tough to nail down the exact time of death. All Bill felt certain of was that the body had been brought here sometime during the night and carefully posed.

He heard a nearby voice.

"Fucking Feds."

Bill glanced up at the three local cops, standing a few yards away. They were whispering inaudibly now, so Bill knew that he was supposed to hear those two choice words. They were from nearby Yarnell, and they clearly weren't happy to have the FBI show up. They thought they could handle this on their own.

The head ranger of Mosby State Park had thought differently. He wasn't used to anything worse than vandalism, litter, and illegal fishing and hunting, and he knew the locals from Yarnell weren't capable of dealing with this.

Bill had made the hundred-plus-mile trip by helicopter, so he could get here before the body was moved. The pilot had followed the coordinates to a patch of meadow on a nearby hilltop, where the ranger and Spelbren had met him. The ranger had driven them a few miles down a dirt road, and when they'd pulled over, Bill could glimpse the murder scene from the road. It was just a short way downhill from the creek.

The cops standing impatiently nearby had already gone over the scene. Bill knew exactly what they were thinking. They wanted to crack this case on their own; a pair of FBI agents was the last thing they wanted to see.

Sorry, you rednecks, Bill thought, *but you're out of your depth here.*

"The sheriff thinks this is trafficking," Spelbren said. "He's wrong."

"Why do you say that?" Bill asked. He knew the answer himself, but he wanted to get an idea of how Spelbren's mind worked.

"She's in her thirties, not all that young," Spelbren said. "Stretch marks, so she's had at least one child. Not the type that usually gets trafficked."

"You're right," Bill said.

"But what about the wig?"

Bill shook his head.

"Her head's been shaved," he replied, "so whatever the wig

9

was for, it wasn't to change her hair color."

"And the rose?" Spelbren asked. "A message?"

Bill examined it.

"Cheap fabric flower," he replied. "The kind you'd find in any low-price store. We'll trace it, but we won't find out anything."

Spelbren looked him over, clearly impressed.

Bill doubted that anything they'd found would do much good. The murderer was too purposeful, too methodical. This whole scene had been laid out with a certain sick style that set him on edge.

He saw the local cops itching to come closer, to wrap this. Photos had been taken, and the body would be removed any time now.

Bill stood and sighed, feeling the stiffness in his legs. His forty years were starting to slow him down, at least a little.

"She's been tortured," he observed, exhaling sadly. "Look at all the cuts. Some are starting to close up." He shook his head grimly. "Someone worked her over for days before doing her in with that ribbon."

Spelbren sighed.

"The perp was pissed off about something," Spelbren said.

"Hey, when are we gonna wrap up here?" one of the cops called out.

Bill looked in their direction and saw them shuffling their feet. Two of them were grumbling quietly. Bill knew the work was already done here, but he didn't say so. He preferred keeping those bozos waiting and wondering.

He turned around slowly and took in the scene. It was a thick wooded area, all pines and cedars and lots of undergrowth, with the creek burbling along its serene and bucolic way toward the nearest river. Even now, in midsummer, it wasn't going to get very hot here today, so the body wasn't going to putrefy badly right away. Even so, it would be best to get it out of here and ship it off to Quantico. Examiners there would want to pick it apart while it was still reasonably fresh. The coroner's wagon was pulled up on the dirt road behind the cop car, waiting.

The road was nothing more than parallel tire tracks through the woods. The killer had almost certainly driven here along it. He had carried the body the short distance along a narrow path to this spot, arranged it, and left. He wouldn't have stayed long. Even though the area looked out of the way, rangers patrolled through here regularly and private cars weren't supposed to be on this road. He had wanted the body to be found. He was proud of his work.

10

And it *had* been found by a couple of early-morning horseback riders. Tourists on rented horses, the ranger had told Bill. They were vacationers from Arlington, staying at a fake Western ranch just outside of Yarnell. The ranger had said that they were a little hysterical now. They'd been told not to leave town, and Bill planned to talk to them later.

There seemed to be absolutely nothing out of place in the area around the body. The guy had been very careful. He'd dragged something behind him when he'd returned from the creek—a shovel, maybe—to obscure his own footprints. No scraps of anything left intentionally or accidentally. Any tire prints on the road had likely been obliterated by the cop car and coroner's wagon.

Bill sighed to himself.

Damn it, he thought. *Where's Riley when I need her?*

His longtime partner and best friend was on involuntary leave, recovering from the trauma of their last case. Yes, that had been a nasty one. She needed the time off, and the truth be told, she might not ever come back.

But he really needed her now. She was a lot smarter than Bill, and he didn't mind admitting it. He loved watching her mind at work. He pictured her picking away at this scene, detail by minuscule detail. By now she'd be teasing him for all the painfully glaring clues that had been staring him in the face.

What would Riley see here that Bill didn't?

He felt stumped, and he didn't like the feeling. But there wasn't anything more he could do about it now.

"Okay, guys," Bill called out to the cops. "Take the body away."

The cops laughed and gave each other high-fives.

"Do you think he'll do it again?" Spelbren asked.

"I'm sure of it," Bill said.

"How do you know?"

Bill took a long deep breath.

"Because I've seen his work before."

CHAPTER TWO

"It got worse for her every day," Sam Flores said, bringing up another horrific image on the huge multimedia display looming above the conference table. "Right up to when he finished her off."

Bill had guessed as much, but he hated to be right.

The Bureau had flown the body to the BAU in Quantico, forensics technicians had taken photos, and the lab had started all the tests. Flores, a lab technician with black-rimmed glasses, ran the grisly slide show, and the gigantic screens were a forbidding presence in the BAU conference room.

"How long was she dead before the body was found?" Bill asked.

"Not long," he replied. "Maybe early evening before."

Beside Bill sat Spelbren, who had flown into Quantico with him after they'd left Yarnell. At the head of the table sat Special Agent Brent Meredith, the team chief. Meredith cut a daunting presence with his broad frame, his black, angular features, and his no-nonsense face. Not that Bill was intimidated by him—far from it. He liked to think that they had a lot in common. They were both seasoned veterans, and had both seen it all.

Flores flashed a series of close-ups of the victim's wounds.

"The wounds on the left were inflicted early on," he said. "Those on the right are more recent, some inflicted hours or even minutes before he strangled her with the ribbon. He seems to have gotten progressively more violent during the week or so that he held her captive. Breaking her arm might have been the last thing he did while she was still alive."

"The wounds look like the work of one perpetrator to me," Meredith observed. "Judging from the mounting level of aggression, probably male. What else have you got?"

"From the light stubble on her scalp, we're guessing her head was shaved two days before she was killed," Flores continued. "The wig was stitched together with pieces of other wigs, all cheap. The contact lenses were probably mail order. And one more thing," he said, looking around at the faces, hesitant. "He covered her with Vaseline."

Bill could feel the tension in the room thicken.

"Vaseline?" he asked.

Flores nodded.

"Why?" Spelbren asked.

Flores shrugged.

"That's your job," he replied.

Bill thought about the two tourists he'd interviewed yesterday. They had been no help at all, torn between morbid curiosity and the edge of panic at what they had seen. They were eager to get back home to Arlington and there hadn't been any reason to detain them. They had been interviewed by every officer on hand. And they'd been duly cautioned to say nothing about what they'd seen.

Meredith exhaled and laid both palms on the table.

"Good work, Flores," Meredith said.

Flores looked grateful for the praise—and maybe a bit surprised. Brent Meredith wasn't given to making compliments.

"Now Agent Jeffreys," Meredith turned to him, "brief us on how this relates to your old case."

Bill took a deep breath and leaned back in his chair.

"A little over six months ago," he began, "on December sixteenth, actually—the body of Eileen Rogers was found on a farm near Daggett. I got called in to investigate, along with my partner, Riley Paige. The weather was extremely cold, and the body was frozen solid. It was hard to tell how long it had been left there, and the time of death was never exactly determined. Flores, show them."

Flores turned back to the slide show. The screen split and alongside the images on the screen, a new series of images appeared. The two victims were displayed side by side. Bill gasped. It was amazing. Aside from the frozen flesh of the one body, the corpses were in almost the same condition, the wounds nearly identical. Both women had their eyes stitched open in the same, hideous manner.

Bill sighed, the images bringing it all back. No matter how many years he was on the force, seeing each victim pained him.

"Rogers's body was found seated upright against a tree," Bill continued, his voice more grim. "Not quite as carefully posed as the one at Mosby Park. No contact lenses or Vaseline, but most of the other details are the same. Rogers's hair was chopped short, not shaved, but there was a similar patched-together wig. She was also strangled with a pink ribbon, and a fake rose was found in front of her."

Bill paused for a moment. He hated what he had to say next.

"Paige and I couldn't crack the case."

Spelbren turned to him.

"What was the problem?" he asked.

"What *wasn't* the problem?" Bill countered, unnecessarily defensive. "We couldn't get a single break. We had no witnesses; the victim's family couldn't give us any useful information; Rogers had no enemies, no ex-husband, no angry boyfriend. There wasn't a single good reason for her to be targeted and killed. The case went cold immediately."

Bill fell silent. Dark thoughts flooded his brain.

"Don't," Meredith said in an uncharacteristically gentle tone. "It's not your fault. You couldn't have stopped the new killing."

Bill appreciated the kindness, but he felt guilty as hell. Why couldn't he have cracked it before? Why couldn't Riley? There were very few times in his career he had been so stumped.

At that moment, Meredith's phone buzzed, and the chief took the call.

Almost the first thing he said was, "Shit."

He repeated it several times. Then he said, "You're positive it's her?" He paused. "Was there any contact for ransom?"

He stood from his chair and stepped outside the conference room, leaving the other three men sitting in perplexed silence. After a few minutes, he came back. He looked older.

"Gentlemen, we're now in crisis mode," he announced. "We just got a positive ID on yesterday's victim. Her name was Reba Frye."

Bill gasped as if he'd been punched in the stomach; he could see Spelbren's shock, too. But Flores looked confused.

"Should I know who that is?" Flores asked.

"Maiden name's Newbrough," Meredith explained. "The daughter of State Senator Mitch Newbrough—probably Virginia's next governor."

Flores exhaled.

"I hadn't heard that she'd gone missing," Spelbren said.

"It wasn't officially reported," Meredith said. "Her father's already been contacted. And *of course* he thinks it's political, or personal, or both. Never mind that the same thing happened to another victim six months ago."

Meredith shook his head.

"The Senator's leaning hard on this," he added. "An avalanche of press is about to hit. He'll make sure of it, to keep our feet to the fire."

Bill's heart sank. He hated feeling as though he were over his head. But that's exactly how he felt right now.

A somber silence fell over the room.

Finally, Bill cleared his throat.

"We're going to need help," he said.

Meredith turned to him, and Bill met his hardened gaze. Suddenly, Meredith's face knotted up with worry and disapproval. He clearly knew what Bill was thinking.

"She's not ready," Meredith answered, clearly knowing that Bill meant to bring her in.

Bill sighed.

"Sir," he replied, "she knows the case better than anyone. And there's no one smarter."

After another pause, Bill came out and said what he was really thinking.

"I don't think we can do it without her."

Meredith thumped his pencil against a pad of paper a few times, clearly wishing he was anywhere but here.

"It's a mistake," he said. "But if she falls apart, it's *your* mistake." He exhaled again. "Call her."

CHAPTER THREE

The teenage girl who opened the door looked as though she might slam it in Bill's face. Instead, she whirled around and walked away without a word, leaving the door open.

Bill stepped inside.

"Hi, April," he said automatically.

Riley's daughter, a sullen, gangly fourteen-year-old, with her mother's dark hair and hazel eyes, didn't reply. Dressed only in an oversized T-shirt, her hair a mess, April turned a corner and plopped herself down on the couch, dead to everything except her earphones and cell phone.

Bill stood there awkwardly, unsure what to do. When he had called Riley, she had agreed to his visiting, albeit reluctantly. Had she changed her mind?

Bill glanced around as he proceeded into the dim house. He walked through the living room and saw everything was neat and in its place, which was characteristic of Riley. Yet he also noticed the blinds drawn, a film of dust on the furniture—and that wasn't like her at all. On a bookshelf he spotted a row of shiny new paperback thrillers he'd bought for her during her leave, hoping they'd get her mind off her problems. Not a single binding looked cracked.

Bill's sense of apprehension deepened. This was not the Riley he knew. Was Meredith right? Did she need more time on leave? Was he doing the wrong thing by reaching out to her before she was ready?

Bill braced himself and proceeded deeper into the dark house, and as he turned a corner, he found Riley, alone in the kitchen, sitting at the Formica table in her housecoat and slippers, a cup of coffee in front of her. She looked up and he saw a flash of embarrassment, as if she had forgotten he was coming. But she quickly covered it up with a weak smile, and stood.

He stepped forward and hugged her, and she hugged him, weakly, back. In her slippers, she was a little shorter than he was. She had become very thin, too thin, and his concern deepened.

He sat down across the table from her and studied her. Her hair was clean, but it wasn't combed, either, and it looked as if she had been wearing those slippers for days. Her face looked gaunt, too pale, and much, much older since he'd last seen her five weeks ago. She looked as if she had been through hell. She had. He tried not to think about what the last killer had done to her.

She averted her gaze, and they both sat there in the thick silence. Bill had been so sure he'd know just what to say to cheer her up, to rouse her; yet as he sat there, he felt consumed by her sadness, and he lost all his words. He wanted to see her look sturdier, like her old self.

He quickly hid the envelope with the files about the new murder case on the floor beside his chair. He wasn't sure now if he should even show her. He was beginning to feel more certain he'd made a mistake coming here. Clearly, she needed more time. In fact, seeing her here like this, he was, for the first time, unsure if his longtime partner would ever come back.

"Coffee?" she asked. He could sense her unease.

He shook his head. She was clearly fragile. When he'd visited her in the hospital and even after she'd come home, he'd been frightened for her. He had wondered if she would ever make her way back from the pain and terror she'd endured, from the depths of her longtime darkness. It was so unlike her; she'd seemed invincible with every other case. Something about this last case, this last killer, was different. Bill could understand: the man had been the most twisted psychopath he had ever encountered—and that was saying a lot.

As he studied her, something else occurred to him. She actually looked her age. She was forty years old, the same age he was, but back when she was working, animated and engaged, she'd always seemed several years younger. Gray was starting to show in her dark hair. Well, his own hair was turning too.

Riley called out to her daughter, "April!"

No reply. Riley called her name several times, louder each time, until she finally answered.

"What?" April answered from the living room, sounding thoroughly annoyed.

"What time's your class today?"

"You know that."

"Just tell me, okay?"

"Eight-thirty."

Riley frowned and looked upset herself. She looked up at Bill.

"She flunked English. Cut too many classes. I'm trying to help dig her out of it."

Bill shook his head, understanding all too well. The agency life took too much of a toll on all of them, and their families were the biggest casualty.

"I'm sorry," he said.

Riley shrugged.

"She's fourteen. She hates me."

"That's not good."

"I hated everybody when I was fourteen," she replied. "Didn't you?"

Bill didn't reply. It was hard to imagine Riley ever hating everybody.

"Wait'll your boys get that age," Riley said. "How old are they now? I forget."

"Eight and ten," Bill replied, then smiled. "The way things are going with Maggie, I don't know if I'll even be in their lives when they get to be April's age."

Riley tilted her head and looked at him with concern. He'd missed that caring look.

"That bad, huh?" she said.

He looked away, not wanting to think about it.

The two of them fell silent for a moment.

"What's that you're hiding on the floor?" she asked.

Bill glanced down then back up and smiled; even in her state, she never missed a thing.

"I'm not hiding anything," Bill said, picking up the envelope and setting it on the table. "Just something I'd like to talk over with you."

Riley smiled broadly. It was obvious that she knew perfectly well what he was really here for.

"Show me," she said, then added, glancing nervously over at April, "Come on, let's go out back. I don't want her to see it."

Riley took off her slippers and walked into the backyard barefoot ahead of Bill. They sat at a weathered wooden picnic table that had been there since well before Riley moved here, and Bill gazed around the small yard with its single tree. There were woods on all sides. It made him forget he was even near a city.

Too isolated, he thought.

He'd never felt that this place was right for Riley. The little ranch-style house was fifteen miles out of town, rundown, and very ordinary. It was just off a secondary road, with nothing else but forests and pastures in sight. Not that he'd ever thought suburban life was right for her either. He had a hard time picturing her doing the cocktail party circuit. She could still, at least, drive into Fredericksburg and take the Amtrak to Quantico when she came back to work. When she still *could* work.

"Show me what you've got," she said.

He spread the reports and photographs across the table.

"Remember the Daggett case?" he asked. "You were right. The killer wasn't through."

He saw her eyes widen as she pored over the pictures. A long silence fell as she studied the files intensely, and he wondered if this might be what she needed to come back—or if it would set her back.

"So what do you think?" he finally asked.

Another silence. She still did not look up from the file.

Finally, she looked up, and when she did, he was shocked to see tears well up in her eyes. He had never seen her cry before, not even on the worst cases, up close to a corpse. This was definitely not the Riley he knew. That killer had done something to her, more than he knew.

She choked back a sob.

"I'm scared, Bill," she said. "I'm so scared. All the time. Of everything."

Bill felt his heart drop seeing her like this. He wondered where the old Riley had gone, the one person he could always rely on to be tougher than him, the rock he could always turn to in times of trouble. He missed her more than he could say.

"He's *dead*, Riley," he said, in the most confident tone he could muster. "He can't hurt you anymore."

She shook her head.

"You don't know that."

"Sure I do," he answered. "They found his body after the explosion."

"They couldn't identify it," she said.

"You know it was him."

Her face fell forward and she covered it with one hand as she wept. He held her other hand across the table.

"This is a new case," he said. "It's got nothing to do with what happened to you."

She shook her head.

"It doesn't matter."

Slowly, as she wept, she reached up and handed him the file, looking away.

"I'm sorry," she said, looking down, holding it out with a trembling hand. "I think you should go," she added.

Bill, shocked, saddened, reached out and took the file back. Never in a million years would he have expected this outcome.

Bill sat there for a moment, struggling against his own tears. Finally, he gently patted her hand, got up from the table, and made his way back through the house. April was still sitting in the living room, her eyes closed, nodding her head to her music.

*

Riley sat crying alone at the picnic table after Bill left.

I thought I was okay, she thought.

She'd really wanted to be okay, for Bill. And she'd thought she could actually carry it off. Sitting in the kitchen talking about trivialities had been all right. Then they had gone outside and when she had seen the file, she'd thought she'd be okay, too. Better than okay, really. She was getting caught up in it. Her old lust for the job was rekindled, she wanted to get back in the field. She was compartmentalizing, of course, thinking of those nearly identical murders as a puzzle to solve, almost in the abstract, an intellectual game. That too was fine. Her therapist had told her she would have to do that if she ever hoped to go back to work.

But then for some reason, the intellectual puzzle became what it really and truly was—a monstrous human tragedy in which two innocent women had died in the throes of immeasurable pain and terror. And she'd suddenly wondered: *Was it as bad for them as it was for me?*

Her body was now flooded with panic and fear. And embarrassment, shame. Bill was her partner and her best friend. She owed him so much. He'd stood by her during the last weeks when nobody else would. She couldn't have survived her time in the hospital without him. The last thing she wanted was for him to see her reduced to a state of helplessness.

She heard April yell from the back screen door.

"Mom, we gotta eat now or I'll be late."

She felt an urge to yell back, *"Fix your own breakfast!"*

But she didn't. She was long since exhausted from her battles with April. She'd given up fighting.

She got up from the table and walked back to the kitchen. She pulled a paper towel off the roll and used it to wipe her tears and blow her nose, then braced herself to cook. She tried to recall her therapist's words: *Even routine tasks will take a lot of conscious effort, at least for a while.* She had to settle for doing things one baby step at a time.

First came taking things out of the refrigerator—the carton of eggs, the package of bacon, the butter dish, the jar of jam, because April liked jam even if she didn't. And so it went until she laid six strips of bacon in a pan on the stovetop, and she turned on the gas

20

range under the pan.

She staggered backward at the sight of the yellow-blue flame. She shut her eyes, and it all came flooding back to her.

Riley lay in a tight crawlspace, under a house, in a little makeshift cage. The propane torch was the only light she ever saw. The rest of the time was spent in complete darkness. The floor of the crawlspace was dirt. The floorboards above her were so low that she could barely even crouch.

The darkness was total, even when he opened a small door and crept into the crawlspace with her. She couldn't see him, but she could hear him breathing and grunting. He'd unlock the cage and snap it open and climb inside.

And then he'd light that torch. She could see his cruel and ugly face by its light. He'd taunt her with a plate of wretched food. If she reached for it, he'd thrust the flame at her. She couldn't eat without getting burned ...

She opened her eyes. The images were less vivid with her eyes open, but she couldn't shake the stream of memories. She continued to make breakfast robotically, her whole body surging with adrenaline. She was just setting the table when her daughter's voice yelled out again.

"Mom, how long's it going to be?"

She jumped, and her plate slipped out of her hand and fell to the floor and shattered.

"What happened?" April yelled, appearing beside her.

"Nothing," Riley said.

She cleaned up the mess, and as she and April sat eating together, the silent hostility was palpable as usual. Riley wanted to end the cycle, to break through to April, to say, *April, it's me, your mom, and I love you.* But she had tried so many times, and it only made it worse. Her daughter hated her, and she couldn't understand why—or how to end it.

"What are you going to do today?" she asked April.

"What do you think?" April snapped. "Go to class."

"I mean after that," Riley said, keeping her voice calm, compassionate. "I'm your mother. I want to know. It's normal."

"Nothing about our lives is normal."

They ate silently for a few moments.

"You never tell me anything," Riley said.

"Neither do you."

That stopped any hope for conversation once and for all.

21

That's fair, Riley thought bitterly. It was truer than April even knew. Riley had never told her about her job, her cases; she had never told her about her captivity, or her time in the hospital, or why she was "on vacation" now. All April knew was that she'd had to live with her father during much of that time, and she hated him even more than she hated Riley. But as much as she wanted to tell her, Riley thought it best that April have no idea what her mother had been through.

Riley got dressed and drove April to school, and they didn't say a word to each other during the drive. When she let April out of the car, she called after her, "I'll see you at ten."

April gave her a careless wave as she walked away.

Riley drove to a nearby coffee shop. It had become a routine for her. It was hard for her to spend any time in a public place, and she knew that was exactly why she had to do it. The coffee shop was small and never busy, even in the mornings like this, so she found it relatively unthreatening.

As she sat there, sipping on a cappuccino, she remembered again Bill's entreaty. It had been six weeks, damn it. This had to change. *She* had to change. She didn't know how she was going to do that.

But an idea was forming. She knew exactly what she needed to do first.

CHAPTER FOUR

The white flame of the propane torch waved in front of Riley. She had to dodge back and forth to escape being burned. The brightness blinded her to everything else and she couldn't even see her captor's face anymore. As the torch swirled about, it seemed to leave lingering traces hanging in the air.

"Stop it!" she yelled. "Stop it!"

Her voice was raw and hoarse from shouting. She wondered why she was wasting her breath. She knew he wouldn't stop tormenting her until she was dead.

Just then, he raised an air horn and blew it in her ear.

A car horn blared. Riley snapped back to the present, and looked out to see the light at the intersection had just turned green. A line of drivers waited behind her vehicle, and she stepped on the gas.

Riley, palms sweating, forced the memory away and reminded herself of where she was. She was going to visit Marie Sayles, the only other survivor of her near-killer's unspeakable sadism. She berated herself for letting the flashback overwhelm her. She had managed to keep her mind on her driving for an hour and a half now, and she had thought she was doing fine.

Riley drove into Georgetown, passing upscale Victorian homes, and parked at the address Marie had given her over the phone—a red brick townhouse with a handsome bay window. She sat in the car for a moment, debating whether to go in, and trying to summon the courage.

Finally, she exited. As she climbed the steps, she was pleased to see Marie meet her at the door. Somberly but elegantly dressed, Marie smiled somewhat wanly. Her face looked tired and drawn. From the circles under her eyes, Riley was pretty sure that she'd been crying. That came as no surprise. She and Marie had seen each other a lot during their weeks of video chats, and there was little they could hide from one another.

When they hugged, Riley was immediately aware that Marie was not as tall and robust as she'd expected her to be. Even in heels Marie was shorter than Riley, her frame small and delicate. That surprised Riley. She and Marie had talked a lot, but this was the first time they had met in person. Marie's slightness made her seem all the more courageous to have survived what she'd been through.

Riley took in her surroundings as she and Marie walked for the dining room. The place was immaculately clean and tastefully furnished. It would normally be a cheery home for a successful single woman. But Marie kept all the curtains closed and the lights low. The atmosphere was strangely oppressive. Riley didn't want to admit it, but it made her think of her own home.

Marie had a light lunch ready on the dining room table, and she and Riley sat down to eat. They sat there in an awkward silence, Riley sweating but unsure why. Seeing Marie was brining it all back.

"So . . . how did it feel?" Marie asked tentatively. "Coming out into the world?"

Riley smiled. Marie knew better than anyone what today's drive took.

"Pretty well," Riley said. "Actually, *quite* well. I only had one bad moment, really."

Marie nodded, clearly understanding.

"Well, you did it," Marie said. "And that was brave."

Brave, Riley thought. That was not how she would have described herself. Once, maybe, when she was an active agent. Would she ever describe herself that way again?

"How about you?" Riley asked. "How much do you get out?"

Marie fell silent.

"You don't leave the house at all, do you?" Riley asked.

Marie shook her head.

Riley reached forward and held her wrist in a grip of compassion.

"Marie, you've got to try," she urged. "If you let yourself stay stuck inside like this, it's like he's still holding you prisoner."

A choked sob forced its way out of Marie's throat.

"I'm sorry," Riley said.

"That's all right. You're right."

Riley watched Marie as they both ate for a moment and a long silence descended. She wanted to think that Marie was doing well, but she had to admit that she seemed alarmingly frail to her. It made her fear for herself, too. Did she look that bad, too?

Riley wondered silently whether it was good for Marie to be living alone. Might she be better with a husband or boyfriend? she wondered. Then she wondered the same thing about herself. Yet she knew the answer for both of them was probably not. Neither of them was in any emotional frame of mind for a sustained relationship. It would just be a crutch.

"Did I ever thank you?" Marie asked after a while, breaking the silence.

Riley smiled. She knew perfectly well that Marie meant for having rescued her.

"Lots of times," Riley said. "And you don't need to. Really."

Marie poked at her food with a fork.

"Did I ever say I'm sorry?"

Riley was surprised. "Sorry? What for?"

Marie spoke with difficulty.

"If you hadn't gotten me out of there, you wouldn't have gotten caught."

Riley squeezed Marie's hand gently.

"Marie, I was just doing my job. You can't go feeling guilty about something that wasn't your fault. You've got too much to deal with as it is."

Marie nodded, acknowledging her.

"Just getting out of bed every day is a challenge," she admitted. "I guess you noticed how dark I keep everything. Any bright light reminds me of that torch of his. I can't even watch television, or listen to music. I'm scared that someone might sneak up on me and I'll not hear it. Any noise at all puts me in a panic."

Marie began to weep quietly.

I'll never look at the world in the same way. Never. There's evil out there, all around us. I had no idea. People are capable of such horrible things. I don't know how I'll ever trust people again."

As Marie cried, Riley wanted to reassure her, to tell her she was wrong. But a part of Riley was not so sure she was.

Finally, Marie looked at her.

"Why did you come here today?" she asked, point-blank.

Riley was caught off guard by Marie's directness—and by the fact that she didn't really know herself.

"I don't know," she said. "I just wanted to visit you. See how you are doing."

"There's something else," Marie said, narrowing her eyes with an uncanny perception.

Maybe she was right, Riley thought. Riley thought of Bill's visit, and she realized she had, indeed, come here because of the new case. What was it she wanted from Marie? Advice? Permission? Encouragement? Reassurance? A part of her wanted Marie to tell her she was crazy, so she could rest easy and forget about Bill. But maybe another part wanted Marie to urge her to do it.

Finally, Riley sighed.

"There's a new case," she said. "Well, not a *new* case. But an old case that never went away."

Marie's expression grew taut and severe.

Riley gulped.

"And you've come to ask if you should do it?" Marie asked.

Riley shrugged. But she also looked up and searched Marie's eyes for reassurance, encouragement. And in that moment she realized that was exactly what she had come here hoping to find.

But to her disappointment, Marie lowered her eyes and slowly shook her head. Riley kept waiting for an answer, but instead there followed an endless silence. Riley sensed that some special fear was working its way inside Marie.

In the silence, Riley looked around the apartment, and her eyes fell upon Marie's landline phone. She was surprised to see it was disconnected from the wall.

"What's the matter with your phone?" Riley asked.

Marie looked positively stricken, and Riley realized she had hit a real nerve.

"He keeps calling me," Marie said, in an almost inaudible whisper.

"Who?"

"Peterson."

Riley's heart jumped up into her throat.

"Peterson is dead," Riley replied, her voice shaky. "I torched the place. They found his body."

Marie shook her head.

"It could have been anyone they found. It wasn't him."

Riley felt a flush of panic. Her own worst fears were being brought back.

"Everybody says it was," Riley said.

"And you really believe that?"

Riley didn't know what to say. Now was no time to confide her own fears. After all, Marie was probably being delusional. But how could Riley convince her of something that she didn't altogether believe herself?

"He keeps calling," Marie said again. "He calls and breathes and hangs up. I know it's him. He's alive. He's still stalking me."

Riley felt a cold, creeping dread.

"It's probably just an obscene phone caller," she said, pretending to be calm. "But I can get the Bureau to check it out anyway. I can get them to send out a surveillance car if you're scared. They'll trace the calls."

"No!" Marie said sharply. "No!"

Riley stared back, puzzled.

"Why not?" she asked.

"I don't want to make him angry," Marie said in a pathetic whimper.

Riley, overwhelmed, feeling a panic attack coming on, suddenly realized it had been a terrible idea to come here. If anything, she felt worse. She knew she could not sit in this oppressive dining room a moment longer.

"I've got to go," Riley said, talking. "I'm so sorry. My daughter's waiting."

Marie suddenly grabbed Riley's wrist with surprising strength, digging her nails into her skin.

She stared back, her icy blue eyes holding such intensity that it terrified Riley. That haunting look seared into her soul.

"Take the case," Marie urged.

Riley could see in her eyes that Marie was confusing the new case and Peterson, blurring them together into one.

"Find that son of a bitch," she added. "And kill him for me."

CHAPTER FIVE

The man kept a short but discreet distance from the woman, glancing her way only fleetingly. He placed a few token items into his handbasket so that he'd look like just another shopper. He congratulated himself on how inconspicuous he was able to make himself. No one would guess his true power.

But then again, he'd never been the kind of man who attracted much attention. As a child, he'd felt practically invisible. Now, at long last, he was able to turn his own innocuousness to his advantage.

Just a few moments ago, he had stood right next to her, scarcely more than two feet away. Rapt in choosing her shampoo, she hadn't noticed him at all.

He knew plenty about her, though. He knew her name was Cindy; that her husband owned an art gallery; that she worked in a free medical clinic. Today was one of her days off. Right now she was on her cell phone talking with somebody—her sister, it sounded like. She was laughing at something the person was saying to her. He burned red with anger, wondering if she were laughing at him, just as all the girls used to. His fury increased.

Cindy wore shorts, a tank top, and expensive-looking running shoes. He'd watched her from his car, jogging, and waited until she'd finished her run and came into the grocery store. He knew her routine for a non-working day like this. She'd take the items home and put them away, take a shower, then drive to meet her husband for lunch.

Her good figure owed a lot to physical exercise. She was no more than thirty years old, but the skin around her thighs wasn't tight anymore. She'd probably lost a lot of weight at one time or another, perhaps pretty recently. She was undoubtedly proud of that.

Suddenly, the woman headed toward the nearest cash register. The man was taken by surprise. She had finished shopping earlier than usual. He rushed to get in line behind her, almost pushing another customer aside to do so. He silently berated himself for that.

As the cashier rang up the woman's items, he inched up and stood extremely close to her—close enough to smell her body, now sweaty and pungent after her vigorous jog. It was a smell that he expected to become much, much better acquainted with very soon. But the smell would then be mixed with yet another odor—one that fascinated him because of its strangeness and mystery.

The smell of pain and terror.

For a moment, the lurker felt exhilarated, even pleasantly light-headed, with eager anticipation.

After paying for her groceries, she pushed her cart out through the automatic glass doors and out into the parking lot.

He felt no hurry now about paying for his own handful of items. He didn't need to follow her home. He'd been there already—had even been inside her house. He had even handled her clothing. He'd take up his vigil again when she got off work.

It won't be long now, he thought. *Not long at all.*

*

After Cindy MacKinnon got into her car, she sat there for a moment, feeling shaken and not knowing why. She remembered the weird feeling she'd just had back in the supermarket. It was an uncanny, irrational feeling of being watched. But it was more than that. It took her a few moments to put her finger on it.

Finally, she realized it was a feeling that someone had meant her harm.

She shivered deeply. During the last few days, that feeling had been coming and going. She chided herself, sure that it was completely groundless.

She shook her head, ridding herself of any vestiges of that feeling. As she started her car, she forced herself to think of something else, and she smiled at her cell phone conversation with her sister, Becky. Later this afternoon, Cindy would help her throw a big birthday party her three-year-old daughter, complete with cake and balloons.

It would be a beautiful day, she thought.

CHAPTER SIX

Riley sat in the SUV beside Bill as he shifted gears, pushing the Bureau's four-wheel-drive vehicle higher into the hills, and she wiped her palms on her pants legs. She didn't know what to make of the sweatiness, and she didn't know what to make of being here. After six weeks off the job, she felt out of touch with what her body was telling her. Being back felt surreal.

Riley was disturbed by the awkward tension. She and Bill had barely spoken during their hour-plus drive. Their old camaraderie, their playfulness, their uncanny rapport—none of that was there now. Riley felt pretty sure she knew why Bill was being so aloof. It wasn't out of rudeness—it was out of worry. He, too, seemed to have doubts about whether she should be back on the job.

They drove toward Mosby State Park, where Bill had told her he had seen the most recent murder victim. As they went, Riley took in the geography all around her and slowly, her old sense of professionalism kicked in. She knew she had to snap out of it.

Find that son of a bitch and kill him for me.

Marie's words haunted her, drove her on, made her choice simple.

But nothing seemed that simple now. For one thing, she couldn't help worrying about April. Sending her to stay at her father's house wasn't ideal for anybody involved. But today was Saturday and Riley didn't want to wait until Monday to see the crime scene.

The deep silence began to add to her anxiety, and she desperately felt the need to talk. Wracking her brain for something to say, finally, she said:

"So are you going to tell me what's going on between you and Maggie?"

Bill turned to her, a surprised look on his face, and she couldn't tell if it was due to her breaking the silence, or her blunt question. Whichever it was, she immediately regretted it. Her bluntness, many people told her, could be off-putting. She never meant to be blunt—she just had no time to waste.

Bill exhaled.

"She thinks I'm having an affair."

Riley felt a jolt of surprise.

"What?"

"With my job," Bill said, laughing a bit sourly. "She thinks I'm having an affair with my job. She thinks I love *all this* more than I love her. I keep telling her she's being silly. Anyway, I can't exactly end it—not my job, anyway."

Riley shook her head.

"Sounds just like Ryan. He used to get jealous as hell when we were still together."

She stopped short of telling Bill the whole truth. Her ex-husband hadn't been jealous of Riley's job. He'd been jealous of Bill. She'd often wondered if Ryan might have had some reason. Despite today's awkwardness, she felt awfully good just being close to Bill. Was that feeling solely professional?

"I hope this isn't a wasted trip," Bill said. "The crime scene's been all cleaned up, you know."

"I know. I just want to see the place for myself. Pictures and reports don't cut it for me."

Riley was starting to feel a bit woozy now. She was pretty sure it was from the altitude, as they climbed still higher. Anticipation had something to do with it, too. Her palms were still sweating.

"How much farther?" she asked, as she watched the woods get thicker, the terrain more remote.

"Not far."

A couple of minutes later, Bill turned off the paved road onto a pair of rough tire tracks. The vehicle bounced along jarringly, then came to a stop about a quarter of a mile into the dense woods.

He switched off the ignition, then turned toward Riley and looked at her with concern.

"You sure you want to do this?" he asked.

She knew exactly what was worrying him. He was afraid she'd flash back to her traumatic captivity. Never mind that this was a different case altogether, and a different killer.

She nodded.

"I'm sure," she said, not at all convinced that she was telling the truth.

She got out of the car and followed Bill off the road onto a brushy, narrow path through the woods. She heard the gurgling of a nearby stream. As the vegetation grew thicker, she had to push her way past low-hanging branches, and sticky little burrs started bunching up on her pants legs. She was annoyed at the thought of having to pick them off.

At last she and Bill emerged onto the creek bank. Riley was immediately struck by what a lovely spot it was. The afternoon

31

sunlight poured in through the leaves, mottling the rippling water with kaleidoscopic light. The steady gurgling of the stream was soothing. It was strange to think of this as a gruesome crime scene.

"She was found right here," Bill said, leading her to a broad, level boulder.

When they got there, Riley stood and looked all around and breathed deeply. Yes, she had been right to come here. She was starting to feel that.

"The pictures?" Riley asked.

She crouched beside Bill on the boulder, and they started leafing through a folder full of photographs taken shortly after Reba Frye's body had been found. Another folder was stuffed with reports and photos of the murder she and Bill had investigated six months ago—the one that they had failed to solve.

Those pictures brought back vivid memories of the first killing. It transported her right back to that farm country near Daggett. She remembered how Rogers had been staged in a similar manner against a tree.

"A lot like our older case," Riley observed. "Both women in their thirties, both with little kids. That seems to be part of his MO. He's got it in for mothers. We need to check with parenting groups, find out if there were any connections between the two women, or between their kids."

"I'll get somebody on it," Bill said. He was taking notes now.

Riley continued poring through the reports and photos, comparing them to the actual scene.

"Same method of strangulation, with a pink ribbon," she observed. "Another wig, and the same type of artificial rose in front of the body."

Riley held up two photographs side by side.

"Eyes stitched open, too," she said. "If I remember right, the technicians found that Rogers's eyes had been stitched postmortem. Was it the same with Frye?"

"Yeah. I guess he wanted them to watch him even after they were dead."

Riley felt a sudden tingle up her spine. She'd almost forgotten that feeling. She got it whenever something about a case was just about to click and make sense. She didn't know whether to feel encouraged or terrified.

"No," she said. "That's not it. He didn't care whether the women saw him."

"Then why did he do it?"

Riley didn't reply. Ideas were starting to rush into her brain.

She was exhilarated. But she wasn't yet ready to put any of it into words—not even to herself.

She laid out pairs of photographs on the boulder, pointing out details to Bill.

"They're *not* exactly the same," she said. "The body wasn't as carefully staged back in Daggett. He'd tried to move that corpse when it was already stiff. My guess is this time he brought her here before rigor mortis set in. Otherwise he couldn't have posed her so …"

She suppressed the urge to finish the sentence with "nicely." Then she realized, that was exactly the kind of word she'd have used when she was on the job before her capture and torture. Yes, she was getting back into the spirit of things, and she felt the same old dark obsession growing inside her. Pretty soon there'd be no turning back.

But was that a good thing or a bad thing?

"What's with Frye's eyes?" she asked, pointing to a photo. "That blue doesn't look real."

"Contacts," Bill answered.

The tingle in Riley's spine grew stronger. Eileen Rogers's corpse hadn't had contact lenses. It was an important difference.

"And the shine on her skin?" she asked.

"Vaseline," Bill said.

Another important difference. She felt her ideas snapping into place with breathtaking speed.

"What has forensics found out about the wig?" she asked Bill.

"Nothing yet, except that it was pieced together out of pieces of cheap wigs."

Riley's excitement grew. For the last murder, the killer had used a simple, whole wig, not something patched together. Like the rose, it had been so cheap that forensics couldn't trace it. Riley felt parts of the puzzle coming together—not the whole puzzle, but a big chunk of it.

"What does forensics plan to do about this wig?" she asked.

"The same as last time—run a search of its fibers, try to track it down through hairpiece outlets."

Startled by the fierce certainty in her own voice, Riley said: "They're wasting their time."

Bill looked at her, clearly caught off guard.

"Why?"

She felt a familiar impatience with Bill, one she felt when she always found herself thinking a step or two ahead of him.

"Look at the picture he's trying to show us. Blue contacts to make the eyes look like they're not real. Eyelids stitched so the eyes stay wide open. The body propped up, legs splayed out freakishly. Vaseline to make the skin look like plastic. A wig pieced together out of pieces of little wigs—not human wigs, *doll's* wigs. He wanted both victims to look like *dolls*—like naked *dolls* on display."

"Jesus," Bill said, feverishly taking notes. "Why didn't we see this last time, back in Daggett?"

The answer seemed so obvious to Riley that she stifled an impatient groan.

"He wasn't good enough at it yet," she said. "He was still figuring out how to send the message. He's learning as he goes."

Bill looked up from his notepad and shook his head admiringly.

"Damn, I've missed you."

As much as she appreciated the compliment, Riley knew that an even bigger realization was on its way. And she knew from years of experience that there was no forcing it. She simply had to relax and let it come to her unbidden. She crouched on the boulder silently, waiting for it happen. As she waited, she picked idly at the burrs on her pants legs.

What a damned nuisance, she thought.

Suddenly her eyes fell on the stone surface under her feet. Other little burrs, some of them whole, others broken into fragments, were lying amid the burrs she was plucking off now.

"Bill," she said, her voice quavering with excitement, "were these little burrs here when you found the body?"

Bill shrugged. "I don't know."

Her hands shaking and sweating more than ever, she grabbed a bunch of pictures and rifled through them until she found a front view of the corpse. There, between her splayed legs right around the rose, was a group of little smudges. Those were the burrs—the very burrs she had just found. But nobody had thought they were important. Nobody had bothered to take a sharper, closer picture of them. And nobody had even bothered to sweep them away when the crime scene was cleaned up.

Riley closed her eyes, bringing her imagination fully into play. She felt lightheaded, even dizzy. It was a sensation that she knew all too well—a feeling of falling into an abyss, into a terrible black void, into the killer's evil mind. She was stepping into his shoes, into his experience. It was a dangerous and terrifying place to be. But it was where she belonged, at least right now. She embraced it.

She felt the killer's confidence as he lugged the body down

the path to the stream, perfectly sure that he wasn't going to get caught, in no hurry at all. He might well have been humming or whistling. She felt his patience, his craft and skill, as he posed the corpse on the boulder.

And she could see the grisly tableau through his eyes. She felt his deep satisfaction at a job well done—the same warm feeling of fulfillment that she always felt when she'd solved a case. He had crouched on this rock, pausing for a moment—or for as long as he liked—to admire his own handiwork.

And as he did, he had plucked the burrs off his pants legs. He took his time about it. He didn't bother to wait until he'd gotten away free and clear. And she could almost hear him saying aloud her own exact words.

"What a damn nuisance."

Yes, he'd even taken the time to pluck off the burrs.

Riley gasped, and her eyes snapped open. Fingering the burr in her own hand, she noted how sticky it was, and that its prickles were sharp enough to draw blood.

"Gather these burrs," she ordered. "We might just get a bit of DNA."

Bill's eyes widened, and he immediately extracted a ziplock bag and tweezers. As he worked, her mind ran in overdrive, not done yet.

"We've been wrong all along," she said. "This isn't his second murder. It's his third."

Bill stopped and looked up, clearly stunned.

"How do you know?" Bill asked.

Riley's whole body tightened as she tried to bring her trembling under control.

"He's gotten too good. His apprenticeship is over. He's a pro now. And he's just hitting his stride. He *loves* his work. No, this is his third time, at least."

Riley's throat tightened and she swallowed hard.

"And there won't be much time now until the next one."

CHAPTER SEVEN

Bill found himself in a sea of blue eyes, none of them real. He didn't usually have nightmares about his cases, and he wasn't having one now—but it sure felt like one. Here in the middle of the doll store, little blue eyes were simply everywhere, all of them wide open and sparkling and alert.

The dolls' little ruby-red lips, most of them smiling, were troubling also. So was all the painstakingly combed artificial hair, so stiff and immobile. Taking in all these details, Bill wondered now how he could have possibly missed the killer's intention—to make his victims look as doll-like as possible. It had taken Riley to make that connection.

Thank God she's back, he thought.

Still, Bill couldn't help but worry about her. He had been dazzled by her brilliant work back at Mosby Park. But afterward, when he drove her home, she'd seemed exhausted and demoralized. She'd barely said a word to him during the whole drive. Maybe it had been too much for her.

Even so, Bill wished that Riley was here right now. She'd decided it would be best for them to split up, to cover more ground more quickly. He couldn't disagree with that. She'd asked him to cover the doll stores in the area, while she would revisit the scene of the crime they'd covered six months ago.

Bill looked around and, feeling in way over his head, wondered what Riley would make of this doll store. It was the most elegant of the ones he'd visited today. Here on the edge of the Capital Beltway, the store probably got a lot of classy shoppers from wealthy Northern Virginia counties.

He walked around and browsed. A little girl doll caught his eye. With its upturned smile and pale skin, it especially reminded him of the latest victim. Although it was fully clothed in a pink dress with lots of lace on the collar, cuffs, and hem, it was also sitting in a disturbingly similar position.

Suddenly, Bill heard a voice to his right.

"I think you're looking in the wrong section."

Bill turned and found himself facing a stout little woman with a warm smile. Something about her immediately told him that she was in charge here.

"Why do you say that?" Bill asked.

The woman chuckled.

"Because you don't have daughters. I can tell a man who doesn't have a daughter from a mile off. Don't ask me how, it's just some kind of instinct, I guess."

Bill was stunned by her insight, and deeply impressed.

She offered Bill her hand.

"Ruth Behnke," she said.

Bill shook her hand.

"Bill Jeffreys. I take it you own this store."

She chuckled again.

"I see you've got some kind of instinct, too," she said. "I'm pleased to meet you. But you *do* have sons, don't you? Three of them, I'd guess."

Bill smiled. Her instincts were pretty sharp, all right. Bill figured that she and Riley would enjoy each other's company.

"Two," he replied. "But pretty damn close."

She chuckled.

"How old?" she asked.

"Eight and ten."

She looked around the place.

"I don't know that I've got much for them here. Oh, actually, I've got a few rather quaint toy soldiers in the next aisle. But that's not the kind of things boys like anymore, is it? It's all video games these days. And violent ones at that."

"I'm afraid so."

She squinted at him appraisingly.

"You're not here to buy a doll, are you?" she asked.

Bill smiled and shook his head.

"You're good," he replied.

"Are you a cop, maybe?" she asked.

Bill laughed quietly and took out his badge.

"Not quite, but a good guess."

"Oh, my!" she said, with concern. "What does the FBI want with my little place? Am I on some kind of list?"

"In a way," Bill said. "But it's nothing to worry about. Your shop came up on our search of stores in this area that sell antique and collectible dolls."

In fact, Bill didn't know exactly *what* he was looking for. Riley had suggested that he check out a handful of these places, assuming the killer might have frequented them—or at least had visited them on some occasion. What she was expecting, he didn't know. Was she expecting the killer himself to be there? Or that one of the employees had met the killer?

Doubtful that they had. Even if they had, it was doubtful that they would have recognized him as a killer. Probably all the men that came in here, if any, were creepy.

More likely Riley was trying to get him to gain more insights into the killer's mind, his way of looking at the world. If so, Bill figured she'd wind up disappointed. He simply did not have the mind that she did, or the talent to easily walk into killers' minds.

It seemed to him as if she were really fishing. There were dozens of doll stores within the radius they had been searching. Better, he thought, to let forensics just continue to track down the doll makers. Though, thus far, that had turned up nothing.

"I'd ask what kind of case this is," Ruth said, "but I probably shouldn't."

"No," Bill said, "you probably shouldn't."

Not that the case was a secret anymore—not after Senator Newbrough's people had put out a press release about it. The media was now saturated with the news. As usual, the Bureau was reeling under an assault of erroneous phone tips, and the internet was abuzz with bizarre theories. The whole thing had become a pain.

But why tell the woman about it? She seemed so nice, and her store so wholesome and innocent, that Bill didn't want to upset her with something so grim and shocking as a serial murderer obsessed with dolls.

Still, there was one thing he wanted to know.

"Tell me something," Bill said. "How many sales do you make to adults—I mean grown-ups without kids?"

"Oh, those are most of my sales, by far. To collectors."

Bill was intrigued. He'd never have guessed that.

"Why do you think that is?" he asked.

The woman smiled an odd, distant smile, and spoke in a gentle tone.

"Because people die, Bill Jeffreys."

Now Bill was truly startled.

"Pardon?" he said.

"As we get older, we *lose* people. Our friends and loved ones die. We grieve. Dolls stop time for us. They make us forget our grief. They comfort and console us. Look around you. I've got dolls that are most of a century old, and some that are almost new. With some of them, at least, you probably can't tell the difference. They're ageless."

Bill looked around, feeling creeped out at all the century-old eyes staring back at him, wondering how many people these dolls had outlived. He wondered what they had witnessed—the love, the anger, the hate, the sadness, the violence. And yet still they stared back with that same blank expression. They didn't make sense to him.

People *should* age, he thought. They should get old and lined and gray, as he had, given all the darkness and horror there was in the world. Given all that he had seen, it would be a sin, he thought, if he still looked the same. The murder scenes had sunk into him like a living thing, had made him not want to stay young anymore.

"They're also—not alive," Bill finally said.

Her smile turned bittersweet, almost pitying.

"Is that really true, Bill? Most of my customers don't think so. I'm not sure I think so, either."

An odd silence fell. The woman broke it with a chuckle. She offered Bill a colorful little brochure with pictures of dolls all over it.

"As it happens, I'm heading to an upcoming convention in D.C. You might want to go, too. Maybe it will give you some ideas for whatever it is you're searching for."

Bill thanked her and left the store, grateful for the tip about the convention. He hoped that Riley would go with him. Bill remembered that she was supposed to interview Senator Newbrough and his wife this afternoon. It was an important appointment—not just because the senator might have good information, but for diplomatic reasons. Newbrough really was making things hot for the Bureau. Riley was just the agent to convince him that they were doing all that they could.

But will she really show up? Bill wondered.

It seemed truly bizarre that he couldn't be sure. Until six months ago, Riley was the one dependable thing in his life. He had always trusted her with his life. But her obvious distress worried him.

More than that, he missed her. Daunted as he sometimes was by her quicksilver mind, he needed her on a job like this. During the last six weeks, he'd also come to realize that he needed her friendship.

Or, deep down, was it more than that?

CHAPTER EIGHT

Riley drove down the two-lane highway, sipping on her energy drink. It was a sunny, warm morning, the car windows were down, and the warm smell of freshly baled hay filled the air. The surrounding modest-sized pastures were dotted with cattle, and mountains edged both sides of the valley. She liked it out here.

But she reminded herself she hadn't come here to feel good. She had some hard work to do.

Riley turned off onto a well-worn gravel road, and after a minute or two, she reached a crossroads. She turned into the national park, drove a short distance, and stopped her car on the sloping shoulder of the road.

She got out and walked across an open area to a tall, sturdy oak that stood on the northeast corner.

This was the place. This was where Eileen Rogers's body had been found—posed rather clumsily against this tree. She and Bill had been here together six months ago. Riley started to recreate the scene in her mind.

The biggest difference was the weather. Back then it had been mid-December, and bitterly cold. A thin blanket of snow covered the ground.

Go back, she told herself. *Go back and feel it.*

She breathed deeply, in and out, until she imagined she could feel a searing coldness passing through her windpipe. She could almost see thick clouds of frost forming with her every breath.

The naked corpse had been frozen solid. It wasn't easy to tell which of the many bodily lesions were knife wounds, and which were cracks and fissures caused by the icy cold.

Riley summoned back the scene, down to every last detail. The wig. The painted smile. The eyes stitched open. The artificial rose lying in the snow between the corpse's splayed legs.

The picture in her mind was now sufficiently vivid. Now she had to do what she'd done yesterday—get a sense of the killer's experience.

Once again, she closed her eyes, relaxed, and stepped off into the abyss. She welcomed that lightheaded, giddy feeling as she slipped into the killer's mind. Pretty soon, she was with him, inside him, seeing exactly what he saw, feeling what he felt.

He was driving here at night, anything but confident. He watched the road anxiously, worried about the ice under his wheels. What if he lost control, skidded into a ditch? He had a corpse on board. He'd be caught for sure. He had to drive carefully. He'd hoped his second murder would be easier than the first, but he was still a nervous wreck.

He stopped the vehicle right here. He hauled the woman's body—already naked, Riley guessed—out into the open. But it was already stiffened from rigor mortis. He hadn't reckoned on that. It frustrated him, shook his confidence. To make matters worse, he couldn't see what he was doing at all well, not even in the glare of the headlights which he directed at the tree. The night was much too dark. He made a mental note to do this in daylight next time if he possibly could.

He dragged the body to the tree and tried to put it into the pose that he'd envisioned. It didn't go at all well. The woman's head was tilted to the left, frozen there by rigor mortis. He yanked and twisted it. Even after breaking its neck, he still couldn't set it staring straight forward.

And how was he to splay the legs properly? One of the legs was hopelessly crooked. He had no choice but to get a tire iron out of his trunk and break the thigh and kneecap. Then he twisted the leg as well as he could, but not to his satisfaction.

Finally, he dutifully left the ribbon around her neck, the wig on her head, and the rose in the snow. Then he got into his car and drove away. He was disappointed and disheartened. He was also scared. In all his clumsiness, had he left any fatal clues behind? He obsessively replayed his every action in his mind, but he couldn't be sure.

He knew that he had to do better next time. He promised himself to do better.

Riley opened her eyes. She let the killer's presence fade away. She was pleased with herself now. She hadn't let herself be shaken and overwhelmed. And she'd gotten some valuable perspective. She'd gotten a sense of how the killer was learning his craft.

She only wished she knew something—anything—about his first murder. She was more certain than ever that he had killed one earlier time. This had been the work of an apprentice, but not a rank beginner.

Just as Riley was about to turn and walk back toward her car, something in the tree caught her eye. It was a tiny dash of yellow peeking out from where the trunk divided in half a little above her head.

41

She walked around to the far side of the tree and looked up.

"He's been back here!" Riley gasped aloud. Chills surged through her body and she glanced around nervously. Nobody seemed to be nearby now.

Nestled up in the branch of a tree staring down at Riley was a naked female doll with blond hair, posed precisely the way the killer had intended the victim to be.

It couldn't have been there long—three or four days at most. It hadn't been shifted by the wind or tarnished by rain. The murderer had returned here when he'd been preparing himself for the Reba Frye murder. Much as Riley had done, he had come back here to reflect on his work, to examine his mistakes critically.

She took pictures with her cell phone. She'd send those to the Bureau right away.

Riley knew why he'd left the doll.

It's an apology for past sloppiness, she realized.

It was also a promise of better work to come.

CHAPTER NINE

Riley drove toward Senator Mitch Newbrough's manor house, and her heart filled with dread as it came into view. Situated at the end of a long, tree-lined drive, it was huge, formal, and daunting. She always found the rich and powerful harder to deal with than folks further down the social ladder.

She pulled up and parked in a well-manicured circle in front of the stone mansion. Yes, this family was very rich indeed.

She got out of the car and walked up to the enormous front doors. After ringing the doorbell, she was greeted by a clean-cut man of about thirty.

"I'm Robert," he said. "The Senator's son. And you must be Special Agent Riley. Come on in. Mother and Father are expecting you."

Robert Newbrough led Riley on into the house, which immediately reminded her how much she disliked ostentatious homes. The Newbrough house was especially cavernous, and the walk to wherever the Senator and his wife were waiting was disagreeably long. Riley was sure that making guests walk such an inconvenient distance was a sort of intimidation tactic, a way of communicating that the inhabitants of this house were far too powerful to tangle with. Riley also found the ubiquitous Colonial furniture and decor to be really quite ugly.

More than anything else, she dreaded what was coming next. To her, talking to victims' families was simply awful—much worse than dealing with murder scenes or even corpses. She found it all too easy to get caught up in people's grief, anger, and confusion. Such intense emotions wrecked her concentration and distracted her from her work.

As they walked, Robert Newbrough said, "Father's been home from Richmond ever since …"

He choked a little in mid-sentence. Riley could feel the intensity of his loss.

"Since we heard about Reba," he continued. "It's been terrible. Mother's especially shaken up. Try not to upset her too much."

"I'm so sorry for your loss," Riley said.

Robert ignored her, and led Riley into a spacious living room. Senator Mitch Newbrough and his wife were sitting together on a huge couch holding each other's hands.

"Agent Paige," Robert said, introducing her. "Agent Paige, let me introduce my parents, the Senator and his wife, Annabeth."

Robert offered Reba a seat, then sat down himself.

"First of all," Riley said quietly, "my deepest condolences for your loss."

Annabeth Newbrough replied with a silent nod of acknowledgment. The Senator just sat staring forward.

In the brief silence that followed, Riley made a quick assessment of their faces. She'd seen Newbrough on television many times, always wearing a politician's ingratiating smile. He wasn't smiling now. Riley hadn't seen so much of Mrs. Newbrough, who seemed to possess the typical docility of a politician's wife.

Both of them were in their early sixties. Riley detected that they'd both gone to painful and expensive lengths to look younger—hair implants, hair dye, facelifts, makeup. As far as Riley was concerned, their efforts had left them looking vaguely artificial.

Like dolls, Riley thought.

"I've got to ask you a few questions about your daughter," Riley said, taking out her notebook. "Were you in close touch with Reba recently?"

"Oh, yes," Mrs. Newbrough said. "We are a very close family."

Riley noted a slight stiffness in the woman's voice. It sounded like something she said a little too often, a little too routinely. Riley felt pretty sure that family life in the Newbrough home had been far from ideal.

"Did Reba say anything recently about being threatened?" Riley asked.

"No," Mrs. Newbrough said. "Not a word."

Riley observed that the Senator hadn't said a word so far. She wondered why he was being so quiet. She needed to draw him out, but how?

Now Robert spoke up.

"She'd been through a messy divorce recently. Things got ugly between her and Paul over custody of their two kids."

"Oh, I never liked him," Mrs. Newbrough said. "He had such a temper. Do you think that possibly—?" Her words trailed off.

Riley shook her head.

44

"Her ex-husband's not a likely suspect," she said.

"Why on earth not?" Mrs. Newbrough asked.

Riley weighed in her mind what she should and should not tell them.

"You may have read that the killer struck before," she said. "There was a similar victim near Daggett."

Mrs. Newbrough was becoming more agitated.

"What's any of this supposed to mean to us?"

"We're dealing with a serial killer," Riley said. "There was nothing domestic about it. Your daughter may not have known the killer at all. There's every likelihood that it wasn't personal."

Mrs. Newbrough was sobbing now. Riley immediately regretted her choice of words.

"Not *personal*?" Mrs. Newbrough almost shouted. "How could it be anything *but* personal?"

Senator Newbrough spoke to his son.

"Robert, please take your mother elsewhere and calm her down. I need to talk with Agent Paige alone."

Robert Newbrough obediently led his mother away. Senator Newbrough said nothing for a moment. He looked Riley steadily in the eyes. She was sure that he was accustomed to intimidating people with that stare of his. But it didn't work especially well on her. She simply returned his gaze.

At last, the Senator reached into his jacket pocket and pulled out a letter-sized envelope. He walked over to her chair and handed it to her.

"Here," he said. Then he walked back to the couch and sat down again.

"What's this?" Riley asked.

The Senator turned his gaze on her again.

"Everything you need to know," he said.

Riley was now completely baffled.

"May I open it?" she asked.

"By all means."

Riley opened the envelope. It contained a single sheet of paper with two columns of names on it. She recognized some of them. Three or four were well-known reporters on the local TV news. Several others were prominent Virginia politicians. Riley was even more perplexed than before.

"Who are these people?" she asked.

"My enemies," Senator Newbrough said in an even voice. "Probably not a comprehensive list. But those are the ones who matter. Somebody there is guilty."

Riley was completely dumbfounded now. She sat there and said nothing.

"I'm not saying that anybody on that list killed my daughter directly, face to face," he said. "But they sure as hell paid somebody to do it."

Riley spoke slowly and cautiously.

"Senator, with all due respect, I believe I just said that your daughter's killing probably wasn't personal. There has already been one murder nearly identical to it."

"Are you saying that my daughter was targeted purely by coincidence?" the Senator asked.

Yes, probably, Riley thought.

But she knew better than to say so aloud.

Before she could reply, he added, "Agent Paige, I've learned through hard experience not to believe in coincidences. I don't know why or how, but my daughter's death was political. And in politics, *everything* is personal. So don't try to tell me it's anything else but personal. It's your job and the Bureau's to find whoever is responsible and bring him to justice."

Riley took a long, deep breath. She studied the man's face in minute detail. She could see it now. Senator Newbrough was a thorough narcissist.

Not that I should be surprised, she thought.

Riley understood something else. The Senator found it inconceivable that anything in his life wasn't specifically about him, and him alone. Even his daughter's murder was about him. Reba had simply gotten caught between him and somebody who hated him. He probably really believed that.

"Sir," Riley began, "with all due respect, I don't think—"

"I don't want you to think," Newbrough said. "You've got all the information you need right in front of you."

They held each other's gaze for several seconds.

"Agent Paige," the Senator finally said, "I get the feeling we're not on the same wavelength. That's a shame. You may not know it, but I've got good friends in the upper echelons of the agency. Some of them owe me favors. I'm going to get in touch with them right away. I need somebody on this case who will get the job done."

Riley sat there, shocked, not knowing what to say. Was this man really that delusional?

The Senator stood.

"I'll send somebody to see you out, Agent Paige," he said. "I'm sorry we didn't see eye to eye."

Senator Newbrough walked out of the room, leaving Riley sitting there alone. Her mouth hung open with shock. The man was narcissistic, all right. But she knew there was more to it than that.

There was something the Senator was hiding.

And no matter what it took, she would find out what it was.

CHAPTER TEN

The first thing that caught Riley's eye was the doll—the same naked doll she had found earlier that day in that tree near Daggett, in exactly the same pose. For a moment, she was startled to see it sitting there in the FBI forensics lab surrounded by an array of high-tech equipment. It looked weirdly out of place to Riley—like some kind of sick little shrine to a bygone non-digital age.

Now the doll was just another item of evidence, protected by a plastic bag. She knew that a team had been sent to retrieve it as soon as she'd called it in from the scene. Even so, it was a jarring sight.

Special Agent Meredith stepped forward to greet her.

"It's been a long time, Agent Paige," he said warmly. "Welcome back."

"It's good to be back, sir," Riley said.

She walked over to the table to sit with Bill and the lab tech Flores. Whatever qualms and uncertainties she might be feeling, it really did feel good to see Meredith again. She liked his gruff, no-nonsense style, and he'd always treated her with respect and consideration.

"How did things go with the Senator?" Meredith asked.

"Not good, sir," she replied.

Riley noticed a twitch of annoyance in her boss's face.

"Do you think he's going to give us any trouble?"

"I'm almost sure of it. I'm sorry, sir."

Meredith nodded sympathetically.

"I'm sure it's not your fault," he said.

Riley guessed that he had a pretty good idea of what had happened. Senator Newbrough's behavior was undoubtedly typical of narcissistic politicians. Meredith was probably all too used to it.

Flores typed rapidly, and as he did, images of grisly photographs, official reports, and news stories came up on large monitors around the room.

"We did some digging, and it turns out you were right, Agent Paige," Flores said. "The same killer did strike earlier, way before the Daggett murder."

Riley heard Bill's grunt of satisfaction, and for a second, Riley felt vindicated, felt her belief in herself returning.

But then her spirits sank. Another woman had died a terrible death. That was no cause for celebration. She had wished, actually, that she had not been right.

Why can't I enjoy being right once in a while? she wondered.

A gigantic map of Virginia spread out over the main flat-screen monitor, then narrowed to the northern half of the state. Flores tagged a spot high up on the map, near the Maryland border.

"The first victim was Margaret Geraty, thirty-six years old," Flores said. "Her body was found dumped in farmland, about thirteen miles outside of Belding. She was killed on June twenty-fifth, nearly two years ago. The FBI wasn't called in for that one. The locals let the case go cold."

Riley peered at the crime scene photos Flores brought up on another monitor. The killer obviously hadn't tried to pose the body. He'd just dumped her in a hurry and left.

"Two years ago," she said, thinking, taking it all in. A part of her was surprised he had been at this for so long. Yet another part of her knew that these sick killers could operate for years. They could have an uncanny patience.

She examined the photos.

"I see that he hadn't developed his style," she observed.

"Right," Flores said. "There's a wig there, and the hair was cropped short, but he didn't leave a rose. However, she was choked to death with a pink ribbon."

"He rushed through the set-up," Riley said. "His nerves got the best of him. It was his first time, and he lacked self-confidence. He did a little better with Eileen Rogers, but it wasn't until the Reba Frye killing that he really hit his stride."

She remembered something that she'd wanted to ask.

"Did you find any connections between the victims? Or between the kids of the two mothers?"

"Not a thing," Flores said. "The check of parenting groups came up empty. None of them seemed to know each other."

That discouraged Riley, but didn't altogether surprise her.

"What about the first woman?" Riley asked. "She was a mother, I take it."

"Nope," Flores said quickly, as though he'd been waiting for that question. "She was married, but childless."

Riley was startled. She was *sure* that the killer was singling out mothers. How could she have gotten that wrong?

She could feel her rising self-confidence suddenly deflate.

As Riley hesitated, Bill asked, "Then how close are we to

identifying a suspect? Were you able to get anything off of those burrs from Mosby Park?"

"No such luck," Flores said. "We found traces of leather instead of blood. The killer wore gloves. He seems to be fastidious. Even at the first scene, he didn't leave any prints or DNA."

Riley sighed. She had been so hopeful that she'd found something that others had overlooked. But now she felt she was striking out. They were back to the drawing board.

"Obsessive about details," she commented.

"Even so, I think we're closing in on him," Flores added.

He used an electronic pointer to indicate locations, drawing lines between them.

"Now that we know about this earlier killing, we've got the order and a better idea of his territory," Flores said. "We've got number one, Margaret Geraty, at Belding to the north here, number two, Eileen Rogers, over to the west at Mosby Park, and number three, Reba Frye, near Daggett, farther south."

As Riley looked, she saw that the three locations formed a triangle on the map.

"We're looking at an area of about a thousand square miles," Flores said. "But that's not as bad as it sounds. We're talking mostly rural areas with a few small towns. In the north you get into some big estates like the Senator's. Lots of open country."

Riley saw a look of professional satisfaction on Flores's face. He obviously loved his work.

"What I'm going to do is bring up all the registered sex offenders who live in this area," Flores said. He typed in a command, and the triangle was dotted with about two dozen little red tags.

"Now let's eliminate the pederasts," he said. "We can be sure that our killer's not one of them."

Flores typed another command, and about half of the dots disappeared.

"Now let's narrow it down to just the hardcore cases—guys who've been in prison for rape or murder or both."

"No," Riley said abruptly. "That's wrong."

All three men stared at her with surprise.

"We're not looking for a violent criminal," she said.

Flores grunted.

"Like hell we're not!" he protested.

A silence fell. Riley felt an insight forming, but it hadn't quite taken shape in her mind. She stared at the doll, which was still sitting grotesquely on the table, looking as out of place as ever.

If only you could talk, she thought.

Then she slowly began to state her thoughts.

"I mean, not *obviously* violent. Margaret Geraty wasn't raped. We already knew that Rogers and Frye weren't either."

"They were all tortured and killed," Flores grumbled.

A tension filled the room, as Brent Meredith looked worried, while Bill was staring fixedly at one of the monitors.

Riley pointed to close-up pictures of Margaret Geraty's hideously mutilated corpse.

"His first killing was his most violent," she said. "These wounds are deep and ugly—worse even than his next two victims. I'll bet your technicians have already determined that he inflicted these wounds really rapidly, one right after another."

Flores nodded with admiration.

"You're right."

Meredith looked at Riley with curiosity.

"What does that tell you?" Meredith asked.

Riley took a deep breath. She found herself slipping into the killer's mind again.

"I'm pretty sure of something," she said. "He's never had sex with another human being in his life. He's probably never even been on a date. He's homely and unattractive. Women have always rejected him."

Riley paused for a moment, collecting her thoughts.

"One day he finally snapped," she said. "He abducted Margaret Geraty, bound her, stripped her, and tried to rape her."

Flores gasped with sudden comprehension.

"But he couldn't do it!" Flores said.

"Right, he's completely impotent," Riley said. "And when he couldn't rape her, he went into a rage. He started stabbing—the closest he could get to sexual penetration. It was the first act of violence he'd ever committed in his life. My guess is he didn't even bother to keep her alive for long."

Flores pointed to a paragraph in the official report.

"Your guess is right," he said. "Geraty's body was found just a couple of days after she disappeared."

Riley felt a deepening terror at her own words.

"And he liked it," she said. "He liked Geraty's terror and pain. He liked all the cutting and stabbing. So he's made it his ritual ever since. And he's learned to take his time about it, to enjoy every minute of it. With Reba Frye, the fear and torture went on for more than a week."

51

A chill of silence settled over the room.

"What about the doll connection?" Meredith asked. "Why are you so sure he's creating a doll?"

"The bodies sure look like dolls," Bill said. "At least the last two. Riley's right about that."

"It is about dolls," Riley said quietly. "But I don't know exactly why. There's probably some sort of revenge element here."

Finally Flores asked, "So do you think we're looking for a registered offender at all?"

"Could be," Riley said. "But not a rapist, not a violent predator. It would be somebody more innocuous, less threatening—a Peeping Tom, or a flasher, or somebody who masturbates in public."

Flores typed vigorously.

"Okay," he said. "I'll get rid of the violent offenders."

The number of red dots on the map lessened to a handful.

"So who have we got left?" Riley asked Flores.

Flores glanced at a few records, then gasped.

"I think I've got him," Flores said. "I think I've got your man. His name's Ross Blackwell. And get this. He was working in a toy store when he got caught posing dolls in kinky positions. Like they were having all kinds of weird sex. The owner called the police. Blackwell got probation, but the authorities have had their eye on him ever since."

Meredith stroked his chin thoughtfully. "Could be our guy," he said.

"Should Agent Paige and I go check on him right now?" Bill asked.

"We don't have enough to bring him in," Meredith said. "Or to get a warrant for any kind of a search. We'd better not alarm him. If he's our guy and he's as smart as we think he is, he's liable to slip through our fingers. Pay him a little visit tomorrow. Find out what he's got to say about himself. Handle him carefully."

CHAPTER ELEVEN

It was very dark by the time Riley got back home into Fredericksburg and, if anything, she felt her night was almost sure to get worse. She felt a spasm of déjà vu as she pulled her car in front of the large house in a respectable suburban neighborhood. She'd once shared this house with Ryan and their daughter. There were a lot of memories here, many of them good. But more than a few of them were not so good, and some were really awful.

Just as she was about to get out of the car and walk up to the house, the front door opened. April came out and Ryan stood silhouetted in the bright light of the doorway. He gave Riley a token wave as April walked away, then he stepped back into the house and closed the door.

It seemed to Riley that he shut the door quite firmly, but she knew that was probably her own mind at work. That door had closed for good some time ago, and that life was gone. But the truth was, she had never really belonged in such a bland, safe, respectable world of order and routine. Her heart was always in the field, where chaos, unpredictability, and danger reigned.

April reached the car and got into the passenger seat.

"You're late," April snapped, crossing her arms.

"Sorry," Riley said. She wanted to say more, to tell April how deeply sorry she really was, not just for this night, not just for her father, but for her whole life. Riley so badly wanted to be a better mother, to be home, to be there for April. But her work life would just not let her go.

Riley pulled away from the curb.

"Normal parents don't work all day and all night too," April said.

Riley sighed.

"I've said before that—" she began.

"I know," April interrupted. "Criminals don't take days off. That's pretty lame, Mom."

Riley drove on in silence for a few moments, wanting to talk to April, but just too tired, too overwhelmed by her day. She didn't even know what to say anymore.

"How did things go with your father?" she finally asked.

"Lousy," April replied.

It was a predictable reply. April seemed to be even more down on her father than she was on her mother these days.

Another long silence fell between them.

Then, in a softer tone, April added, "At least Gabriela's there. It's always nice to see a friendly face for a change."

Riley smiled ever so slightly. Riley really did appreciate Gabriela, the middle-aged Guatemalan woman who had worked as their housemaid for years. Gabriela was always wonderfully responsible and grounded, which was more than Riley could say about Ryan. She was glad that Gabriela was still in their lives—and still there to look after April whenever she stayed at her father's house.

During the drive home, Riley felt a palpable need to communicate with her daughter. But what could she say to break through to her? It wasn't as if she didn't understand how April felt—especially on a night like tonight. The poor girl simply had to feel unwanted, getting shuttled back and forth between her parents' homes. That had to be hard on a fourteen-year-old who was already angry about so many things in her life. Fortunately, April agreed to go to her father's house after her class each day until Riley picked her up. But today, the very first day of the new arrangement, Riley had been so very late.

Riley found herself close to tears as she drove. She couldn't think of anything to say. She was simply too exhausted. She was *always* too exhausted.

When they got home, April stalked wordlessly off to her room and shut the door noisily behind her. Riley stood in the hallway for a moment. Then she knocked on April's door.

"Come on out, sweetie," she said. "Let's talk. Let's sit down in the kitchen for a little bit, have a cup of peppermint tea. Or maybe in the backyard. It's a pretty night out. It's a shame to waste it."

She heard April's voice reply, "You go ahead and do that, Mom. I'm busy."

Riley leaned wearily against the doorframe.

"You keep saying I don't spend enough time with you," Riley said.

"It's past midnight, Mom. It's really late."

Riley felt her throat tighten and tears well up in her eyes. But she wasn't going to let herself cry.

"I'm trying, April," she said. "I'm doing my best—with everything."

A silence fell.

"I know," April finally said from inside her room.

Then all was quiet. Riley wished she could see her daughter's face. Was it possible that she heard just a trace of sympathy in those two words? No, probably not. Was it anger, then? Riley didn't think so. It was probably just detachment.

Riley went to the bathroom and took a long hot shower. She let the steam and the pounding hot droplets massage her body, which ached all over after such a long and difficult day. By the time she got out and dried her hair she felt better physically. But inside she still felt empty and troubled.

And she knew that she wasn't ready to sleep.

She put on slippers and a bathrobe and went to the kitchen. When she opened a cabinet the first thing she saw was a mostly-full bottle of bourbon. She thought about pouring herself a straight double shot of whiskey.

Not a good idea, she told herself firmly.

In her current frame of mind, she wouldn't stop with one. Through all her troubles of the last six weeks, she'd managed not to let alcohol get the best of her. This was no time to lose control. She fixed herself a cup of hot mint tea instead.

Then Riley sat down in the living room and began to pore over the folder full of photographs and information about the three murder cases.

She already knew quite a bit about the victim of six months ago near Daggett—the one they now knew to be the second of three murders. Eileen Rogers had been a married mother with two children who owned and managed a restaurant with her husband. And of course, Riley had also seen the site where the third victim, Reba Frye, had been left. She'd even visited Frye's family, including the self-absorbed Senator.

But the two-year-old Belding case was new to her. As she read the reports, Margaret Geraty began to come into focus as a real human being, a woman who had once lived and breathed. She'd worked in Belding as a CPA, and had recently moved to Virginia from upstate New York. Her surviving family aside from her husband included two sisters, a brother, and a widowed mother. Friends and relatives described her as good-natured but rather solitary—possibly even lonely.

Sipping on her tea, Riley couldn't help but wonder—what would have become of Margaret Geraty if she had lived? At thirty-six, life still held all kinds of possibilities—children, and so much else.

Riley felt a chill as another thought dawned on her. Just six weeks ago, her own life story had come fearfully close to ending up in a folder just like the one now open in front of her. Her whole existence might well have been reduced to a stack of horrible photos and official prose.

She closed her eyes, trying to shake it away as she sensed the memories come flooding back. But try as she did, she could not stop them.

As she crept through the dark house, she heard a scratching below the floorboards, then a cry for help. After probing the walls, she found it—a small, square door that opened into a crawlspace under the house. She shined a flashlight inside.

The beam fell upon a terrified face.

"I'm here to help," Riley said.

"You've come!" the victim cried. "Oh, thank God you've come!"

Riley scuttled across the dirt floor toward the little cage in the corner. She fumbled with the lock for a moment. Then she pulled out her pocketknife and pried at the lock until she forced it open. A second later, the woman was crawling out of the cage.

Riley and the woman headed for the square opening. But the woman was scarcely out before a threatening male figure blocked Riley's way.

She was trapped, but the other woman had a chance.

"Run!" Riley screamed. "Run!"

Riley yanked herself back to the present. Would she ever be free from those horrors? Certainly, working on a new case involving torture and death wasn't making it easier for her.

Even so, there was one person she could always turn to for support.

She got out her phone and texted Marie.

Hey. You still awake?

After a few seconds, the reply came.

Yes. How are U?

Riley typed: *Pretty shaky. And you?*

Too scared to sleep.

Riley wanted to type something to make both of them feel better. Somehow, just texting like this didn't seem to be enough.

Do U want to talk? she typed. *I mean TALK—not just text?*

It took several long seconds before Marie replied.

No, I don't think so.

Riley was surprised for a moment. Then she realized that her voice might not always be comforting for Marie. Sometimes it might even trigger awful flashbacks for her.

Riley remembered Marie's words the last time they had spoken. *Find that son of a bitch. And kill him for me.* And as she pondered them, Riley did have news that she thought Marie might want to hear.

I'm back on the job, Riley typed.

Marie's words poured out in a rush of typed phrases.

Oh good! So glad! I know it's not easy. I'm proud. U r very brave.

Riley sighed. She didn't feel so brave—not just at this moment, anyway.

Marie's words continued.

Thank U. Knowing you're working again makes me feel much better. Maybe I can sleep now. Goodnight.

Riley typed: *Hang in there.*

Then she put her phone down. She felt a bit better, too. After all, she'd accomplished something, getting back to work like this. Slowly but surely, she really was starting to heal.

Riley drank the rest of her tea, then went straight to bed. She let her exhaustion overtake her and fell asleep quickly.

Riley was six years old, in a candy store with Mommy. She was so happy about all the candy Mommy was buying for her.

But then a man walked toward them. A big, scary man. He wore something over his face—a nylon stocking, just like Mommy wore on her legs. He pulled a gun. He yelled at Mommy to give him her purse. But Mommy was so scared that she couldn't move. She couldn't give it to him.

And so he shot her in the chest.

She fell to the floor bleeding. The man snatched up the purse and ran.

Riley started screaming and screaming and screaming.

Then she heard Mommy's voice.

"There's nothing you can do, dear. I'm gone and you can't help it."

Riley was still in the candy store but she was all grown up now. Mommy was right in front of her, standing over her own corpse.

"I've got to bring you back!" Riley cried.

Mommy was smiling sadly at Riley.

"You can't," Mommy said. "You can't bring back the dead."

Riley sat up, breathing hard, startled from her sleep by a rattling noise. She looked all around, on edge. The house was silent now.

But she'd heard something, she was sure. Like a noise at the front door.

Riley jumped to her feet, her instincts kicking in. She got a flashlight and her gun out of the dresser and moved carefully through the house toward the front door.

She peered through the small glass pane in the door, but saw nothing. All was silent.

Riley braced herself and quickly opened the door wide, shining the light outside. No one. Nothing.

As she moved the light around something on the front stoop caught her attention. A few pebbles were scattered there. Had somebody tossed them at the door, causing that rattling?

Riley wracked her brain, trying to remember if those pebbles had been there when she'd gotten home last night. In her haze, she simply couldn't be sure one way or the other.

Riley stood there for a few moments, but there was no sign of anybody anywhere.

She closed and locked the front door and headed back down the short hallway to her bedroom. As she reached the end, she was startled to see that April's bedroom door was slightly open.

Riley pulled the door open wide and looked inside.

Her heart pounded with terror.

April was gone.

CHAPTER TWELVE

"April!" Riley screamed. "April!"

Riley ran to the bathroom and looked inside. Her daughter wasn't there either.

She ran desperately through the house, opening doors, looking into every room and every closet. She found nothing.

"April!" she screamed again.

Riley recognized the bitter flavor of bile in her mouth. It was the taste of terror.

At last, in the kitchen, she noticed an odd smell wafting in through an open window. She recognized that smell from long-ago college days. Her terror ebbed away, replaced by sad annoyance.

"Oh, Jesus," Riley murmured aloud, feeling immense relief.

She jerked the back door open. In the early morning light she could see her daughter, still in her pajamas, sitting at the old picnic table. April looked guilty and sheepish.

"What do you want, Mom?" April asked.

Riley strode across the yard, holding out her hand.

"Give it to me," Riley said.

April awkwardly tried to display an innocent expression.

"Give you what?" she asked.

Riley's voice choked back more sadness than anger. "The joint you're smoking," she said. "And please—don't lie to me about it."

"You're crazy," April said, doing her best to sound righteously indignant. "I wasn't smoking anything. You're always assuming the worst about me. You know that, Mom?"

Riley noticed how her daughter was hunched forward as she sat on the bench.

"Move your foot," Riley said.

"What?" April said, feigning incomprehension.

Riley pointed at the suspicious foot.

"Move your foot."

April groaned aloud and obeyed. Sure enough, her bedroom slipper had been covering a freshly crushed marijuana joint. A wisp of smoke rose from it, and the smell was stronger than ever.

Riley bent down and snatched it up.

"Now give me the rest of it."

April shrugged. "The rest of what?"

Riley couldn't quite keep her voice steady. "April, I mean it. Don't lie to me. Please."

April rolled her eyes and reached into her shirt pocket. She pulled out a joint that hadn't been lit.

"Oh, for Christ's sake, here," she said, handing it to her mother. "Don't try to tell me you're not going to smoke it yourself as soon as you get a chance."

Riley shoved both joints into her bathrobe pocket.

"What else have you got?" she demanded.

"That's it, that's all there is," April snapped back. "Don't you believe me? Well, go ahead, search me. Search my room. Search everywhere. This is all I've got."

Riley was trembling all over. She struggled to bring her emotions under control.

"Where did you get these?" she asked.

April shrugged. "Cindy gave them to me."

"Who's Cindy?

April let out a cynical laugh. "Well, you wouldn't know, would you, Mom? It's not like you know much of anything about my life. What do you care, anyway? I mean, does it make any difference to you if I get high?"

Riley was stung now. April had gone right for the jugular, and it hurt. Riley couldn't hold back the tears anymore.

"April, why do you hate me?" she cried.

April looked surprised, but hardly repentant. "I don't hate you, Mom."

"Then why are you *punishing* me? What did I ever do to deserve this?"

April stared off into space. "Maybe you ought to spend some time thinking about that, Mom."

April got up from the bench and walked toward the house.

Riley wandered through the kitchen, mechanically getting out everything she needed to make breakfast. As she took the eggs and bacon out of the refrigerator, she wondered what to do about this situation. She ought to ground April immediately. But how exactly could she do that?

When Riley had been off the job, she'd been able to keep tabs on April. But everything was different now. Now that Riley was back at work, her schedule would be wildly unpredictable. And apparently, so would her daughter.

Riley mulled over her choices as she laid strips of bacon in the pan to sizzle. One thing seemed certain. Since April would be spending so much time with her father, Riley really ought to tell Ryan what had happened. But that would open up another world of problems. Ryan was already convinced that Riley was domestically incompetent, both as a wife and mother. If Riley told him that she'd caught April smoking pot in the backyard, he'd feel absolutely sure of it.

And maybe he'd be right, she thought miserably as she pushed two slices of bread down into the toaster.

So far, Ryan and Riley had managed to avoid a custody battle over April. She knew that although he'd never admit it, Ryan was enjoying his freedom as a bachelor too much to want to be bothered with raising a teenager. He hadn't been thrilled when Riley told him that April would be spending more time with him.

But she also knew that her ex-husband's attitude could change very fast, especially if he had an excuse to blame her for something. If he found out that April had been smoking pot, he might try to take her away from Riley altogether. That thought was unbearable.

A few minutes later, Riley and her daughter were sitting at the breakfast table eating. The silence between them was even more awkward than usual.

Finally April asked, "Are you going to tell Dad?"

"Do you think maybe I should?" Riley replied.

It seemed like an honest enough reply under the circumstances.

April hung her head, looking worried.

Then April pleaded, "Please don't tell Gabriela."

The words struck Riley straight to the heart. April was more worried about their housemaid finding out than she was about what her father might think—or her own mother, for that matter.

So things have gotten this bad, Riley thought miserably.

What precious little that was left of her family life was disintegrating right before her eyes. She felt as if she were barely a mother at all anymore. She wondered if Ryan had any such feelings about being a father.

Probably not. Feeling guilty wasn't Ryan's style. She sometimes envied him his emotional indifference.

After breakfast, as April got ready for school, the house fell silent, and Riley began to obsess about the other thing that had happened that morning—*if* it had happened. What or who had caused that rattling at the front door? *Had* there been a rattling at the front door? Where had those pebbles suddenly come from?

She recalled Marie's panic over strange phone calls, and an

obsessive fear was growing inside her, getting out of control. She got out her cell phone and called a familiar number.

"Betty Richter, FBI Forensics Tech," came the curt reply.

"Betty, this is Riley Paige." Riley swallowed hard. "I think you know why I'm calling."

After all, Riley had been making this exact same phone call every two or three days for the last six weeks now. Agent Richter had been in charge of closing up the details on the Peterson case, and Riley desperately wanted resolution.

"You want me to tell you that Peterson's really dead," Betty said in a sympathetic tone. Betty was the very soul of patience, understanding, and good humor, and Riley had always been grateful to have her to talk to about this.

"I know it's ridiculous."

"After all you went through?" Betty said. "No, I don't think so. But I don't have anything new to tell you. Just the same old thing. We found Peterson's body. Sure, it was burned to a cinder, but it was exactly his height and build. There's really nobody else it could have been."

"How sure are you? Give me a percentage."

"I'd say ninety-nine percent," she said.

Riley took a long, slow breath.

"You can't make that a hundred?" she asked.

Betty sighed. "Riley, I can't give you a hundred percent certainty about much of *anything* in life. Nobody can. Nobody's a hundred percent sure the sun is going to rise tomorrow morning. Earth might get smacked by a giant asteroid in the meantime, and we'll all be dead."

Riley emitted a rueful chuckle.

"Thanks for giving me something else to worry about," she said.

Betty laughed a little too. "Any time," she said. "Glad to be of help."

"Mom?" April called out, ready to go to school.

Riley ended the phone call, feeling a bit better, and prepared to go. After drop-off, she had agreed to pick up Bill today. They had a suspect to interview that fit all the demographics.

And Riley had a feeling he just might be the savage killer they were looking for.

CHAPTER THIRTEEN

Riley turned off the engine and sat before Bill's house, admiring his pleasant two-story bungalow. She'd always wondered how he managed to keep that front lawn such a healthy green and those ornamental shrubs so immaculately trimmed. Bill's domestic life might be in turmoil, but he sure did keep a nice yard, a perfect fit for this picturesque residential neighborhood. She couldn't help wondering what all the backyards looked like in this little community so close to Quantico.

Bill came out, his wife, Maggie, appearing behind him and giving Riley a ferocious glare. Riley looked away.

Bill got in and slammed the door behind him.

"Let's get the hell out of here," he growled.

Riley started the car and pulled away from the curb.

"I take it all is not well at home," she said.

Bill shook his head.

"We had a big fight when I got home so late last night. It all started up again this morning."

He was silent for a moment, then added grimly, "She's talking about divorce again. And she wants full custody of the boys."

Riley hesitated, but then she went ahead and asked the question that was on her mind, "And I'm part of the problem?"

Bill was silent.

"Yeah," he finally admitted. "She wasn't happy to hear that we're working together again. She says you're a bad influence."

Riley didn't know what to say.

Bill added, "She says I'm at my worst when I'm working with you. I'm more distracted, more obsessed with my job."

True enough, Riley thought. She and Bill were both obsessed with their jobs.

Silence fell again as they drove. After a few minutes, Bill opened up his laptop.

"I've got some details about the guy we're going to talk to. Ross Blackwell."

He scanned the screen.

"A registered sex offender," he added.

Riley's lip curled in disgust.

"What charges?"

"Possession of child pornography. He was suspected of more but nothing was ever proved. He's in the database but no restrictions on his activity. It was ten years back, and this photo is pretty old."

Sneaky, she thought. *Maybe hard to trap.*

Bill continued reading.

"Fired from several jobs, for vague reasons. The last time he was working in a chain store in a big mall in the Beltway—really mainstream commercial stuff, and its market is mostly families with kids. When they caught Blackwell posing dolls in kinky positions, they fired and reported him."

"A man with a quirk about dolls and a record of child pornography," Riley muttered.

So far, Ross Blackwell fit the profile that she was starting to put together.

"And now?" she asked.

"He's got a job in a hobby and model shop," Bill replied. "Another chain store in another mall."

Riley was a bit surprised.

"Didn't the managers know about Blackwell's record when they hired him?"

Bill shrugged.

"Maybe they don't care. His interests seem to be entirely heterosexual. Maybe they don't figure he'll do much harm in a place that's all about model cars and airplanes and trains."

She felt a chill run through her body. Why would a guy like that even be able to get another job? This man seemed likely to be a vicious killer. Why would he be let out every day to cruise around among those who were vulnerable?

They finally made their way through the relentless traffic to Sanfield. The D.C. suburb struck Riley as a typical example of an "edge city," largely made up of malls and corporate headquarters. She found it to be soulless, plastic, and depressing.

She parked outside the huge shopping mall. For a moment, she just sat in the driver's seat and stared at the old photograph of Blackwell on Bill's laptop. There was nothing distinctive about his face, just a white guy with dark hair and an insolent expression. Now he would be in his fifties.

She and Bill got out of the car and made their way on foot through the consumers' utopia, until they saw the scale model store.

"I don't want to let him get away," Riley said. "What if he spots us and bolts?"

"We should be able to corner him inside," Bill replied. "Immobilize him and get the customers out."

Riley put one hand on her gun.

Not yet, she told herself. *Don't cause a panic if we don't have to.*

She stood there for a moment, watching the store's customers coming and going. Was one of those guys Blackwell? Was he already escaping them?

Riley and Bill walked in through the door of the model shop. Most of the space was taken up by a sprawling and detailed reproduction of a small town, complete with a running train and flashing traffic lights. Model airplanes hung from the ceiling. There wasn't a doll in sight.

Several men seemed to be working in the store, but none of them fit the image she held in her mind.

"I can't spot him," Riley said.

At the front desk Bill asked, "Do you have a certain Ross Blackwell working here?"

The man at the cash register nodded and pointed toward a rack with scale modeling kits. A short, pudgy man with graying hair was sorting the merchandise. His back was to them.

Riley touched her gun again, but left it in the holster. She and Bill spread out so they could block any escape attempt Blackwell might make.

Her heart beat faster as she approached.

"Ross Blackwell?" Riley asked.

The man turned around. He wore thick glasses and his belly protruded over his belt. Riley was especially struck by the dull, anemic pallor of his skin. She thought that he didn't seem likely to run, but her judgment of "creep" fit him just fine.

"It depends," Blackwell replied with a wide smile. "What's your business?"

Riley and Bill both showed him their badges.

"Wow, the Feds, huh?" Blackwell said, sounding almost pleased. "This is new. I'm used to dealing with the local authorities. You're not here to arrest me, I hope. Because I really thought all those weird misunderstandings were a thing of the past."

"We'd just like to ask you a few questions," Bill said.

Blackwell smirked a little and tilted his head inquiringly.

"A few questions, huh? Well, I know the Bill of Rights pretty much by heart. I don't have to talk to you if I don't want to. But hey, why not? It might even be fun. If you'll buy me a cup of coffee, I'll go along with it."

Blackwell walked toward the front desk, and Riley and Bill followed close behind him. Riley was alert for any attempt at evading them.

"I'm taking a coffee break, Bernie," Blackwell called out to the cashier.

Riley could tell by Bill's expression that he was wondering if they'd gotten the right guy. She understood why he might feel that way. Blackwell didn't seem the least bit upset to see them. In fact, he seemed to be rather pleased.

But as far as Riley was concerned, this made him seem all the more amoral and sociopathic. Some of the vilest serial killers in history had displayed plenty of charm and self-assurance. The last thing she expected was for the killer to *seem* the least bit guilty.

It was only a short way to the food court. Blackwell escorted Bill and Riley straight to a coffee counter. If the man was nervous about being with two FBI agents, he didn't show it.

A little girl who was trailing along behind her mother stumbled and fell just in front of them.

"Whoops!" Blackwell cried out cheerfully. He bent over and lifted the child to her feet.

The mother said an automatic thanks, then led her daughter off by the hand. Riley watched Blackwell eye the little girl's bare legs beneath her short skirt, and she felt sick to her stomach. Her suspicion deepened.

Riley grabbed Blackwell's arm hard, but he gave her a look of bewilderment and innocence. She shook his arm and let him go.

"Get your coffee," she said, nodding to nearby the cafe counter.

"I'd like a cappuccino," Blackwell said to the young woman behind the counter. "These folks are buying."

Then, turning to Bill and Riley, he asked, "What are you two having?"

"We're fine," Riley said.

Bill paid for the cappuccino, and the three of them headed toward a table that didn't have other people seated nearby.

"Okay, so what do you want to know about me?" Blackwell asked. He seemed relaxed and friendly. "I hope you're not going to get all judgmental, like the authorities I'm used to. People are so closed-minded these days."

"Closed-minded about putting dolls in obscene poses?" Bill asked.

Blackwell looked sincerely hurt. "You make it sound so

66

dirty," he said. "There wasn't anything obscene about it. Have a look for yourselves."

Blackwell got out his cell phone and started showing photographs of his handiwork. They included little pornographic tableaus he had created inside of dollhouses. The little human figures were in various states of undress. They had been posed in an imaginative array of groupings and positions in different parts of the houses. Riley's mind boggled at the variety of sex acts portrayed in the pictures—some of them quite probably illegal in many states.

Looks plenty obscene to me, Riley thought.

"I was being satirical," Blackwell explained. "I was making an important social statement. We live in such a crass and materialistic culture. *Somebody's* got to make this kind of protest. I was exercising my right to free speech in a thoroughly responsible way. I wasn't abusing it. It's not like I was yelling 'fire' in a crowded theater."

Riley noticed that Bill was starting to look indignant.

"What about the little kids who stumbled across these little scenes of yours?" Bill asked. "Don't you think you were harming them?"

"No, as a matter of fact, I don't," Blackwell said rather smugly. "They get worse things out of the media every single day. There's no such thing as childhood innocence anymore. That's exactly what I was trying to tell the world. It breaks my heart, I tell you."

He actually sounds like he means it, Riley thought.

But it was obvious to her that he didn't mean it at all. Ross Blackwell didn't have a single moral or empathetic bone in his body. Riley suspected his guilt more and more with every passing moment.

She tried to read his face. It wasn't easy. Like all true sociopaths, he masked his feelings with amazing skill.

"Tell me, Ross," she said. "Do you like the outdoors? I mean like camping and fishing."

Blackwell's face lit up with a broad smile. "Oh, yeah. Ever since I was a kid. I was an Eagle Scout back in the day. I sometimes go off into the wilderness alone for weeks at a time. Sometimes I think I was Daniel Boone in a previous life."

Riley asked, "Do you like to go hunting, too?"

"Sure, all the time," he said enthusiastically. "I've got lots of trophies at home. You know, mounted heads of elks and deer. I mount them all myself. I've got a real flare for taxidermy."

Riley squinted at Blackwell.

"Do you have any favorite places? Forests and such, I mean. State and national parks."

Blackwell stroked his chin thoughtfully.

"I go to Yellowstone a lot," he said. "I suppose that's my favorite. Of course, it's hard to beat the Great Smoky Mountains. Yosemite, too. It's not easy to choose."

Bill put in, "How about Mosby State Park? Or maybe that national park near Daggett?"

Blackwell suddenly looked a bit wary.

"Why do you want to know?" he asked uneasily.

Riley knew that the moment of truth—or its opposite—had finally arrived. She reached into her purse and pulled out photographs of the murder victims, taken when they were alive.

"Can you identify any of these women?" Riley asked.

Blackwell's eyes widened with alarm.

"No," he said, his voice shaking. "I've never seen them in my life."

"Are you sure?" Riley prodded. "Maybe their names will refresh your memory. Reba Frye. Eileen Rogers. Margaret Geraty."

Blackwell seemed on the edge of sheer panic.

"Nope," he said. "I've never seen them. Never heard their names."

Riley studied his face closely for a moment. Finally, she fully understood the situation. She knew all she needed to know about Ross Blackwell.

"Thank you for your time, Ross," she said. "We'll be in touch if we need to know anything else."

Bill looked dumbfounded as he followed her out of the food court.

"What was going on back there?" he snapped. "What are you thinking? He's guilty and he knows that we're on to him. We can't let him out of our sight until we can nail him."

Riley let out a sigh of mild impatience.

"Think about it, Bill," she said. "Did you get a look at that pale skin of his? Not even a solitary freckle. That guy's scarcely spent a whole day outdoors in his life."

"So he's not really an Eagle Scout?"

Riley chuckled slightly. "Nope," she said. "And I can promise you he's never been to Yellowstone or Yosemite or the Great Smoky Mountains. And he doesn't know a thing about taxidermy."

Bill looked positively embarrassed now.

"He really had me believing him," Bill said.

Riley nodded in agreement.

"Of course he did," she said. "He's a great liar. He can make people believe he's telling the truth about anything. And he just loves to lie. He does it whenever he gets a chance—and the bigger the lies, the better."

She paused for a moment.

"The trouble is," Riley added, "he's lousy at telling the truth. He's not used to it. He loses his cool when he tries to do it."

Bill walked silently beside her for a moment, trying to take this in.

"So you're saying—?" he began.

"He was telling the truth about the women, Bill. That's why he sounded so guilty. The truth always sounds like a lie when he tries to tell it. He really and truly never saw any of those women in his life. I'm not saying he's not capable of murder. He probably is. But he didn't do *these* murders."

Bill growled under his breath.

"Damn," he said.

Riley didn't say anything the rest of the way to the car. This was a serious setback. The more she thought about it, the more alarmed she felt. The real killer was still out there, and they still didn't have a clue who or where he was. And she knew, she just knew, that he would soon kill again.

Riley was getting frustrated with her inability to figure this case out, but as she wracked her brain, it suddenly occurred to her who she needed to talk to. Right now.

CHAPTER FOURTEEN

They were just a short distance out of Sanfield when Riley suddenly crossed two lanes and veered onto an exit ramp.

Bill was surprised. "Where are we going?" he asked.

"Belding," Riley said.

Bill stared at her from the passenger's seat, waiting for more of an explanation.

"Margaret Geraty's husband still lives there," she said. "Roy's his name, right? Roy Geraty. And doesn't he own a filling station or something?"

"Actually, it's an auto repair and supply store," Bill said.

Riley nodded. "We're going to pay him a visit," she said.

Bill shrugged doubtfully.

"Okay, but I'm not sure why," he said. "The locals did a pretty thorough job interviewing him about his wife's murder. They didn't get any leads."

Riley didn't say anything for a while. She knew all this already. Still, she felt as if there was something yet to be learned. Some sort of loose end must have been left hanging in Belding, just a short drive away through Virginia farm country. She just had to find out what it was—if she could. But she was starting to doubt herself.

"I'm rusty, Bill," Riley muttered as she drove. "For a while back there, I was really sure that Ross Blackwell was our killer. I ought to have known better at first glance. My instincts are shot."

"Don't be too hard on yourself," Bill replied. "He seemed to fit your profile."

Riley groaned under her breath. "Yeah, but my profile was wrong. Our guy wouldn't pose dolls like that—and not in a public place."

"Why not?" Bill asked.

Riley thought for a moment.

"Because he takes dolls too seriously," she said. "They hold some really deep significance for him. It's something personal. I think he'd be offended by little stunts like Blackwell's, the way he posed them. He'd consider it vulgar. Dolls aren't toys to him. They're ... I don't know. I can't quite get it."

"I know how your mind works," Bill said. "And whatever it is

70

will come to you eventually."

Riley fell silent as she mentally replayed some of the events of the last few days. That only heightened her sense of insecurity.

"I've been wrong about other stuff, too," she told Bill. "I thought the killer was targeting mothers. I was sure of it. But Margaret Geraty wasn't a mother. How could I get that wrong?"

"You'll hit your stride soon," Bill said.

They reached the outskirts of Belding. It was a tired-looking little town that must have been there for generations. But the nearby farms had been bought up by wealthy families who wanted to be "gentleman farmers" and still commute to power jobs in D.C. The town was fading away and one might almost drive through it without noticing it.

Roy Geraty's auto repair and supply store was impossible to miss.

Riley and Bill got out of the car and went into the rather seedy front office. No one was there. Riley rang a little bell on the counter. They waited, but no one came. After a few minutes, they ventured into the garage. A single pair of feet poked out from beneath one vehicle.

"Are you Roy Geraty?" Riley asked.

"Yeah," came a voice from under the car.

Riley looked around. There wasn't another employee in sight. Had things gotten so bad that the owner had to do everything by himself?

Geraty came rolling out from under the car and squinted at them suspiciously. He was a bulky man in his middle to late thirties, and he was wearing oil-stained coveralls. He wiped his hands on a dirty cloth and got to his feet.

"You're not local," he said. Then he added, "Well, what can I help you with?"

"We're with the FBI," Bill said. "We'd like to ask you some questions."

"Ah, Jesus," the man growled. "I don't need this."

"It won't take long," Riley said.

"Well, come on," the man grumbled. "If we've got to talk, we've got to talk."

He led Riley and Bill into a little employee break area with a couple of banged-up vending machines. They all sat down on plastic chairs. Almost as if nobody else was there, Roy picked up a remote and turned on an old television. He fumbled around switching channels until he found an old sitcom. Then he stared at the screen.

"Just ask what you want and let's get it over with," he said. "These last few days have been hell."

Riley found it easy to guess what he meant.

"I'm sorry your wife's murder is back in the news," she said.

"The papers say there have been two more like it," Geraty said. "I can't believe it. My phone's been ringing off the hook with reporters and just plain assholes. My email inbox is flooded too. There's no respect for privacy anymore. And poor Evelyn—my wife—she's really shook up about it."

"You've remarried?" Bill asked.

Geraty nodded, still staring at the TV screen. "We tied the knot seven months after Margaret ..."

He couldn't make himself finish the sentence.

"Folks around here thought it was too fast," he said. "It didn't seem too fast to me. I'd never been lonelier in my life. Evelyn's been a gift from heaven. I don't know what would have become of me without her. I guess maybe I'd have died."

His voice grew thick with emotion.

"We've got a baby girl now. Six months old. Her name's Lucy. The joy of my life."

The sitcom laugh track on the TV erupted with inappropriate laughter. Geraty sniffed and cleared his throat and leaned back in his chair.

"Anyway, I sure can't figure what you want to ask me about," he said. "Seems to me I answered every kind of question you can think of two years ago. It didn't do any good. You couldn't catch the guy then, and you're not going to catch him now."

"We're still trying," Riley said. "We'll bring him to justice."

But she could feel the hollowness in her own words.

She paused a moment, then asked, "Do you live near here? I was wondering if we might be able to visit your house, have a look around."

Geraty knitted his brow in thought.

"Do I have to? Or do I have a choice about it?" he asked.

His question took Riley slightly aback.

"It's just a request," she said. "But it might be helpful."

Geraty shook his head firmly.

"No," he said. "I've got to draw a line. The cops practically moved into my place back in those days. Some of them were sure I'd killed her. Maybe some of you guys are thinking the same thing now. That I killed somebody."

"No," Riley reassured him. "That's not why we're here."

She saw that Bill was watching the mechanic very closely.

Geraty didn't look up. He just went on. "And poor Evelyn—she's home with Lucy, and she's already a nervous wreck from all the phone calls. I won't put her through any more of it. I'm sorry, I don't mean to be uncooperative. It's just that enough is enough."

Riley could tell that Bill was about to insist. She spoke before he could.

"I understand," she said. "It's all right."

Riley felt sure that she and Bill probably were not likely to learn anything important from a visit to the Geraty home anyhow. But maybe he would answer a question or two.

"Did your wife—Margaret, your first wife—like dolls?" Riley asked cautiously. "Did she collect them, maybe?"

Geraty turned toward her, looking away from the TV for the first time.

"No," he said, looking surprised at the question.

Riley realized that no one would have asked that particular question before. Of all the theories the police might have had two years ago, dolls wouldn't have been among them. And even in the harassment he was undergoing now, no one else would have made a connection with dolls.

"She didn't like them," Geraty continued. "It wasn't like she hated them. It's just that they made her sad. She couldn't—*we* couldn't—have children, and dolls always made her think about that. They reminded her. Sometimes she'd even cry when she was around dolls."

With a deep sigh, he turned back toward the TV again.

"She was unhappy about it during those last years," he said in a low, faraway voice. "Not having kids, I mean. So many friends and relatives, having kids of their own. It seemed like everybody except us was having babies all the time, or had kids growing up. There were always baby showers to go to, mothers always asking her to help out with birthday parties. It really got her down."

Riley felt a lump of sympathy form in her throat. Her heart went out to this man who was still trying to put his life back together after an incomprehensible tragedy.

"I think that will be all, Mr. Geraty," she said. "Thanks so much for your time. And I know it's awfully late to be saying so, but I'm sorry for your loss."

A few moments later, Riley and Bill were driving away.

"A wasted trip," Riley said to Bill.

Riley looked in the rearview mirror and saw the little town of Belding vanishing behind them. The killer wasn't there, she knew. But he was somewhere in the area that Flores had shown them on

73

the map. Somewhere close. Perhaps they were driving by his trailer right now and didn't even know it. The thought tortured Riley. She could almost feel his presence, his eagerness, his urge to torture and kill that was becoming an ever more compelling need.

And she had to stop it.

CHAPTER FIFTEEN

The man was awakened by his cell phone alarm. At first he didn't know where he was. But he knew right away that today was going to be important. It was the kind of day he lived for.

He knew that he had awakened in this strange place for a very good reason—because it was to be that kind of day. It would be a day of delicious satisfaction for him, and of sheer terror and indescribable pain for someone else.

But where was he? Still half-asleep, he couldn't remember. He was lying on a couch in a small, carpeted room, looking at a refrigerator and a microwave. Morning light streamed through a window.

He got up, opened the door to the room, and looked out into a dark hallway. He flipped on the room light beside the doorframe. Light shined out into the hallway and into an open door across the hallway. He could make out a black-upholstered medical examination table with some sterilized white paper stretched along it.

Of course, he thought. *The free medical clinic.*

Now he remembered where he was and how he'd gotten here. He congratulated himself on his stealth and cunning. Yesterday he'd arrived at the clinic late in the day, when it was especially busy. In the midst of the bustle of patients, he had asked for a simple blood pressure test. And *she* had been the nurse who tested him.

The very woman he had come here to see. The woman he had been watching for days, at her home, when she was shopping, when she came here to work.

After the blood pressure test he'd squeezed himself into a tight space deep inside a supply closet. How innocent all the staff had been. The clinic had closed and everyone had gone home without even checking the closets. Then he'd crept out and made himself at home right here, in the little staff lounge. He'd slept well.

And today was going to be a very remarkable day.

He turned the ceiling light off immediately. No one outside must know that anyone was in the building. He looked at the time on his cell phone. It was just a few minutes before seven a.m.

She would arrive any minute now. He knew this from his days

75

of surveillance. It was her job to get the clinic ready for both physicians and patients every morning. The clinic itself didn't open until eight. Between seven and eight, she was always alone here.

But today was going to be different. Today she would not be alone.

He heard a car pull into the parking lot outside. He adjusted the venetian blinds just enough to look outside. It was her, all right, stepping out of the car.

He had no trouble steadying his nerves. This was not like those first two times, when he had felt so fearful and apprehensive. Ever since the third time, when everything had flowed so smoothly, he knew he had really hit his stride. Now he was seasoned and skillful.

But there was one thing he wanted to do a little differently, just to vary his routine, to make this time a little different from the others.

He was going to surprise her with a little token—his own personal calling card.

*

As Cindy MacKinnon walked through the empty parking lot, she mentally rehearsed her daily routine. After getting all the supplies in place, her first order of business would be to sign refill requests from pharmacies and make sure the appointment calendar was up to date.

Patients would be waiting outside the door by the time they opened at eight. The rest of the day would be devoted to sundry tasks, including taking vital signs, drawing blood, giving shots, making appointments, and fulfilling the often unreasonable demands of the registered nurses and physicians.

Her work here as a licensed practical nurse was hardly glamorous. Even so, she loved what she did. It was deeply gratifying to help people who otherwise couldn't afford medical care. She knew that they saved lives here, even with the basic services that they offered.

Cindy took the clinic keys out of her purse and unlocked the glass front door. She stepped inside quickly and locked the door behind her. Someone else would unlock it again at eight o'clock. Then she immediately punched in the code to deactivate the building alarm.

As she walked into the waiting area, something caught her

eye. It was a small object lying on the floor. In the dim light, she couldn't make out what it was.

She switched on the overhead lights. The object on the floor was a rose.

She walked over to it and picked it up. The rose wasn't real. It was artificial, made of cheap fabric. But what was it doing there?

Probably a patient had dropped it yesterday. But why hadn't someone picked it up after the clinic closed at five p.m.?

Why hadn't *she* seen it yesterday? She had waited until the cleaning woman was finished. She had been the last to leave and she was sure the rose hadn't been there.

Then came a rush of adrenaline and an explosion of pure fear. She knew what the rose meant. She wasn't alone. She knew she had to get out. She didn't have a split second to lose.

But as she turned to run toward the door, a strong hand seized her arm from behind, stopping her in her tracks. There was no time to think. She had to let her body act on its own.

She raised her elbow and whirled around, throwing her whole weight to the side and back. She felt her elbow strike a hard but pliable surface. She heard a fierce, loud groan and felt the weight of her attacker's body tilting upon her.

Had she been lucky and hit his solar plexus? She couldn't turn around to see. There wasn't time—a few seconds, if even that.

She ran toward the door. But time slowed down, and it didn't feel like running at all. It felt like moving through thick, clear gelatin.

Finally she reached the door and tried to pull it open. But of course she had locked it after coming inside.

She groped frantically through her purse until she found her keys. Then her hands shook so badly that she couldn't hold them. They fell clattering to the ground. Time stretched out even further as she bent over and picked them up. She fumbled among the keys until she found the right one. Then she stabbed the key at the lock.

It was useless. Her hand was useless from shaking. She felt as if her body were betraying her.

At last, her eye caught a glimpse of movement outside. On the sidewalk beyond the parking lot a woman was walking her dog. Still gripping the keys, she raised her fists and pounded against the impossibly hard glass. She opened her mouth to scream.

But her voice was stifled by something tight across her mouth, pulling painfully at the corners. It was cloth—a rag or a handkerchief or a scarf. Her attacker had gagged her with merciless and implacable force. Her eyes bulged, but instead of a scream, all she could emit was a horrible groan.

She flailed her arms, and the keys fell again from her hand. She was pulled helplessly backward, away from the morning light into a dark, murky world of sudden and unimaginable horror.

CHAPTER SIXTEEN

"Do you feel kind of out of place?" Bill asked.

"Yeah," Riley said. "And I'm sure we both look it, too."

A seemingly random mix of dolls and people were seated in the leather-upholstered furniture of the ostentatious hotel lobby. The people—mostly women, but a few men—were drinking tea and coffee and chatting with one another. Dolls of sundry types, both male and female, sat among them like perfectly behaved children. Riley thought it looked like some bizarre kind of family reunion in which none of the children were real.

Riley couldn't help staring at the odd scene. With no more leads to follow, she and Bill had decided to come here, to this doll convention, hoping she might stumble upon some lead, however remote.

"Are you two registered?" he asked

Riley turned to see a security guard eyeing Bill's jacket, undoubtedly having detected his concealed weapon. The guard held his hand near his own holstered gun.

She thought that with this many people around, the guard had good reason to worry. A crazed shooter really could wreak havoc in a place like this.

Bill flashed his badge. "FBI," he said.

The guard chuckled.

"Can't say I'm surprised," he said.

"Why not?" Riley asked.

The guard shook his head.

"Because this is just about the weirdest bunch of people I ever saw in one place."

"Yeah," Bill agreed. "And they're not even all people."

The guard shrugged and replied, "You can bet that *somebody* here has done something they shouldn't have."

The man jerked his head to one side then the other, scanning the room.

"I'll be glad when it's all over." Then he strode away, looking wary and alert.

As she wandered with Bill into an adjoining hallway, Riley wasn't sure what the guard was so worried about. Generally speaking, the attendees looked more eccentric than menacing. The women in view ranged from young to elderly. Some were stern and dour looking, while others seemed open and friendly.

"Tell me again what you hope to find out here," Bill muttered.

"I'm not sure," Riley admitted.

"Maybe you're making too much of the whole doll thing," he said, clearly unhappy to be here. "Blackwell was creepy about dolls, but he wasn't the perp. And yesterday we learned that the first victim didn't even like dolls."

Riley didn't reply. Bill might well be right. But when he had showed her a brochure announcing this convention and show, she somehow couldn't help following through. She wanted to make another try.

The men Riley saw tended to look bookish and professorial, most of them wearing glasses and more than a few of them sporting goatees. None of them appeared quite capable of murder. She passed a seated woman who was lovingly rocking a baby doll in her arms and singing a lullaby. A little farther on, an elderly woman was carrying on a rapt conversation with a life-sized monkey doll.

Okay, Riley thought, *so there is a little bit of weirdness going on.*

Bill pulled the brochure out of his jacket pocket and browsed it as they walked along.

"Anything interesting happening?" Riley asked him.

"Just talks, lectures, workshops—that kind of thing. Some big manufacturers are here to bring store owners up to date on trends and crazes. And there are some folks who seem to have gotten famous in the whole doll scene. They're giving talks of one kind or another."

Then Bill laughed.

"Hey, here's a lecture with a real doozy of a title."

"What is it?"

"'The Social Construction of Victorian Gender in Period Porcelain Dolls.' It's going to start in a few minutes. Want to check it out?"

Riley laughed as well. "I'm sure we wouldn't understand a word of it. Anything else?"

Bill shook his head. "Not really. Nothing to help understand the motives of a sadistic killer, anyway."

Riley and Bill moved on into the next big open room. It was a gigantic maze of booths and tables, where every conceivable kind of doll or puppet was on exhibit. They ranged from as tiny as a single finger to life size, from antique to fresh out of the factory. Some of them were walking and some were talking, but most of them just hung or sat or stood there, staring back at the viewers who clustered in front of each one.

For the first time Riley saw that actual children were present—no boys, only small girls. Most were under their parents' immediate supervision, but a few wandered loose in unruly little groups, putting exhibitors' nerves on edge.

Riley picked up a miniature camera from a table. The attached tag claimed that it worked. On the same counter were tiny newspapers, stuffed toys, handbags, wallets, and backpacks. On the next table were doll-sized bathtubs and other bathroom fixtures.

The T-shirt station printed shirts for dolls and for full-size people, but the hair salon was for dolls only. The sight of several small carefully styled wigs gave Riley chills. The FBI had already found the manufacturers of the wigs from the murder scenes and knew that they were sold in countless stores everywhere. Seeing them lined up like this brought back images that Riley knew that other people here didn't share. Images of dead women, naked, sitting splayed like dolls, wearing ill-fitting wigs made out of doll hair.

Riley felt sure that those images would never fade from her mind. The women treated so callously, yet so carefully arranged to represent … something she couldn't quite pin down. But of course that was why she and Bill were even here.

She stepped forward and spoke to the perky young woman who seemed to be charge of the doll-hair salon.

"Do you sell these wigs here?" Riley asked.

"Of course," the woman responded. "Those are just for display, but I have brand new ones in boxes. Which one would you like?"

Riley wasn't sure what to say next. "Do you style these little wigs?" she finally asked.

"We can change the style for you. It's a very small additional charge."

"What kind of people buy them?" Riley said. She wanted to ask whether any creepy guys had been around to buy doll wigs.

The woman looked at her, wide-eyed. "I'm not sure what you mean," she said. "All kinds of people buy them. Sometimes they bring in a doll they already have to get the hair changed."

"I mean, do men often buy them?" Riley asked.

The young woman was looking distinctly uncomfortable now.

"Not that I recall," she said. Then she turned abruptly away to deal with a new customer.

Riley just stood there for a moment. She felt like an idiot, accosting someone with such questions. It was as though she had thrust her own dark world into one that was supposed to be sweet and simple.

She felt a touch on her arm. Bill said, "I don't think you're going to find the perp here."

Riley could feel her face flush. But as she turned away from the doll-hair salon, she realized that she wasn't the only strange lady that the exhibitors here had to deal with. She almost walked into a woman desperately clutching a newly bought doll, weeping passionately, apparently with joy. At another table, a man and a woman had gotten into a shouting match over which of them would get to buy a particularly rare collector's item. They were engaged in a physical tug-of-war that threatened to tear the merchandise apart.

"Now I begin to see why that security guard was worried," she said to Bill.

She saw that Bill was intently watching someone nearby.

"What?" she asked him.

"Check out that guy," Bill said, nodding toward a man standing at a nearby display of large dolls in frilly dresses. He was in his mid-thirties and quite handsome. Unlike most of the other males here, he didn't look bookish or scholarly. Instead, he cut the appearance of a prosperous and confident businessman, properly dressed in an expensive suit and tie.

"He looks as out of place as we do," Bill muttered. "Why is a guy like that playing with dolls?"

"I don't know," Riley replied. "But he also looks like he could hire a real live playmate if he wanted to." She watched the businessman for a moment. He had stopped to look at a display of little girl dolls in frilly dresses. He glanced around, as if to be sure that no one was watching.

Bill turned his back to the man and leaned forward as if talking animatedly with Riley. "What's he doing now?"

"Checking out the merchandise," she said. "In a way I really don't like."

The man bent toward one doll and peered at it closely— maybe a little too closely—and his thin lips curled up into a smile. Then he again scanned the others in the room.

"Or looking for prospective victims," she added.

Riley was sure she detected a certain furtiveness in the man's manner as he fingered the doll's dress, examining the fabric in a sensuous manner.

Bill glanced at the man again. "Jesus," he murmured. "Is this guy creepy or what?"

A chilly feeling seized Riley. Rationally, she knew perfectly well that this couldn't be the murderer. After all, what were the chances of stumbling across him in public like this? Still, at that moment Riley was convinced that she was in the presence of evil.

"Don't let him get out of sight," Riley said. "If he gets weird enough, we'll ask him some questions."

But then, reality blew those dark thoughts away. A little girl about five years old came running up to the man.

"Daddy," she called him.

The man's smile widened, and his face beamed innocently with love. He showed his daughter the doll he had found, and she clapped her hands and laughed with delight. He handed it to her and she hugged it tightly. The father took out his wallet and got ready to pay the vendor.

Riley stifled a groan.

My instincts miss again, she thought.

She saw that Bill was listening to someone on his cell phone. His face looked stricken as he turned toward her.

"He's taken another woman."

CHAPTER SEVENTEEN

Riley cursed under her breath as she pulled into the parking lot beside a long, flat-roofed building. Three people wearing FBI jackets were standing outside, mingling with several local cops.

"This can't be good," Riley said. "I wish we'd gotten here before the hordes descended."

"No joke," Bill agreed.

They'd been told that a woman had been kidnapped from inside this small-town medical clinic, taken early this morning.

"At least we're getting on it faster this time," Bill said. "Maybe we stand a chance of getting her back alive."

Riley silently agreed. In the earlier cases, no one had known exactly when or where the victim was kidnapped. The women had just disappeared and later turned up dead accompanied by cryptic signs of the killer's mindset.

Maybe it will be different this time, she thought.

She was relieved that someone had witnessed enough of the crime to call 911. The local police knew about an alert for a serial kidnapper and killer, and they had called in the FBI. They were all assuming that this was the same deviant at work.

"He's still way ahead of us," Riley said. "If it's really him. This is not the kind of place I expected our perp to grab someone."

She had thought the killer would be stalking a parking garage or an isolated jogging trail. Maybe even a poorly lit neighborhood.

"Why a community clinic?" she asked. "And why in daylight? Why would he take the chance of entering a building?"

"Sure doesn't seem like a random choice," Bill agreed. "Let's get moving."

Riley parked as close to the taped-off area as she could. As she and Bill got out of the car, she recognized Special Agent in Charge Carl Walder.

"This is *really* bad," Riley muttered to Bill as they walked toward the building.

Riley didn't think much of Walder—a babyish, freckled-faced man with curly, copper-colored hair. Neither Riley nor Bill had personally worked a case under him, but he had a bad reputation. Other agents said that he was the worst kind of boss—someone who had no idea what he was doing, and was therefore all the more determined to throw his weight around and assert his authority.

To make matters worse for Riley and Bill, Walder outranked their own team chief, Brent Meredith. Riley didn't know how old Walder was, but she was sure that he had risen up the FBI food chain too fast for his own good, or for anybody else's.

As far as Riley was concerned, it was a classic example of the Peter Principle at work. Walder had successfully risen to the level of his incompetence.

Walder stepped forward to meet Riley and Bill.

"Agents Paige and Jeffreys, I'm glad you could make it," he said.

Without niceties, Riley went right ahead and asked Walder the question that was nagging at her.

"How do we know it's the same perp that took the other three women?"

"Because of this," Walder said, holding out an evidence bag holding a cheap little fabric rose. "It was lying on the floor just inside."

"Oh, shit," Riley said.

The Bureau had been careful not to leak to the press that detail of his MO—how he'd left roses at the scenes where he'd posed the bodies. This was not the work of a copycat or of a brand new killer.

"Who was it this time?" Bill asked.

"Her name is Cindy MacKinnon," Walder said. "She's an LPN. She was abducted when she came in early to set up the clinic."

Then Walder indicated the other two agents, a young female and an even younger male. "Perhaps you've met Agents Craig Huang and Emily Creighton. They'll be joining you on this case."

Bill audibly murmured, "What the—"

Riley poked Bill in the ribs to shut him up.

"Huang and Creighton have already been briefed," Walder added. "They know as much about these murders as you do."

Riley fumed silently. She wanted to tell Walder that no, Huang and Creighton did *not* know as much as she did. Not even as much as Bill did. They couldn't know that much without having spent as much time at the crime scenes, or without having spent uncounted hours poring over evidence. They didn't have anything resembling the professional investment she and Bill had already put into this case. And she was sure that neither of these youngsters had ever summoned up the mind of a killer to get a sense of his experience.

Riley took a deep breath to stifle her anger.

"With due respect, sir," she said, "Agent Jeffreys and I have got a pretty good handle on it and we'll need to work fast. Extra help … won't help." She'd almost said that extra help would just slow them down, but had stopped herself in time. No point in insulting the kids.

Riley detected a trace of a smirk on Walder's babyish face.

"With due respect, Agent Paige," he replied, "Senator Newbrough doesn't agree."

Riley's heart sank. She remembered her unpleasant interview with the Senator and something he had said. *"You may not know it, but I've got good friends in the upper echelons of the agency."*

Of course Walder had to be one of those "good friends."

Walder lifted his chin and spoke with borrowed authority. "The Senator says that you're having trouble grasping the full magnitude of this case."

"I'm afraid the Senator is letting his emotions run away with him," Riley said. "It's understandable, and I sympathize. He's distraught. He thinks that his daughter's killing was political or personal or both. It obviously wasn't."

Walder squinted his eyes skeptically.

"How is it obvious?" he said. "It seems obvious to me that he's right."

Riley could hardly believe her ears

"Sir, the Senator's daughter was the third woman taken out of what are now four," she said. "His time frame has been spread out over more than two years. It's purely coincidence that his daughter happened to be one of the victims."

"I beg to differ," Walder said. "And so do Agents Huang and Creighton."

As if on cue, Agent Emily Creighton piped in.

"Doesn't this kind of thing happen from time to time?" she said. "Like, sometimes a perpetrator will stage another murder before killing his intended victim? Just to make it look serial and not personal?"

"This last abduction could serve the same purpose," added Agent Craig Huang. "A final decoy."

Riley managed not to roll her eyes at the kids' naiveté.

"That's an old, old story," she said. "A work of fiction. It doesn't happen in real life."

"Well," Walder said in an authoritative tone, "it happened *this* time."

"We don't have time for this," Riley snapped. Her patience had run out. "Have we got any witnesses?"

"One," Walder said. "Greta Tedrow made the 911 call but she didn't actually see much. She's sitting inside. The receptionist is in there too, but she didn't see it happen. By the time she showed up at eight o'clock, the cops were already here."

Through the clinic's glass doors, Riley could see two women sitting in the waiting room. One was a slim woman in running clothes, with a cocker spaniel on a leash beside her. The other was large, middle-aged, and Hispanic-looking.

"Have you interviewed Ms. Tedrow?" Riley asked Walder.

"She's been too shaken up to talk," Walder said. "We're going to take her back to the BAU."

Riley actually did roll her eyes this time. Why make an innocent witness feel like a suspect? Why play the bully, as if that wouldn't shake her up even more?

Ignoring Walder's gesture of protest, she swung a door open and strode through the entrance.

Bill followed her in, but he left the interview to Riley while he checked a couple of adjoining offices, then poked around the waiting room.

The woman with the dog looked at Riley anxiously.

"What's going on?" Greta Tedrow asked. "I'm ready to answer questions. But nobody's asking me anything. Why can't I go home?"

Riley sat in a chair beside her and patted her hand.

"You will go home, Ms. Tedrow, and soon," she said. "I'm Agent Paige, and I'll ask you a few questions right now."

Greta Tedrow nodded shakily. The cocker spaniel just lay there on the floor looking up at Riley in a friendly manner.

"Nice dog," Riley said. "Very well behaved. How old is he— or is it a she?"

"It's he. Toby's his name. He's five years old."

Riley slowly held her hand toward the dog. With the animal's silent permission, she petted his head lightly.

The woman nodded an unspoken thank-you. Riley got out her pencil and notepad.

"Now take your time, don't rush," Riley said. "Tell me in your own words how it happened. Try to remember everything you can."

The woman spoke slowly and haltingly.

"I was walking Toby." She pointed outside. "We were just coming around the corner beyond the hedges, over that way. The clinic had just come into view. I thought I heard something. I looked. There was a woman in the clinic doorway. She was pounding on the glass. I think her mouth was gagged. Then someone pulled her backward out of sight."

Riley patted the woman's hand again.

"You're doing great, Ms. Tedrow," she said. "Did you see her attacker at all?"

The woman wrestled with her memory.

"I didn't see his face," she said. "I *couldn't* see his face. The light was on in the clinic, but …"

Riley could see a flash of recollection cross the woman's face.

"Oh," the woman said. "He was wearing a dark ski mask."

"Very good. What happened next?"

The woman became slightly more agitated.

"I didn't stop to think. I got out my cell phone and called 911. It seemed like a long time before I could get an operator. I was on the phone talking to the operator when a truck came tearing out from behind the building. Its tires screeched going out of the parking lot, and it turned to the left."

Riley was taking notes rapidly. She was aware that Walder and his two young favorites had come into the room and were just standing there, but she ignored them.

"What kind of truck?" she asked.

The woman knitted her forehead. "A Dodge Ram, I think. Yes, that's right. Pretty old—maybe from the late nineties. It was very dirty, but I think it was a really deep navy blue color. And it had something on its bed. Kind of like a camper, only it wasn't a camper. One of those aluminum tops with windows."

"A cap?" Riley suggested.

The woman nodded. "I think that's what they're called."

Riley was pleased and impressed by the woman's memory.

"What about a license number?" Riley asked.

The woman looked a little bit taken aback.

"I—I didn't catch it," she said, sounding disappointed with herself.

"Not even one letter or number?" Riley asked.

"I'm sorry, but I didn't see it. I don't know how I missed it."

Walder stooped down and whispered intensely in Riley's ear.

"We've *got* to take her to the BAU," he said.

He backed up a little as Riley rose to her feet.

"Thank you, Ms. Tedrow," Riley said. "That's all for now. Have the police already taken your contact information?"

The woman nodded.

"Then go home and get some rest," Riley said. "We'll be in touch again soon."

The woman walked her dog out of the clinic and headed home. Walder looked ready to explode with rage and exasperation.

"What the hell was that all about?" he demanded. "I said we had to take her to the BAU."

Riley shrugged. "I can't imagine why we would do that," she said. "We've got to keep moving on this case and she's told us all she can."

"I want one of our hypnotists to work with her. To help her remember the license number. It's in her brain somewhere."

"Agent Walder," Riley said, trying not to sound as impatient as she felt, "Greta Tedrow is one of the most observant witnesses I've interviewed in a very long time. She said she didn't see the license plate number, didn't 'catch' it. Not even one number. That bothered her. She didn't know how she could miss it. Coming from someone with a memory as sharp as hers, that can only mean one thing."

She paused, challenging Walder to guess what that "one thing" might be. She could tell by his vacant expression that he had no idea.

"There *was* no license plate to see," she finally said. "Either the attacker had removed it or it had been muddied up and made unreadable. All she saw was a blank space where the license plate should have been. If a legible license plate had been there, that woman would have caught at least part of it."

Bill let out a snort of quiet admiration. Riley wanted to shush him, but figured that would only make matters worse. She decided to change the subject.

"Has the victim's next of kin been contacted?" she asked Walder.

Walder nodded. "Her husband. He came here for a few minutes. But he couldn't handle it. We sent him home. He lives only a few blocks away. I'll send Agents Huang and Creighton to interview him."

The two younger agents had been standing apart enthusiastically discussing something. At that moment, they turned toward Riley, Bill, and Walder. They looked very happy with themselves.

"Emily—er, Agent Creighton and I have got it figured out," Huang said. "There was no sign of a break-in, nothing resembling forced entry. That means the perp's got local connections. In fact, he knows somebody who works in this clinic. He just might work here himself."

"Somehow he got his hands on a key," Creighton put in. "Maybe he stole it, or maybe he borrowed it and copied it, something like that. And he knew the code for the alarm. He got in and out without setting it off. We'll interview the staff with that in mind."

"And we know just who we're looking for," Huang said. "Someone with some kind of grudge against Senator Newbrough."

Riley choked back her anger. These two were jumping to unfounded conclusions. Of course, they could be right. But what had they overlooked? She looked around at the clinic waiting room and adjoining hallway and a different possibility formed in her mind. She turned toward the Hispanic receptionist.

"*Perdóneme, señora,*" she said to the woman. "*Dónde está el cuarto de provisiones?*"

"*Allá,*" the woman said, pointing to a hallway door.

Riley went to the door and opened it. She looked inside, then turned to Walder and said, "I can tell you exactly how he got into the building. He came in through here."

Walder looked annoyed. By contrast, Bill looked anything but annoyed—positively delighted, in fact. Riley knew that Bill disliked Walder as much as she did. He was undoubtedly looking forward to seeing Walder get a good lesson in detective work.

The two young agents stared into the open doorway, then turned toward Riley.

"I don't get it," complained Emily Creighton.

"It's just a closet," echoed Craig Huang.

"Look at those boxes in the back," Riley said. "Don't touch anything."

Bill and Walder joined the cluster of people looking into the big supply closet. Paper supplies and bandages were stored on wide shelves. Clinicians' apparel was stacked in one area. But several large boxes on the floor looked out of place. Although everything else in the closet was arranged neatly, those boxes sat at odd angles and space was visible behind them.

"Boxes pushed away from the back wall," Bill commented. "Somebody could have hidden back in there pretty easily."

"Get the evidence crew in here," Walder snapped to the younger agents. Then he asked Riley, "What's your theory?"

Her brain was clicking away as the scenario rapidly took shape for her. She started laying it out.

"He arrived at the clinic yesterday," she said. "Probably late in the day, at some especially busy hour. In the midst of the bustle of patients, he asked the receptionist for something simple. A blood pressure test, maybe. And *she* might well have been the nurse who administered that test—Cindy MacKinnon, the woman he had been stalking, the woman he came here to abduct. He would have enjoyed that."

"You can't know that for sure," Walder said.

"No," Riley agreed. "And of course he wouldn't give his real name, but have someone check the clinic records for her services to anyone the other staff members don't recognize. In fact, we should check on everyone who was a patient here yesterday."

That would take time, she knew. But they had to follow up on every possibility as fast as they could. This man had to be stopped.

"He was here," Riley said, "mingling with all the patients. Maybe someone will remember something odd. And when no one was looking, he managed to get into this supply room."

"It isn't drug storage and I don't see anything else that would be valuable enough to steal," Bill added. "So it probably isn't watched very carefully."

"He squeezed himself into a tight space right under the bottom shelf and behind those boxes," Riley said. "The staff had no idea he was there. The clinic closed at the usual hour, and everyone went home without noticing. When he was sure that everyone had left, the perp pushed the boxes aside, crept out, and made himself at home. He waited all night. My guess is that he slept just fine."

The evidence team came in, and the agents moved aside to let them do their search for hairs, fingerprints, or anything else that might carry DNA or provide some other clue.

"You might be right," Walder muttered. "We'll also need to go over anywhere he might have been during the night. That means everywhere."

"It's the simplest solution," Riley said. "That's usually the best."

She put on her plastic gloves and went on down the hallway, looking into each room. One was a staff lounge, with a comfortable-looking couch.

"This is where he spent the night," she said with a feeling of certainty.

Walder looked inside. "Everybody stay out of this room until the team has been over it," he said, doing his best to sound efficient.

Riley returned to the waiting room. "He was already here when Cindy MacKinnon showed up this morning, right on schedule. He grabbed her."

Riley pointed toward the end of the hallway.

"Then he made off with her through the back entrance. He had his truck waiting right out there."

Riley closed her eyes for a moment. She could almost see him in her mind, a shadowy image she couldn't quite bring into focus. If he stood out someone would notice. So he wasn't extreme in appearance. Not obese, not unusually tall or short, no weird hairstyle, not marked by odd tattoos or coloring. He would be dressed in well-worn clothes, but nothing that would identify with a particular job. Old casual clothes. That would be natural to him, she thought. That was how he usually dressed.

"What is his connection with these women?" she muttered. "Where does his fury come from?"

"We'll find out," Bill said firmly.

Walder was completely silent now. Riley knew why. His protégés' overwrought theory about the abductor having an inside connection now seemed perfectly ridiculous. When Riley spoke again, it was in a tone that bordered on patronizing.

"Agent Walder, I appreciate the youthful spirit of your two agents," she said. "They're learning. They'll get good at this someday. I really believe that. But I think you'd better leave interviewing the husband to Agent Jeffreys and myself."

Walder sighed and gave her a slight, barely visible nod.

Without another word, Riley and Bill left the scene of the abduction. She had some important questions to ask the victim's husband.

CHAPTER EIGHTEEN

As she drove to the address the clinic receptionist had given her, Riley felt her usual dread at having to interview victims' families or spouses. She somehow sensed that this time was going to be even worse than usual. But the abduction was fresh.

"Maybe this time, we'll find her before he kills her," she said.

"If the evidence team can get a clue on this guy," Bill replied.

"Somehow, I doubt that he's going to turn up in any database." The image that Riley was forming in her mind wasn't of a habitual offender. This thing was deeply personal to the killer in some way that she hadn't been able to identify. She would figure it out, she was sure. But she needed to figure it out fast enough to stop the terror and agony that Cindy was going through right now. No one else should have to endure the pain of that knife … or of that darkness … of that searing flame …

"Riley," Bill said sharply, "that's it right there."

Riley jerked back to the present. She pulled the car over to the curb and looked around at the neighborhood. It was a little rundown but all the more warm and inviting because of that. It was the sort of low-rent area where young people without a lot of money could pursue their dreams.

Of course, Riley knew that the neighborhood wouldn't stay this way. Gentrification was undoubtedly scheduled to kick in any day now. But maybe that would be good for an art gallery. If the victim got back home alive.

Riley and Bill got out of the car and approached the little storefront gallery. A handsome metal sculpture was displayed in the front window behind a sign that announced "CLOSED."

The couple's apartment was upstairs. Riley rang the doorbell, and she and Bill waited for a few moments. She wondered who was going to come to the door.

When the door opened, she was relived to be greeted by the compassionate face of FBI victim specialist Beverly Chaddick. Riley had worked with Beverly before. The specialist had been in this job for at least twenty years, and she had a wonderful way dealing with distraught victims and family members.

"We need to ask Mr. MacKinnon some questions," Riley said. "I hope he's up for it."

"Yes," Beverly said. "But go easy on him."

Beverly led Bill and Riley upstairs to the little apartment. It immediately struck Riley as heartbreakingly cheerful, decorated with a marvelous clutter of paintings and sculptures. The people who lived here loved to celebrate life and all of its possibilities. Was all that over now? Her heart ached for the young couple.

Nathaniel MacKinnon, a man in his late twenties, was sitting in the combined living and dining room. His lankiness made him look all the more broken.

Beverly announced in a gentle voice, "Nathaniel, Agents Paige and Jeffreys are here."

The young man looked at Bill and Riley expectantly. His voice croaked with desperation.

"Have you found Cindy? Is she okay? Is she alive?"

Riley realized that she could say nothing helpful. She was all the more grateful that Beverly was here, and that she'd already established a rapport with the distraught husband.

Beverly sat down next to Nathaniel MacKinnon.

"Nobody knows anything yet, Nathaniel," she said. "They're here to help."

Bill and Riley sat down nearby.

Riley asked, "Mr. MacKinnon, has your wife said anything recently about feeling fearful or threatened?"

He shook his head mutely.

Bill put in, "This is a difficult question, but we have to ask. Do either you or your wife have any enemies, anybody who might wish you harm?"

The husband seemed to have trouble understanding the question.

"No, no," he stammered. "Look, there are sometimes little feuds in my line of work. But it's all just stupid little things, squabbles among artists, not people who would do something like …"

He stopped in mid-sentence.

"And everybody … *loves* Cindy," he said.

Riley detected his anxiety and uncertainty about using the present tense. She sensed that questioning this man was probably futile and possibly insensitive. She and Bill should probably cut things short and leave the situation in Beverly's capable hands.

Meanwhile, though, Riley looked around the apartment, trying to pick up the slightest trace of a clue.

She didn't need to be told that Cindy and Nathaniel MacKinnon didn't have children. The apartment wasn't big enough, and besides, the surrounding artworks were anything but childproof.

She suspected, though, that the situation was not the same as with Margaret and Roy Geraty. Riley's gut told her that Cindy and Nathaniel were childless by choice, and only temporarily. They were waiting for the right time, more money, a bigger home, a more settled lifestyle.

They thought they had all kinds of time, Riley thought.

She thought back to her early assumption that the killer targeted mothers. She wondered yet again how she could have gotten it so wrong.

Something else about the apartment was starting to dawn on her. She saw no photographs anywhere of Nathaniel or Cindy. This wasn't especially surprising. As a couple, they were more interested in the creativity of others than in pictures of themselves. They were anything but narcissistic.

Even so, Riley felt the need to get a clearer image of Cindy.

"Mr. MacKinnon," she asked cautiously, "do you have any recent photographs of your wife?"

He looked at her blankly for a moment. Then his expression brightened.

"Why, yes," he said. "I've got a new one right here on my cell phone."

He brought up the photograph on his phone and passed it along to Riley.

Riley's heart jumped up in her throat when she saw it. Cindy MacKinnon was sitting with a three-year-old girl on her lap. Both she and the child were glowing with delight as they held a beautifully dressed doll between them.

It took Riley a moment to start breathing again. The kidnapped woman, a child, and a doll. She hadn't been wrong. At least not completely. There had to be a connection between this killer and dolls.

"Mr. MacKinnon, who is the child in this picture?" Riley asked, as calmly as she could manage.

"That's Cindy's niece, Gale," Nathaniel MacKinnon replied. "Her mother is Cindy's sister, Becky."

"When was this photograph taken?" Riley asked.

The man stopped to think. "I think Cindy sent it to me on Friday," he said. "Yes, I'm sure that's when she sent it. It was at Gale's birthday party. Cindy helped her sister with the party. She left work early to help out."

Riley struggled with her thoughts, unsure for a moment just

what to ask next.

"Was the doll a gift for Cindy's niece?" she asked.

Nathaniel nodded. "Gale was thrilled with it. That made Cindy so happy. She just loves to see Gale happy. The girl's almost like a daughter to her. She called me right away to tell me. That's when she sent the photograph."

Riley struggled to keep her voice steady. "It's a lovely doll. I can see why Gale was so happy with it."

She hesitated again, staring at the doll's image as though it could tell her whatever it was that she needed to know. Surely that painted smile, those blank blue eyes, held a key to her questions. But she didn't even know what to ask.

Out of the corner of her eye she could see Bill watching her intently.

Why would a brutal killer pose his victims to look like dolls?

Finally Riley asked, "Do you know where Cindy bought the doll?"

Nathaniel looked genuinely puzzled. Even Bill looked surprised. Doubtless he wondered where Riley was going with this. The truth was, Riley wasn't entirely sure yet herself.

"I've got no idea," Nathaniel said. "She didn't tell me. Is that important?"

"I'm not sure," Riley admitted. "But I think it could be."

Nathaniel was growing more agitated now. "I don't understand. What's this all about? Are you saying my wife was abducted over a little girl's doll?"

"No, I'm not saying that." Riley tried to sound calm and convincing. Of course, she realized, she *was* saying that. She thought that his wife probably was abducted over some little girl's doll, even though that made no sense at all.

Nathaniel was visibly distressed. Riley saw that Beverly Chaddick, the victim specialist who was seated nearby, was eyeing her uneasily. With a slight shake of her head, Beverly seemed to be trying to communicate that Riley needed to go easier on the distraught husband. Riley reminded herself that interviewing victims and their families was not her own forte.

I've got to be careful, she told herself. But she also felt an urgent need to hurry. The woman was in captivity. Caged or tied, that didn't matter. She didn't have long to live. Was this any time to hold back on any source of information?

"Is there any way to find out where Cindy bought it?" Riley asked, trying to speak in a gentler tone. "Just in case we do need that information."

"Cindy and I keep some receipts," Nathaniel said. "Just for tax-deductible expenses. I don't think she would have kept the receipt for a family gift. But I'll look."

Nathaniel went to a closet and took down a shoebox. He sat down again and opened the box, which was full of paper receipts. He started looking through the them, but his hands were trembling uncontrollably.

"I don't think I can do this," he said.

Beverly gently took the box away from him.

"That's all right, Mr. MacKinnon," she said. "I'll look for it."

Beverly began to rummage through the box. Nathaniel was near tears.

"I don't understand," he said in a broken voice. "She just bought a gift. It could have been anything. From anywhere. I think she was considering several possibilities, but she finally decided on a doll."

Riley felt sick to her stomach. Somehow, deciding on a doll had led Cindy MacKinnon into a nightmare. If she had decided on a stuffed animal instead, would she be at home today, alive and happy?

"Will you please explain to me what this doll business is all about?" Nathaniel insisted.

Riley knew that the man more than deserved an explanation. She could think of no gentle way to put it.

"I think—" she began haltingly. "I think that your wife's abductor—might be obsessed with dolls."

She was aware of the instant responses from the others in the room. Bill shook his head and turned his gaze downward. Beverly's head snapped up in shock. Nathaniel gazed at her with an expression of hopeless despair.

"What makes you think that?" he asked in a choked voice. "What do you know about him? What aren't you telling me?"

Riley searched for a helpful reply, but she could see an awful dawning realization in his eyes.

"He's done this before, hasn't he?" he said. "There have been other victims. Has this got something to do with—?"

Nathaniel struggled to remember something.

"Oh my God," he said. "I've been reading about it in the news. A serial killer. He killed other women. Their bodies were found in Mosby Park, and in that national park near Daggett, and somewhere around Belding."

He doubled over and began to sob uncontrollably.

"You think that Cindy's his next victim," he cried. "You think

97

she's already dead."

Riley shook her head insistently.

"No," Riley said. "No, we don't think that."

"Then what *do* you think?"

Riley's thoughts were in turmoil. What could she tell him? That his wife was probably alive, but utterly terrified, and about to be hideously tortured and mutilated? And that the cutting and the stabbing would go on and on—until Cindy was rescued or dead, whichever came first?

Riley opened her mouth to speak, but no words at all came out. Beverly leaned forward and put one hand on Riley's arm. The specialist's face was still warm and friendly, but the fingers were quite firm.

Beverly spoke very slowly, as if explaining something to a child.

"I can't find the receipt," she said. "It's not here."

Riley understood Beverly's unspoken meaning. With her eyes, Beverly was telling her that the interview had gotten out of control, and that it was time for her to leave.

"I'll take it from here," Beverly mouthed in a barely audible whisper.

Riley whispered back to her, "Thank you. I'm sorry."

Beverly smiled and nodded sympathetically.

Nathaniel sat with his face buried in his hands. He didn't even look up at Riley as she and Bill stood up to leave.

They left the apartment and went back down the stairs to the street. They both got into Riley's car but she didn't start the engine. She felt her own tears welling up.

I don't know where to go, she thought. *I don't know what to do.*

It seemed to be the story of her life these days.

"It's dolls, Bill," she said. She was trying to explain her new theory to herself as much as to him. "It's definitely got something to do with dolls. Do you remember what Roy Geraty told us in Belding?"

Bill shrugged. "He said that his first wife—Margaret—didn't like dolls. They made her sad, he said. He said they sometimes made her cry."

"Yeah, because she couldn't have kids of her own," Riley said. "But he said something else. He said she had all kinds of friends and relatives having kids of their own. He said that she was always having to go to baby showers, and to help out with birthday parties."

Riley could see by Bill's expression that he was starting to understand now.

"So she sometimes had to *buy* dolls," he said. "Even if they did make her sad."

Riley struck the steering wheel with her fist.

"They all bought dolls," she said. "He *saw* them buying dolls. And he saw them buy the dolls in the same place, in the same store."

Bill nodded. "We've got to find that store," he said.

"Right," Riley said. "Somewhere in our thousand-plus-square-mile area, there's a doll store that all the kidnapped women went to. And he went there too. If we can find it, maybe—just maybe—we can find him."

At that moment, Bill's cell phone rang.

"Hello?" he said. "Yeah, Agent Walder, this is Jeffreys."

Riley stifled a moan. She wondered what kind of hassle Walder was about to cause them now.

She saw Bill's mouth drop open with stunned surprise.

"Jesus," he said. "Jesus. Okay. Okay. We'll be right there."

Bill ended the call and stared at Riley, dumbstruck for a few seconds.

"Walder and those kids he brought along," he said. "They've caught him."

CHAPTER NINETEEN

Riley and Bill arrived at the Behavioral Analysis Unit to find Walder waiting for them at the door.

"We've got him," Walder said, ushering them into the building. "We've got the guy."

Riley could hear both elation and relief in his voice.

"How?" she demanded.

"Agent Paige, you've seriously underestimated Huang and Creighton," Walder said. "After you left, the receptionist told them about a creepy guy who'd been hanging around the clinic recently. His name is Darrell Gumm. Women patients had complained about him. He was always getting too close to them, they said, not respecting their personal space. He also said some pretty unsavory things to them. And once or twice he actually sneaked into the women's restroom."

Riley mulled this over, checking it against her own assumptions about the perpetrator. *It could be him,* she thought. She felt a flutter of excitement in her throat.

Bill asked Walder, "Didn't anybody at the clinic call the police about Gumm?"

"They were letting their own security guy handle it. The guard told Gumm to stay away. At that kind of facility they do get oddballs from time to time. But Huang and Creighton picked up on the description. They realized he sounded like the guy we're looking for. They got his address from the receptionist, and we all headed over to his apartment."

"How do you know it's him?" Riley asked.

"He confessed," Walder said firmly. "We got a confession out of him."

Riley began to feel a touch of relief herself. "And Cindy MacKinnon?" she asked. "Where is she?"

"We're working on it," Walder said.

Riley's relief faded. "What do you mean, 'working on it'?" she asked.

"We've got field agents sweeping the neighborhood. We don't think he could have taken her very far. Anyhow, he'll tell us very soon. He's doing plenty of talking."

This had better be the guy, Riley thought. Cindy MacKinnon simply had to be alive. They couldn't lose yet another innocent woman to this twisted brute. His timeline was tightening up, but surely she wouldn't already be dead this soon after the abduction. He hadn't had the pleasure of torturing her yet.

Bill asked Walder, "Where is the suspect now?"

Walder pointed the way. "We've got him over in the detention center," he said. "Come on. I'm headed there now."

Walder filled them in as they walked through the extensive BAU complex to the building where suspects were held.

"When we flashed our badges," Walder said grimly, "he invited us to come right in and make ourselves at home. Self-confident bastard."

Riley thought that sounded right. If Darren Gumm really was the perp, the agents' arrival might have been just the denouement he'd been hoping for. He might well have intended to get caught all along, after an all-too-clever, two-year game of cat and mouse with the authorities. Maybe the reward he'd been hoping for all along was fame—a lot more than fifteen minutes of fame.

The trouble was, Riley knew, he could still use his latest captive to toy with them all. And he could well be the type who would do that.

"You should have seen his place," Walder went on. "A filthy little one-room pit, with a fold-out couch and a tiny bathroom that stinks to high heaven. And on the walls, absolutely everywhere, he's got news clippings about assaults and rapes and murders from all over the country. No sign of a computer, he's completely off the grid, but I've got to say, he's got an analog database of psychopathic criminality that a lot of police departments would envy."

"And let me guess," Bill put in. "He had a cluster of stories posted up about our killings—pretty much all the information that's been made public about them for all of two years."

"He sure as hell did," Walder said. "Creighton and Huang asked him a few questions, and he acted as suspicious as hell. Finally Huang asked what he knew about Cindy MacKinnon and he clammed up. It was obvious he knew who we meant. We had enough to arrest him. And he confessed almost as soon as we got him here."

At that moment Walder led Riley and Bill into a little room with a one-way window that looked into an interrogation room.

The interrogation was already well under way. On one side of the table sat Agent Emily Creighton. Agent Craig Huang was pacing the floor behind her. Riley thought that the two young agents actually looked more capable than they had before. On the other side of the table sat Darrell Gumm. His wrists were cuffed to the tabletop.

Riley was repelled by him immediately. He was a little toad of a man, somewhere around thirty, of medium build, and somewhat pudgy. But he looked sufficiently sturdy to be a plausible physical threat, especially to defenseless women caught by surprise. His forehead sloped sharply backwards, making his skull look like that of some long extinct hominid. His chin was all but nonexistent. All in all, he certainly fit Riley's expectations. And his confession did seem to wrap things up.

"Where is she?" Creighton shouted at Gumm.

Riley could tell by the impatient crackle in Creighton's voice that she had already asked that question many times.

"Where is who?" Gumm asked in a high and unpleasant voice. His expression fairly reeked of contempt and insolence.

"Stop playing games with us," Huang said sharply.

"I don't have to say anything without a lawyer present, right?" Gumm said.

Creighton nodded. "We already told you that. We'll bring in a lawyer any time you ask for one. You keep saying you don't want one. That's your right too. You can waive your right to an attorney. Have you changed your mind?"

Gumm tilted his head and looked at the ceiling, mock-thoughtfully.

"Let me think about that. No, I don't think so. Not yet, anyway."

Huang leaned across the table toward him, trying hard to look menacing.

"I'm asking for the last time," he said. "Where did you hide the truck?"

Gumm shrugged. "And I'm *saying* for the last time—what truck? I don't own a truck. I don't even own a car. Shit, I don't even have a driver's license."

Speaking in a low voice, Walder informed Riley and Bill, "That last bit is true. No driver's license, no voter registration, no credit cards, nothing at all. He really does live off the grid. No wonder the truck didn't have a license plate. He probably stole it. But he couldn't have driven it far in the time he had. It has to be somewhere near his apartment."

Agent Creighton was scowling at Gumm now.

"You think this is funny, don't you?" she said. "You've got some poor woman tied up somewhere. You've admitted that much already. She's scared to death, and I'll bet she's hungry and thirsty too. How long are you going to let her suffer? Are you really willing to let her die like that?"

Gumm snickered.

"Is this the part where you knock me around?" he asked. "Or is this when you tell me that you can get me to talk without leaving any visible marks?"

Riley had tried to keep quiet, but she couldn't contain herself any longer.

"They're not asking the right questions," she said.

She pushed past Walder and headed through the door that led into the interrogation room.

"Hold it, Agent Paige," Walder commanded.

Ignoring him, Riley charged into the room. She rushed toward the table, planted both hands on it, and leaned intimidatingly toward Gumm.

"Tell me, Darrell," she snarled. "Do you like dolls?"

For the first time, Darrell's face showed a trace of alarm.

"Who the hell are you?" he asked Riley.

"I'm somebody you don't want to lie to," Riley said. "Do you like dolls?"

Darrell's eyes darted around the room.

"I dunno," he said. "Dolls? They're cute, I guess."

"Oh, you think they're more than cute, don't you?" Riley said. "You were that kind of boy when you were little—the kind who liked to play with dolls, the kind that all the kids make fun of."

Darrell turned toward the mirror that was on his side of the one-way window.

"I know somebody's back there," he called out, sounding scared now. "Will somebody get this crazy woman away from me?"

Riley walked around the table, pushed Huang aside, and stood right next to Gumm. Then she shoved her face toward his face. He leaned back, trying to escape her gaze. But she wouldn't give him room to breathe. Their faces were only three or four inches apart.

"And you *still* like dolls, don't you?" Riley hissed, pounding her fist on the table. "Little girl dolls. You like to take their clothes off. You like to see them naked. What do you like to do with them when they're naked?"

Darrell's eyes widened.

Riley held his gaze for a long moment. She hesitated, trying to read his expression clearly. Was that contempt or disgust that turned his mouth down so sharply?

103

She opened her mouth to ask more, but the door to the interrogation room burst open behind her. She heard Walder's stern voice.

"Agent Paige, I want you out of here right now."

"Give me just another minute," she said.

"Now!"

Riley stood over Gumm in silence for a moment. Now he just looked bewildered. She looked around and saw that Huang and Creighton were staring at her in dumbfounded disbelief. Then she turned away and followed Walder out into the adjoining room.

"What the hell was that all about?" Walder demanded. You're reaching. You don't want this case to be closed. It *is* closed. Get over it. All we've got to do now is find the victim."

Riley groaned aloud.

"I think you've got it wrong," she said. "I don't think this guy reacts to dolls the way the killer would. I need more time to be sure."

Walder stared at her for a moment, then shook his head.

"This really hasn't been your day, has it, Agent Paige?" he said. "In fact, I'd say you haven't been at your best during this whole case. Oh, you *were* right about one thing. Gumm doesn't seem to have had a connection to the Senator—neither political nor personal. Well, that hardly matters. I'm sure the Senator will be gratified that we brought his daughter's killer to justice."

It was all Riley could do to hold her temper.

"Agent Walder, with all due respect—" she began.

Walder interrupted. "And that's just your problem, Agent Paige. Your respect toward me has been severely lacking. I'm tired of your insubordination. Don't worry, I'm not going to file a negative report. You've done good work in the past and I'm giving you the benefit of the doubt now. I'm sure you're still traumatized from all you went through yourself. But you can go home now. We'll handle things from here."

Then Walder patted Bill on the shoulder.

"I'd like you to stay, Agent Jeffreys," he said.

Bill was fuming now. "If she's going, I'm going," he growled.

Bill led Riley out into the hallway. Walder stepped out of the room to watch them leave. But a short distance down the hallway, certainty caught up with Riley. The suspect's face had showed disgust, she was sure of that now. Her questions about naked dolls had not excited him. They had just confused him.

Riley was shaking all over. She and Bill continued on their way out of the building.

"He's not the guy," she uttered softly to Bill. "I'm sure of it."

Bill looked back, shocked, and she stopped and stared at him with full intensity.

"*She's* still out there," she added. "And they have no idea where she is."

*

Long after dark, Riley paced the floor at home, replaying every detail of the case in her mind. She'd even fired off emails and text messages in an effort to alert members of the Bureau that Walder had brought in the wrong man.

She had driven Bill home and been very late yet again picking up April. Riley was grateful that April hadn't made a fuss about it this time. Still subdued from the pot-smoking incident, April had even been rather pleasant as they put together a late supper and shared small talk.

Midnight came and went, and Riley felt as if her mind were going in circles. She wasn't getting anywhere. She needed someone to talk to, someone to bounce ideas off of. She thought about calling Bill. Surely he wouldn't mind getting called this late.

But no, she needed someone else—someone with insights that weren't easy to come by, someone whose judgment she'd learned to trust from past experience.

At last, she realized who that someone was.

She called a number on her cell phone and was dismayed to hear yet another recorded message.

"You've reached the number of Michael Nevins. Please leave a message at the tone."

Riley took a deep breath, then said, "Mike, could we talk? If you're there, please pick up. It's really an emergency."

No one answered. She wasn't surprised that he wasn't available. He often worked all hours. She just wished this weren't one of those times.

Finally she said, "I'm working on a bitch of a case, and I think maybe you're the only one who can help me. I'll drive up to your office first thing tomorrow morning. I hope that's okay. Like I said, it's an emergency."

She ended the call. There was nothing more she could do right now. She only hoped she could get a few hours of sleep.

CHAPTER TWENTY

The chair was comfortable and the surroundings were elegant, but the soft lighting in Mike Nevins's office did nothing to raise Riley's spirits. Cindy was still missing. God only knew what was happening to her right now. Was she being tortured? The way Riley had been?

The agents sweeping the neighborhood still hadn't found her, not even after twenty-four hours. That came as no surprise to Riley. She knew they were looking in the wrong area. The problem was that neither she nor anyone else had any clues to the right area. She didn't want to wonder how far away the killer had taken her—or if she was still alive.

"We're losing her, Mike," Riley said. "With every minute that goes by, she's in more pain. She's closer to death."

"What makes you so sure they've got the wrong man?" forensic psychiatrist Michael Nevins asked her.

Always immaculately groomed and wearing an expensive shirt with a vest, Nevins had a meticulous, fussy persona. Riley liked him all the more because of it. She found him refreshing. They had first met over a decade ago, when he was a consultant on a high-profile FBI case that she worked on. His office was in D.C., so they didn't get together often. But over the years they'd often found that weaving together her instincts and his deep background knowledge gave them a unique insight into devious minds. She'd driven to see him first thing this morning.

"Where do I begin?" Riley replied with a shudder.

"Take your time," he said.

She sipped at a mug of the delicious hot tea he had given her.

"I saw him," she said. "I asked him some questions, but Walder wouldn't let me spend any time with him."

"And he doesn't fit your profile?"

"Mike, this Darrell Gumm guy is a wannabe," she continued. "He's got some kind of fanboy fantasy about psychopaths. He wants to be one. He wants to be famous for it. But he doesn't have what it takes. He's creepy, but he's not a killer. It's just that right now he gets to act out his fantasy to the hilt. It's his dream come true."

Mike stroked his chin thoughtfully. "And you don't think the

106

real killer wants fame?"

She said, "He might be interested in fame, and he might even want it, but it's not what makes him tick. He's driven by something else, something more personal. The victims represent something to him, and he enjoys their pain because of who or what they stand for. They're not chosen randomly."

"Then how?"

Riley shook her head. She wished she could put it into words better than she could.

"It's got something to do with dolls, Mike. The guy's obsessed with them. And dolls have something to do with how he targets the women."

Then she sighed. At this point, this didn't even sound very convincing to her. And yet she was sure that was the right track.

Mike was silent for a moment. Then he said, "I know that you have a talent for recognizing the nature of evil. I've always trusted your instincts. But if you're right, this suspect they're holding has got everybody else fooled. And not all FBI agents are fools."

"But some of them are," Riley said. "I can't get the woman he took yesterday out of my mind. I keep thinking about what she's going through right now." Then she blurted out the point of her visit with the psychiatrist. "Mike, could you question Darrell Gumm? You'd see through him in a second."

Mike looked startled. "They haven't called me in on this one," he said. "I checked on the case this morning and I was told that Dr. Ralston interviewed him yesterday. Apparently he agrees that Gumm's the killer. He even got Gumm to sign a written confession. The case is closed as far as the Bureau is concerned. They think that now they just need to find the woman. They're sure they'll get Gumm to talk."

Riley rolled her eyes with exasperation.

"But Ralston's a quack," she said. "He's Walder's toady. He'll come to any conclusion Walder wants."

Mike didn't say anything. He just smiled at Riley. Riley was pretty sure that Mike held Ralston in the same contempt as she did. But he was too professional to say so.

"I haven't been able to figure this one out," Riley said. "Will you at least read the files and tell me what you think?"

Mike seemed deep in thought. Then he said, "Let's talk about you a little. How long have you been back on the job?"

Riley had to think about that. This case had consumed her but it was still new.

"About a week," she said.

He tilted his head with concern. "You're pushing very hard. You always do."

"The man has killed one woman in that time and taken another. I should have stayed on the case since I first saw his work six months ago. I should never have dropped out on it."

"You were interrupted."

She knew he was referring to her own capture and torture. She had spent hours describing that to Mike and he had helped her through it.

"I'm back now. And another woman is in trouble."

"Who are you working with now?"

"Bill Jeffreys again. He's terrific but his imagination isn't as active as mine is. He hasn't come up with anything either,"

"How is that working for you? Being with Jeffreys every day?"

"Fine. Why wouldn't it be?"

Mike gazed quietly at her for a moment, then leaned toward her with an expression of concern.

"I mean, are you sure your head is clear? Are you sure you're in this game? I guess what I'm asking is—which criminal are you really after?"

Riley squinted, a little surprised by this apparent change of topic.

"What do you mean, which?" she asked.

"The new one, or the old one?"

A silence fell between them.

"I think that maybe you're actually here to talk about you," Mike said softly. "I know that you've always had trouble believing that Peterson died in that explosion."

Riley didn't know what to say. She hadn't expected this; she hadn't expected the tables to turn on her.

"That's beside the point," Riley said.

"What about your meds, Riley?" Mike asked.

Again, Riley didn't reply. She hadn't taken her prescribed tranquilizer for days. She didn't want to blunt her concentration.

"I'm not sure I like where you're going with this," Riley said.

Mike took a long sip from his mug of tea.

"You're carrying a lot of emotional baggage," he said. "You got divorced this year, and I'm aware that your feelings about that are conflicted. And of course, you lost your mother in such a horrible, tragic way all those years ago."

Riley's face flushed with irritation. She didn't want to get into this.

108

"We've talked about the circumstances of your own abduction," Mike went on. "You pushed the limits. You took a huge risk. Your actions were really pretty foolhardy."

"I got Marie out," she said.

"At great cost to yourself."

Riley took a long, deep breath.

"You're saying maybe I brought it on myself," she said. "Because my marriage fell apart, because of how my mother got killed. You're saying maybe I think I deserved it. So I attracted this to myself. I put myself in this situation."

Mike smiled back with a sympathetic smile.

"I'm just saying you need to take a good hard look at yourself right now. Ask yourself what's really going on inside."

Riley struggled for breath, fighting back tears. Mike was right. She had been wondering all these things. That's why his words were hitting her so hard. But she'd been ignoring those half-submerged thoughts. And it was high time she figured out if any of it was true.

"I was doing my job, Mike," she said in a choked voice.

"I know," he said. "None of it was your fault. Do you know that? It's the self-blame I worry about. You attract what you feel you deserve. You create your own life circumstances."

Riley stood, unable to hear any more.

"I wasn't taken, Doctor, because I attracted it," she said. "I was taken because there are psychos out there."

*

Riley hurried to the nearest exit, into the open courtyard. It was a beautiful summer day. She took several long, slow breaths, calming herself a little. Then she sat down on a bench and buried her head in her hands.

At that moment her cell phone buzzed.

Marie.

Her gut told her right away that the call was urgent.

Riley answered and heard nothing but convulsive gasps.

"Marie," Riley asked, concerned, "what is it?"

For a moment, Riley only heard sobs. Marie was obviously in an even worse state than she was.

"Riley," Marie finally gasped, "have you found him? Have you been looking for him? Has *anybody* been looking for him?"

Riley's spirits sank. Of course Marie was talking about Peterson. She wanted to assure her that he was really dead, killed in that explosion. But how could she say so positively when she harbored doubts herself? She remembered what forensics tech agent Betty Richter had told her a few days ago about the odds that Peterson was really dead.

I'd say ninety-nine percent.

That figure hadn't given Riley any comfort. And it was the last thing Marie wanted or needed to hear right now.

"Marie," Riley said miserably, "there's nothing I can do."

Marie let out a wail of despair that chilled Riley to the bone.

"Oh, God, then it *is* him!" she cried. "It can't be anybody else."

Riley's nerves quickened. "What are you talking about, Marie? What's happened?"

Marie's words poured out in a frantic rush.

"I *told* you he'd been calling me. I cut off my landline, but somehow he's got my cell phone number. He keeps calling all the time. He doesn't say anything, he just calls and breathes, but I know it's him. Who else can it be? And he's been here, Riley. He's been to my house."

Riley's alarm mounted by the second.

"What do you mean?" she asked.

"I hear noises at night. He throws things at the door and my bedroom window. Pebbles, I think."

Riley's heart jumped as she remembered the pebbles on her own front stoop. Was it possible that Peterson was really alive? Were both she and Marie in danger all over again?

She knew she had to choose her words carefully. Marie was clearly teetering on an extremely dangerous brink.

"I'm coming to you right now, Marie," she said. "And I'll get the Bureau to look into this."

Marie let out a harsh, desperate, and bitter laugh.

"Look into it?" she echoed. "Forget it, Riley. You said it already. There's nothing you can do. You're not going to do anything. Nobody's going to do anything. Nobody *can* do anything."

Riley got in her car and put the phone on speaker so she could talk and drive.

"Stay on the phone," she said, as she started her car and headed for Georgetown. "I'm coming for you."

110

CHAPTER TWENTY ONE

Riley struggled against traffic while trying to keep Marie on the phone. She drove through an intersection after a yellow light switched to red; she was driving dangerously and she knew it. But what else could she do? She was in her own car, not an agency vehicle, so she had no lights and siren.

"I'm hanging up, Riley," Marie said for the fifth time.

"No!" Riley barked yet again, fighting down a surge of despair. "Stay on the phone, Marie."

Marie's voice sounded weary now.

"I can't do this anymore," she said. "Save yourself if you can, but I really can't do this. I'm through with this. I'm going to stop it all right now."

Riley felt ready to explode from panic. What did Marie mean? What was she going to do?

"You *can* do this, Marie," Riley said.

"Goodbye, Riley."

"No!" Riley shouted. "Just wait. Wait! It's all you have to do. I'll be right there."

She was driving much faster than the flow of traffic, wending among the lanes like a madwoman. Several times, other drivers honked at her.

"Don't hang up," Riley demanded fiercely. "Do you hear me?"

Marie said nothing. But Riley could hear her sobbing and keening.

The sounds were perversely reassuring. At least Marie was still there. At least she was still on the phone. But could Riley keep her there? She knew that the poor woman was plummeting into an abyss of pure animal terror. Marie no longer had a rational thought in her head; she seemed to be almost insane with fear.

Riley's own memories swarmed into her mind. Terrible days in a beastlike state in which the world of humanity simply didn't exist. Total darkness, the feeling of the very existence of a world outside of the darkness slipping away, and a complete loss of any sense of the passage of time.

I've got to fight it, she told herself.

The memories enveloped her …

With nothing to hear or see, Riley tried to keep her other senses engaged. She felt the sour taste of fear back in her throat, rising up in her mouth until it turned into an electrical tingling on the tip of her tongue. She scratched at the dirt floor she was sitting on, exploring its dampness. She sniffed the mold and mildew that surrounded her.

Those sensations were all that still kept her in the world of the living.

Then in the midst of the blackness, came a blinding light and the roar of Peterson's propane torch.

A sharp bump shook Riley out of her hideous reverie. It took her a second to realize that her car had struck against a curb and that she was in danger of veering into oncoming traffic. Horns blared.

Riley regained control of her car and looked around. She wasn't far from Georgetown.

"Marie," she shouted. "Are you still there?"

Again, she heard only a muffled sob. That was good. But what could Riley do now? She wavered. She could call for FBI help in D.C., but by the time she explained the problem and got agents sent to the address, God only knew what would happen. Besides, that would mean ending the call with Marie.

She had to keep her on the phone, but how?

How was she going to pull Marie out of that abyss? She had almost fallen into it herself.

Riley remembered something. Long ago, she had been trained in how to keep crisis callers on the line. She'd never had to use that training until now. She struggled to remember what she was supposed to do. Those lessons had been so long ago.

Part of a lesson came back to her. She was taught to do anything, *say* anything, to keep the caller talking. It didn't matter how meaningless or irrelevant it might be. What mattered was that the caller kept hearing a concerned human voice.

"Marie, there's something you need to do for me," Riley said.

"What's that?"

Riley's brain was rushing frantically, making up what to say as she went along.

"I need for you to go to your kitchen," she said. "I want you to tell me exactly what herbs and spices you've got in your rack."

Marie didn't answer for a moment. Riley worried. Was Marie in the right state of mind to go along with such an irrelevant distraction?

"Okay," Marie said. "I'm going there now."

Riley breathed a sigh of relief. Perhaps this would buy her some time. She could hear the clinking of spice jars over the phone. Marie's voice sounded truly strange now—hysterical and robotic at the same time.

"I've got dried oregano. And crushed red pepper. And nutmeg."

"Excellent," Riley said. "What else?"

"Dried thyme. And ground ginger. And black peppercorns."

Marie paused. How could Riley keep this going?

"Have you got curry powder?" Riley asked.

After a clink of bottles, Marie said, "No."

Riley spoke slowly, as if giving life-and-death instructions—because really, she was doing exactly that.

"Well, get a pad of paper and a pencil," Riley said. "Write that down. You'll need to get it when you buy groceries."

Riley heard the sound of scribbling.

"What else have you got?" Riley asked.

Then came a deathly pause.

"This is no good, Riley," Marie said in a tone of numb despair.

Riley stammered helplessly. "Just—just humor me, okay?"

Another pause fell.

"He's here, Riley."

Riley felt a rock-hard knot in her throat.

"He's where?" she asked.

"He's in the house. I get it now. He's been here all along. There's nothing you can do."

Riley's thoughts churned as she tried to make sense of what was happening. Marie might be slipping into paranoid delusions. Riley understood this all too well from her own struggles with PTSD.

On the other hand, Marie might be telling the truth.

"How do you know that, Marie?" Riley asked, looking for an opportunity to pass a slow-moving truck.

"I hear him," Marie said. "I hear his footsteps. He's upstairs. No, he's in the front hallway. No, he's in the basement."

Is she hallucinating? Riley wondered.

It was entirely possible. Riley had heard more than her share of nonexistent noises in the days after her abduction. Even recently she sometimes couldn't trust her five senses. Trauma played awful tricks on the imagination.

113

"He's everywhere in the house," Marie said.

"No," Riley replied firmly. "He can't be everywhere."

Riley managed to pass a sluggish delivery truck. A sense of futility was rolling over her in what felt like tidal waves. It was a terrible feeling, almost like drowning.

When Marie spoke again, she was no longer sobbing. She sounded resigned now, even mysteriously tranquil.

"Maybe he's like a ghost, Riley. Maybe that's what happened when you blew him up. You killed his body but you didn't kill his evil. Now he can be in a whole lot of places at once. Now there's no stopping him, ever. You can't fight a ghost. Give it up, Riley. You can't do anything. I can't either. All I can do is not let the same thing happen to me again."

"Don't hang up! I need you to do something else for me."

There was a moment's silence. Then Marie said, "What? What now, Riley?"

"I need you to stay on this line, but I need you to call 911 on your landline."

Marie's voice turned into a slight growl. "Jesus, Riley. How many times do I have to tell you that I cut off my landline?"

In her confusion, Riley had forgotten. Marie actually sounded a little irritated. That was good. Anger was better than panic.

"Besides," Marie continued, "what good's it going to do to call 911? What can they do to help me? Nobody can help. He's everywhere. He'll get me sooner or later. He'll get you too. We both might as well give up."

Riley felt stymied. Marie's delusions were taking on an intractable logic of their own. And she didn't have time to persuade Marie that Peterson was not a ghost.

"We're friends, aren't we, Marie?" Riley finally said. "You once told me that you'd do anything for me. Was that true?"

Marie started crying again.

"Of course it's true."

"Then hang up and call 911. There doesn't have to be a reason. It doesn't have to do any good. Just do it because I want you too."

A long pause fell. Riley couldn't even hear Marie breathing.

"I know you want to give up, Marie. I understand. That's your choice. But *I* don't want to give up. Maybe it's stupid, but I don't. That's why I'm asking you to call 911. Because you said you'd do anything for me. And I want you to do it. I *need* you to do it. For me."

The silence continued. Was Marie even still on the line?

114

"Do you promise?" she asked.

The call ended with a click. Whether Marie would call for help or not, Riley couldn't leave anything to chance. She picked up her cell phone and punched in 911.

"This is Special Agent Riley Paige, FBI," she said when the operator answered. "I'm calling about a possible intruder. Someone extremely dangerous."

Riley gave the operator Marie's address.

"We'll have a team there right away," the operator said.

"Good," Riley said, and ended the call.

Riley then tried Marie's number again, but got no response.

Someone has to get there in time, she thought. *Someone has to get there right now.*

Meanwhile, she struggled against a renewed flood of dark memories. She had to get control of herself. Whatever was about to happen next, she needed to keep her wits about her.

When Marie's red brick townhouse came into view, Riley felt a surge of alarm. No emergency vehicles had yet arrived. She heard police sirens wailing in the distance. They were on their way.

Riley double-parked her car and dashed for the front door, realizing she was the first responder. When she tried the doorknob, the door swung open. But why was it unlocked?

She stepped inside and drew her gun.

"Marie!" Riley called out. "Marie!"

No answer came.

Riley knew for certain that something awful had happened here—or was happening right now. She stepped further into the front hallway.

"Marie!" she called again. The house remained silent.

The police sirens were louder now, but no help had yet arrived.

Riley was starting to believe the worst now—that Peterson had been here, and perhaps still was here.

She made her way along the dimly lit hallway. She kept calling Marie's name as she studied every door. Might he be in the closet to the left? What about the bathroom door over to the right?

If she encountered Peterson, she wouldn't be taken by him again.

She would kill the bastard once and for all.

CHAPTER TWENTY TWO

In spite of Riley's calls, no answer came from Marie. There were no sounds in the house other than those she made herself. The place felt empty. She made her way up the stairs and turned carefully into an open doorway.

As she turned the corner, Riley's breath stopped in her throat. She felt as if the world were collapsing beneath her.

There was Marie: suspended in mid-air, hanging by her neck from a cord tied to a light fixture on the high ceiling. An overturned stepladder lay on the floor.

Time seemed to stop as Riley's mind rejected reality.

Then her knees buckled and she caught herself against the door frame. She let out a long harsh sound.

"NOOOO!"

She dashed across the room, turned the ladder upright and scrambled up on it. She wrapped an arm around Marie's body to relieve the pressure and fingered Marie's neck, searching for any sign of a pulse.

Riley was sobbing now. "Be alive, Marie. Be alive, goddammit."

But it was too late. Marie's neck was broken. She was dead.

"Christ," Riley said, collapsing back onto the ladder. Pain surged up from somewhere deep in her abdomen. She wanted to die here, too.

As moments passed, Riley became dimly aware of sounds downstairs. The first responders had arrived. A familiar emotional mechanism kicked in. Basic human fear and grief gave way to a cold, professional efficiency.

"Up here!" she shouted.

She wiped her sleeve across her face to blot the tears.

Five heavily-armed, Kevlar-clad officers charged up the stairs. The woman in front was visibly surprised to see Riley.

"I'm Officer Rita Graham, the team chief," she said. "Who are you?"

Riley got off the ladder and flashed her badge. "Special Agent Riley Paige, FBI."

The woman looked uneasy.

"How did you get here before we did?"

"She was a friend of mine," Riley said, fully in professional mode now. "Her name was Marie Sayles. She called me. She told me something was wrong, and I was already on the way when I called 911. I didn't get here on time. She's dead."

The responder team quickly checked and confirmed Riley's declaration.

"Suicide?" Officer Graham asked.

Riley nodded. She had no doubt at all that Marie had killed herself.

"What's this?" the team leader asked, pointing at a folded notecard sitting on an end table next to the bed.

Riley looked at the card. Written in a barely legible scrawl was a message:

This is the only way.

"A suicide note?"

Riley nodded again grimly. But she knew that it wasn't the usual kind of suicide note. It wasn't an explanation, and it certainly wasn't an apology.

It's advice, Riley thought. *It's advice for me.*

The team took pictures and made notes. Riley knew that they would wait for the coroner before removing the body.

"Let's talk downstairs," Officer Graham said. She led Riley down to the living room, sat down on a chair, and gestured for Riley to sit down too.

The curtains were still drawn and no lights were on in the room. Riley wanted to throw open the curtains and let in some sunlight, but she knew better than to change anything. She sat down on the sofa.

Graham turned on a table lamp beside her chair.

"Tell me what happened," the officer said, taking out a notepad and a pencil. Although she had the toughened face of a seasoned cop, there was a sympathetic look in her eyes.

"She was the victim of an abduction," Riley said. "Almost eight weeks ago. We both were victims. You may have read about it. The Sam Peterson case."

Graham's eyes widened.

"Oh, my God," she said. "The guy who tortured and killed all those women, the guy with the blowtorch. So that was you—the agent who escaped and blew him up?"

"Right," Riley said. Then, after a pause, she said, "The trouble is, I'm not sure I really did blow him up. I'm not positive that he's

117

dead. Marie didn't believe that he was. That's what finally got to her. She just couldn't take not knowing. And maybe he *was* stalking her again."

As Riley continued her explanation, the words flowed automatically, almost as if she'd learned the whole thing by heart. She now felt completely detached from the scene, listening to herself report how this horrible thing had happened.

After helping Officer Graham get a handle on the case, Riley told her how to contact Marie's next of kin. But as she talked, anger was building beneath her professional veneer—a cold, icy anger. Peterson had claimed another victim. Whether he was dead or alive didn't matter. He'd killed Marie.

And Marie had died absolutely certain that Riley was doomed to be his next victim, whether by his hand or her own. Riley wanted to take hold of Marie and physically shake this wretched idea out of her head.

This is not *the only way!* she wanted to tell her.

But did she believe that? Riley didn't know. There seemed to be too damned much she didn't know.

The coroner arrived while Riley and Officer Graham were still talking. Graham got up and went to meet him. Then she turned to Riley and said, "I'll be upstairs for a few minutes. I'd like you to hang around and fill me in a bit more."

Riley shook her head.

"I've got to go," she said. "There's someone I need to talk to." She pulled out her card and put it down on the table. "You can get in touch with me."

The officer began to object, but Riley didn't give her a chance; she got up and walked out of Marie's dark home. She had urgent business.

*

An hour later, Riley was driving west through the Virginia countryside.

Do I really want to do this? she asked herself again.

She was exhausted. She hadn't slept well last night, and now she had been through a waking nightmare. Thank goodness she'd talked with Mike in between. He had helped steady her, but she was sure he'd never approve of what she was going to do now. She wasn't altogether sure she was fully in her right mind.

She was taking the quickest route from Georgetown to Senator Mitch Newbrough's manor house. That narcissistic politician had a

118

lot to answer for. He was hiding something, something that might lead to the real killer. And that made him partly responsible for this new victim.

Riley knew that she was headed for trouble. She didn't care.

It was late afternoon when she pulled into the circular drive in front of the stone mansion. She parked, got out of the car, and walked up to the enormous front doors. When she rang the doorbell, she was greeted by a formally dressed gentleman—Newbrough's butler, she assumed.

"What may I do for you, ma'am?" he asked stiffly.

Riley flashed her badge at him.

"Special Agent Riley Paige," she said. "The Senator knows me. I need to talk with him."

With a skeptical look, the butler turned away from her. He raised a walkie-talkie to his lips, whispered, and then listened. The butler turned back toward Riley with a rather superior smirk.

"The Senator does not wish to see you," he said. "He's quite emphatic about it. Good day, ma'am."

But before the man could shut the doors, Riley pushed straight past him and strode on into the house.

"I'm going to notify security," the butler called after her.

"You go right ahead and do that," Riley shouted over her shoulder.

Riley had no idea where to look for the Senator. He could be anywhere in the cavernous mansion. But she figured it didn't matter. She could probably get him to come to her.

She headed into the living room where she had met with him before and plopped herself down on the huge couch. She fully intended to make herself right at home until the Senator showed himself.

Only a few seconds passed before a big man clad in a black suit stepped into the room. Riley knew by his manner that he was the Senator's security man.

"The Senator has asked for you to leave," he said, crossing his arms.

Riley didn't budge from the couch. She looked the man over, assessing just how much of a threat he really was. He was big enough to probably be able to remove her by force. But her own self-defense skills were very good. If he took her on, more than one of them was going to get pretty badly hurt, and doubtless some of the Senator's antiques would be damaged.

"I hope they told you that I'm FBI," she said, locking eyes with him. She doubted very much that he'd actually draw his weapon on an FBI agent.

Not easily intimidated, the man stared back at her. But he didn't move toward her.

Riley heard footsteps approaching behind her, and then the sound of the Senator's voice.

"What is it this time, Agent Paige? I'm a very busy man."

The security man stepped aside as Newbrough walked in front of her and stood there. His photogenic politician's smile had a sarcastic cast to it. He was silent for a moment. Riley sensed right away that they were about to engage in a battle of wills. She was determined not to move from the couch.

"You were wrong, Senator," Riley said. "There wasn't anything political about your daughter's murder—and nothing personal either. You gave me an enemies list, and I'm sure you passed along that same list to your lapdog at the Bureau."

Newbrough's smile twisted into a slight sneer.

"I take it you mean Special Agent in Charge Carl Walder," he said.

Riley knew that her choice of words was rash and that she'd live to regret it. But right now she didn't care.

"That list was a waste of the Bureau's time, Senator," Riley said. "And meanwhile another victim has been abducted."

Newbrough stood firmly rooted to his spot.

"I understand that the Bureau has made an arrest," he said. "The suspect has confessed. But he hasn't said much, has he? There's some connection to me, you can be sure of it. He'll tell all in due time. I'll make sure that Agent Walder follows through on it."

Riley tried to hide her amazement. After yet another abduction, Newbrough still considered himself to be the primary target of the killer's wrath. The man's ego was truly outrageous. His capacity to believe that *everything* was about him had no limits.

Newbrough tilted his head with seeming curiosity.

"But you seem to be blaming me somehow," he said. "I take umbrage at that, Agent Paige. It's not my fault that your own fecklessness has led to the capture of another victim."

Riley's face tingled with rage. She didn't dare reply. She'd say something far too rash.

He walked over to a liquor cabinet and poured himself a large glass of what Riley assumed to be extremely expensive whiskey. He was obviously making a point of not asking Riley if she wanted a drink.

Riley knew that it was high time for her to get to the point.

"The last time I was here, there was something you didn't tell me," she said.

Newbrough turned to face her again, taking a long sip from his glass.

"Didn't I answer all your questions?" he said.

"It's not that. You just didn't tell me something. About Reba. And I think it's time you did."

Newbrough held her in a penetrating stare.

"Did she like dolls, Senator?" Riley asked.

Newbrough shrugged. "I suppose all little girls do," he said.

"I don't mean as a little girl. I mean as an adult. Did she collect them?"

"I'm afraid I wouldn't know."

Those were the first words Newbrough had said so far that Riley truly believed. A man this pathologically self-centered knew little about anybody else's likes and interests—not even those of his own daughter.

"I'd like to talk to your wife," Riley said.

"Certainly not," Newbrough snapped. He was adopting a new expression now—one that Riley had seen him use on television. Much like his smile, this expression was carefully rehearsed, undoubtedly practiced thousands of times in a mirror. It was meant to convey moral outrage.

"You really have no decency, do you, Agent Paige?" he said, his voice shaking with calculated anger. "You come into a house of grief, bringing no comfort, no answers to a bereaved family. Instead you make veiled accusations. You blame perfectly innocent people for your own incompetence."

He shook his head in a gesture of injured righteousness.

"What a mean, cruel little woman you are," he said. "You must have brought terrible pain to a great many people."

Riley felt as if she'd been punched in the stomach. This was a tactic she hadn't been prepared for—a complete turning of the moral tables. And he'd hit her own genuine guilt and self-doubt.

He knows exactly how to play me, she thought.

She knew that she had to leave right now or she'd do something she'd regret. He was practically goading her in that direction. Without a word, she got up from the couch and walked out of the living room toward the front entrance.

She heard the Senator's voice call after her.

"Your career is over, Agent Paige. I want you to know that."

Riley brushed past the butler and charged out the front door.

121

She got in her car and started to drive.

Waves of rage, frustration, and exhaustion crashed over her. A woman's life was at stake, and nobody in the world was rescuing her. She was sure that Walder was just expanding the search area around Gumm's apartment. And Riley was sure they were looking in the wrong place. It was up to her to do something. But she no longer had any idea what to do. Coming here certainly hadn't helped. Could she trust her own judgment anymore?

Riley hadn't driven for more than ten minutes before her cell phone buzzed. She looked down at it and saw that it was a text from Walder. She had no trouble guessing what it was about.

Well, she thought bitterly. *At least the Senator didn't waste any time.*

CHAPTER TWENTY THREE

When Riley reached Quantico and walked into the Behavioral Analysis Unit, both the chief and Bill were waiting for her in Walder's office. She realized that Bill must have been called in especially for this meeting.

Special Agent in Charge Carl Walder rose from his desk.

"The Senator's lapdog?" Walder said, his babyish face knotted with anger.

Riley lowered her eyes. She really had gone too far with that remark.

"I'm sorry, sir," she said.

"Sorry isn't going to cut it, Agent Paige," Walder said. "You've completely gone off the rails. What were you thinking, going to the Senator's house to confront him like that? Do you have any idea the damage you've done?"

By "damage," Riley was sure that Walder meant his own personal embarrassment. She couldn't get very worried about that.

"Have you found Cindy McKinnon yet?" she asked in a low voice.

"No, as a matter of fact, we haven't," Walder said sharply. "And frankly, you're not helping us find her."

Riley was stung.

"*I'm* not helping?" she replied. "Sir, I keep telling you, you're charging the wrong man, and you're looking in the wrong—"

Riley stopped herself in mid-sentence

Cindy MacKinnon was what mattered right now, not Riley's ongoing battles with Walder. This was no time for petty squabbling. When she spoke again, it was in a milder tone.

"Sir, even though I feel he may be withholding something, I may have been wrong to unilaterally go and see the Senator without checking with you, and I apologize. But forget about me for a moment. That poor woman's been missing for well over twenty-four hours. What if I'm right, and someone else is holding her captive? What's she going through right now? How long has she got?"

His voice cautious, Bill added, "We've got to consider the possibility, sir."

Walder sat down and said nothing for a moment. Riley could

see by his expression that he, too, was concerned about the possibility. Then he spoke very slowly, giving weight to each word.

"The Bureau will handle it."

Riley didn't know what to say. She didn't even quite understand what Walder meant. Was he acknowledging his possible mistake? Or was he still determined not to veer from his present course?

"Sit down, Agent Paige," Walder said.

Riley sat in the chair next to Bill, who glanced at her with mounting concern.

Walder said, "I heard about what happened with your friend today, Riley."

Riley was jolted a little. She wasn't surprised that Walder knew about Marie's death. After all, word that she'd been first on the scene was sure to make its way back to the Bureau. But why was he bringing it up now? Did she detect a note of sympathy in his voice?

"What happened?" Walder asked. "Why did she do it?"

"She couldn't deal with it anymore," Riley said in a whisper.

"Couldn't deal with what?" Walder asked.

A silence fell. Riley couldn't shape an answer to that question.

"I've heard you don't think Peterson is dead," Walder said. "I guess I can understand why you can't shake that idea. But you've got to know that it doesn't make sense."

There came another pause.

"Did you tell your friend about it?" Walder asked. "Did you tell her about this obsessive idea of yours?"

Riley's face flushed. She knew what was coming next.

"She was too fragile for that, Agent Paige," Walder said. "You should have known it would make her snap. You should have used better judgment. But frankly, Agent Paige, your judgment is shot to hell. I hate to say it, but it's true."

He is blaming me for Marie's death, Riley realized.

Riley was fighting back tears now. Whether they were tears of grief or indignation, she didn't know. She had no idea what to say. Where could she begin? She hadn't planted that idea in Marie's head and she knew it. But how could she make Walder understand? How could she explain that Marie had her own reasons to doubt that Peterson was dead?

Bill spoke up again. "Sir, go easy on her, okay?"

"I think I've been going too easy on her, Agent Jeffreys," Walder said, his voice becoming stern. "I think I've been too patient."

Walder held her gaze for a long moment.

"Give me your gun and your badge, Agent Paige," he finally said.

Riley heard Bill let out a gasp of disbelief.

"Sir, this is crazy," Bill said. "We need her."

But Riley didn't need to be told twice. She rose from her chair and took out her gun and her badge. She placed them on Walder's desk.

"You can clean out your office in your own good time," Walder said, his voice steady and unemotional. "Meanwhile, you should go home and get some rest. And get back into therapy. You need it."

As Riley turned to leave the room, Bill stood up as if to go with her.

"You stay, Agent Jeffreys," Walder demanded.

Riley eyes met Bill's. With a look, she told him not to disobey. Not this time. He nodded back to her with a stricken expression. Then Riley left the office. As she walked down the hall, she felt cold and numb, wondering what to do now.

When she stepped out into the cool night air, tears finally started to flow. But she was surprised to realize that they were tears of relief, not despair. For the first time in days, she felt liberated, free from frustrating limitations.

If nobody else was going to do what had to be done, it was still up to her. But at long last, nobody was going to tell her how to do her job. She'd find the killer, and she'd save Cindy MacKinnon—no matter what it took.

*

After Riley, later again, picked up April and drove home, she found as they arrived home that she couldn't deal with fixing dinner. Marie's face still haunted her and she felt more exhausted than she had ever been.

"It's been a bad day," she told April. "A terrible day. Will you settle for grilled cheese sandwiches?"

"I'm not really hungry," April said. "Gabriela keeps me stuffed all the time."

Riley felt a deep pang of despair. *Another failure*, she thought.

But then April took another look at her mother, this time with a hint of compassion.

"Grilled cheese will be good," she said. "I'll fix them."

"Thank you," Riley said. "You're a sweetheart."

She felt her spirits lift a little. At least there would be no conflict here at home tonight. She really needed that little break.

They had a quick and quiet supper, then April went to her room to finish homework and go to bed.

As exhausted as she was, Riley felt she had little time to waste. She went to work. She opened her laptop, pulled up a map of the victims' locations, and printed out the section she wanted to study.

Riley slowly drew a triangle on the map. Its lines linked the three places where the victims had been found. The northernmost point marked where Margaret Geraty's body had been dumped in farmland two years ago. A point to the west marked where Eileen Rogers had been more carefully placed near Daggett some six months back. Finally, the point to the south marked where the killer had achieved full mastery, posing Reba Frye by a stream in Mosby Park.

Riley circled the area again and again, thinking, wondering. Another woman might soon be found dead somewhere in this area—if she wasn't dead already. There was no time to lose.

Riley hung her head. She was so tired. But a woman's life was at stake. And it now seemed to be up to Riley to save her—without official help or sanction. She wouldn't even have Bill to help her. But could she solve this case entirely on her own?

She had to try. She had to do it for Marie. She had to prove to Marie's spirit—and maybe even to herself—that suicide wasn't the only option.

Riley frowned at that triangle. It was a good guess that the victim was now being held somewhere in that area of a thousand square miles.

I've just got to look in the right place, she thought. *But where?*

She knew that she would have to condense her search area, and it wasn't going to be easy to do. At least she was familiar with some of the general area.

The uppermost part of the triangle, the point closest to Washington, was mostly upscale, rich, and privileged. Riley was all but sure that the killer didn't come from that kind of background. Besides, he had to be holding the victim in a place where no one could hear her scream. Forensics had found no sign of the other women's mouths being gagged or taped. Riley drew an X through that well-to-do area.

The two southern points were both parklands. Might the killer be holding the woman in a rented hunting cabin or on a campsite?

Riley thought it over.

No, she decided. *That would be too temporary.*

Her every instinct told her that this man operated out of his own home—perhaps a house where he had lived all his life, where he had passed an unusually miserable childhood. He would enjoy taking his victims there. Taking them home with him.

So she crossed out the park areas. What was left was primarily farmland and small towns. Riley strongly suspected that she was looking for a farmhouse somewhere in that area.

She looked again at the map on her computer, then zoomed in closely on the area under consideration. Her heart sank at the sight of a tangle of secondary roads. If she was right, the killer lived on some old dirt farm in that maze. But there were too many roads for her to search quickly by car—and besides, the farm might not even be visible from the road.

She groaned aloud with despair. The whole thing seemed more hopeless by the moment. The terrible pain of loss and failure threatened to surge up again.

But then she said aloud, "Dolls!"

She reminded herself of the conclusion she had come to yesterday—that the killer had probably spotted all of his victims in a single store that sold dolls. Where might that store be?

She drew another smaller shape on the paper map. It lay just to the east of the large triangle, and its corners marked the places where the four women had lived. Somewhere in that area, she felt pretty sure, was a store where all the women had bought dolls, and where the killer had targeted them. She would have to find that store first, before she could track down the place where he took the women.

Again, she brought up the map on her computer and zoomed in on it. The easternmost point of the smaller area wasn't very far from where Riley lived. She saw that a state road formed an arc that reached westward through several small towns, none of them wealthy or historic. They were just the sorts of towns she was looking for. And each of them undoubtedly had some kind of toy or doll store.

She printed out the smaller map, then ran another search, locating stores in every town. Finally, Riley shut down her computer. She had to get some sleep.

Tomorrow she would go out in search of Cindy MacKinnon.

CHAPTER TWENTY FOUR

Dusk was falling by the time Riley pulled into Glendive. It had been a long day, and she was feeling desperate. Time was passing much too fast, and so was any possibility of finding any life-saving clues.

Glendive was the eighth town on her route. In every town so far, Riley had gone into stores that sold toys and dolls, questioning anyone who would talk to her. She felt sure that she hadn't found the store she was looking for.

Nobody in any of the stores remembered seeing the women in the photographs she had showed them. Of course, the women in question were similar in age and appearance to a dozen others that a storekeeper might meet in any given week. To make matters worse, none of the dolls Riley saw on display struck her as the likely inspiration for the arrangement of the victims.

When she drove into Glendive, Riley had an odd sense of déjà vu. The main street looked uncannily like those in most of the other towns, with a brick church flanked on one side by a movie theater and on the other side by a drug store. All these towns were starting to blur together in her exhausted mind.

What was I thinking? she asked herself.

Last night she had been desperate to sleep, and she had taken her prescription tranquilizers. That hadn't been a bad idea. But following it with a couple of shots of whiskey had been unwise. Now she had a severe headache, but she had to keep going.

As she parked her car near the store she planned to check out, she saw that daylight was waning. She sighed with discouragement. She had one more town and one more store to check out tonight. It would be at least three hours before she could get back to Fredericksburg to pick up April at Ryan's house. How many nights had she been late now?

She took out her cell phone and dialed the house number. She hoped against hope that Gabriela would answer. Instead, she heard Ryan's voice.

"What is it, Riley?" he asked.

"Ryan," Riley sputtered, "I'm terribly sorry, but—"

"You're going to be late again," Ryan said, finishing her sentence.

"Yeah," Riley said. "I'm sorry."

A silence fell.

"Look, it's really important," Riley finally said. "A woman's life is in danger. I've got to do what I'm doing."

"I've heard it before," Ryan said in a disapproving tone. "It's always a matter of life and death. Well, go ahead. Take care of it. It's just that I'm starting to wonder why you bother to pick up April at all. She might as well just stay right here."

Riley felt her throat tighten. Just as she had feared, Ryan sounded like he was gearing up for a custody fight. And it wasn't out of any sincere desire to raise April. He was too busy living it up to concern himself with his daughter. All he wanted was to cause Riley pain.

"I'll come and get her," Riley said, trying to steady her voice. "We can talk about all this later."

She ended the call.

Then she stepped out of the car and walked the short distance to the store—Debbie's Doll Boutique, it was called. She went inside and saw that the name was a little presumptuous for a store that sold pretty standard, brand-name merchandise.

Nothing quaint or fancy here, she realized.

It seemed unlikely that this was the place she was looking for. The store she had in mind had to be at least a little bit special, a place that inspired a word-of-mouth reputation that attracted customers from surrounding towns. Still, Riley had to check this one out to be absolutely sure.

Riley walked up to the counter, where a tall, elderly woman with thick glasses and birdlike features was at the cash register.

"I'm Special Agent Riley Paige, FBI," she said, once again feeling naked without her badge. So far, other clerks had been willing to talk to her without it. She hoped that this woman would as well.

Riley pulled out four photographs and put them on the counter.

"I wonder if you've seen any of these women," she said, pointing to the pictures one by one. "You probably wouldn't remember Margaret Geraty—she would have been here two years ago. But Eileen Rogers would have come here about six months ago, and Reba Frye would have bought a doll six weeks ago. This last woman, Cindy MacKinnon, would have been here late last week."

The woman peered at the pictures closely.

"Oh, dear," she said. "My eyes aren't what they used to be.

Let me take a closer look."

She picked up a magnifying glass and examined the photos. Meanwhile, Riley noticed that there was someone else in the store. He was a rather homely man of average height and build. He was wearing a T-shirt and well-worn jeans. Riley might well have overlooked him if it weren't for one important detail.

He was carrying a bunch of roses.

These roses were real, but the combination of roses and dolls could signal a killer's obsession.

The man wasn't looking at her. He had surely heard her announce herself as FBI. Was he avoiding eye contact?

Just then the woman's voice piped up.

"I don't *think* I've seen any of them," she said. "But then, like I said, I don't see at all well. And I've never been any good with faces. I'm sorry not to be of more help."

"It's all right," Riley said, putting the photos back in her purse. "Thank you for your time."

She turned to look again at the man, who was now browsing a nearby rack. Her pulse quickened.

It definitely could be him, she thought. *If he buys a doll, I'll know it's him.*

But it wouldn't do for her to stand here and watch him. If he was guilty, he wasn't likely to give himself away. He might slip away from her.

She smiled at the storekeeper and left.

Outside, Riley walked a short distance down the block and stood there waiting. Only a few minutes passed before the store's door opened and the man came out. He was still holding the roses in one hand. In the other he held a bag of newly purchased merchandise. He turned and started walking along the sidewalk, moving away from Riley.

Taking long strides, Riley walked after him. She assessed his size and build. She was slightly taller than he was, and possibly a good bit stronger. She was probably better trained. She wasn't going to let him get away.

Just as he was passing a narrow alley, the man must have heard steps behind him. He turned suddenly and glanced back at her. He stepped to one side, as though to get out of her way.

Riley pushed him sideways into the alley—pushed him hard and roughly. The space was narrow, dirty, and dim.

Startled, the man dropped both the package and the roses. The flowers scattered across the pavement. He raised an arm as though to ward her off.

She took hold of that arm and twisted it behind his back, pushing him face-first against a brick wall.

"I'm Special Agent Riley Paige, FBI," she snapped. "Where are you holding Cindy MacKinnon? Is she still alive?"

The man was shaking from head to foot.

"Who?" he asked, his voice trembling. "I don't know what you mean."

"Don't play games with me," Riley snapped, feeling more naked than ever without her badge—and especially without her gun. How was she supposed to bring this guy in without drawing a weapon? She was a long way from Quantico, and she didn't even have a partner to help her.

"Lady, I don't know what this is all about," the man said, bursting into tears.

"What are these roses for?" Riley demanded. "*Who* are they for?"

"My daughter!" the man cried out. "Her first piano recital is tomorrow."

Riley was still holding him by his right arm. The man's left hand was flat against the wall. Riley suddenly noticed something that hadn't caught her eye until now.

The man was wearing a wedding ring. She'd been all but sure that the murderer wasn't married.

"Piano recital?" she said.

"Mrs. Tully's students," he cried. "You can ask anyone in town."

Riley loosened her grip a little.

The man went on, "I bought her roses to celebrate. For when she takes her bow. I bought her a doll too."

Riley released the man's arm and walked over to where he had dropped the package. She picked it up and pulled out its contents.

It was a doll, all right—one of those teenage-girl dolls that always offended and disturbed her, all sexed up with full lips and an ample bosom. But as creepy as it was, it looked nothing like the kind of doll she'd seen near Daggett. That doll was of a little girl. So was the doll she'd seen in the picture of Cindy MacKinnon and her niece—all frilly and golden-haired and dressed in pink.

She had the wrong man. She gasped for breath.

"I'm sorry," she said to the man. "I was wrong. I'm so, so sorry."

Still shaking with shock and confusion, the man was picking up the roses. Riley bent over to help him.

"No! No!" the man exclaimed. "Don't help! Stay away!

Just—get away from me!"

Riley turned and walked out of the alley, leaving the forlorn man to gather up his daughter's roses and doll. How could she have let this happen? Why did she go so far with it? Why had she not noticed the man's wedding ring the moment she saw him?

The answer was simple. She was exhausted, and her head was splitting. She wasn't thinking straight.

As she walked dazedly down the sidewalk, a neon storefront sign for a bar caught her eye. She wanted a drink. She felt like she needed a drink.

She went into the dimly lit place and sat down at the bar. The bartender was busy waiting on another customer. Riley wondered what the man she had just accosted was doing right now. Was he calling the police? Was she about to be apprehended herself? That would certainly be a bitter irony.

But she guessed that the man probably wouldn't call the police. After all, he'd have a hard time explaining what had happened. He might even feel embarrassed at having been attacked by a woman.

Anyway, if he had called the police, and they were on their way to get her, it wouldn't do to make a run for it. If she had to, she'd face the consequences of her actions. And maybe she deserved to be arrested. She remembered her conversation with Mike Nevins, how he'd drawn her attention to her own feelings of worthlessness.

Maybe I'm right to feel worthless, she thought. *Maybe it would have been better if Peterson had just killed me.*

The bartender stepped toward her.

"What will you have, ma'am?" he asked.

"A bourbon on the rocks," Riley said. "Make that a double."

"Coming right up," the bartender said.

She reminded herself that it wasn't like her to drink on the job. Her agonizing recovery from PTSD had been marked by occasional bouts of intense drinking, but she'd thought that was behind her.

She took a sip. The rough drink felt comforting going down.

She still had one more town to visit, and at least one more person to interview. But she needed something to calm her nerves.

Well, she thought with a bitter smile, *at least I'm not officially on duty.*

She finished the drink quickly, then talked herself out of ordering another. The toy store in the next town would close soon, and she had to get there right away. Time was running out for

Cindy MacKinnon—if it hadn't run out already.

As she left the bar, Riley sensed that she was walking on the edge of a familiar abyss. She had thought she'd left all that horror, pain, and self-loathing far behind. Was it catching up with her again?

How much longer, she wondered, could she evade its deadly pull?

CHAPTER TWENTY FIVE

Riley's cell phone buzzed early the next morning. She was sitting at her coffee table, looking at the map she had followed yesterday, planning a new route for today. When she saw that the call was from Bill, her nerves quickened. Would this be good or bad news?

"Bill, what's going on?"

She heard her former partner sigh miserably.

"Riley, are you sitting down?"

Riley's heart sank. She was glad that she *was* sitting down. She knew now that Bill's tone of voice could only mean one terrible thing, and she felt her muscles weaken with dread.

"They've found Cindy MacKinnon," Bill said.

"And she's dead, isn't she?" Riley said with a gasp.

Bill said nothing for a moment. But his silence answered Riley's question. Riley felt tears welling up—tears of shock and helplessness. She fought against them, determined not to cry.

"Where did they find her?" Riley asked.

"Pretty far to the west of the other victims, in the national forest, almost to the West Virginia line."

She looked at her map. "What's the nearest town?" He told her and she found the approximate location. It wasn't inside the triangle made by the other three sites where bodies had been found. But still, there must be some sort of relationship with the other sites. She couldn't quite place what it was.

Bill continued describing the discovery.

"He put her next to a cliff in an open area, no trees around it. I'm at the scene right now. It's horrible. He's getting bolder, Riley."

And acting faster, Riley thought with despair. He'd only kept this victim alive for a few days.

"So Darrell Gumm really is the wrong guy," Riley said.

"You're the only one who said so," Bill replied. "You were right."

Riley struggled to comprehend the situation.

"So has Gumm been released?" she asked.

Bill grunted with annoyance.

"Not a chance," he said. "He'll be facing obstruction charges. He's got a lot to answer for. Not that he seems to care. But we'll try to keep his name out of the news as much as we can. That amoral prick doesn't deserve the publicity."

A silence fell between them.

"Damn it, Riley," Bill said at last, "if only Walder had listened to you, maybe we could have saved her."

Riley doubted that. It wasn't as if she'd had any solid leads of her own; but maybe with all that redirected manpower, something could have been turned up in those precious hours.

"Have you got any photos?" she asked. Her heart was pounding.

"Yeah, Riley, but—"

"I know you're not supposed to show them to me. But I've got to see them. Could you send them to me?"

After a pause, Bill said, "Done."

A few moments later, Riley was looking at a series of ghastly images on her cell phone. The first was a close-up of that face she had seen in a picture just a few days back. Then the woman had been beaming with love over a happy little girl and her brand new doll. But now that face was pallid, its eyes stitched open, a hideous smile painted over its lips.

As she looked through more pictures, she saw that the display was a match for how Reba Frye's corpse had been arranged. All of the details were there. The pose was precise. The body was naked and splayed, sitting stiffly upright like a doll. An artificial rose was on the ground between her legs.

This was the killer's true signature, his message. This was the effect he'd wanted to achieve all along. He'd achieved mastery with his victims number three and four. Riley knew perfectly well he was all ready to do it again.

After looking at the pictures, Riley got back on the phone with Bill.

"I'm so sorry," she said, her voice choked with horror and sadness.

"Yeah, me too," he said. "But have you got any ideas at all?"

Riley ran the images she had just seen through her mind.

"I assume the wig and rose are the same as the others," she said. "The ribbon, too."

"Right. They look the same."

She paused again. What clues could Bill's team hope to find?

"Did you get the call early enough to check for tracks, footprints?" she asked.

"The scene was secured early this time. A ranger spotted her and called the Bureau directly. No local cops tromping around. But we didn't find anything useful. This guy is careful."

Riley thought hard for a few moments. The photos had showed a woman's body sitting in the grass, leaning against a rock formation. Questions were buzzing through her mind.

"Was the body cold?" she asked.

"It was by the time we got to it."

"How long do you think it had been there?"

She could hear Bill thumbing through his notebook.

"I don't know for sure, but she was put into this pose soon after death. According to discoloration, within a few hours. We'll know more after the coroner gets to work."

Riley felt her familiar impatience well up. She wanted to get a clearer sense of the killer's chronology.

She asked, "Could he have posed her where he killed her and then brought her to the location after the body was in rigor mortis?"

"Probably not," Bill said. "I don't see anything awkward about the position. I don't think she could have already been stiff before he brought her here. Why? Do you think he brought her here and then killed her?"

Riley closed her eyes and thought hard.

Finally she said, "No."

"You're sure?"

"He killed her wherever he kept her and then brought her to the site. He wouldn't have brought her there alive. He wouldn't want to struggle with a human being in his truck or on the site."

Her eyes still shut tight, Riley reached inside herself for a sense of the killer's mind.

"He would only want to bring the raw materials for the statement he was making," she said. "Once she was dead, that's what she was to him. Like a piece of artwork, no longer a woman. So he killed her, washed her down, dried her, prepared the body just the way he wanted it, all covered with Vaseline."

The scene was starting to play out in her imagination in vivid detail.

"He got her to the location when rigor mortis was setting in," she said. "He timed it perfectly. After killing three other women, he understood just how that would work. He made the onset of rigor part of his creative process. He posed her as she hardened, little by little. He molded her like clay."

Riley found it hard to say what she saw happening next in her mind—or the killer's mind. The words came out slowly and painfully.

"By the time he'd finished sculpting the rest of her body, her chin still rested on her chest. He felt the muscles of her shoulders and neck, sensing the exact state of remaining pliability, and tilted the head up. He held it there until it stiffed. It might have taken two or three minutes. He was patient. Then he stepped back and enjoyed his handiwork."

"Jesus," Bill murmured in a hushed, shocked voice. "You're good."

Riley sighed bitterly and didn't reply. She didn't think she was good—not anymore. All she was good at was getting into a sick mind. What did that say about her? How did it do anybody any good? It certainly hadn't helped Cindy MacKinnon.

Bill asked, "How far away do you think he holds the victims while they're still alive?"

Riley did some swift mental calculations, visualizing a map of the area in her head.

"Not very far from where he posed her," she said. "Probably under two hours away."

"That still covers a lot of territory."

Riley's spirits were ebbing by the second. Bill was right. She wasn't saying a single thing that could be any help.

"Riley, we need you back on this case," Bill said.

Riley groaned under her breath.

"I'm sure Walder doesn't think so," she said.

I don't think so, either, she thought.

"Well, Walder's wrong," Bill said. "And I'm going to tell him he's wrong. I'm going to get you back on the job."

Riley let Bill's words sink in for a moment.

"It's too much of a risk for you," she said at last. "Walder's liable to fire you too if you make waves."

Bill stammered, "But—but Riley—"

"No 'buts,' Bill. If you get yourself fired, this case will never get solved."

Bill sighed. His voice was tired and resigned.

"Okay," he said. "But have you got any ideas at all?"

Riley thought for a moment. The abyss she'd been peering into for the last couple of days yawned wider and deeper. She felt what little was left of her resolve slipping away through her fingers. She'd failed, and a woman was dead.

Still, maybe there was one more thing she could do.

"I have some ideas brewing," she said. "I'll let you know."

As they ended the call, the smell of coffee and fried bacon reached Riley from the kitchen. April was in there. She'd been making breakfast ever since Riley had gotten out of bed.

Without even being asked! Riley thought.

Maybe spending time with her father was making her appreciate Riley, at least a little. April never liked having to be around Ryan. Whatever the reason, Riley was grateful for even the smallest comfort on a morning like this.

She sat there thinking about what to do next. She'd been planning to drive west again today, following the new route she'd mapped out. But she felt defeated, completely beaten down by this terrible turn of events. Yesterday she hadn't been at her best, and had even succumbed to that drink in Glendive. She couldn't do the same thing today, not in her present state of mind. She'd surely make mistakes. And too many mistakes had been made already.

But the location of the store was still important—maybe more important than ever. The killer would target his next victim there, if he hadn't already. Riley got on her computer and composed an email for Bill, with a copy of her map attached.

She explained to Bill which towns and which stores ought to be checked. Bill himself should probably stay focused on finding the killer's house, she wrote. But maybe he could persuade Walder to send someone else along Riley's route—as long as Walder didn't find out that it was her idea.

She sat there, staring at the map again and again, and slowly she began to spot a pattern she had not seen before. It was not that the sites related to each other, but that they were spread out in a lopsided fan from another mark on her map—the area enclosed by the four women's addresses. As she studied it, it made her more convinced than ever that the selection of victims was centered around some particular place that they all went, a particular doll store. And wherever the killer took his victims, it probably wasn't a long distance from where he first saw them.

But why hadn't she been able to find the store? Was she taking the wrong approach? Was she so stuck on a single idea that she couldn't see any other clues? Was she just imagining a pattern that was leading her completely astray?

Riley scanned her map and sent it along to Bill with her notes.

"Breakfast is ready, Mom."

As she sat down with her daughter, Riley found herself fighting back tears again.

"Thank you," she said. She began to eat silently.

"Mom, what's wrong?" April asked.

Riley was surprised at the question. Did she hear a note of concern in her daughter's voice? The girl was still pretty taciturn with Riley most of the time, but at least she hadn't been openly rude for a few days.

"Nothing's wrong," Riley said.

"That's not true," April said.

Riley said nothing in reply. She didn't want to drag April into the horrible reality of the case. Her daughter was troubled enough already.

"Was that Bill on the phone?" April asked.

Riley nodded silently.

"What did he call about?" April asked.

"I can't talk about it."

A long silence fell between them. They both kept on eating.

Finally April said, "You keep trying to get me to talk to you. That cuts both ways, you know. You never talk to me, not really. Do you ever talk to *anybody* anymore?"

Riley stopped eating and stifled a sob as it rose up in her throat. It was a good question. And the answer was no. She didn't talk to anybody at all, not anymore. But she couldn't bring herself to say so.

She reminded herself that it was Saturday, and she wasn't taking April to school. And she'd made no plans for April to stay with her father. And even though Riley wasn't going to drive west in search of clues, there was still something she had to do.

"April, I've got to go somewhere," she said. "Will you be okay here by yourself?"

"Sure," April said. Then, in a truly sad voice, she asked, "Mom, could you at least tell me where you're going?"

"I'm going to a funeral."

CHAPTER TWENTY SIX

Riley arrived at the parlor in Georgetown shortly before Marie's service was scheduled to begin. She dreaded funerals. To her, they were worse than arriving at a crime scene with a freshly murdered body. They always got inside her gut in some terrible way. Yet Riley felt she still owed something—she wasn't sure what—to Marie.

The funeral parlor had a facade of prefab brick panels and white columns on the front portico. She entered a carpeted, air-conditioned foyer that led into a hallway wallpapered in muted pastel colors gauged to be neither depressing nor cheery. The effect backfired on Riley, adding to her feeling of despair. She wondered why funeral homes couldn't just be the gloomy and uninviting places they really ought to be, like mausoleums or morgues, with none of this phony sanitization.

She passed several rooms, some with caskets and visitors, others empty, until she arrived where Marie's service was to be held. At the far end of the room she saw the open casket, made out of burnished wood with a long brass handle along the sides. Perhaps two dozen people had showed up, many of them seated, some of them mingling and whispering. Bland organ music was being pumped into the room. A small viewing line was passing the coffin.

She got in line and soon found herself standing beside the coffin, looking down at Marie. For all of Riley's mental preparation, it still gave her a jolt. Marie's face was unnaturally passive and serene, not twisted and agonized, as it had been when she was hanging from that light fixture. This face was not stressed and fearful, as it had been when they had talked in person. It seemed wrong. Actually, it seemed worse than wrong.

She quickly moved past the coffin, noticing a somewhat elderly couple sitting in the front row. She assumed that they were Marie's parents. They were flanked by a man and woman closer to Riley's age. She took them to be Marie's brother and sister. Riley reached back into memories of conversations with Marie and recalled that their names were Trevor and Shannon. She had no idea what Marie's parents' names were.

Riley thought of stopping to offer the family her condolences.

But how would she introduce herself? As the woman who rescued Marie from captivity, only to find her corpse later? No, surely she was the last person they wanted to see right now. It was best to leave them to grieve in peace.

As she made her way to the back of the room, Riley realized that she didn't recognize a single person there. That seemed strange and terribly sad. After all their countless hours of video chatting and their single face-to-face meeting, they didn't have one friend in common.

But they did have one terrible enemy in common—the psychopath who had held them both. Was he here today? Riley knew that killers commonly visited the funerals and graves of victims. Deep down, as much as she owed it to Marie, she also had to admit that that was the real reason she had come here today. To find Peterson. It was also why she was carrying a concealed weapon—her personal Glock that she normally kept boxed in her car trunk.

As she walked toward the back of the room, she scanned the faces of those already seated. She had glimpsed Peterson's face in the glare of his torch, and she'd seen pictures of him. But she'd never gotten a really good look at him face to face. Would she recognize him?

Her heart pounded as she looked at all the faces suspiciously, searching for a murderer in each one. They all soon became a blur of grief-stricken faces, staring back puzzlingly at her.

Seeing no obvious suspects, Riley sat down in an aisle seat in the back row, separated from anyone else, where she could watch anyone who entered or exited.

A young minister stepped up to a podium. Riley knew that Marie hadn't been religious, so the minister must have been her family's idea. The stragglers sat down, and everybody became quiet.

In a hushed and rather professional-sounding voice, the minister began with familiar words.

"'Even though I walk through the valley of the shadow of death, I will fear no evil, for you are with me; your rod and your staff, they comfort me.'"

The minister paused for a moment. In the brief silence, a single phrase echoed through Riley's mind …

"I will fear no evil."

Somehow, it struck Riley as a grotesquely inappropriate thing to say. What did it even mean to "fear no evil"? How could it possibly be a good idea? If Marie had been more fearful months ago, more wary, maybe she wouldn't have fallen into Peterson's clutches at all.

This was definitely a time to be fearful of evil. There was plenty of it out there.

The minister began to speak again.

"My friends, we have gathered here to mourn the loss and celebrate the life of Marie Sayles—daughter, sister, friend, and colleague ..."

The minister then launched into a boilerplate homily about loss, friendship, and family. Although he described Marie's "passing" as "untimely," he made no mention of the violence and terror that had haunted the last weeks of her life.

Riley quickly tuned out his sermon. As she did, she remembered the words in Marie's suicide note.

"This is the only way."

Riley felt a knot of guilt swelling inside of her, growing so large that she almost couldn't breathe. She wanted to rush up to the front of the room, push the minister aside, and confess to the congregation that this was all, all her own fault. She had failed Marie. She had failed everyone who loved Marie. She had failed herself.

Riley fought back the urge to confess, but her unease started to take on a brutal clarity. First there had been the funeral home's prefab bricks, silly white columns, and pastel-colored wallpaper. Next had been Marie's face, so unnatural and waxy in the coffin. And now here was the preacher, gesturing and talking like some kind of toy, a miniature automaton, and the congregation of little heads bobbing as he spoke to them.

It's like a doll house, Riley now realized.

And Marie was posed in the coffin—not a real corpse, but a pretend one, in a pretend funeral.

Horror cascaded over Riley. The two murderers—Peterson and whoever had killed Cindy MacKinnon and the others—merged together in her mind. It didn't matter that the pairing was completely groundless and irrational. She couldn't disentangle them. They became one to her.

It seemed as though this well-crafted funeral was the monster's final touch. It announced that there would be many more victims and many more funerals to follow.

As she sat there, Riley noticed out of the corner of her eyes someone slip in quietly to the service and sit on the other end of the back row. She turned her head slightly to see who had arrived in the middle of the service and saw a man dressed casually, wearing a baseball cap drawn low, shielding his eyes. Her heart beat faster. He looked large and strong enough to be the one who overpowered her when he caught her. His face was hard, jaws clenched, and she thought that he had a guilty look about him. Could it be the killer she was looking for?

Riley realized that she was almost hyperventilating. She slowed her breathing down until her head cleared. She had to restrain herself from leaping up and arresting the latecomer. The service was obviously coming to a close, and she couldn't disrupt it and disrespect Marie's memory. She had to wait. What if it wasn't him?

But then, to her surprise, he suddenly got to his feet and quietly left the room. Had he spotted her?

Riley jumped up and followed him. She sensed heads turn at her sudden commotion, but that didn't matter now.

She trotted through the funeral parlor hallway toward the front entrance, and as she threw open the front door, she saw that the man was walking briskly away along the city sidewalk. She drew her handgun and charged after him.

"FBI!" she shouted. "Stop right there!"

The man whirled around to face her.

"FBI!" she repeated, once again feeling naked without her badge. "Keep your hands where I can see them."

The man facing her looked utterly baffled.

"ID!" she demanded.

His hands were shaking—whether from fear or indignation, Riley couldn't tell. He fished out a wallet with a driver's license and as she scanned it, she saw it identified him as a Washington resident.

"Here's my ID," he said. "Where's yours?"

Riley's resolution started to slip away. Had she ever seen this man's face before? She wasn't sure.

"I'm an attorney," the man said, still very shaken. "And I know my rights. You'd better have a good reason for pulling a gun on me for no reason. Right here on a city street."

"I'm Agent Riley Paige," she said. "I need to know why you were attending that funeral."

The man looked at her more closely.

"Riley Paige?" he asked. "The agent who rescued her?"

Riley nodded. The man's face suddenly sagged with despair.

"Marie was a friend," he said. "Months ago, we were close. And then this terrible thing happened to her and …"

The man choked back a sob.

"I'd lost touch with her. It was my fault. She was a good friend, and I didn't stay in touch. And now I'll never get a chance to …"

The man shook his head.

"I wish I could go back and do everything differently. I just feel so bad about it. I couldn't even make it all the way through the funeral. I had to leave."

This man was feeling guilty, Riley realized, and in pain. For reasons very much like her own.

"I'm sorry," Riley said softly, deflated, lowering her gun. "I really am. I will find the bastard who did this to her."

As she turned to walk away, she heard him call out in a perplexed tone.

"I thought he was already dead?"

Riley didn't reply. She left the bereaved man standing on the sidewalk.

And as she walked away, she knew exactly where she needed to go. A place where no one else on earth, except Marie, could possibly understand.

*

Riley drove through city streets that transitioned from Georgetown's elegant homes to a ramshackle neighborhood in a once-thriving industrial area. Many buildings and stores were abandoned, and the local residents were poor. The deeper she drove, the worse it became.

She finally parked along a block that consisted entirely of condemned row houses. She got out of the car and quickly found what she was looking for.

Two vacant homes flanked a broad, barren area. Not very long ago, three deserted houses had stood here. Peterson had lived as a squatter in the middle house, using it as his secret lair. It had been the perfect spot for him, too separated from living inhabitants for anyone to hear the screams coming from beneath the house.

Now the space had been leveled flat, all evidence of the houses cleared away, and grass was starting to grow there. Riley tried to visualize what it had looked like when the houses had been there. It wasn't easy. She'd only been here once when the houses were standing. And then it had been night.

As she walked into the clearing, memories started to come back to her …

144

*Riley had been trailing him all day and into the night. Bill
had been called away on an unrelated emergency, and Riley
had unwisely decided to follow the man here alone.*

*She watched him enter the wretched little house with
boarded up windows. Then, just a few moments later, he left
again. He was on foot, and she didn't know where he was
going.*

*She briefly considered calling for backup. She decided
against it. The man had gone away, and if the victim was
really inside that house, she couldn't leave her alone and in
torment for another minute. She walked up onto the porch and
squeezed her way between boards that only partially blocked
the doorway.*

*She turned on her flashlight. The beam reflected against
at least a dozen tanks of propane gas. It was no surprise. She
and Bill knew that the suspect was obsessed with fire.*

*Then she heard a scratching below the floorboards, then
a weak cry ...*

Riley paused the flow of memories. She looked around. She
felt sure—uncannily sure—that she was now standing on the very
spot that she both dreaded and sought. It was here where both she
and Marie had been caged in that dark and filthy crawlspace.

The rest of the story was still raw in her mind. Riley had been
captured by Peterson when she set Marie free. Marie had staggered
a couple of miles in a state of complete shock. By the time she was
found, she had no idea where she had been held captive. Riley was
left alone in the dark to find her own way out.

After a seemingly endless nightmare, tormented repeatedly by
Peterson's torch, Riley had gotten loose. When she did, she had
beaten Peterson nearly unconscious. Every blow gave her a great
sense of vindication. Maybe those blows, that small vindication,
she reflected, had allowed her to heal better than Marie.

Then, crazed and maddened with fear and exhaustion, Riley
had opened all the tanks of propane. As she fled the house, she
threw a lighted match back inside. The explosion threw her all the
way across the street. Everyone was amazed that she'd survived.

Now, two months after that explosion, Riley stood looking
around at her grim handiwork—a vacant space where nobody lived
or was likely to live for a long time. It seemed like a perfect image
of what her life had become. In a way, it seemed like the end of the
road—at least for her.

A sickening feeling of vertigo came over her. Still standing in

145

that grassy spot, she felt as if she were falling, falling, falling. She tumbled straight into that abyss that had been yawning open for her. Even in broad daylight, the world seemed terribly dark—even darker than it had been in that cage in that crawlspace. There seemed to be no bottom to the abyss, and no end to her fall.

Riley recalled once again Betty Richter's assessment of the odds that Peterson had been killed.

I'd say ninety-nine percent.

But that nagging one percent somehow rendered the other ninety-nine meaningless and absurd. And besides, even if Peterson really had died, what difference did it make? Riley remembered Marie's awful words on the phone on the day of her suicide.

Maybe he's like a ghost, Riley. Maybe that's what happened when you blew him up. You killed his body but you didn't kill his evil.

Yes, that was it. She had been fighting a losing battle all her life. Evil, after all, haunted the world, as surely as it did this place where she and Marie had suffered so horribly. It was a lesson she should have learned as a little girl, when she couldn't stop her mother from being murdered. The lesson was hammered home by Marie's suicide. Rescuing her had been pointless. There was no point in rescuing anybody, not even herself. Evil would prevail in the end. It was just as Marie had told her over the phone.

You can't fight a ghost. Give it up, Riley.

And Marie, so much braver than Riley had known, finally took matters into her own hands. She'd explained her choice in five simple words.

This is the only way.

But that was not courage, to take your life own life. That was cowardice.

A voice broke through Riley's darkness.

"You all right, lady?"

Riley looked up.

"What?"

Then, slowly, she realized that she was on her knees in a vacant city lot. Tears were running down her face.

"Should I call someone for you?" the voice asked. Riley saw that a woman had stopped on the nearby sidewalk, an older woman in shabby clothes but with a concerned look on her face.

Riley got her sobbing under control and rose to her feet, and the woman shuffled off.

Riley stood there, numb. If she couldn't put an end to her own horror, she knew a way that she could numb herself against it. It

146

wasn't courageous, and it wasn't honorable, but Riley was past caring. She wasn't going to resist it any longer. She got into her car and drove toward home.

CHAPTER TWENTY SEVEN

Hands still shaking, Riley reached into a kitchen cabinet for the bottle of vodka she'd stashed, the one she promised she would never touch again. She unscrewed the bottle cap and tried to pour it quietly into a glass, so that April wouldn't hear. Since it looked so much like water, she hoped she could drink it openly without lying about it. She didn't want to lie. But the bottle gurgled indiscreetly.

"What's going on, Mom?" April asked from behind her at the kitchen table.

"Nothing," Riley answered.

She heard April groan a little. She could tell that her daughter knew what she was doing. But there was no pouring the vodka back into the bottle. Riley wanted to throw it away, she really did. The last thing she wanted to do was drink, especially in front of April. But she had never felt so low, so shaken. She felt as if the world were conspiring against her. And she really needed a drink.

Riley slipped the bottle back into the cabinet, then went to the table and sat down with her glass. She took a long sip, and it burned her throat in a comforting way. April stared at her for a moment.

"That's vodka, isn't it, Mom?" she said.

Riley said nothing, guilt creeping over her. Did April deserve this? Riley had left her at home all day, calling occasionally to check up on her, and the girl had been perfectly responsible and had stayed out of trouble. Now Riley was the one being furtive and reckless.

"You got mad at me for smoking pot," April said.

Riley still said nothing.

"Now is when you're supposed to tell me that this is different," April said.

"It *is* different," Riley said wearily.

April glared.

"How?"

Riley sighed, knowing her daughter was right, and feeling a deepening sense of shame.

"Pot's illegal," she said. "This isn't. And—"

"And you're an adult and I'm a kid, right?"

Riley didn't reply. Of course, that was exactly what she had been starting to say. And of course, it was hypocritical and wrong.

"I don't want to argue," Riley said.

"Are you really going to start into this kind of thing again?" April said. "You drank so much when you were going through all those troubles—and you never even told me what it was all about."

Riley felt her chin clench. Was it from anger? What on earth did she have to be angry with April about, at least right now?

"There are some things I just can't tell you," Riley said.

April rolled her eyes.

"Jesus, Mom, why not? I mean, am I *ever* going to be grown up enough to learn the awful truth about what you do? It can't be much worse that what I imagine. Believe me, I can imagine a lot."

April got up from her chair and stomped over to the cabinet. She pulled down the vodka bottle and started to pour herself a glass.

"Please don't do that, April," Riley said weakly.

"How are you going to stop me?"

Riley got up and gently took the bottle away from April. Then she sat down again and poured the contents of April's glass into her own glass.

"Just finish eating your food, okay?" Riley said.

April was tearing up now.

"Mom, I wish you could see yourself," she said. "Maybe you'd understand how it hurts me to see you like this. And how it hurts that you never tell me anything. It just hurts so much."

Riley tried to speak but found that she couldn't.

"Talk to somebody, Mom," April said, beginning to sob. "If not to me, to somebody. There must be *somebody* you can trust."

April fled into her room and slammed the door behind her.

Riley buried her face in her hands. Why did she keep failing so badly with April? Why couldn't she keep the ugly parts of her life separate from her daughter?

Her whole body heaved with sobs. Her world had spun completely out of control and she couldn't form a single coherent thought.

She sat there until the tears stopped flowing.

Taking the bottle and the glass with her, she went into the living room and sat on the couch. She clicked on the TV and watched the first channel that came up. She had no idea what movie or TV show she'd happened upon, and she didn't care. She just sat there staring blankly at the pictures and letting the meaningless voices wash over her.

149

But she couldn't stop the images flooding through her mind. She saw the faces of the women who had been killed. She saw the blinding flame of Peterson's torch moving toward her. And she saw Marie's dead face—both when Riley had found her hanging and when she'd been so artfully displayed in the coffin.

A new emotion started to crawl along her nerves—an emotion that she dreaded above all others. It was fear.

She was terrified of Peterson, and she could feel his vengeful presence all around her. It didn't much matter whether he was alive or dead. He'd taken Marie's life, and Riley couldn't shake the conviction that she was his next target.

She also feared, perhaps even more, the abyss that she was falling into now. Were the two really separate? Hadn't Peterson caused this abyss? This was not the Riley she knew. Did PTSD ever have an end?

Riley lost track of time. Her whole body buzzed and ached with her multifaceted fear. She drank steadily, but the vodka wasn't numbing her at all.

She finally went to the bathroom and combed the medicine cabinet and found what she was looking for. Finally, with shaking hands, she found it: her prescription tranquilizers. She was supposed to take one at bedtime, and to never mix it with alcohol.

With shaking hands, she took two.

Riley went back to the living room couch and stared at the TV again, waiting for the medication to take effect. But it wasn't working.

Panic seized her in an icy grip.

The room seemed to be spinning now, making her feel nauseous. She closed her eyes and stretched out on the couch. Some of the dizziness went away, but the darkness behind her eyelids was impenetrable.

How much worse can things get? she asked herself.

She knew right away that it was a stupid question. Things were going to get worse and worse and worse for her. Things would never ever get better. The abyss was bottomless. All she could do was surrender to the fall and give herself over to cold despair.

The pitch-blackness of intoxication folded itself around her. She lost consciousness and soon began to dream.

Once again, the white flame of the propane torch cut through the darkness. She heard someone's voice.

"Come on. Follow me."

It wasn't Peterson's voice. It was familiar, though—extremely familiar. Had somebody come to her rescue? She rose to her feet and began to follow whoever was carrying the torch.

But to her horror, the torch cast its light on one corpse after another—first Margaret Geraty, then Eileen Rogers, then Reba Frye, then Cindy MacKinnon—all of them naked and horribly splayed. Finally the light fell on Marie's body, suspended in mid-air, her face horribly contorted.

Riley heard the voice again.

"Girl, you sure as hell botched things up."

Riley turned and looked. In the sizzling glare, she saw who was holding the torch.

It wasn't Peterson. It was her own father. He was wearing the full dress uniform of a Marine colonel. That struck her as odd. He'd been retired for many years now. And she hadn't seen or spoken to him in more than two years.

"I saw some bad shit in 'Nam," he said with a shake of his head. "But this really makes me sick. Yeah, you botched it bad, Riley. Of course I learned long ago not to expect anything from you."

He waved the torch so that it shone on one last body. It was her mother, dead and bleeding from the bullet wound.

"You might as well have shot her yourself, for all the good you did her," her father said.

"I was just a little girl, Daddy," Riley wailed.

"I don't want to hear any of your damn excuses," her father barked. "You never brought a single human soul a moment of joy or happiness, you know that? You never did anybody a lick of good. Not even yourself."

He turned the knob of the torch. The flame went out. Riley was in pitch-darkness again.

Riley opened her eyes. It was night, and the only light in the living room came from the TV. She remembered her dream clearly. Her father's words kept ringing in her ears.

You never brought a single human soul a moment of joy or happiness.

Was it true? Had she failed everybody so miserably—even the people she loved most?

You never did anybody a lick of good. Not even yourself.

Her mind was foggy and she couldn't think straight. Maybe she couldn't bring anybody any real joy and happiness. Maybe there was simply no real love inside of her. Maybe she wasn't

151

capable of love.

On the verge of despair, reeling for a crutch, Riley recalled April's words.

Talk to somebody. Somebody you can trust.

In her drunken haze, not thinking clearly, almost automatically Riley tapped a number on her cell phone. After a few moments, she heard Bill's voice.

"Riley?" he asked, sounding more than half-asleep. "Do you know what time it is?"

"I've got no idea," Riley said, slurring her words badly.

Riley heard a woman ask groggily, "Who is that, Bill?"

Bill said to his wife, "I'm sorry, I've got to take this."

She heard the sound of Bill's footsteps and a door closing. She guessed that he was going somewhere to talk privately.

"What's this all about?" he asked.

"I don't know, Bill, but—"

Riley stopped for a moment. She felt herself on the brink of saying things that she'd regret—maybe forever. But somehow she couldn't pull herself back.

"Bill, do you think you could get away for a while?"

Bill let out a growl of confusion.

"What are you talking about?"

Riley drew a deep breath. What *was* she talking about? She was finding it hard to collect her thoughts. But she knew that she wanted to see Bill. It was a primal instinct, an urge she could not control.

With what little awareness she had left she knew she should say *I'm sorry* and hang up. But fear, loneliness, and desperation overtook her, and she plunged ahead.

"I mean…" she continued, slurring her words, trying to think coherently, "just you and me. Spend some time together."

There was only silence on the line.

"Riley, it's the middle of the night," he said. "What do you mean *spend time together*?" he demanded, his irritation clearly rising.

"I mean…" she began, searching, wanting to stop, but unable to. "I mean…I think about you, Bill. And not just at work. Don't you think about me, too?"

Riley felt a terrible weight crushing upon her as soon as she had said it. It was wrong, and there was no taking it back.

Bill sighed bitterly.

"You're drunk, Riley," he said. "I'm not going to meet you anywhere. You're not going to drive anywhere. I've got a marriage

I'm trying to save, and you … well, you've got your own problems. Pull yourself together. Try to get some sleep."

Bill ended the call abruptly. For a moment, reality seemed to hang in a state of suspension. Then Riley was seized by a horrible clarity.

"What have I done?" she whimpered aloud.

In but a few moments, she had thrown away a ten-year professional relationship. Her best friend. Her only partner. And probably the most successful relationship of her life.

She'd been sure that the abyss she'd fallen into had no bottom. But now she knew she was wrong. She'd hit the bottom, and shattered the floor. Still, she was falling. She didn't know if she'd ever be able to get up again.

She reached for the vodka bottle on the coffee table—she didn't know whether to drink the last of its contents or to pour it out. But her hand-eye coordination was completely shot. She couldn't take hold of it.

The room swam around her, there came a crash, and everything went black.

CHAPTER TWENTY EIGHT

Riley opened her eyes, then squinted, shielding her face with her hand. Her head was splitting, her mouth dry. The morning light from the window was blinding and painful, reminding her uncannily of the white flash of Peterson's torch.

She heard April's voice say, "I'll take care of that, Mom."

There came a slight rattling and the glare diminished. She opened her eyes.

She saw that April had just closed the venetian blinds, shutting out the direct sunlight. She came over to the couch and sat down beside where Riley still lay. She picked up a cup of coffee and offered it to her.

"Careful, it's hot," April said.

Riley, the room spinning, slowly eased herself into a sitting position and reached for the mug. Handling the cup gingerly, she took a small sip. It was hot, all right. It burned both her fingertips and her tongue. Still, she was able to hold it, and she took another sip. At least the pain gave her a feeling of coming to life again.

April was staring off into space.

"Are you going to want some breakfast?" April asked in a distant, vacant voice.

"Maybe later," Riley said. "I'll fix it."

April smirked a bit sadly. Doubtless she could see that Riley was in no condition to fix much of anything.

"No, I'll do it," April said. "Just let me know when you feel like eating."

They both fell silent. April kept on staring elsewhere. Humiliation gnawed at Riley's gut. She vaguely remembered her disgraceful phone call to Bill last night, then her last thoughts before passing out—that hideous knowledge that she'd truly hit rock bottom. And now, to make matters worse, her daughter was here to witness her ruin.

Still sounding distant, April asked, "What are you planning to do today?"

It seemed both an odd question and a good one. It was time for Riley to make plans. If this was rock bottom, she needed to start pulling herself out.

She flashed back to her dream, her father's words, and as she did, she realized it was time to confront some of her demons.

Her father. The darkest presence of her life. The one who had always lingered in the back of her consciousness. The driving force, she sometimes felt, behind all the darkness she had manifested in her life. He, of all people, was the one she needed to see. Whether it was a primal urge for a father's love, her urge to face head-on the darkness in her life, or a desire to shake off being haunted by her dream, she did not know. But the urge consumed her.

"I think I'll drive out to see Grandpa," she said.

"Grandpa?" she asked, shocked. "You haven't seen him for years. Why would you go see him? I think he hates me."

"I don't think so," Riley said. "He's always been too busy hating me."

Another silence fell, and Riley sensed that her daughter was gathering her resolve.

"I want you to know something," April said. "I dumped out the rest of the vodka. There wasn't much left. I also poured out the whiskey you still had in the cabinet. I'm sorry. I guess it was none of my business. I shouldn't have done that."

Tears came to Riley's eyes. This was surely the most grown-up and responsible thing she'd ever known April to do.

"No, you should have," Riley said. "It was the right thing to do. Thank you. I'm sorry I couldn't do it myself."

Riley wiped away a tear and gathered up her own resolve.

"I think it's time we really talked," Riley said. "I think it's time I told you some of the things you've wanted me to tell you." She sighed. "But it won't be pleasant."

April finally turned and looked at her, anticipation in her eyes.

"I really wish you would, Mom," she said.

Riley took a long, deep breath.

"A couple of months back, I was working on a case," she said. Relief poured through her as she began to tell April about the Peterson case. She realized that this was much too long overdue.

"I got too eager," she continued. "I was by myself and I came across a situation, and I wasn't willing to wait. I didn't call for backup. I thought I could take care of it by myself."

April said, "That's what you do all the time. You try to take care of everything alone. Without me even. Without even talking to me."

"You're right."

Riley steeled herself.

"I got Marie out of captivity."

Riley hesitated, then finally plunged ahead. She heard her own voice shaking.

"I got caught," she continued. "He held me in a cage. There was a torch."

She broke down crying, all her pent-up terror rushing to the surface. She was so embarrassed, but couldn't stop.

To her surprise, she felt April's reassuring hand on her shoulder, and heard April crying herself.

"It's okay, mom," she said.

"They couldn't find me," Riley continued, between sobs. "They didn't know where to look. It was my fault."

"Mom, nothing's your fault," April said.

Riley wiped away her tears, trying to get a hold of herself.

"Finally, I got away finally. I blew up the place. They say the man is dead. That he can't hurt me now."

There came a silence.

"Is he?" April asked.

Riley so desperately wanted to say yes, to reassure her daughter. But instead she found herself saying:

"I don't know."

The silence thickened.

"Mom," April said, a new tone to her voice, one of kindness, of compassion, of strength, one Riley had never heard before, "you saved someone's life. You should be so proud of yourself."

Riley felt a new dread as she slowly shook her head.

"What?" April asked.

"That's where I was yesterday," Riley said. "Marie. Her funeral."

"She's dead!?" she asked, flabbergasted.

Riley could only nod.

"How?"

Riley hesitated. She didn't want to say it, but she had no choice. She owed April the whole truth. She was done withholding things.

"She killed herself."

She heard April gasp.

"Oh, Mom," she said, crying. "I'm so, so sorry."

They both cried for a long, long time, until finally they settled into a relaxed silence, each spent.

Riley took a deep breath, leaned over, and smiled at April, pulling the hair off her wet cheeks with love.

"You'll have to understand that there will be things I can't tell you," Riley said. "Either because I can't tell anybody, or because it wouldn't be safe for you to know, or maybe just because I don't think you should be thinking about them. I have to learn how to be the mother here."

"But something as big as this," April said. "You should have told me. You're my mother, after all. How was I supposed to know what you were going through? I'm old enough. I can understand. "

Riley sighed.

"I guess I thought you had enough to worry about. Especially with Dad and I splitting up."

"The split wasn't as hard as having you not talk to me," April countered. "Dad's always ignored me except when he felt called upon to give orders. But you—it's like suddenly you weren't there anymore."

Riley took April's hand and squeezed it tightly.

"I'm sorry," Riley said. "For everything."

April nodded.

"I'm sorry too," she said.

They hugged, and as Riley felt April's tears flow down her neck, she vowed to be different. She vowed to make a change. When this case was behind her, she would become the mother she always wanted to be.

CHAPTER TWENTY NINE

Riley drove reluctantly into the heart of her early childhood. What she expected to find there she didn't know. But she knew this was a crucial errand—for herself, anyway. She braced herself at the idea of seeing her father. Yet she knew she needed to face him.

Sloping all around her were the Appalachian Mountains, far to the south of her recent investigations. The trip down here had been a tonic in some ways, and with the windows down, she was beginning to feel better. She'd forgotten how beautiful the Shenandoah Valley was. She found herself steering upward through rocky passes and alongside flowing streams.

She passed through a typical mountain town—little more than a cluster of buildings, a gas station, a grocery store, a church, a handful of houses, a restaurant. She remembered how she'd spent her earliest childhood years in a town much like this.

She also remembered how sad she'd been when they'd moved to Lanton. Mother had said it was because it was a university town and had a whole lot more to offer. That had reset Riley's life expectations when she was still very young. Might things have gone better if she'd been able to spend her whole life in this simpler and more innocent world? A world where her mother wasn't likely to get gunned down in a public place?

The town disappeared behind her in multiple curves of the mountain roads. After a few miles, Riley turned off onto a winding dirt road.

Before too long she arrived at the cabin her father had bought after retiring from the Marines. A battered old utility vehicle was parked nearby. She hadn't been here in more than two years, but she knew the place well.

She parked and got out of her car. As she walked toward the cabin, she breathed in the clean forest air. It was a beautiful sunny day, and at this altitude the temperature was cool and pleasant. She basked in the splendid quiet, broken by nothing more than bird songs and the rustle of leaves in the breeze. It felt good to be surrounded on all sides by deep forest.

She walked toward the door, past a tree stump where her father cut his firewood. There was a pile of wood nearby—his only source of heat in colder weather. He also lived without electricity, but spring water was piped into the cabin.

Riley knew that this simple life was a matter of choice, not poverty. With his excellent benefits, he could have retired anywhere he'd liked. He'd chosen here, and Riley couldn't blame him. Maybe someday she'd do the same. Of course, a substantial pension looked markedly less likely, now that she'd lost her badge.

She pushed at the door and it opened freely. Out in these parts, there was little to fear from intruders. She stepped inside and looked around. The spare but comfortable single room was dim, with several unlit gas lanterns here and there. The pine paneling gave off a warm and pleasant woody smell.

Nothing had changed since the last time she'd been here. There were still no mounted deer heads or any other signs of game animals. Her father killed more than his share of animals, but solely for food and clothing.

The quiet was broken by a gunshot outside. She knew it wasn't deer season. He was probably shooting at smaller game—squirrels, crows, or groundhogs. She left the cabin and walked uphill past the smokehouse where he stored his meat, then followed a trail into the woods.

She passed by the covered spring that his fresh water came from. She arrived at the edge of what remained of an old apple orchard. Small lumpy fruit hung from the trees.

"Daddy!" she called out.

No reply came. She pushed on into the overgrown orchard. Soon she saw her father standing nearby—a tall, gangly man wearing a hunting cap and a red vest and holding a rifle. Three dead squirrels lay at his feet.

He turned his lined, hard, weathered face toward her, looking not the least bit surprised to see her—and not the least bit pleased.

"You shouldn't be up here without a red vest, girl," he growled. "Lucky thing I didn't shoot you dead."

Riley didn't reply.

"Well, there's nothing out here to shoot now," he said irritably, unloading his gun. "You've run them all off, with your yelling and crashing through the brush. At least I've got squirrels for dinner."

He started to walk downhill toward his cabin. Riley followed after him, barely able to keep up with his long, swift strides. After years of retirement, he still walked with his old military bearing, his whole body coiled like a huge steel spring.

When they got to the cabin, he didn't invite her in, nor did she expect him to. Instead, he tossed the squirrels into a basket by the door, then walked over to the stump near the woodpile and sat there. He took off his cap, revealing gray hair that was still cropped short, Marine-style. He didn't look at Riley.

With no place else to sit, Riley plopped down on the front steps.

"It looks nice inside your cabin," she said, trying to find something to talk about. "I see you're still not mounting trophies."

"Yeah, well," he said with smirk, "I never took trophies when I killed in 'Nam. I'm not going to start now."

Riley nodded. She'd heard this remark often, always delivered with his typical grim humor.

"So what are you doing here?" her father asked.

Riley started to wonder. What on earth had she expected from this hard man, so incapable of basic affection?

"I've got some troubles, Daddy," she said.

"With what?"

Riley shook her head and smiled sadly. "I don't know where to start," she said.

He spit on the ground.

"It was a damn fool thing you did, getting caught by that psychopath," he said.

Riley was surprised. How did he know? She'd had no communication with him for a year.

"I thought you lived completely off the grid," she said.

"I get into town from time to time," her father said. "I hear things."

She almost said that her "damn fool thing" had saved a woman's life. But she quickly remembered—that wasn't true at all, not in the long run.

Still, Riley found it interesting that he knew about this. He'd actually gone to the trouble to find out something that had happened to her. What else might he know about her life?

Probably not much, she thought. *Or at least nothing I've done right according to his standards.*

"So did you fall to pieces after that whole thing with the killer?" he asked.

Riley bristled at this.

"If you mean did I suffer from PTSD, yes, I did."

"PTSD," he repeated, chuckling cynically. "I can't even remember just what those damn letters stand for. Just a fancy way of saying you're weak, as far as I'm concerned. I never suffered from this PTSD thing, not after I got home from the war, not after all the stuff I saw and did and got done to me. Don't see how anybody gets away with using that as an excuse."

He fell silent, looking off into space as if she weren't there. Riley figured this visit wasn't going to end well. She might as well talk a little about what was going on in her life. He wouldn't have anything encouraging to say about it, but at least it would make conversation.

"I'm having trouble with a case, Daddy," she said. "It's another serial killer. He tortures women, strangles them, and poses them outdoors."

"Yeah, I heard about that too. Poses them naked. Sick business." He spit again. "And let me guess. You're at odds with the Bureau about it. The powers-that-be don't know what they're doing. They won't listen to you."

Riley was startled. How did he guess?

"It was the same with me in 'Nam," he said. "The brass didn't seem to even get that they were fighting a damn war. Christ, if they'd left it up to the likes of me, we'd have won it. Makes me sick to think about it."

Riley heard something in his voice that she hadn't heard often—or at least had seldom noticed. It was regret. He actually felt regret about not winning the war. It didn't matter that he was in no way to blame. He felt responsible.

As Riley studied his face she realized something. She looked like him, more than she'd looked like her mother. But it was more than that. She *was* like him—not just in her horrible way with relationships, but with her cussed determination, her overweening sense of responsibility.

And that wasn't altogether a bad thing. In this rare moment of felt kinship, she wondered if maybe he really could tell her something she needed to know.

"Daddy, what he does—it's so ugly, leaving bodies naked and so horribly posed, but—"

She stopped, trying to find the right words.

"The places he leaves them are always so beautiful—forests and creeks, natural scenes like that. Why do you suppose he picks such places do something so ugly and evil?"

Her father's eyes turned inward. He seemed to be exploring his own thoughts, his own memories, talking as much about himself as about anybody else.

"He wants to start all over again," he said. "He wants to go all the way back to the beginning. Isn't it the same with you? Don't you just want to go back to where you started and begin all over again? Go back to where you were a kid? Find the place where everything went wrong and make life go all different?"

He paused for a moment. Riley remembered her thoughts driving here—how sad she'd been as a little girl when she'd had to leave these mountains. There really was some elemental truth in what her father was saying.

"That's why *I* live here," he said, slipping deeper into reverie.

Riley sat there quietly, taking this in. Her father's words started to bring something into focus. She'd long assumed that the killer kept and tortured the women in his childhood home. It hadn't occurred to her that he chose that setting for a reason—to somehow reach back into his past and change everything.

Still not looking at her, her father asked, "What does your gut tell you?"

"It's something to do with dolls," Riley said. "It's something that the Bureau's not getting. They're chasing after everything wrong. He's obsessed with dolls. That's the key somehow."

He grunted and shuffled his feet.

"Well, you just keep following that gut of yours," he said. "Don't let the bastards tell you what to do."

Riley was dumbstruck. It wasn't as if he were paying her a compliment. It wasn't as if he meant to be nice. He was the same irascible jerk he'd always been. But somehow, he was saying exactly what she needed to hear.

"I'm not going to quit," she said.

"You'd damn well better not quit," he snarled in a whisper.

There was nothing more to say. Riley got to her feet.

"It was good to see you, Daddy," she said. And she actually halfway meant it. He didn't reply, just sat there looking at the ground. She got into her car and drove away.

As she drove, she realized that she felt different from when she'd come—and in some odd way, much better. Something, she felt, had been resolved between them.

She also knew something that she hadn't known before. Wherever the killer lived, it wasn't in some tenement, some sewer, or even some wretched, rundown shack out in the woods somewhere.

It was going to be a place of beauty—a place where beauty and horror were poised equally, side by side.

*

A little while later, Riley was sitting at the counter in a cafe in the town nearby. Her father had offered her nothing to eat, which was no surprise, and now she was hungry and needed some nutrition for the drive home.

Just when the waitress set her bacon, lettuce, and tomato sandwich on the counter in front of her, Riley's cell phone buzzed. She looked to see who was calling, but there was no identification. She took the call warily.

"Is this Riley Paige?" asked a woman with an efficient voice.

"Yes," Riley said.

"I've got Senator Mitch Newbrough on the line. He wants to speak with you. Could you hold, please?"

Riley felt a jolt of alarm. Of all the people she did *not* want to hear from, Newbrough was at the top of her list. She had the urge to end the call without another word, but then thought better of it. Newbrough was already a powerful enemy. Making him hate her even more wasn't a good idea.

"I'll hold," Riley said.

A few seconds later, she heard the Senator's voice.

"Senator Newbrough here. I'm talking to Riley Paige, I assume."

Riley didn't know whether to be furious or terrified. He was talking as if she were the one calling him.

"How did you get this number?" she asked.

"I get things when I want them," Newbrough said in a typically cold voice. "I want to talk to you. In person."

Riley's dread mounted. What possible reason could he have for wanting to see her? This couldn't be good. But how could she say no without making things worse?

"I could drop by your house," he said. "I know where you live."

Riley almost asked how he knew her address. But she reminded herself that he'd already answered that question.

"I'd rather we just took care of this right now on the phone," Riley said.

"I'm afraid that's not possible," Newbrough said. "I can't talk about it on the phone. How soon can you meet me?"

Riley felt herself in the grip of Newbrough's powerful will. She wanted to refuse, but somehow couldn't make herself do so.

"I'm out of town right now," she said. "I won't be getting home until much later. Tomorrow morning I drive my daughter to school. We could meet in Fredericksburg. Maybe in a coffee shop."

"No, not a public place," Newbrough said. "It needs to be

somewhere less conspicuous. Reporters tend to follow me around. They get all over me whenever they get a chance. I'd rather stay off their radar. How about Quantico, the BAU headquarters?"

Riley couldn't keep a note of bitterness out of her voice.

"I don't work there anymore, remember?" she said. "You should know that better than anybody."

There came a brief pause.

"Do you know the Magnolia Gardens Country Club?" Newbrough asked.

Riley sighed at the absurdity of the question. She certainly didn't move in those kinds of circles.

"I can't say I do," she said.

"It's easy to find, about halfway between Quantico and my farm. Be there at ten-thirty a.m."

Riley liked this less and less. He wasn't asking, he was giving an order. After wrecking her career, what business did he have demanding anything of her?

"Is that too early?" Newbrough asked when Riley didn't reply.

"No," Riley said, "it's just that—"

Newbrough interrupted, "Then be there. It's members only, but I'll notify them to let you in. You'll want to do this. You'll see that it's important. Trust me."

Newbrough ended the call without saying goodbye. Riley was flabbergasted.

"Trust me," he'd said.

Riley might have found it funny if she weren't so unnerved. Next to Peterson and whatever other killer she was trailing, Newbrough was possibly the person she least trusted in the world. She trusted him even less than she did Carl Walder. And that was really saying something.

But she didn't appear to have any choice. He had something to tell her, she could feel it. Something, she sensed, that might even lead to the killer.

CHAPTER THIRTY

Riley neared the Magnolia Gardens Country Club and was stopped at a little white building at the gate. A green and white striped boom barrier blocked the way, and a uniformed security guard holding a clipboard stepped out of the building and walked up to the driver's side of her car.

Riley opened the window.

"Your name?" the guard said brusquely.

Riley was not at all certain about the protocol needed to get into the club, but Newbrough had said he'd let them know she was coming.

"I'm Riley Paige," she said. Then she stammered, "I'm a, uh, guest of Senator Newbrough."

The guard scanned the list, then nodded.

"Go on in," he said.

The boom gate lifted and Riley drove on through.

The entry lane wound through the namesake gardens, extremely luxurious, colorful, and fragrant this time of year. At last she pulled up at a brick building with white columns. Unlike those on the funeral parlor she'd visited recently, these columns were the real thing. Riley felt as if she'd stumbled upon some sort of nineteenth-century Southern plantation.

A valet hurried up to her car, gave her a card, and took her keys. He drove the car away.

Riley stood alone in front of the grand entrance, feeling as out of her element as she had at the Senator's home. Dressed in casual jeans, she wondered if she'd even be allowed to enter. Wasn't there some kind of a dress code in places like this? It was a good thing her jacket draped loosely over her shoulder holster.

A uniformed doorman stepped out to meet her.

"Your name, ma'am?" he asked.

"Riley Paige," she said, wondering if he'd ask for some sort of identification.

The doorman glanced at his own list. "Right this way, ma'am," he said.

He escorted her inside, down a long corridor, and to a small, private dining room. She had no idea whether to tip the doorman or not. But then, she had no idea how much the man was paid.

Might he make more than she did as an FBI agent? She thought it possible that offering a tip might be more gauche than not tipping him at all. It seemed best not to take chances.

"Thank you," she said to the man.

He nodded, showing no sign of disappointment, and went back the way they'd come.

The room was small but by far the most posh dining area she'd ever ventured into. There were no windows, but the single painting on the wall was an original oil of the namesake gardens she's passed outside.

The single table was set with silver, china, crystal, and linen. She chose a plush covered chair that faced the door and sat down. She wanted to see Senator Newbrough when he arrived.

If he arrives, she thought. She had no real reason to think he wouldn't. But this whole situation seemed so unreal, she didn't know what to expect.

A white-suited waiter came in and placed a tray with cheeses and a variety of crackers on her table.

"Would you like something to drink, ma'am?" he asked politely.

"Just water, thanks," Riley said. The waiter went out and within seconds popped back in with a crystal pitcher of water and two matching glasses. He poured water for her and left the pitcher and the other glass on the table.

Riley sipped at her water. She had to admit to herself that she enjoyed the feel of the elegant glass in her hand. She only had to wait a minute or two before the Senator arrived, looking every bit as cold and severe as he had before. He closed the door behind him and sat down on the opposite side of her table.

"I'm glad you came, Agent Paige," he said. "I've brought something for you."

Without further ceremony, Newbrough placed a thick, leather-bound notebook on the table. Riley stared at it warily. She remembered the list of enemies that Newbrough had given her the first time they'd met. Was this going to be something equally problematic?

"What is this?" she asked.

"My daughter's diary," Newbrough said. "I picked it up at her house after she was … found. I took it because I didn't want anyone to see it. Mind you, I don't know what's in it. I've never read it. But I'm quite sure it includes things that I'd rather not have become public knowledge."

Riley didn't know what to say. She had no idea why he might

want her to have this. She could tell that Newbrough was weighing whatever he was about to say next carefully. From the first time she met with him, she'd been sure that he'd been withholding information from her. She tingled with expectancy that he might now tell her what that was.

Finally he said, "My daughter was having trouble with drugs during the last year of her life. Cocaine, heroin, Ecstasy, all kinds of hard stuff. Her husband put her on that route. It was one of the reasons her marriage failed. Her mother and I had been hoping she was pulling out of it when she died."

Newbrough paused, staring at the diary.

"At first I thought that her death was somehow connected with all that," he said. "The users and dealers in her circle were an unsavory bunch. I didn't want it to get out. You understand, I'm sure."

Riley wasn't at all sure that she did understand. But she was certainly surprised.

"Drugs had nothing to do with your daughter's murder," she said.

"I realize that now," Newbrough said. "Another woman was found dead, wasn't she? And doubtless there will be more victims. It appears that I was wrong in thinking this had anything to do with me or my family."

Riley was stunned. How often did this incredibly egotistical man ever admit that he was wrong about anything?

He patted the diary with his hand.

"Take this with you. It might have some information to help you with your case."

"It's not *my* case anymore, Senator," Riley said, allowing a trace of her bitterness to emerge. "I think you know that I was fired from the Bureau."

"Oh, yes," Newbrough said, tilting his head thoughtfully. "My mistake, I'm afraid. Well, it's nothing I can't fix. You'll be reinstated. Give me a little time with it. Meanwhile, I hope you can make use of this."

Riley was overwhelmed by the gesture. She took a deep breath.

"Senator, I believe I owe you an apology. I—I wasn't at my best the last time we met. I'd just been to a friend's funeral, and I was distraught. I said some things I shouldn't have."

Newbrough nodded in silent acceptance of her apology. It was apparent that he wasn't going to apologize to her, as much as she knew that she deserved it. She had to be content with his admission that he'd made a mistake. At least he was trying to make amends. That mattered more than an apology, anyway.

Riley picked up the diary without opening it.

"There's just one thing I'd like to know, Senator," she said. "Why are you giving this to me and not to Agent Walder?"

Newbrough's lips twisted into a slight semblance of a smile.

"Because there's one thing I've learned about you, Agent Paige," he said. "You're nobody's lapdog."

Riley couldn't reply. This sudden respect from a man who otherwise seemed to only have regard for himself simply stunned her.

"And now perhaps you'd like some lunch," the Senator said.

Riley thought it over. As grateful as she was for Newbrough's change of heart, she still felt far from comfortable around him. He remained a cold, brittle, and unpleasant man. And besides, she had work to do.

"If you don't mind, I think I'd better excuse myself," she said. Indicating the diary, she added, "I need to start making use of this right away. There's no time to lose. Oh—and I promise not to let anything I find here become public."

"I appreciate that," Newbrough said.

He politely rose from his chair as Riley left the room. She exited the building and handed the ticket to the valet. While she waited for him to fetch her car, she opened the diary.

As she flipped through its pages, she saw right away that Reba Frye had written quite a bit about her illicit drug use. Riley also got the immediate impression that Reba Frye was a very self-absorbed woman who seemed to be obsessed with petty resentments and dislikes. But after all, wasn't that the whole point of a diary? It was a place where one had every right to be self-absorbed.

Besides, Riley thought, even if Reba had been as narcissistic as her father, she certainly didn't deserve such a terrible fate. Riley felt a chill as she remembered the photos she'd seen of the woman's corpse.

Riley continued flipping through the diary. Her car pulled up on the gravel driveway, but she ignored the valet, mesmerized. She stood there, hands trembling, and read all the way through to the end, desperate for any mention of the killer, of anything, any clue at all. But she was crestfallen to find none.

She began to lower the heavy book, feeling crushed. She couldn't stand another dead end.

Just then, as she lowered it, a small piece of paper, tucked between two pages, began to slip out of the book. She caught it and studied it, curious.

As she examined it, her heart suddenly slammed in her chest.

In utter shock, she dropped the diary.

She was holding a receipt.

To a doll store.

CHAPTER THIRTY ONE

There it was. After all the dead ends, Riley could barely believe what she was holding. At the top of the handwritten receipt was the name and address of the store: Madeline's Fashions in Shellysford, Virginia.

Riley was stumped. It didn't sound like a doll or toy store.

On her cell phone she found the website for Madeline's Fashions. It was, oddly, a women's clothing shop.

But she looked closer and saw that they also dealt in collectible dolls. They could only be viewed by appointment.

A chill ran up Riley's spine.

This has got to be the place, she thought.

She picked up the diary and with shaking hands, flipped through the pages to find the entry for the date on the receipt. There it was:

Just bought the perfect little doll for Debbie. Her birthday's not for a month, but she's so hard to shop for.

There it was, in plain English. Reba Frye had bought a doll for her daughter at a store in Shellysford. Riley felt certain that all the other victims had bought dolls there, too. And that that was where the murderer had first spotted them.

Riley pulled up a map on her phone, and it showed Shellysford a hour's drive away. She had to get there as soon as she possibly could. For all she knew, the murderer had already spotted another victim.

But she needed to get some information in the works. And she needed to make a painful phone call that she'd put off too long already.

She took her keys from the baffled valet, jumped in her car, and pulled out, her tires screeching on the club's manicured drive. As she sped past the gate, she punched in Bill's cell phone number, wondering if he'd bother to answer. She couldn't blame him if he never wanted to speak to her again.

To her relief, Bill's voice came over the phone.

"Hello," he said.

Riley's heart jumped. She didn't know whether to be relieved or terrified to hear his voice.

"Bill, this is Riley," she said.

"I know who this is," Bill replied.

A silence fell. This wasn't going to be easy. And she knew she didn't deserve for it to be easy.

"Bill, I don't know how to start," she said. Her throat swelled with emotion and she found it hard to speak. "I'm so, so terribly sorry. It's just that— well, everything had gotten so bad, and I just wasn't in my right mind, and—"

"And you were drunk," Bill said, interrupting.

Riley sighed miserably.

"Yes, I was drunk," she said. "And I apologize. I hope you can forgive me. I'm so sorry."

Another silence came.

"Okay," Bill finally said.

Riley's heart sank. She knew Bill better than she knew anybody else in the world. So she could hear a world of meaning in those two blunt syllables. He wasn't forgiving her, and he wasn't even accepting her apology—at least not yet. All he was doing was acknowledging that she *had* apologized.

Anyway, now was no time to be hashing it out. There was a far more urgent matter to take care of.

"Bill, I've got a lead," she said.

"What?" he asked in a stunned voice.

"I found the store."

Bill sounded worried now.

"Riley, are you out of your mind? What are you doing, still working this case? Walder *fired* you, for God's sake."

"Since when have I ever waited for permission? Anyway, it looks like I'm going to be reinstated."

Bill snorted with disbelief.

"Who says?"

"Newbrough."

"What are you talking about?" Bill asked, sounding more and more agitated. "Christ, Riley, you didn't go to his house again, did you?"

Riley thoughts became jangled. There was too much to explain. She had to stick to the basics.

"No, and he was different this time," she said. "It was weird, and I can't get into it right now. But Newbrough gave me some new information. Bill, Reba Frye bought a doll at a store in Shellysford. I've got proof. I've got the name of the store."

"That's crazy," Bill said. "We've had agents scouring that

whole area. They've been to every town out there. I don't think they even found a doll store in Shellysford."

Riley was finding it harder and harder to contain her own excitement.

"That's because there isn't one," she said. "It's a clothing store that sells dolls, but you can only see them by appointment. Madeline's Fashions, it's called. Are you at the BAU right now?"

"Yes, but—"

"Then get somebody checking into the place. Get whatever you can on everybody who's ever worked there. I'm going there right now."

Bill's voice was loud and frantic.

"Riley, don't! You've got no authorization. You don't even have a badge. And what if you find the guy? He's liable to be dangerous. And Walder took your gun."

"I've got my own gun," Riley said.

"But you won't be able to detain anybody."

With a growl of determination, Riley said, "I'll do whatever I have to do. Another life might be at stake."

"I don't like this," Bill said, sounding more resigned now.

Riley ended the phone call and stepped on the gas.

*

Bill sat in his office staring dumbly at his cell phone. He realized that his hands were shaking. He wasn't sure why. Anger and frustration? Or was it from fear for Riley, for whatever reckless thing she was about to do?

Her drunken phone call two nights ago had left him confused and devastated. It was something of a cliché that law enforcement partners often felt closer to one another than to their own spouses. And Bill knew that it was true. For a long time, he'd felt closer to Riley than he'd ever felt to anyone in his life.

But there was no room for romance in their line of work. Complications or hesitations on the job could have deadly results. He'd always kept things professional between them and always trusted Riley to do the same. But now she had broken that trust.

Well, she was obviously aware of her mistake. But what had she meant when she said she would be reinstated? Would they work together again? He wasn't sure if he wanted to. Was the dynamic and comfortable professional rapport they'd long shared ruined forever?

But he couldn't worry about all of that now. Riley had asked him to check on the employees of a store. He'd pass that request on, but not to Carl Walder. Bill got on the phone and called the extension for Special Agent Brent Meredith. Meredith wasn't in the proper chain of command on this case, but Bill knew he could count on him to get the job done.

He planned to keep the call short and efficient. He had to drive to Shellysford right now and he only hoped he could get there before Riley Paige did something really stupid.

Like get herself killed.

CHAPTER THIRTY TWO

Riley's heart was pounding in anticipation as she pulled into the little town of Shellysford. Madeline's Fashions was easy to spot. It was in plain view on the main street, and its name was displayed across the front window. Shellysford was a bit more upscale than she'd expected. Some apparently historic buildings had been kept in good repair, and the main street verged on elegance. The rather chic-looking clothing store fit in well with its prosperous surroundings.

Riley parked at the curb in front of the store, got out of her car, and took in her surroundings. She immediately noticed that one of the store's window mannequins was actually holding a doll—a princess in a pink dress, wearing a sparkly tiara. The agents combing this town, though, may have easily have taken this as mere window dressing. Only a small sign in the window suggested otherwise: *Collectible Dolls Shown By Appointment.*

A bell above the door rang as Riley walked inside, and the woman at the counter glanced in her direction. She looked middle-aged but remarkably youthful, and her graying hair was full and healthy.

Riley weighed her options. Without her badge, she had to be careful. True, she'd managed to get other retailers to talk to her without it. But she absolutely did not want to spook this woman.

"Excuse me," Riley said. "Are you Madeline?"

The woman smiled. "Well, my name is actually Mildred, but I go by Madeline. I like it better. And it sounds better for the name of a store. 'Mildred's Fashions' just wouldn't have the same ring." The woman chuckled and winked. "It wouldn't draw quite the clientele I'm aiming for."

So far so good, Riley thought. The woman was open and talkative.

"Lovely place," Riley said, looking around. "But seems like a lot of work for one person. Have you got any help? Surely you don't do all this by yourself."

The woman shrugged.

"Mostly I do," she said. "Sometimes I've got a teenage girl who works the register while I help customers. This is a quiet day, though. There was no need for her to come in."

Still considering the right approach, Riley walked over to a clothing rack and fingered some of the merchandise.

"Beautiful outfits," she said. "Not many stores carry dresses like these."

Madeline looked pleased.

"No, you're not likely to find anything like them elsewhere," she said. "They're all high fashion, but I buy them from outlets when styles have been discontinued. So by big city standards, these would be yesterday's fashion." Then with another wink and a grin, she added, "But in a little town like Shellysford—well, they might as well be the latest thing."

Madeline pulled a lavender-colored cocktail dress off the rack.

"You'd look wonderful in this," she said. "It's perfect for your coloring—and for your personality too, I suspect."

Riley didn't think so. In fact, she couldn't see herself wearing any of the store's rather posh outfits. Still, she was sure that this dress would have been more appropriate at the country club than what she was now wearing.

"Actually," Riley said, "I was hoping to look at some of your dolls."

Madeline looked slightly surprised.

"Did you make an appointment?" she asked. "If you did, it seems to have slipped my mind. And how did you find out about our doll collection?"

Riley pulled the receipt out of her handbag and showed it to Madeline.

"Someone gave this to me," Riley said.

"Oh, a referral," Madeline said, obviously pleased. "Well, I can make an exception, then."

She walked to the back of the store and opened a wide folding door, and Riley followed her into a small back room. Its shelves were lined with dolls, and a couple of racks standing on the floor were filled with doll accessories.

"I started this little side business a few years back," Madeline said. "I had the opportunity to buy out the stock of a manufacturer that went out of business. The owner was a cousin of mine, so when they closed down I got a special deal. I'm happy to pass on those savings to my customers."

Madeline picked up a doll and looked it over proudly.

"Aren't they lovely?" she said. "Little girls love them. Their parents too. And these dolls are no longer being made, so they're truly collectibles, even though they're not antiques. And look at all these costumes. Any of my dolls can wear any of these outfits."

Riley scanned the rows of dolls. They looked much alike, although their hair color varied. So did their clothes, which included modern dress, princess gowns, and historical outfits. Among the accessories, Riley saw doll furniture to go with each style. The prices of the dolls were all above a hundred dollars.

"I hope you understand why I don't keep this section open," Madeline explained. "Most of my walk-in clients aren't shopping for dolls. And just between you and me," she added, lowering her voice to a whisper, "many of these smaller items are awfully easy to steal. So I'm careful about who I show all this to."

Fluffing up a doll's dress, Madeline asked, "By the way, what is your name? I like to know the names of all my customers."

"Riley Paige."

Then Madeline squinted with an inquisitive smile.

"And who was the customer who referred you?" she asked.

"Reba Frye," Riley said.

Madeline's face darkened.

"Oh, dear," she said. "The state senator's daughter. I remember when she came in. And I heard about ..." She fell silent for a moment. "Oh, dear," she added, shaking her head sadly.

Then she looked at Riley warily.

"Please tell me you're not a reporter," she said. "If so, I must ask you to leave. It would be terrible publicity for my store."

"No, I'm an FBI agent," Riley said. "And the truth is, I'm here to investigate Reba Frye's murder. I met with her father, Senator Newbrough, just a little while ago. He gave me this receipt. That's why I'm here."

Madeline looked more and more uneasy.

"Would you show me your badge?" she asked.

Riley held back a sigh. She had to bluff her way through this somehow. She had to lie at least a little.

"I'm off duty," she said. "We don't carry badges when we're off duty. It's standard procedure. I just came here on my own time to find out whatever I could."

Madeline nodded sympathetically. She seemed to believe her—or at least not to disbelieve her. Riley tried not to show her relief.

"What can I do to help?" Madeline asked.

"Just tell me anything you can about that day. Who else came in to work? How many customers came in?"

Madeline held out her hand. "May I see the receipt? For the date, I mean."

Riley handed her the receipt.

"Oh, yes, I remember," Madeline said as she looked at it. "That was a crazy day, several weeks ago."

Riley's attention quickened.

"Crazy?" Riley asked. "How so?"

Madeline knitted her brow as she recollected.

"A collector came in," she said. "He bought twenty dolls at once. I was surprised that he had the money. He didn't look all that rich. He was just a rather sad-looking older man. I gave him a special price. Things were really a mess while my girl and I rang up all that merchandise. We're not used to that kind of business. Everything was in turmoil for a little while there."

Riley's mind clicked away, putting this information together.

"Was Reba Frye in the store at the same time as this collector?" she asked.

Madeline nodded. "Why yes," she said. "Now that you mention it, she was here right then."

"Do you keep a record of your customers?" Riley asked. "With contact information?"

"Yes, I do," Madeline said.

"I need to see the man's name and address," Riley said. "It's very important."

Madeline's expression grew more wary.

"You said the Senator gave you this receipt?" she asked.

"How else could I have gotten it?" Riley asked.

Madeline nodded. "I'm sure that's true, but still ..."

She paused, struggling with her decision.

"Oh, I'm sorry," she blurted, "but I can't do it—let you look at the records, I mean. You don't even have any identification, and my customers deserve their privacy. No, really, Senator or no Senator, I can't let you look at it without a warrant. I'm sorry, but it just doesn't seem right to me. I hope you understand."

Riley took a long breath as she tried to assess the situation. She didn't doubt that Bill would show up here as soon as he could. But how soon would that be? And would the woman still insist on seeing a warrant? How much more time might that involve? For all Riley knew, someone's life might be hanging in the balance right that very minute.

"I understand," Riley said. "But is it okay if I just look around here a bit? I might find some clues."

Madeline nodded. "Of course," she said. "Take as long as you like."

A distraction tactic quickly took shape in Riley's mind. She began to browse among the dolls while Madeline tidied up some of the accessories. Riley reached up onto a high shelf as if trying to fetch down a doll. Instead, she managed to knock a whole row of dolls off the shelf.

"Oh!" Riley said. "I'm so sorry!"

She backed away in the clumsiest manner she could muster. She collided with a rack of accessories and knocked them all over.

"Oh, I'm so, so sorry!" Riley said again.

"It's all right," Madeline said with more than a note of irritation. "Just—just let me take care of it."

Madeline started to pick up the scattered merchandise. Riley hastily left the room and headed for the front desk. Glancing to make sure that Madeline wasn't watching her, Riley dived behind the desk. She quickly spotted a ledger book on a shelf under the cash register.

Her fingers shaking, Riley thumbed through the ledger. She quickly found the date, the name of the man, and his address. She didn't have time to write it down, so she committed it to memory.

She had just stepped out from behind the counter when Madeline returned from the back room. Madeline looked genuinely suspicious now.

"You'd really better leave," she said. "If you come back with a warrant, I'll be able to help. I certainly want to help the Senator and his family in any way I can. I feel terrible about all they're going through. But right now—well, I think you should leave."

Riley made a beeline toward the front door.

"I—I understand," she stammered. "I'm terribly sorry."

She rushed to her car and got in. She took out her cell phone and called Bill's number.

"Bill, I've got a name!" she almost shouted when he answered. "His name is Gerald Cosgrove. And I've got his address."

Remembering carefully, Riley recited the address to Bill.

"I'm only a few minutes away," Bill said. "I'll call in his name and address, see what kind of information the Bureau can turn up. I'll get back to you right away."

Bill ended the phone call. Riley fidgeted, waiting impatiently. She looked back at the store and noticed that Madeline was standing near the window, looking out at her suspiciously. Riley couldn't blame Madeline for her mistrust. Her behavior just now had been more than a little odd.

Riley's cell phone buzzed. She answered it.

"Bingo," Bill said. "The guy's a registered sex offender. The address you gave me isn't far. You're maybe a little closer to him than I am."

"I'm driving there right now," Riley said, stepping on the gas.

"For Christ's sake, Riley, don't go in there alone!" he barked back. "Wait for me outside. I'll get there as soon as I can. Do you hear me?"

Riley ended the call and drove away. No, she could not wait.

*

Less than fifteen minutes later, Riley pulled up to a dusty, isolated lot. A shabby-looking mobile home sat in the middle of it. Riley parked her car and got out.

An old car was parked on the street in front of the lot, but Riley didn't see any sign of the truck the witness described after Cindy MacKinnon's abduction. Of course, Cosgrove might well be keeping it somewhere else. Or perhaps he had dumped it for fear that it might be traced.

Riley shuddered when she saw a couple of sheds with padlocked doors at the back of the lot. Was that where he had kept the women? Was he holding one right now, torturing her and preparing to kill her?

Riley looked around, taking in the area. The lot wasn't completely isolated. There were a few houses and mobile homes not far away. Even so, it seemed likely that no one live near enough to hear a woman screaming in one of those sheds.

Riley drew her gun and approached the trailer. It was set up on a permanent foundation, and it looked like it had been there for many years. Some time ago, someone had planted a flower bed alongside the trailer to make it look more like a regular house. But now the bed was overrun with weeds.

So far, the place matched her expectations. She felt certain that she'd come to the right place.

"It's all over for you, you bastard," she murmured under her breath. "You'll never take another victim."

When she reached the trailer, she banged on the metal door.

"Gerald Cosgrove!" she yelled. "This is the FBI. Are you in there?"

There was no answer. Riley edged her way up onto the cinderblock steps and peered through the door's little window. What she saw inside chilled her to the bone.

The place seemed to be packed full of dolls. She didn't see a living soul, just dolls of all shapes and sizes.

Riley shook the door handle. It was locked. She banged on the door again. This time she heard a man's voice.

"Go away. Leave me alone. I didn't do anything."

Riley thought she heard someone scrambling around inside. The trailer door was designed to open outward, so she couldn't kick it in. She fired her gun at the locked handle. The door fell open.

Riley burst into the small main room. She was momentarily dazzled by the sheer number and array of dolls. There must have been hundreds of them. They were simply everywhere—on shelves, on tables, and even on the floor. It took a moment for her to see a man among them, cowering on the floor against a partition wall.

"Don't shoot," Cosgrove pleaded, his hands raised and shaking. "I didn't do it. Don't shoot me."

Riley sprung at him and yanked him to his feet. She spun him around and pulled one hand behind his back. She holstered her handgun and got out her cuffs.

"Give me your other hand," she said.

Shaking from head to foot, he obeyed without hesitation. Riley quickly had him cuffed and sitting awkwardly in a chair.

He was a weak-looking man in his sixties with thin gray hair. He cut a pathetic figure, sitting there with tears running down his face. But Riley wasted no pity on him. The spectacle of all these dolls was enough to tell her that he was a sick, twisted man.

Before she could ask any questions, she heard Bill's voice.

"Jesus, Riley. Did you blow open this door?"

Riley turned and saw Bill stepping into the trailer.

"He wouldn't open up," Riley said.

Bill growled under his breath. "I thought I told you to wait outside," he said.

"And I thought you knew better than to think I would," Riley said. "Anyway, I'm glad you're here. This looks like our guy."

The man was wailing now.

"I didn't do it! It wasn't me! I did my time! I put all that stuff behind me!"

Riley asked Bill, "What did you find out about him?"

"He did some time for attempted child molestation. Nothing since—until now."

This made good enough sense to Riley. This monstrous little man had undoubtedly moved on to bigger prey—and to greater cruelty.

"That was years ago," the man said. "I've been good ever since. I take my meds. I don't get those urges anymore. It's all in the past. You've made a mistake."

Bill asked in a cynical tone, "So you're an innocent man, eh?"

"That's right. Whatever you think I did, it wasn't me."

"So what's with all the dolls?" Riley asked.

Through his tears, Cosgrove smiled brokenly.

"Aren't they beautiful?" he said. "I collected them little by little. I got lucky a few weeks back, found this great store over in Shellysford. So many dolls and so many different dresses. I spent my whole Social Security check right there and then, bought as many as my money could get me."

Bill shook his head. "I sure as hell don't want to know what you do with them," he said.

"It's not what you think," Cosgrove said. "They're like my family. My only friends. They're all I've got. I just stay home with them. It's not like I can afford to go anywhere. They treat me right. They don't judge me."

Again, Riley worried. Was Cosgrove holding a victim right now?

"I want to check your sheds out back," she told him.

"Go ahead," he said. "There's nothing there. I've got nothing to hide. The keys are right over there."

He nodded toward a bunch of keys hanging next to the wounded door. Riley walked over and grabbed them.

"I'm going out there for a look," she said.

"Not without me, you're not," Bill said.

Together, Bill and Riley used Bill's cuffs to fasten Cosgrove to his refrigerator door. Then they stepped outside and walked around the trailer. They opened the first shed's padlock and looked inside. There was nothing in there except a garden rake.

Bill stepped into the shed and looked around.

"Nothing," he said. "Not even any sign of blood."

They walked over to the next shed, unlocked it, and looked inside. Aside from a rusty hand lawnmower, the shed was completely empty.

"He must have held them somewhere else," Bill said.

Bill and Riley went back to into the trailer. Cosgrove was still sitting there, gazing wretchedly at his family of dolls. Riley found him a troubling sight—a man with no real life of his own, and certainly no future.

Still, he struck her as an enigma. She decided to ask him a couple of questions.

"Gerald, where were you last Wednesday morning?"

"What?" Cosgrove replied. "What do you mean? I don't

know. I don't remember Wednesday. Here, I guess. Where else would I be?"

Riley gazed at him with increasing curiosity.

"Gerald," she said, "what day is today?"

Cosgrove's eyes darted around in desperate confusion.

"I—I don't know," he stammered.

Riley wondered—could it possibly be true? Did he not know what day it was? He sounded perfectly sincere. He certainly didn't seem bitter or angry. She saw no fight in him at all. Just fear and desperation.

Then she sternly reminded herself not to let him take her in. A true psychopath could sometimes fool even a seasoned veteran with a total lie.

Bill unfastened Cosgrove from the refrigerator. Cosgrove was still cuffed behind his back.

Bill barked out, "Gerald Cosgrove, you're under arrest for the murders of three women …"

Bill and Riley escorted him roughly out of the trailer as Bill continued with the victims' names and Cosgrove's rights. Then they shoved him to the car Bill had driven here—a well-equipped Bureau vehicle with mesh caging between the back and front seats. Riley and Bill pushed him into the back seat. They strapped and cuffed him in securely. Afterwards they both just stood for a moment without saying a word.

"Damn it, Riley, you did it," Bill muttered with admiration. "You caught the bastard—even without your badge. The Bureau's going to welcome you back with open arms."

"Do you want me to ride with you?" Riley asked.

Bill shrugged. "Naw, I've got him under control. I'll get him into custody. You just take your own car back."

Riley decided not to argue, wondering if Bill still harbored resentment toward her for the other night.

As she watched Bill pull away, Riley wanted to congratulate herself on her success, and her redemption. But any feeling of satisfaction evaded her. Something kept nagging at her. She kept hearing her father's words.

You just keep following that gut of yours.

Little by little as she drove, Riley started to realize something.

Her gut was telling her that they'd gotten the wrong man.

CHAPTER THIRTY THREE

The next morning Riley drove April to school, and as she dropped her off, that gut feeling was still nagging at her. It had bothered her all night, not letting her sleep.

Is he the guy? she kept asking herself.

Before April got out of the car, she turned to her with an expression of genuine concern.

"Mom, what's wrong?" she asked.

Riley was a little taken aback by the question. She and her daughter seemed to have entered into a whole new phase of their relationship—a much better one than they'd had before. Still, Riley wasn't used to having April worry about her feelings. It felt good, but strange.

"It shows, huh?" Riley said.

"It sure does," April said. She gently held her mother's hand. "Come on. Tell me."

Riley thought for a moment. That feeling of hers still wasn't easy to put into words.

"I..." she began, then trailed off, unsure what to say. "I'm not sure I arrested the right man."

April's eyes widened.

"I'm...not sure what to do," Riley added.

April took a long breath.

"Don't doubt yourself, Mom," April replied. "You do it a lot. And you always wish you hadn't. Isn't that what you always tell me, too?"

April smiled, and Riley smiled back.

"I'll be late if I don't get to class," April said. "We can talk about this later."

April kissed Riley on the cheek, got out of the car, and dashed toward school.

Riley sat there, thinking. She didn't drive away immediately. Instead, she called Bill.

"Anything?" she asked when she got him on the line.

She heard Bill heave a long sigh.

"Cosgrove is a strange character," he said. "Right now he's a real mess—exhausted and depressed, and crying a lot. I think he'll probably crack soon. But ..."

Bill paused. Riley sensed that he, too, was struggling with doubt.

"But what?" Riley asked.

"I don't know, Riley. He seems so disoriented, and I'm not sure even knows what's going on. He slips in and out of reality. Sometimes he doesn't seem to understand that he's been arrested. Maybe all those meds he's taking are messing him up. Or maybe it's just plain old psychosis."

Riley's own doubts kicked in again.

"What is he telling you?" she asked.

"Mostly, he just keeps asking for his dolls," Bill said. "He's worried about them, like they're children or pets that he shouldn't leave at home alone. He keeps saying they can't do without him. He's completely docile, not the least bit belligerent. But he's not giving us any information. He's not saying anything about the women, or whether he's holding one right now."

Riley turned Bill's words over in her mind for a moment.

"So what do you think?" she finally asked. "Is he the one?"

Riley detected growing frustration in Bill's voice.

"How could he not be? I mean, everything points to him and nobody else. The dolls, the criminal record, everything. He was in the store the same time as her. What more could you ask for? How could we have got it wrong?"

Riley said nothing. She couldn't argue. But she could tell that Bill was struggling with his own instincts.

Then she asked: "Did somebody run a search on Madeline's past employees?"

"Yeah," Bill said. "But that didn't lead anywhere. Madeline always hires high school girls to work the register. She's been doing it pretty much since she's been in business."

Riley groaned with discouragement. When were they going to get a break in this case?

"Anyway," Bill said, "a bureau psychologist will interview Cosgrove today. Maybe he can get some insights, tell us where we stand."

"Okay," Riley said. "Keep me in the loop."

She ended the phone call. Her car engine was running, but she still hadn't driven away from the school. Where was she going to go? If Newbrough really was trying to get her reinstated, he hadn't gotten it done yet. She still didn't have a badge—or a job.

I might as well go home, she thought.

But as soon as she started driving, her father's words came rushing back again.

You just keep following that gut of yours.

Right now, her gut was telling her loud and clear that she needed to get back to Shellysford. She didn't know exactly why, but she just had to.

*

The bell above the fashion store door rang as Riley walked inside. She saw no customers. Madeline looked up from her work at the front desk and frowned. Riley could see that the shop owner was not at all happy to see her again.

"Madeline, I'm sorry about yesterday," Riley said, walking to the desk. "I was so clumsy, and I'm sorry. I hope I didn't actually break anything."

Madeline folded her arms and glared at Riley.

"What do you want this time?" she asked.

"I'm still struggling with this case," Riley said. "I need your help."

Madeline didn't reply for a few seconds.

"I still don't know who you are, or even if you're FBI," she said.

"I know, and I don't blame you for not trusting me," Riley pleaded. "But I did have Reba Frye's receipt, remember? I could only have gotten it from her father. He really did send me here. You know that much is true."

Madeline shook her head warily.

"Well, I guess that must mean something. What do you want?"

"Just let me look at the doll collection again," Riley said. "I promise not to make a mess this time."

"All right," Madeline said. "But I'm not leaving you alone."

"That's fair," Riley said.

Madeline went to the back of the store and opened the folding doors. As Riley moved in among the dolls and accessories, Madeline stood in the doorway watching her like a hawk. Riley understood the woman's misgivings, but this scrutiny wasn't good for her concentration—especially since she really didn't know what she ought to be looking for.

Just then the bell above the front door rang. Three rather boisterous customers burst into the store.

"Oh, brother," Madeline said. She hurried back into the dress store to tend to her customers. Riley had the dolls all to herself, at least for the moment.

She studied them closely. Some were standing, but others were seated. All of the dolls were decked out in dresses and gowns. But even though they were clothed, the seated dolls were in exactly the same pose as the naked murder victims, their legs splayed stiffly. The killer had obviously taken his inspiration from this kind of doll.

But that wasn't enough for Riley to go on. There had to be some other clue lurking here.

Riley's eyes fell on a row of picture books on a lower shelf. She stooped down and began to pull them off the shelf one by one. The books were beautifully illustrated adventure stories about little girls who looked exactly like the dolls. The dolls and the girls on the covers even wore the same dresses. Riley realized the books and the dolls were originally meant to be sold together as a set.

Riley froze at the sight of one book cover. The girl had long blond hair and wide-open bright blue eyes. Her pink and white ball gown had a spray of roses draped across the skirt. She had a pink ribbon in her hair. The book was titled *A Grand Ball for a Southern Belle.*

Riley's skin crawled as she looked more closely at the girl's face. Her eyes were bright blue, opened extremely wide, with enormous black lashes. Her lips, shaped into an exaggerated smile, were thick and bright pink. There was no doubt about it. Riley knew for certain that the killer was fixated on this very image.

At that moment, the bell rang again as the three customers left the store. Madeline trotted to the back room, visibly relieved that Riley hadn't caused any damage. Riley showed her the book.

"Madeline, do you have the doll that goes with this book?" she asked.

Madeline looked at the cover, then scanned the shelves.

"Well, I must have had several of them at one time or another," she said. "I don't see any of them right now." She thought for a moment, then added, "Now that I think of it, I sold the last of those a long time ago."

Riley could barely keep her voice from shaking.

"Madeline, I know you don't want to do this. But you've *got* to help me look for names of people who might have bought this doll. I can't begin to tell you how important this is."

Madeline now seemed to sympathize with Riley's agitation.

"I'm sorry, but I can't," she said. "It's not that I don't want to, but I can't. It's been ten or fifteen years now. Even my ledger doesn't go back that far."

Riley's spirits fell. Another dead end. She had taken it as far as she could possibly take it. Coming here had been a waste of time.

Riley turned to go. She crossed the store and opened the door, and as the fresh air hit her, something struck her. The smell. The fresh air outside made her realize how stale the air was in here. Not stale, but...pungent. It seemed out of place in a frilly, feminine store like this. What was it?

Then Riley realized. Ammonia. But what did that mean?

Follow your gut, Riley.

Halfway out the door, she stopped and turned, looking back at Madeline.

"Did you mop the floors today?" she asked.

Madeline shook her head, puzzled.

"I use a temp agency," she said. "They send over a janitor."

Riley's heart pounded faster.

"A janitor?" she asked, her voice barely above a whisper.

Madeline nodded.

"He comes in during our morning hours. Not every day. Dirk is his name."

Dirk. Riley's heart pounded and her skin grew cold.

"Dirk what?" she asked.

Madeline shrugged.

"I'm afraid I don't know his last name," she replied. "I don't write his checks. The temp agency might, but it's a rather slipshod outfit, really. Dirk's not very reliable, if you want to know the truth. "

Riley took long slow breaths to steady her nerves.

"Was he here this morning?" she asked.

Madeline nodded mutely.

Riley approached her, and summoned all her intensity.

"Madeline," she urged, "whatever you do, do *not* let that man back in your store. Ever again."

Madeline staggered back with shock.

"Do you mean he's—?"

"He's dangerous. Extremely dangerous. And I've got to find him right away. Do you have his phone number? Do you have any idea where he lives?"

"No, you'd have to ask the temp agency," Madeline said in a fearful voice. "They'll have all his information. Here, I'll give you their business card."

Madeline rummaged around on her desk and found a card for the Miller Staffing Agency. She handed it to Riley.

"Thank you," Riley said with a gasp. "Thank you so much."

Without another word, Riley rushed out of the store and got in the car and tried calling the temp office. The phone rang and rang. There was no voicemail.

She made a mental note of the address and started to drive.

*

The Miller Staffing Agency was a mile away on the other side of Shellysford. Housed in a brick storefront building, it looked like it had been in business for many years.

As Riley went inside, she saw that it was a decidedly low-tech operation that hadn't kept up with the times. There was only one nearly obsolete computer in sight. The place was pretty crowded, with several would-be workers filling out application forms at a long table.

Three other people—clients, apparently—were crowded around the front desk. They were complaining loudly and all at once about problems they were having with the agency's employees.

Two longhaired men worked at the desk, fending off complainers and trying to keep up with phone calls. They looked like twenty-something slackers, and they didn't appear to be managing things at all well.

Riley managed to push her way to the front, where she caught one of the young men between phone calls. His nametag said "Melvin."

"I'm Agent Riley Paige, FBI," she announced, hoping that in the confusion, Melvin wouldn't ask to see her badge. "I'm here on a murder investigation. Are you the manager?"

Melvin shrugged. "I guess."

From his vacant expression, Riley guessed that he was either stoned or not very bright, or possibly both. At least he didn't seem to be worried about seeing any ID.

"I'm looking for the man you've got working at Madeline's," she said. "A janitor. His first name is Dirk. Madeline doesn't seem to know his last name."

Melvin muttered to himself, "Dirk, Dirk, Dirk … Oh, yeah. I remember him. 'Dirk the Dick,' we used to call him." Calling out to the other young man, he asked, "Hey, Randy, whatever happened to Dirk the Dick?"

"We fired him," Randy replied. "He kept showing up late for jobs, when he bothered to show up at all. A real pain in the ass."

"That can't be right," Riley said. "Madeline says he's still working for her. He was just there this morning."

Melvin looked puzzled now.

"I'm sure we fired him," he said. He sat down at the old computer and began some kind of a search. "Yeah, we sure did fire him, about three weeks ago."

Melvin squinted at the screen, more puzzled than before.

"Hey, this is weird," he said. "Madeline keeps sending us checks, even though he's not working anymore. Somebody should tell her to stop doing that. She's blowing a lot of money."

The situation was becoming clearer to Riley. Despite being fired and no longer getting paid, Dirk still kept going to work at Madeline's. He had his own reasons for wanting to work there—sinister reasons.

"What's his last name?" Riley asked.

Melvin's eyes roamed about the computer screen. He was apparently looking at Dirk's defunct employee records.

"It's Monroe," Melvin said. "What else do you want to know?"

Riley was relieved that Melvin wasn't being too scrupulous about sharing what ought to be confidential information.

"I need his address and phone number," Riley said.

"He didn't give us a phone number," Melvin said, still looking at the screen. "I've got an address, though. Fifteen-twenty Lynn Street."

By now, Randy had taken interest in the conversation. He was looking over Melvin's shoulder at the computer screen.

"Hold it," Randy said. "That address is completely bogus. The house numbers on Lynn Street don't go anywhere near that high."

Riley wasn't surprised. Dirk Monroe obviously didn't want anyone to know where he lived.

"What about a Social Security number?" she asked.

"I've got it," Melvin said. He wrote the number down on a piece of paper and handed it to Riley.

"Thanks," Riley said. She took the paper and walked away. As soon as she set foot outside, she called Bill.

"Hey, Riley," Bill said when he answered. "I wish I could give you some good news But our psychologist interviewed Cosgrove, and he's convinced that the man is not capable of killing anyone, let alone four women. He said—"

"Bill," she interrupted. "I've got a name—Dirk Monroe. He's our guy, I'm sure of it. I don't know where he lives. Can you run his Social? Now?"

Bill took the number and put Riley on hold. Riley paced up

and down the sidewalk anxiously as she waited. Finally Bill came back on the line.

"I've got the address. It's a farm about thirty miles west of Shellysford. A rural road."

Bill read her the address.

"I'm going," Riley said.

Bill sputtered.

"Riley, what are you talking about? Let me get some backup there. This guy's dangerous."

Riley felt her whole body tingle with an adrenaline rush.

"Don't argue with me, Bill," she said. "You ought to know better by now."

Riley ended the call without saying goodbye. Already, she was driving.

CHAPTER THIRTY FOUR

When the farmhouse came into view, Riley felt jarred in a way that she hadn't expected. It was as if she'd driven into an oil painting of an ideal rural America. The white wood-frame house was nestled cozily in a small valley. The house was old, but obviously kept in decent condition.

A few outbuildings were scattered on the nearby grounds. They were not in as good repair as the house. Neither was a large barn that looked ready to collapse. But those structures looked all the more charming because of their dilapidation.

Riley parked a short distance from the house. She checked the gun in her holster and got out of the car. She breathed in the clear, clean country air.

It shouldn't be this lovely here, Riley thought. And yet she knew that it made perfect sense. Ever since she'd talked to her father, she'd dimly realized that the killer's lair might well be a place of beauty.

Still, there was a kind of danger here that she hadn't prepared herself for. It was the danger of being lulled by the sheer charm of her surroundings, of letting down her guard. She had to remind herself that a hideous evil coexisted with this beauty. She knew she was about to find herself face to face with the true horror of the place. But she had no idea just where she'd find it.

She turned and looked all around. She didn't see any truck on the grounds. Either Dirk was out driving somewhere, or the truck was inside one of the outbuildings or the barn. The man himself could be anywhere, of course—in one of the outbuildings, possibly. But she decided to check the house first.

A noise startled her, and her peripheral vision caught a flurry of rapid movement. But it was only a handful of loose chickens. Several hens were pecking the ground nearby. Nothing else moved except tall blades of grass and leaves on the trees as a gentle breeze blew through them. She felt utterly alone.

Riley approached the farmhouse. When she arrived at the steps, she drew her gun, then walked up on the porch. She knocked on the front door. There was no response. She knocked again.

"I've got a delivery for Dirk Monroe," she called out. "I need a signature to leave it."

Still no response.

Riley stepped off the porch and began to circle the house. The windows were too high to see into, and she found that the back door was also locked.

She returned to the front door and knocked again. There was still only silence. The door lock was a simple, old-fashioned type for a skeleton key. She carried a little lock-picking set in her handbag for just such situations. She knew that the hook of a small flat tension wrench would do the trick.

She slipped her gun back into its holster and found the wrench. She inserted it into the lock, then groped and twisted it until the lock rotated. When she turned the doorknob the door swung open. Drawing her gun again, she walked inside.

The interior had much the same picturesque quality as the landscape outside. It was a perfect little country home, remarkably neat and clean. There were two big soft chairs in the living room with white crocheted pieces on the arms and back.

The room made her feel as though friendly family members might step out at any second to welcome her, to invite her to make herself at home. But as Riley studied her surroundings, that feeling waned. This house actually did not look as if it were lived in at all. Everything was just too neat.

She remembered her father's words.

He wants to start all over again. He wants to go all the way back to the beginning.

That's exactly what Dirk was trying to do right here. But he was failing, because his life had somehow been hopelessly flawed from the start. Surely he knew that and was tormented by it.

Instead of finding his way back into a happier childhood, he'd trapped himself in an unreal world—a display that might be in some historical museum. A framed cross-stitch embroidery even hung on the living room wall. Riley stepped closer to look at it.

The little stitched x's made up the image of a woman in a long gown and holding a parasol. Beneath her were embroidered words …

A Southern Belle is always
gracious
courteous
genteel …

The list went on, but Riley didn't bother to read the rest. She got the message that mattered to her. The stitchery was nothing more wishful thinking. Obviously, this farm had never been a plantation. No so-called Southern belle had ever lived here, sipping sweet tea and ordering servants about.

Still, the fantasy must be dear to someone who lived here—or had lived here in the past. Maybe that someone had once bought a doll—a doll that represented a Southern belle in a storybook.

Listening for any sound, Riley moved quietly into the hallway. On one side, an arched doorway opened into a dining room. Her sense of being in a past time grew even stronger. Sunlight streamed in through lace curtains hanging over the windows. A table and chairs were positioned perfectly, as if awaiting a family dinner. But like everything else, the dining room looked as though it hadn't been used for a long time.

A large old-fashioned kitchen was on the other side of the hallway. There, too, everything was in its proper place, and there was no sign of recent use.

Ahead of her, at the end of the hall, was a closed door. As Riley moved in that direction, a cluster of framed photographs on the wall drew her attention. She examined them as she edged by. They appeared to be ordinary family photos, some black and white, some in color. They reached far back in time—perhaps as long as a century.

They were just the sort of pictures one might find in any home—parents, elderly grandparents, children, and the dining room table laden with feasts of celebration. Many of the images were faded.

A picture that didn't look more than a couple of decades old appeared to be a boy's school picture—a cleaned-up student with a new haircut and a stiff, unfelt smile. The picture to the right of it was a woman hugging a girl in a frilly dress.

Then, with a slight shock, Riley noticed that the girl and the boy had exactly the same face. They were actually the same child. The girl with the woman wasn't a girl at all, but the schoolboy wearing a dress and a wig. Riley shuddered. The expression on the costumed boy's face told her that this was not a case of a harmless dress-up or comfortable cross-dressing. In this photograph, the child's smile was anguished, wretched—even angry and hateful.

The final snapshot showed the boy at about age ten. He was holding a doll. The woman stood behind the boy, smiling a smile that glowed with entirely misplaced, uncomprehending joy. Riley leaned closer to view the doll and gasped.

There it was—a doll that matched the picture on the book in the store. It was exactly the same, with long blond hair, bright blue eyes, roses, and pink ribbons. Years ago, the woman had given the boy this doll. She must have forced it upon him, expecting him to cherish and love it.

The tortured expression on the boy's face told the real story. He couldn't fake a smile this time. His face was knotted with disgust and self-loathing. This picture captured the moment when something broke apart in him, never to be made whole again. Right then and there, the image of the doll fastened itself onto his unhappy young imagination. He couldn't shake it off, not ever. It was an image that he was recreating with dead women.

Riley turned away from the pictures. She moved toward the closed door at the end of the hall. She swallowed hard.

There it is, she thought.

She was sure of it. That door was the barrier between the dead, artificial, unreal beauty of this country home and the hideously ugly reality that crept behind it. That room was where the false mask of blissful normalcy fell away once and for all.

Holding her gun in her right hand, she opened the door with her left hand. The room was dark, but even in the dim light from the hall, she could see that it was completely unlike the rest of the house. The floor was littered with debris.

She found a light switch to the side of the door and flicked in on. A single overhead bulb revealed a nightmare spread out before her. The first thing that registered on her mind was a metal pipe standing in the middle of the space, bolted to the floor and to the ceilings. Bloodstains on the floor marked what happened there. The unheeded screams of women echoed through her mind, nearly overwhelming her.

No one was inside the room. Riley steadied herself and stepped forward. The windows were boarded up, and no sunlight entered. The walls were pink, with storybook images painted on them. But they were defaced by ugly smears.

Pieces of a child's furniture—frilly chairs and stools really meant for a little girl—were overturned and broken. Scraps of dolls had been thrown everywhere—amputated limbs and heads and snatches of hair. Small doll wigs were nailed to the walls.

Heart pounding with fear, with rage, remembering her own captivity too well, Riley stepped deeper into the room, mesmerized by the scene, by the fury, by the agony that she sensed here.

There came a sudden rustle behind her, and suddenly, the lights went out.

Riley, panic-stricken, spun around to fire her gun but missed her chance. Something heavy and hard struck her arm an agonizing blow. Her weapon went skittering into the darkness.

Riley tried to dodge the next blow, but a rigid, weighty, object glanced across her head, cracking noisily against her skull. She fell and scrambled toward a dark corner of the room.

The blow kept echoing between her ears. Concussive sparkles flickered in the darkness of her mind. She'd been hurt and she knew it. She struggled to hold onto consciousness, but it felt like sand slipping between her fingers.

There it was again—that hissing white flame cutting through the darkness. Little by little, the shimmering light revealed who was carrying it.

This time it was Riley's mother. She was standing right in front of Riley, the fatal bullet wound bleeding in the middle of her chest, her face pale and dead-looking. But when her mother spoke, it was with Riley's father's voice.

"Girl, you're doing this all wrong."

Riley was seized by nauseating dizziness. Everything kept spinning. Her world made no sense at all. What was her mother doing, holding this awful instrument of torture? Why was she speaking with her father's voice?

Riley cried out, "Why aren't you Peterson?"

Suddenly, the flame was extinguished, leaving only lingering traces of phantom light.

Again, she heard her father's voice growling in pitch-blackness.

"That's your trouble. You want to take on all the evil in the world—all at the same time. You've got to make your choice. One monster at a time."

Her head still swimming, Riley tried to grasp that message.

"One monster at a time," she murmured.

Her consciousness ebbed and flowed, taunting her with bursts of lucidity. She saw that the door was slightly ajar and a man was silhouetted there against the dim hallway light. She couldn't make out his face.

He held something in his hand—a crowbar, she now realized. He seemed to be in his stocking feet. He must have been somewhere in the house all along, waiting for the right moment to come and take her by surprise.

Her arm and her head hurt horribly. She felt a sticky, liquid warmth on the side of her skull. She was bleeding, and bleeding badly. She struggled against unconsciousness.

She heard the man laugh, and the laughter wasn't a familiar voice. Her thoughts became hopelessly confused. It wasn't Peterson's voice, so cruel and mocking in that darkness. And where was his torch? Why was everything so different?

She groped about in her mind for the truth of her situation.

It's not Peterson, she told herself. *It's Dirk Monroe.*

She whispered aloud to herself, "One monster at time."

This monster was bent on killing her.

She clawed around on the floor. Where was her gun?

The man moved toward her, swinging the crowbar with one hand, slicing the air with it. Riley got halfway to her feet before he landed a blow across her shoulder and knocked her down again. She braced herself for another blow, but then heard the sound of the crowbar falling to the floor.

Something was looped around her left foot, pulling her. He'd gotten a rope around that foot and was dragging her slowly across the floor, through the litter and toward the pipe in the middle of the room. It was the place where four women had already suffered and died.

Riley tried to probe his thoughts. He hadn't scouted her or chosen her. He'd never seen her buying one of those dolls he so deeply loathed. Even so, he intended to make the most of her arrival. He was going to make her his next victim. He was determined to make her suffer. She was going to die in pain.

Even so, Riley caught a glimmer of impending justice. Bill and a team would get here soon. What would Dirk do when the FBI stormed the house? He'd kill her, of course, and instantly. He'd never allow her to be rescued. But he was doomed all the same.

But why did Riley have to be his last victim? She saw faces of people she loved—April, Bill—even her father. Now Riley knew she shared with him a stubborn bond of dark wisdom, a comprehension of limitless evil in the world. She thought of the work she lived each day to do, and slowly, a new determination rose up in her. She wouldn't let him claim her easily. She'd die on her own terms, not his.

She groped around the floor with her hand. She found something solid—not part of a doll, but something hard and sharp. She gripped the handle of the knife. It was surely the very knife he'd used on four women.

Time slowed down to a mind-numbing crawl. She realized that Dirk had just passed the rope around the central pipe. Now he was pulling her foot up against it.

He was turned away from her, too sure that she was defeated already. His mind was occupied with tying her to the post—and on what he would do to her then.

His unwariness gave Riley a moment, and one moment only, before he turned back her way. Still prone on the floor, she wrenched her body into a seated position. He noticed this and started to turn, but she moved quicker. She wrestled her free right foot beneath her, then rose up to face him.

She plunged the knife into his stomach, then drew it out and stabbed him again and again. She heard him shriek and moan. She kept stabbing madly until she blacked out.

CHAPTER THIRTY FIVE

Riley opened her eyes. Her whole body was in pain, especially her shoulder and her head. Bill's face filled her vision. Was she dreaming?

"Bill?" she asked.

He smiled, looking relieved. He was holding something soft against her head, staunching the flow of blood.

"Welcome back," he said.

Riley realized that she was still in the room, with the post nearby. She was seized by a moment of panic.

"Where's Dirk?" she asked.

"Dead," Bill said. "You gave him just what he deserved."

Riley still wondered if she was dreaming.

"I've got to see," she gasped. She managed to turn her head. She saw Dirk stretched out across the floor face down in a pool of his own blood. Eyes opened. Unblinking.

Bill turned her head back toward him.

"Don't try to move," he said. "You're hurt pretty bad. You're going to be okay. But you've lost a lot of blood."

A spasm of nauseated dizziness told her that Bill was right. She managed to whisper five words before she lost consciousness again.

"One monster at a time."

CHAPTER THIRTY SIX

Special Agent Brent Meredith shut the thick manila envelope stuffed with photographs and written reports with a note of satisfied finality. Riley felt the same satisfaction, and she was sure that Bill and Flores did too. They were all seated at the table in the Behavioral Analysis Unit conference room. If only Riley weren't bandaged up and hurting all over, the moment would have felt perfect.

"So Dirk's mother wanted a daughter instead of a son," Meredith said. "She tried to turn him into a Southern belle. That was probably just the tip of the iceberg. God knows what else he went through as a kid."

Bill leaned back in his chair.

"Let's not give him too much sympathy," he said. "Not everybody with a lousy childhood turns into a murderous sadist. He made his own choices."

Meredith and Flores nodded in agreement.

"But does anybody know whatever happened to Dirk's mother?" Riley asked.

"Records show that she died five years ago," Flores said. "His father disappeared long before that, when Dirk was still a baby."

A sober silence settled over the group. Riley understood exactly what it meant. She was in the presence of three people whose lives were devoted to destroying evil. Even in their satisfaction, the specter of more evil, and much more work to do, hung over all of them. It would never be over. Not for them.

The door opened, and Carl Walder walked in. He was all smiles.

"Great work, everybody," he said. He slid Riley's gun and badge across the table toward her. "These belong to you."

Riley smiled a wry smile. Walder was not going to apologize, much less acknowledge any fault of his own. But that was just as well. Riley didn't know just how she'd respond if he actually said he was sorry. Probably not gracefully.

"By the way, Riley," Walder said. "The Senator called me this morning, and he sends you his best wishes for your recovery, and his thanks. He seems to think the world of you."

Riley now had to stifle her amusement. That call, she was

sure, was exactly why Walder was giving her back her gun and her badge. She remembered one of the last things Newbrough had said to her.

"You're nobody's lapdog."

The same thing could never be said of Carl Walder.

"Stop by my office soon," Walder said. "Let's talk promotion. An administrative position, maybe. You deserve it."

Without another word, Walder left the office. Riley heard her companions breathe a shared sigh of relief that he was gone so quickly.

"You should think about it, Riley," Meredith said.

Riley chuckled.

"Can you really see me in an administrative job?"

Meredith shrugged.

"You've more than paid your dues. You've done more tough field work than most agents do in a lifetime. Maybe you should become an instructor. You'd be great at training agents, with your experience and insight. What do you think?"

Riley thought it over. What would she really have to teach young agents? Her instincts were all she had, and as far as she knew, instincts couldn't be taught. There was no way to train people to follow their gut. They either had it or they didn't.

Besides, did she really wish her own gut instincts on anybody? She lived too much in terror of her own thoughts, haunted by her troubling capacity to grasp an evil mind. It was a hard thing to live with.

"Thanks," Riley said, "but I like it just where I am."

Meredith nodded, and rose from his chair. "Well, let's call it a day. Get some rest, folks."

The meeting broke up, and Riley and Bill found themselves walking down the hall together silently. They left the building and sat down together on a bench outside. Whole minutes passed. Neither of them seemed to know what to say. There was too much to say.

"Bill," she asked tentatively, "do you think we can be partners again?"

After a pause, Bill said, "What do you think?"

They turned and looked into each other's eyes. Riley could see lingering pain in Bill's face. The wound she'd inflicted with her drunken phone call still hadn't healed. It was going to take a long time.

But she now knew something else—something that had long been true, but that she'd never let herself admit before. Her bond to

Bill was intense and powerful, and he almost certainly felt the same. It was no longer a secret that they could keep from themselves. There was no way for them to go back to their former ways.

Their partnership was over. They both knew it. Neither one of them had to say it aloud.

"Go home, Bill," Riley said gently. "Try to put things back together with your wife. You've got your kids to think of."

"I will," Bill said. "But I hope I don't lose you—your friendship, I mean."

Riley patted his hand and smiled.

"There's no chance of that," she said.

They both got up from the bench and walked away to their cars.

*

"What's on your mind, Mom?" April asked.

Riley and April had been sitting in the living room long into the night watching television. Earlier that evening, Riley had told April all that had happened—or at least all that she felt she could tell her.

Riley hesitated before answering April's question. But she knew that she had to say it aloud. Besides, April knew about it already. It wasn't a secret. It was just something Riley couldn't shake off her mind.

"I killed a man today," Riley said.

April looked at her with love and concern.

"I know," she said. "What does that feel like?"

"It's hard to put into words," Riley said. "It's terrible. It's something no one has a right to do—not ever, really. But sometimes it's the only thing."

Riley paused. "I feel something else," she said. "I'm not sure I should say it."

April laughed quietly. "I thought we weren't going to do the silent thing anymore, Mom."

Riley steadied herself and said, "I feel alive. God help me, it makes me feel alive. And any day now, I know that some woman will walk into Madeline's store and buy a doll and never be in any danger. I'm just … well, I'm just happy for her. I'm glad that I could give her that, even if she'll never know it."

Riley squeezed April's hand.

"It's late, and you've got school tomorrow," she said.

April kissed her mother on the cheek.

"Goodnight, Mom," she said, then went to her bedroom.

Riley felt a new wave of pain and exhaustion. She realized that she'd better get to bed or she'd fall asleep right there on the couch.

She picked herself up and walked toward her bedroom. She was already in her nightgown, and she didn't bother to stop at the bathroom to brush her teeth. She just wanted to go straight to bed.

When she entered her bedroom and turned on the light, something caught her eye immediately. Her heart skipped a beat.

There, in her bed, was something awry.

It was a handful of small pebbles.

ONCE TAKEN

(A RILEY PAIGE MYSTERY—BOOK 2)

BLAKE PIERCE

.

PROLOGUE

Captain Jimmy Cole had just finished telling his passengers an old Hudson River ghost story. It was a good one, about an ax murderer in a long, dark coat, perfect for a foggy night like this. He sat back in his chair and rested his knees for a moment, too creaky from too many surgeries, and pondered, for the millionth time, his retirement. He'd seen nearly every hamlet the Hudson had to offer, and one of these days, even a small fishing boat like his, the *Suzy*, would get the best of him.

Done for the night, he steered his ship for shore, and as it chugged steadily for the dock at Reedsport, one of his passengers called out, jarring him from his reverie.

"Hey, Cap'n—isn't that your ghost right over there?"

Jimmy didn't bother to look. All four of his passengers—two young vacationing couples—were pretty drunk. Doubtless one of the guys was just trying to scare the girls.

But then one of the women added: "I see it too. Isn't it weird?"

Jimmy turned toward his passengers. Goddamn drunks. Last time he'd charter his boat this late at night.

The second man pointed.

"It's over there," he said.

His wife covered her eyes.

"Oh, I can't look!" she said with a nervous and embarrassed laugh.

Jimmy, exasperated, realizing he wasn't going to get any rest, finally turned and looked where the man was pointing.

In a gap between the shoreline trees, something did catch his eye. It glistened, he thought, and it had a vaguely human shape. Whatever it was, it seemed to float above the ground. But it was too far away to see clearly.

Before Jimmy could reach for his binoculars, the object disappeared behind the trees along the bank.

The truth was, Jimmy had had a few beers himself. That wasn't a problem as far as he was concerned. He knew this river well. And he liked his job. He especially enjoyed being out on the Hudson at this time of night, when the water was so still and peaceful. Few things out here could shatter his sense of calm.

205

He slowed and steered the *Suzy* carefully against the bumpers as he hit the dock. Proud of himself for a gentle landing, he stopped the engine and lashed the boat to the cleats.

The passengers tumbled off the boat giggling and laughing. They staggered down the dock to shore and headed toward their B&B. Jimmy was glad they'd paid in advance.

But he couldn't stop thinking about that strange object he'd spotted. It was far back down the shoreline and impossible to see from here. Who or what might it be?

Annoyed by it, he knew he wouldn't get any rest until he figured it out. That was just the way he was.

Jimmy sighed loudly, twice as annoyed, and set off on foot, trudging back along the riverbank, following the train tracks that bordered the water. Those tracks had been in use a hundred years ago when Reedsport was mostly bordellos and gambling houses. Now, they were just another relic to a bygone time.

Jimmy finally rounded a curve and approached an old warehouse near the tracks. A few security lamps on the building cast a dim light, and he saw it: a glistening human shape that seemed to be floating in mid-air. The shape was suspended from one of the crossbeams of a power pole.

As he neared and got a good look, a chill ran up his spine. The shape was truly human—yet it didn't show any signs of life. The body faced away from him, bound in some kind of fabric and wrapped around and around with heavy chains that crisscrossed and connected far beyond any need to hold a prisoner. The chains glittered in the light.

Oh, God, not again.

Jimmy could not help but remember a gruesome murder that had rocked the whole area several years ago.

His knees weakening, Jimmy walked around to the other side of the body. He stepped close enough to see its face—and he almost fell to the tracks in shock. He recognized her. It was a local woman, a nurse, and a friend of many years. Her throat was slashed, and her dead mouth was gagged open with a chain that wrapped around her head.

Jimmy gasped in grief and horror.

The murderer was back.

CHAPTER ONE

Special Agent Riley Paige froze in place, staring in shock. The handful of pebbles on her bed shouldn't have been there. Someone had broken into her home and placed them—someone who meant her harm.

She knew immediately the pebbles were a message, and that the message was from an old enemy. He was telling her that she had not killed him after all.

Peterson is alive.

She felt her body tremble at the thought.

She'd long suspected it, and now she was absolutely sure. Worse, he'd been inside her house. The thought made her want to throw up. Was he still here now?

Her breathing became short with fear. Riley knew that her physical resources were limited. Just that day she had survived a deadly encounter with a sadistic killer, and her head was still bandaged and her body bruised all over. Would she be ready to face him if he were inside her house?

Riley immediately drew her gun from its holster. Hands trembling, she went to her closet and opened it. Nobody was in there. She checked under her bed. Nobody there either.

Riley stood there and forced herself to think clearly. Had she been in the bedroom since she had gotten home? Yes, she had, because she had put her gun holster on top of the dresser next to the door. But she hadn't turned on the light and hadn't even looked into the room. She had simply stepped into the doorway and deposited her weapon on the dresser top, then left. She'd changed into her nightgown in the bathroom.

Could her nemesis have been in the house this whole time? After she and April got home, the two of them had talked and watched TV late into the night. Then April had gone to bed. In a tiny house like hers, staying hidden would require amazing stealth. But she couldn't discount the possibility.

Then she was seized by a new fear.

April!

Riley snatched the flashlight that she kept on the side table. With her gun in her right hand and the flashlight in her left, she stepped out of her bedroom and switched on the hall light. When she heard nothing awry, she quickly made her way to April's bedroom and threw open the door. The room was pitch dark. Riley turned on the overhead light.

Her daughter was already in bed.

"What is it, Mom?" April asked, squinting with surprise.

Riley stepped into the bedroom.

"Don't get out of bed," she said. "Stay right where you are."

"Mom, you're scaring me," April said, her voice trembling.

That was just fine as far as Riley was concerned. She was plenty scared herself, and her daughter had every reason to be as scared as she was. She went to April's closet, shined her flashlight around inside, and saw that no one was there. No one was under April's bed either.

What should she do next? She had to check every nook and corner in the rest of the house.

Riley knew what her one-time partner Bill Jeffreys would say.

Damn it, Riley, call for help.

Her longstanding tendency to go things alone had always infuriated Bill. But this time, she was going to heed his advice. With April in the house, Riley wasn't going to take any chances.

"Put on a bathrobe and some shoes," she said to her daughter. "But don't leave this room—not yet."

Riley went back into her bedroom and picked up her phone from the side table. She punched autodial for the Behavioral Analysis Unit. As soon as she heard a voice on the line, she hissed, "This is Special Agent Riley Paige. There's been an intruder in my home. He might still be here. I need someone here fast." She thought for a second, then added, "And send an evidence team."

"We'll get right on it," came the reply.

Riley ended the phone call and stepped out into the hall again. Except for the two bedrooms and the hallway, the house was still dark. He could be anywhere, lurking, waiting to attack. This man had caught her off guard once before, and she had nearly died at his hands.

Switching lights on as she went and keeping her gun at the ready, Riley moved efficiently through the house. She aimed her flashlight into every closet and unlit corner.

Finally, she glanced up at the hallway ceiling. The door above her led to the attic, with a pull-down ladder tucked away inside. Did she dare climb up there for a look?

 At that moment Riley heard police sirens. She breathed a huge sigh of relief at the sound. She realized that the agency had called in the local police, because BAU headquarters was more than half an hour away.

She went to her bedroom and pulled on a pair of shoes and her bathrobe, then returned to April's room.

"Come with me," she said. "Stay close."

Still holding her gun, Riley wrapped her left arm around April's shoulders. The poor girl was trembling with fear. Riley led April to the front door and opened it just as several uniformed police officers came dashing up the sidewalk.

The male officer in charge came into the house, his gun drawn.

"What's the problem?" he asked.

"Someone was in the house," Riley said. "He might still be here."

The officer eyed the gun in her hand uneasily.

"I'm FBI," Riley said. "BAU agents will be here soon. I've already searched the house, except the attic." She pointed. "There's a door in the ceiling over in the hall."

The officer called out, "Bowers, Wright, get in here and check the attic. The rest of you search outside, back and front."

Bowers and Wright went straight to the hallway and pulled down the ladder. Both drew their weapons. One waited at the bottom of the ladder while the other climbed upward and flashed a light around. In a few moments, the man disappeared into the attic.

Soon a voice called out, "No one here."

Riley wanted to feel relieved. But the truth was, she more than half wished that Peterson had been up there. He could be arrested right here and now—or better yet, shot. She was all but sure that he wasn't going to turn up in the front yard or the back.

"Have you got a basement?" the lead officer asked.

"No, just a crawl space," Riley said.

The officer called outside, "Benson, Pratt, check under the house."

April was still holding onto her mother for dear life.

"What's going on, Mom?" she asked.

Riley hesitated. For years she'd avoided telling April much of the ugly truth about her work. But she had recently realized that she'd been overly protective. So she'd told April about her traumatic captivity at Peterson's hands—or at least as much as she thought she could handle. She'd also confided her doubts that the man was really dead.

But what should she tell April now? She wasn't sure.

Before Riley could make up her mind, April said, "It's Peterson, isn't it?"

Riley hugged her daughter tightly. She nodded back, trying to hide the shiver that ran through her whole body.

"He's still alive."

CHAPTER TWO

An hour later, Riley's house was swarming with people wearing uniforms or FBI labels. Heavily armed Federal agents and an evidence team were working with the police.

"Bag those pebbles on the bed," Craig Huang called out. "They'll need to be examined for prints or DNA."

At first, Riley hadn't been pleased to see that Huang was in charge. He was very young, and her previous experience working with him hadn't gone well. But now she saw that he was giving solid orders and organizing the scene effectively. Huang was growing into his job.

The evidence team was already at work combing every inch of the house and dusting for fingerprints. Other agents had disappeared into the darkness behind the house, trying to find vehicle tracks or some hint of a trail through the woods. Now that things seemed to be running smoothly, Huang led Riley away from the others into the kitchen. He and Riley sat down at the table. April joined them there, still badly shaken.

"So what do you think?" Huang asked Riley. "Is there any chance that we'll still find him?"

Riley sighed with discouragement.

"No, I'm afraid he's long gone. He must have been here earlier this evening, before my daughter and I got home."

Just then a Kevlar-clad female agent came in from the back of the house. She had dark hair, dark eyes, and a dark complexion, and she looked even younger than Huang.

"Agent Huang, I found something," the woman said. "Scratches on the back door lock. It looks like someone picked it open."

"Good work, Vargas," Huang said. "Now we know how he got in. Could you stay with Riley and her daughter for a little while?"

The young woman's face lit up with delight.

"I'll be glad to," she said.

She sat at the table, and Huang left the kitchen to rejoin the others.

"Agent Paige, I'm Agent María de la Luz Vargas Ramírez." Then she grinned. "I know, it's a mouthful. It's a Mexican thing.

People call me Lucy Vargas."

"I'm glad you're here, Agent Vargas," Riley said.

"Just Lucy, please."

The young woman fell silent for a moment and just kept gazing at Riley. Finally she said, "Agent Paige, I hope I'm not out of line in saying this, but ... it's a real honor to meet you. I've been following your work ever since I went into training. Your whole record is just so amazing."

"Thank you," Riley said.

Lucy smiled with admiration. "I mean, the way you wrapped up the Peterson case—the whole story just amazes me."

Riley shook her head.

"I wish things were that simple," she said. "He's not dead. He was the intruder here today."

Lucy stared back, stunned.

"But everybody says—" Lucy began.

Riley interrupted.

"Someone else thought he was alive. Marie, the woman I rescued. She was sure he was still out there taunting her. She ..."

Riley paused, painfully remembering the sight of Marie's body hanging in her own bedroom.

"She committed suicide," Riley said.

Lucy looked both horrified and surprised. "I'm sorry," she said.

Just then, Riley heard a familiar voice call out to her.

"Riley? You okay?"

She turned and saw Bill Jeffreys standing in the kitchen archway, looking anxious. The BAU must have alerted him about the trouble, so he'd driven here on his own.

"I'm okay, Bill," she said. "So is April. Sit down."

Bill sat down at the table with Riley, April, and Lucy. Lucy stared at him, apparently in awe to meet Riley's former partner, yet another FBI legend.

Huang stepped back into the kitchen.

"Nobody's in the house, or outside either," he told Riley. "My people have gathered up whatever evidence they can find. They say it won't be much to go on. It'll be up to the lab technicians to see what they can make of it."

"I was afraid of that," Riley said.

"Looks like it's time for us to wrap things up for tonight," Huang said. Then he left the kitchen to give his final orders to the agents.

Riley turned toward her daughter.

"April, you're going to stay at your father's house tonight."

April's eyes widened.

"I'm not leaving you here," April said. "And I sure don't want to stay with Dad."

"You've got to," Riley said. "You might not be safe here."

"But Mom—"

Riley interrupted. "April, there are still things I haven't told you about this man. Terrible things. You'll be safe with your father. I'll pick you up tomorrow after your class."

Before April could protest further, Lucy spoke.

"Your mother's right, April. Take it from me. In fact, consider it an order from me. I'll handpick a couple of agents who can drive you there. Agent Paige, with your permission, I'll call your ex-husband and tell him what's going on."

Riley was surprised by Lucy's offer. She was also pleased. Almost uncannily, Lucy seemed to understand that this would be an awkward call for her to make. Ryan would undoubtedly take this news more seriously from any agent other than Riley. Lucy had also handled April well.

Not only had Lucy had spotted the picked lock, she also demonstrated empathy. Empathy was an excellent quality in a BAU agent, and it was all too often worn away by the stress of the job.

This woman is good, Riley thought.

"Come on," Lucy said to April. "Let's go call your dad."

April stared daggers at Riley. Even so, she got up from the table and followed Lucy into the living room, where they started making the call.

Riley and Bill were left sitting at the kitchen table alone. Even though there seemed to be nothing left to do, it seemed right to Riley that Bill was there. They had worked together for years and she had always thought of them as something like a matched pair—both were forty with touches of gray showing in dark hair. They were both dedicated to their jobs and troubled in their marriages. Bill was solid in build and temperament.

"It was Peterson," Riley said. "He was here."

Bill said nothing. He looked unconvinced.

"You don't believe me?" Riley said. "There were pebbles in my bed. He must have put them there. They couldn't have gotten there any other way."

Bill shook his head.

"Riley, I'm sure there really was an intruder," he said. "You weren't imagining that part. But Peterson? I doubt that very much."

Riley's anger was rising now.

"Bill, listen to me. I heard rattling against the door one night, and I looked outside, and I found pebbles there. Marie heard someone throw pebbles at her bedroom window. Who else could it be?"

Bill sighed and shook his head.

"Riley, you're tired," he said. "And when you're tired and you get an idea fixed in your head, it's easy to believe just about anything. It can happen to anybody."

Riley found herself fighting back tears. In better days, Bill would have trusted her instincts without question. But those days were over. And she knew why. A few nights ago she'd called him drunk and suggested that they act on their mutual attraction and begin an affair. It had been an awful thing to do, and she knew it, and she'd not had a drink since then. Even so, things hadn't been right between her and Bill after that.

"I know what this is about, Bill," she said. "It's because of that stupid phone call. You don't trust me anymore."

Now Bill's voice crackled with anger.

"Damn it, Riley, I'm just trying to be realistic."

Riley was seething. "Just go, Bill."

"But Riley—"

"Believe me or don't believe me. Take your pick. But right now I want you to go."

With an air of resignation, Bill got up from the table and left.

Through the kitchen doorway, Riley could see that almost everybody had left the house, including April. Lucy came back into the kitchen.

"Agent Huang is leaving a couple of agents here," she said. "They'll watch the house from a car for the rest of the night. I'm not sure it's a good idea for you to be alone inside. I'll be glad to stay."

Riley sat and thought for a moment. What she wanted—what she *needed* right now—was for somebody to believe that Peterson wasn't dead. She doubted that she could convince even Lucy of that. The whole thing seemed hopeless.

"I'll be all right, Lucy," Riley said.

Lucy nodded and left the kitchen. Riley heard the sound of the last agents leaving the house and shutting the door behind them. Riley got up and checked both the front door and back door to make sure they were locked. She moved two chairs up against the back door. They would make noise enough if anybody picked the lock again.

Then she stood in the living room and looked all around. The house looked weirdly bright, with every single light burning.

I ought to turn some of them off, she thought.

But as she reached for the living room light switch, her fingers froze. She just couldn't do it. She was paralyzed with terror.

Peterson, she knew, was coming for her again.

CHAPTER THREE

Riley hesitated for a moment as she entered the BAU building, wondering if she was really ready to face anyone today. She hadn't slept all night, and was bone-tired. The sensation of terror that had kept her awake all night had run her adrenaline until there was nothing left. Now, she just felt hollowed out.

Riley took a deep breath.

The only way out is through.

She gathered her resolve and walked into the busy maze of FBI agents, specialists, and support staff. As she wound her way through the open bay area, familiar faces looked up from their computers. Most smiled to see her and several gave her a thumbs-up. Riley slowly felt glad she had decided to come in. She'd needed something to lift to her spirits.

"Way to go with the Dolly Killer," one young agent said.

It took Riley a couple of seconds to understand what he meant. Then she realized that "Dolly Killer" must be the new nickname for Dirk Monroe, the psychopath she had just taken down. The name made sense.

Riley also noticed that some of the faces looked at her more warily. Doubtless they had heard about the incident at her house last night when a whole team had raced to her frantic call for backup. *They probably wonder if I'm in my right mind,* she thought. As far as she knew, absolutely no one else in the Bureau believed that Peterson was still alive.

Riley stopped by the desk of Sam Flores, a lab technician with black-rimmed glasses, hard at work at his computer.

"What news have you got for me, Sam?" Riley said.

Sam looked up from the screen at her.

"You mean about your break-in, right? I'm just now looking at some preliminary reports. I'm afraid there won't be much. The lab guys didn't get anything off the pebbles—no DNA or fibers. No fingerprints, either."

Riley sighed with discouragement.

"Let me know if anything changes," she said, patting Flores on the back.

"I wouldn't count on it," Flores said.

Riley continued on to the area shared by senior agents. As she passed by the small glass-walled offices, she saw that Bill wasn't in. That was actually a relief, but she knew that sooner or later she would have to clear up the recent awkwardness between them.

When she set foot in her own neat, well-organized office, Riley immediately noticed that she had a phone message. It was from Mike Nevins, the D.C. forensic psychiatrist who sometimes consulted on BAU cases. Over the years, she had found him a source remarkable insight, and not only into cases. Mike had helped Riley through her own bout of PTSD after Peterson had captured and tortured her. She knew he was calling to check up on her, as he often did.

She was about to call him back, when the broad frame of Special Agent Brent Meredith appeared in her doorway. The unit commander's black, angular features hinted at his tough, no-nonsense personality. Riley felt relieved at the sight of him, always reassured by his presence.

"Welcome back, Agent Paige," he said.

Riley got up to shake his hand. "Thanks, Agent Meredith."

"I hear you had another little adventure last night. I hope you're all right."

"I'm fine, thanks."

Meredith looked at her with warm concern, and Riley knew that he was trying to assess her readiness for work.

"Would you like to join me in the break area for some coffee?" he asked.

"Thanks, but there are some files I really need to review. Some other time."

Meredith nodded and said nothing. Riley knew he was waiting for her to speak. Doubtless he had also heard about her belief that Peterson had been the intruder. He was giving her a chance to voice her opinion. But she was sure that Meredith wouldn't be any more inclined than anybody else to agree with her about Peterson.

"Well, I'd better be going," he said. "Let me know whenever you're up for coffee or lunch."

"I'll do that."

Meredith paused and turned back toward Riley.

Slowly and carefully, he said, "Do be careful, Agent Paige."

Riley detected a world of meaning in those words. Not long ago, another higher-up in the agency had suspended her for subordination. She'd been reinstated, but her position could be still tenuous. Riley sensed that Meredith was giving her a friendly warning. He didn't want her to do anything to jeopardize herself. And raising a lot of fuss about Peterson might cause trouble with those who had declared the case closed.

As soon as she was alone, Riley went to her filing cabinet and pulled out the thick file on the Peterson case. She opened it up on her desk and browsed through it, refreshing her memory about her nemesis. She didn't find much that was helpful.

The truth was that the man remained an enigma. There hadn't even been any records of his existence until Bill and Riley finally tracked him down. Peterson might not even be his real name, and they'd turned up several different first names supposedly connected with him.

As Riley looked through the file, she came across photographs of his victims—women who had been found in shallow graves. They had all borne burn scars, and the cause of death had been manual strangulation. Riley shuddered with the memory of the large, powerful hands that had caught her and caged her like an animal.

Nobody knew just how many women he had killed. There might be many more corpses yet to be found. And until Marie and Riley had been captured and lived to tell about it, nobody knew about how he liked to torment women in the dark with a propane torch. And nobody else was willing to believe that Peterson was still alive.

The whole thing was really getting her down. Riley was known for her ability to get into the minds of killers—an ability that sometimes scared her. Even so, she'd never been able to get into Peterson's mind. And as of right now, she felt that she understood him even less.

He had never struck Riley as an organized psychopath. The fact that he left his victims in shallow graves suggested quite the opposite. He was no perfectionist. Even so, he was meticulous enough not to leave clues behind. The man was truly paradoxical.

She remembered something that Marie had said to her shortly before her suicide …

"Maybe he's like a ghost, Riley. Maybe that's what happened when you blew him up. You killed his body but you didn't kill his evil."

He wasn't a ghost, and Riley knew it. She was sure—more sure than ever—that he was out there, and that she was his next target. Even so, he might as well be a ghost as far as she was concerned. Aside from herself, nobody else even believed that he existed.

"Where are you, you bastard?" she whispered aloud.

She didn't know, and she had no way to find out. She was

completely stymied. She had no choice but to let the whole thing go for now. She closed the folder and put it back in its place in her filing cabinet.

Then her office phone rang. She saw that the call was coming through on a line shared by all the special agents. It was the line that the BAU phone bank used to forward appropriate call-ins to agents. As a rule of thumb, whichever agent picked up such a call first would take the case.

Riley glanced around at the other offices. Nobody else seemed to be in at the moment. The other agents were all either taking a break or out working other cases. Riley answered the phone.

"Special Agent Riley Paige. What can I do to help you?"

The voice on the line sounded harried.

"Agent Paige, this is Raymond Alford, Chief of Police in Reedsport, New York. We've got a real problem here. Would it be okay for us to do this by video chat? I think maybe I could explain it better. And I've got some images that you'd better see for yourself."

Riley's curiosity was piqued. "Certainly," she said. She gave Alford her contact information. A few moments later she was talking to him face to face. He was a slender, balding man who appeared to be well along in years. At the moment, his expression was anxious and tired.

"We had a murder here last night," Alford told her. "A real ugly one. Let me show you."

A photograph came up on Riley's computer screen. It showed what appeared to be a woman's body hanging from a chain over railroad tracks. The body was wrapped in a multitude of chains, and it seemed to be oddly dressed.

"What's the victim wearing?" Riley asked.

"A straitjacket," Alford said.

Riley was startled. Looking closer at the photograph, she could see that it was true. Then the picture disappeared, and Riley found herself face to face with Alford again.

"Chief Alford, I appreciate your alarm. But what makes you think this is a case for the Behavioral Analysis Unit?"

"Because this exact same thing happened very near here five years ago," Alford said.

An image appeared of another woman's corpse. She, too, was chained all over and bound in a straitjacket.

"Back then it was a part-time prison worker, Marla Blainey. The MO was identical—except that she was just dumped on the riverbank, not hung up."

Alford's face reappeared.

"This time it was Rosemary Pickens, a local nurse," he said. "Nobody can imagine a motive, not for either of the women. They were both well-liked."

Alford slumped wearily and shook his head.

"Agent Paige, my people and I are really out of our depth here. This new killing must be a serial or copycat. The trouble is, neither of those makes any sense. We don't get that kind of problem in Reedsport. This is just a little Hudson River tourist town with a population of about seven thousand. Sometimes we have to break up a fight or fish a tourist out of the river. That's about as bad as things usually get here."

Riley thought about it. This actually did look like a case for the BAU. She really ought to refer Alford directly to Meredith.

But Riley glanced toward Meredith's office and saw that he hadn't returned yet. She'd have to alert him about this later. In the meantime, maybe she could help a little.

"What were the causes of death?" she asked.

"Throats slashed, both of them."

Riley tried not to show her surprise. Strangulation and blunt force strike were far more common than slashing.

This seemed to be a highly unusual killer. Even so, it was the kind of psychopath that Riley knew well. She specialized in just such cases. It seemed a shame that she wasn't going to be able to bring her skills to this one. In the wake of her recent trauma, she wouldn't get the assignment.

"Have you taken the body down?" Riley asked.

"Not yet," Alford said. "She's still hanging there."

"Then don't. Leave it there for now. Wait till our agents get there."

Alford didn't look pleased.

"Agent Paige, that's going to be a tall order. It's right next to the train tracks and it can be seen from the river. And the town doesn't need this kind of publicity. I'm under a lot of pressure to take it down."

"Leave it," Riley said. "I know it's not easy, but it's important. It won't be long. We'll get agents there this afternoon."

Alford nodded in mute compliance.

"Have you got any more photos of the latest victim?" Riley asked. "Any close-ups?"

"Sure, I'll bring them up."

Riley found herself looking at a series of detail shots of the corpse. The local cops had done a good job. The photos showed how tightly and elaborately the chains were wrapped around the corpse.

Finally came a close-up of the victim's face.

Riley felt as though her heart jumped up into her throat. The victim's eyes bulged, and her mouth was gagged by a chain. But that wasn't what shocked Riley.

The woman looked a lot like Marie. She was older and heavier, but even so, Marie might have looked a lot like this if she'd only lived another decade or so. The image hit Riley like an emotional blow to the gut. It was as if Marie was calling out for her, demanding that she get this killer.

She knew that she had to take this case.

CHAPTER FOUR

Peterson coasted his car along, not too fast, not too slow, feeling good as he finally had the girl back in his sights. Finally, he had found her. There she was, Riley's daughter, alone, walking toward her high school, with no clue at all that he was stalking her. That he was about to end her life.

As he watched, she suddenly stopped in her tracks and turned around, as if suspicious she were being watched. She stood there, as if undecided. A few other students passed her and filtered into the building.

He coasted the car along, waiting to see what she would do next.

Not that the girl mattered to him especially. Her mother was the true target of his revenge. Her mother had thwarted him badly, and she had to pay. She already had, in a way—after all, he'd driven Marie Sayles to suicide. But now he had to take from her the girl who mattered to her most.

The girl, to his delight, began to turn around and walk away from school. Apparently she had decided not to go to class today. His heart pounded—he wanted to pounce. But he could not. Not yet. He had to tell himself to be patient. Other people were still in sight.

Peterson drove ahead and circled a block, forcing himself to be patient. He suppressed a smile at the joy to come. With what he had in mind for her daughter, Riley would suffer in ways she didn't think possible. Although she was still gangly and awkward, the girl looked a lot like her mother. That would make it extra satisfying.

As he circled around, he saw that the girl was walking briskly along the street. He pulled over to the curb and watched her for a few minutes, until he realized that she was taking a road that led out of town. If she was going to walk home alone, then this might be the perfect moment to take control of her.

His heart pounding, wanting to savor the delightful anticipation, Peterson circled another block with his car.

People needed to learn to put off certain pleasures, Peterson knew, to wait until just the right time. Delayed gratification made everything more pleasurable. He had learned that from years of delicious, lingering cruelty.

There's just so much to look forward to, he thought contentedly.

When he came back around and saw her again, Peterson laughed aloud. She was hitchhiking! God was smiling down upon him on this day. Taking her life was clearly meant to be.

He pulled the car up beside her and gave her his most pleasant smile.

"Give you a lift?"

The girl smiled back broadly. "Thanks. That would be great."

"Where are you headed?" he asked.

"I live just a little way out of town."

The girl told him the address.

He said, "I'm going right past there. Hop in."

The girl got into the front seat. With increasing satisfaction, he observed that she even had her mother's hazel eyes.

Peterson pressed the buttons to lock the doors and windows. Over the quiet rumble of the air conditioner, the girl didn't even notice.

*

April felt a pleasant rush of adrenaline as she fastened the safety harness. She'd never hitchhiked before. Her mother would have a fit if she found out.

Of course, it served Mom right, April figured. It was really rotten to make her stay at Dad's last night—and all because of some crazy idea of hers that Peterson had been in their home. It wasn't true, and April knew it. The two agents who had driven her to Dad's house had said so. From what they'd said to each other, it sounded kind of like the whole agency thought Mom was a bit bonkers.

The man said, "So what brings you into Fredericksburg?"

April turned and looked at him. He was an agreeable-looking, big-jawed guy with shaggy hair and a stubble of beard. He was smiling.

"School," April said.

"A summer class?" the man asked.

"Yeah," April said. She certainly wasn't going to tell him that she'd decided to skip the class. Not that he looked like the kind of guy who wouldn't understand. He seemed pretty cool. Maybe he'd even get a kick out of helping her defy parental authority. Still, it was best not to take any chances.

The man's smile turned a bit mischievous.

"So what does your mother think about hitchhiking?" he asked.

April flushed with embarrassment.

"Oh, she's fine with it," she said.

The man chuckled. It wasn't a very pleasant sound. And something occurred to April. He'd asked what her *mother* thought, not what her *parents* thought. What made him say it that way?

The traffic was fairly heavy this close to the school at this time of morning. It was going to take a while to get home. April hoped that the man wasn't going to make a whole lot of conversation. That could get really awkward.

But after a couple of blocks of silence, April felt even more uncomfortable. The man had stopped smiling, and his expression seemed rather grim to her. She noticed that all the doors were locked. She surreptitiously fingered the button of the passenger-side window. It didn't budge.

The car came to a stop behind a line of cars waiting for a light to change. The man clicked on the left turn signal. April was seized by a sudden burst of anxiety.

"Um ... we have to go straight here," she said.

The man said nothing. Had he simply not heard her? Somehow, she couldn't get up the nerve to say it again. Besides, maybe he planned to go by a different route. But no, she couldn't think of how he could drive her home from that direction.

April wondered what to do. Should she scream for help? Would anybody hear her? And what if the man hadn't heard what she said? Didn't mean any harm after all? The whole thing would be horribly embarrassing.

Then she saw someone familiar slouching along the sidewalk, his backpack slung over his shoulder. It was Brian, her sort-of-boyfriend these days. She rapped sharply on the window.

She gasped with relief when Brian looked around and saw her.

"Do you want a ride?" she mouthed to Brian.

Brian grinned and nodded.

"Oh, that's my boyfriend," April said. "Could we stop and pick him up, please? He's on his way to my house anyway."

It was a lie. April really had no idea where Brian was headed. The man scowled and grunted. He wasn't at all happy with this. Was he going to stop? April's heart beat wildly.

Brian was talking on his cell phone as he stood on the sidewalk and waited. But he was looking straight at the car and April was sure that he could see the driver pretty clearly. She was glad to have a potential witness just in case the man had something ugly in mind.

The man studied Brian, and he clearly saw him talking on his cell, and saw him looking back right at him.

Without saying a word, the man unlocked the doors. April signaled for Brian to get in the back seat, so he opened the door and jumped in. He shut the door just as the light changed and the line of cars started to move again.

"Thanks for the ride, mister," Brian said brightly.

The man didn't say anything at all. He kept on scowling.

"He's taking us to my house, Brian," April said.

"Awesome," Brian replied.

April felt safe now. If the man really had bad intentions, he surely wasn't going to snatch both her and Brian. He'd surely drive them straight to Mom's house.

Thinking ahead, April wondered whether she should tell her mother about the man and her suspicions about him. But no, that would mean admitting to skipping her class and hitchhiking. Mom would ground her for good.

Besides, she thought, the driver couldn't be Peterson.

Peterson was a psychotic killer, not a regular man driving a car.

And Peterson, after all, was dead.

CHAPTER FIVE

Brent Meredith's tight, grim expression told Riley that he didn't like her request at all.

"It's an obvious case for me to take," she said. "I have more experience than anybody else with this kind of kinky serial killer."

She had just described the call from Reedsport, Meredith's jaw set the entire time.

After a long silence, Meredith finally sighed.

"I'll allow it," he said reluctantly.

Riley breathed a sigh of relief.

"Thank you, sir," she said.

"Don't thank me," he growled. "I'm doing this against my better judgment. I'm only going along with it because you've got the special skills to deal with this case. Your experience with this kind of killer is unique. I'll assign you a partner."

Riley felt a jolt of discouragement. She knew that working with Bill wasn't an option right now, but she wondered if Meredith knew why there was tension between the long-time partners. She thought it more likely that Bill had simply told Meredith that he wanted to stay close to home for now.

"But sir—" she began.

"No buts," Meredith said. "And no more of your lone wolf shenanigans. It's not smart, and it's against policy. You've nearly gotten yourself killed more than once. Rules are rules. And I'm breaking enough of them right now as it is, not putting you on leave after your recent incidents."

"Yes, sir," Riley said quietly.

Meredith rubbed his chin, obviously considering all the options. He said, "Agent Vargas will go with you."

"Lucy Vargas?" Riley asked.

Meredith just nodded. Riley didn't much like the idea.

"She was on the team that showed up at my house last night," Riley said. "She seems very impressive, and I liked her—but she's a rookie. I'm used to working with someone more experienced."

Meredith smiled broadly. "Her marks at the academy were off the charts. And she's young, all right. It's rare that students right out of the academy get accepted to BAU. But she really is that good. She's ready for experience in the field."

Riley knew she had no choice.

Meredith continued, "How soon can you be ready to go?"

Riley ran the necessary preparations through her mind. Talking to her daughter was at the top of her list. And what else? Her travel kit wasn't here in her office. She'd have to drive to Fredericksburg, stop at home, then make sure that April would stay at her father's and drive back to Quantico.

"Give me three hours," she said.

"I'll call for a plane," Meredith said. "I'll notify the police chief in Reedsport that we have a team on the way. Be at the airstrip in exactly three hours. If you're late, there'll be hell to pay."

Riley rose nervously from her chair.

"I understand, sir," she said. She almost thanked him again, but hastily remembered his command not to. She left his office without another word.

*

Riley made it to her house in half an hour, parked outside, and made a beeline for the front door. She had to grab her travel kit, a small suitcase she always kept packed with toiletries, a robe, and a change of clothes. She had to get them super fast and then go into town, where she'd explain things to April and Ryan. She wasn't looking forward to that part at all, but she needed to be sure that April was safe.

When she turned the key in the front door, she found that it was already unlocked. She knew she had locked it when she left. She always did, without fail. All of Riley's senses snapped into alertness. She pulled out her gun and stepped inside.

As she moved stealthily into the house, peering around at every nook and corner, she became aware of a long, continuous noise. It seemed to be coming from outside the house, in back. It was music—very loud music.

What the hell?

Still on the lookout for any intruder, she went through the kitchen. The back door was partly open and a pop song was blaring outside. She smelled a familiar aroma.

"Oh, Jesus, not this again," she said to herself.

She put her gun back into its holster and walked outside. Sure enough, there was April, sitting at the picnic table with a skinny boy about her age. The music was coming from a pair of little speakers sitting on the picnic table.

Upon seeing her mother, April's eyes lit up with panic. She reached under the picnic table to extinguish the joint in her hand, obviously hoping to make it disappear.

"Don't bother to hide it," Riley said, striding toward the table. "I know what you're doing."

She could barely make herself heard over the music. She reached over to the player and turned it off.

"This isn't what it looks like, Mom," April said.

"This is *exactly* what it looks like," Riley said. "Give me the rest of it."

Rolling her eyes, April handed over a plastic bag with a small amount of pot in it.

"I thought you were working," April said, as if that explained everything.

Riley didn't know whether to feel more angry or disappointed. She'd caught April smoking pot just once before. But things had gotten better between them, and she'd thought those days were behind them.

Riley stared at the boy.

"Mom, this is Brian," April said. "He's a friend from school."

With a vacant grin and glassy eyes, the boy reached out to shake hands with Riley.

"Pleased to meet you, Ms. Paige," he said.

Riley kept her own hands at her sides.

"What are you even doing here?" Riley asked April.

"This is where I live," April said with a shrug.

"You know what I mean. You're supposed to be at your dad's house."

April didn't reply. Riley looked at her watch. Time was running short. She had to resolve this situation quickly.

"Tell me what happened," Riley said.

April was starting to look somewhat embarrassed. She really wasn't prepared for this situation.

"I walked to school from Dad's house this morning," she said. "I ran into Brian in front of the school. We decided to skip today. It's okay if I miss it once in a while. I'm acing it already. The final exam isn't till Friday."

Brian let out a nervous, inane laugh.

"Yeah, April really is doing great in that class, Ms. Paige," he said. "She's awesome."

"How did you get here?" Riley asked.

April looked away. Riley easily guessed why she was reluctant to tell her the truth.

228

"Oh, God, you kids hitchhiked here, didn't you?" Riley said.

"The driver was a really nice guy, very quiet," April said. "Brian was with me the whole time. We were safe."

Riley struggled to keep her nerves and her voice steady.

"How do you *know* you were safe? April, you're *never* supposed to accept rides from strangers. And why would you come here after the scare we got last night? That was incredibly foolish. Suppose Peterson was still around?"

April smiled as if she knew better.

"C'mon, Mom. You worry too much. The other agents say so. I heard two of them talking about it—the guys who drove me to Dad's house last night. They said Peterson was definitely dead, and you just couldn't accept it. They said whoever left those stones probably did it as a prank."

Riley was steaming. She wished she could get her hands on those agents. They had a lot of nerve, contradicting Riley within earshot of her daughter. She thought about asking April for their names, but she decided to let that go.

"Listen to me, April," Riley said. "I've got to go out of town on a job for a few days. I have to leave right now. I'm taking you to your Dad's house. I need for you to stay there."

"Why can't I go with you?" April asked.

Riley wondered how on earth teenage kids could be so stupid about some things.

"Because you've got to finish this class," she said. "You've got to pass it or you'll be behind in school. English is a requirement, and you blew it for no good reason. And besides, I'm working. Being around while I'm on the job isn't always safe. You ought to know that by now."

April said nothing.

"Come on inside," Riley said. "We've only got a few minutes. I've got to get some things together, and so do you. Then I'm taking you to your father's house."

Turning to Brian, Riley added, "And I'm driving you home."

"I can hitch," Brian said.

Riley simply glared at him.

"Okay," Brian said, looking rather cowed. He and April got up from the table and followed Riley into the house.

"Go on and get in the car, both of you," she said. The kids obediently left the house.

She latched the new slide bolt that she'd added to the back door and went from room to room making sure that all the windows were fastened.

In her own bedroom, she picked up her travel bag and made sure that everything she needed was still inside. As she left, she glanced nervously at her bed as though the pebbles might have returned. For a moment, she wondered why she was headed off to another state instead of staying here and trying to track the killer who had put them there to taunt her.

Besides, this stunt of April's had her scared. Could she trust her daughter to stay safe in Fredericksburg? She'd thought so before, but now she had her doubts.

Still, there wasn't anything she could do to change things. She was committed to the new case and had to leave. As she walked outside to the car, she glanced into the thick, dark woods, scanning them for any sign of Peterson.

But there was none.

CHAPTER SIX

Riley glanced at her car clock as she drove the kids into an upscale part of Fredericksburg and shuddered to see how little time she had left. Meredith's words came rushing back.

If you're late, there'll be hell to pay.

Maybe—just maybe—she'd get to the airstrip on time. She had planned to just stop at home and grab a bag, and now things were getting a lot more complicated. She wondered if she should she call Meredith and warn him that family problems might hold her up. No, she decided; her boss had been reluctant enough as it was. She couldn't expect him to cut her any slack.

Luckily, Brian's address was on the route to Ryan's house. When Riley pulled up to a big front yard and stopped the car, she said, "I ought to come in and tell your parents what happened."

"They're not at home," Brian said with a shrug. "Dad's gone for good, and Mom isn't there much."

He got out of the car, then turned and said, "Thanks for the ride." As he walked toward his house Riley wondered what kind of parents would leave a kid like that on his own. Didn't they know what kind of trouble a teenager could get into?

But maybe his mother doesn't have much choice in that matter, Riley thought miserably. *Who am I to judge?*

As soon as Brian went inside his house, Riley drove away. April had said nothing during the whole drive so far, and she didn't seem to be in any mood to talk now. Riley couldn't tell whether that silence was due to sullenness or shame. She realized that there seemed to be a lot she didn't know about her own daughter.

Riley was upset with both herself and April. Just yesterday they'd seemed to be getting along better. She'd thought that April was beginning to understand the pressures on an FBI agent. But then Riley had insisted that April go to her father's house last night, and today April was rebelling against being forced to do that.

Riley reminded herself that she ought to be a whole lot more sympathetic. She'd always been something of a rebel herself. And Riley knew what it was like to lose a mother and to have a distant father. April was bound to be afraid that the same thing would happen to her.

She's terrified for my safety, Riley realized. During recent months, April had seen her mother endure both physical and emotional injuries. After last night's intruder scare, April was surely worried sick. Riley reminded herself that she needed to pay closer attention to how her daughter might be feeling. Anyone of any age might have a hard time coping with the complications of Riley's life.

Riley pulled in front of the house she had once shared with Ryan. It was a large, handsome house with a portico at the side door, or *porte-cochère* as Ryan called it. These days, Riley chose to park on the street instead of pulling into the driveway and under the shelter.

She had never felt at home here. Somehow, living in a respectable suburban neighborhood had never suited her. Her marriage, the house, the neighborhood, all had represented so many expectations that she'd never felt able to fulfill.

Over the years Riley had realized that she was better at her job than she would ever be at living a normal life. Finally she had left the marriage, house, and neighborhood, and that made her all the more determined to live up to the expectations of being a mother to a teenage daughter.

As April started to open the car door, Riley said, "Wait."

April turned and looked at her expectantly.

Without so much as stopping to think, Riley said, "I get it. I understand."

April stared at her with a stunned expression. For a moment, she seemed on the verge of tears. Riley felt almost as surprised as her daughter. She didn't know quite what had come over her. She only knew that now was no time for parental lectures, even if she had time to deliver one, which she didn't. She also felt in her gut that she'd said exactly the right thing.

Riley and April got out of the car and walked together to the house. She didn't know whether to hope Ryan would be at home or not. She didn't want to get into an argument with him, and she'd already decided not to tell him about the marijuana incident. She knew she ought to, but there simply wasn't time to deal with his reactions. Still, she really did have to explain to him that she was going to be gone for a few days.

Gabriela, the stout, middle-aged Guatemalan woman who had worked as the family's housekeeper for years, greeted Riley and April at the door. Gabriela's eyes were wide with worry.

"*Hija*, where have you been?" she asked in her heavy accent.

232

"I'm sorry, Gabriela," April said meekly.

Gabriela looked closely at April's face. Riley saw by her expression that she detected that April had been smoking pot.

"*Tonta!*" Gabriela said sharply.

"*Lo siento mucho,*" April said, sounding genuinely repentant.

"*Vente conmigo,*" Gabriela said. As she led April away, she turned and gave Riley a look of bitter disapproval.

Riley withered under that look. Gabriela was one of the few people in the world who truly daunted her. The woman also had a wonderful way with April, and at the moment, she seemed to be doing a better job of parenting than Riley was.

Riley called after Gabriela, "Is Ryan here?"

As she walked away, Gabriela replied, "*Sí.*" Then she called into the house, "Señor Paige, your daughter is back."

Ryan appeared in the hallway, dressed and coiffed to leave. He looked surprised to see Riley.

"What are you doing here?" he asked. "Where was April?"

"She was at my house."

"What? After everything that happened last night, you took her home?"

Riley's jaw clenched with exasperation.

"I didn't take her anywhere," she said. "Ask her, if you want to know how she got there. I can't help it if she doesn't want to live with you. You're the only one who can fix that."

"This is all your fault, Riley. You've let her get completely out of control."

For a split second, Riley was furious. But her fury gave way to a sinking feeling that he might be right. It wasn't fair, but he really did know how to push her buttons that way.

Riley took a long, deep breath and said, "Look, I'm leaving town for a few days. I've got a case in Upstate New York. April has got to stay here, and she's got to stay put. Please explain the situation to Gabriela."

"*You* explain the situation to Gabriela," Ryan snapped. "I've got a client to meet. Right now."

"And I've got a plane to catch. Right now."

They stood staring at each other for a moment. Their argument had reached a stalemate. As she looked into his eyes, Riley reminded herself that she'd once loved him. And he'd seemed to love her just as much. That had been back when both of them were young and poor, before he had become a successful lawyer and she had become an FBI agent.

She couldn't help noting that he was still a very good-looking

233

man. He went to a lot of trouble to look that way and spent many hours at the gym. Riley also knew perfectly well that he had lots of women in his life. That was part of the problem—he was enjoying his freedom as a bachelor too much to worry about parenting.

Not that I'm doing all that much better, she thought.

Then Ryan said, "It's always about your job."

Riley choked back her anger. They'd gone around and around about this. Her job was somehow both too dangerous and too trivial. His job was all that mattered, because he was making a lot more money, and because he claimed to be making a real difference in the world. As if handling lawsuits for wealthy clients amounted to more than Riley's never-ending war against evil.

But she couldn't let herself get dragged into this tired old argument right now. Neither of them ever won it anyway.

"We'll talk when I get back," she said.

She turned and walked out of the house. She heard Ryan shut the door behind her.

Riley got into her car and drove. She had less than an hour to get back to Quantico. Her head was reeling. So much was happening so fast. Just a little while ago she had decided to take a new case. Now she wondered if it was the right thing to do. Not only was April having trouble coping, but she was sure that Peterson was back in her life.

But in a way, it made good sense. As long as April stayed with her father, she'd be safe from Peterson's clutches. And Peterson wasn't going to take any other victims during Riley's absence. As puzzled as she was by him, Riley knew one thing for certain. She alone was his target for revenge. She, and no one else, was his intended next victim. And it would feel good to be far away from him for a while.

She also reminded herself of a hard lesson she had learned during her last case—not to take on all the evil in the world, all at the same time. It boiled down to a simple motto: *One monster at a time.*

And right now, she was going after an especially vicious brute. A man she just knew would strike again soon.

CHAPTER SEVEN

The man began to spread lengths of chains out on the long worktable in his basement. It was dark outside, but all those links of stainless steel were bright and shiny under the glare of a bare light bulb.

He pulled one of the chains out to its full length. The rattling sound stirred terrible memories of being shackled, caged, and tormented with chains like these. But it was like he kept telling himself: *I've got to face my fears.*

And to do that he had to prove his mastery over the chains themselves. Too often in the past, chains had held mastery over him.

It was a shame that anyone had to suffer on account of this. For five years, he'd thought he'd put the whole matter behind him. It had helped so much when the church hired him to be a night watchman. He'd liked that job, proud of the authority that came with it. He'd liked feeling strong and useful.

But last month, they'd taken that job away from him. They needed someone with security skills, they'd said, and better credentials—someone bigger and stronger. They promised to keep him working in the garden. He'd still be making enough money to pay the rent on this tiny little house.

Even so, the loss of that job, the loss of the authority it gave him, had shaken him, made him feel helpless. That urge broke loose again—that desperation not to be helpless, that frantic need to assert mastery over the chains so they couldn't take him again. He'd tried before to outrun the urge, as if he could leave his inner darkness right here in his basement. This last time, he'd driven all the way down to Reedsport, hoping to escape it. But he couldn't.

He didn't know why he couldn't. He was a good man, with a good heart, and he liked to do favors. But sooner or later, his kindness always turned against him. When he'd helped that woman, that nurse, carry groceries to her car in Reedsport, she'd smiled and said, "What a good boy!"

He winced at the memory of the smile and those words.

"What a good boy!"

His mother had smiled and said such things, even while she kept the chain on his leg too short for him to reach any food or even see outside. And the nuns, too, had smiled and said things like that when they peered at him through the little square opening in the door to his small prison.

"What a good boy!"

Not everyone was cruel, he knew that. Most people really meant well toward him, especially in this little town where he'd long since settled. They even liked him. But why did everyone seem to think of him as a child—and a handicapped child at that? He was twenty-seven years old, and he knew that he was exceptionally bright. His mind was full of brilliant thoughts, and he scarcely ever encountered a problem he couldn't solve.

But of course he knew why people saw him the way they did. It was because he could barely speak at all. He'd stammered hopelessly all his life, and he hardly ever tried to talk, although he understood everything that other people said.

And he was small, and weak, and his features were stubby and childish, like those of someone who had been born with some congenital defect. Caged in that slightly misshapen skull was a remarkable mind, thwarted in its desire to do brilliant things in the world. But nobody knew that. Nobody at all. Not even the doctors at the psychiatric hospital had known it.

It was *ironic.*

People didn't think he knew words like *ironic.* But he did.

Now he found himself nervously fingering a button in his hand. He'd plucked it off the nurse's blouse when he hung her up. Reminded of her, he looked around at the cot where he'd kept her chained up for more than a week. He'd wished he could talk to her, explain that he didn't mean to be cruel, and it was just that she was so much like his mother and the nuns, especially in that nurse's uniform of hers.

The sight of her in that uniform had confused him. It was the same with the woman five years ago, the prison guard. Somehow both women had merged in his mind with his mother and the nuns and the hospital workers. He'd fought a losing battle simply to tell them apart.

It was a relief to be through with her. It was a terrible responsibility, keeping her bound like that, giving her water, listening to her moaning through the chain he'd used to gag her. He only undid the gag to put a straw in her mouth for water now and again. Then she'd try to scream.

If only he could have explained to her that she *mustn't* scream, that there were neighbors across the street who mustn't hear. If he could only have told her, maybe she'd have understood. But he couldn't explain, not with his hopeless stammer. Instead, he'd mutely threatened her with a straight-edged razor. In the long run, even the threat hadn't worked. That was when he'd had to slit her throat.

Then he'd taken her back to Reedsport and hung her up like that, for everyone to see. He wasn't sure just why. Perhaps it was a warning. If only people could understand. If they did, he wouldn't have to be so cruel.

Perhaps it was also his way of telling the world how sorry he was.

Because he *was* sorry. He'd go to the florist tomorrow and buy flowers—a cheap little bouquet—for the family. He couldn't talk to the florist, but he could write out simple instructions. The gift would be anonymous. And if he could find a good place to hide, he'd stand near the grave when they buried her, bowing his head like any other mourner.

He pulled another chain taut on his workbench, clenching its ends as tightly as he could, applying all his strength to it, silencing its rattle. But deep down, he knew that this wasn't enough to make him master of the chains. For that, he'd have to put the chains to use again. And he'd use one of the straitjackets still in his possession. Someone must be bound, as he'd been bound.

Someone else would have to suffer and die.

CHAPTER EIGHT

As soon as Riley and Lucy stepped off the FBI plane, a young uniformed cop came dashing toward them across the tarmac.

"Boy, am I glad to see you guys," he said. "Chief Alford's fit to be tied. If somebody doesn't take Rosemary's body down directly, he's liable to have a stroke. Reporters are already all over this. I'm Tim Boyden."

Riley's heart sank as she and Lucy introduced themselves. Media on the scene so quickly was a sure sign of trouble. The case was off to a rocky start.

"Can I help you carry anything?" Officer Boyden asked.

"We're good," Riley said. She and Lucy had only a couple of small bags.

Officer Boyden pointed across the tarmac.

"The car's right over there," he said.

The three of them walked briskly to the car. Riley got in on the front passenger side, while Lucy took the back seat.

"We're just a couple of minutes from town," Boyden said as he started to drive. "Man, I can't believe this is happening. Poor Rosemary. Everybody liked her so much. She was always helping people. When she disappeared a couple of weeks ago, we were all scared for the worst. But we couldn't have imagined …"

His voice trailed off and he shook his head in horrified disbelief.

Lucy leaned forward from the back seat.

"I understand that you had a murder like this before," she said.

"Yeah, back when I was still in high school," Boyden said. "Not right here in Reedsport, though. It was near Eubanks, farther south along the river. A body in chains, just like Rosemary. Wearing a straitjacket too. Is the chief right? Do we have a serial on our hands?"

"We're not ready to say," Riley said.

The truth was, she thought that the chief must be right. But the young officer seemed upset enough already. There seemed no point in alarming him further.

"I can't believe it," Boyden said, shaking his head again. "A nice little town like ours. A nice lady like Rosemary. I can't believe it."

As they drove into town, Riley saw a couple of vans with TV news crews on its little main street. A helicopter with a TV station logo was circling above the town.

Boyden drove to a barricade where a small cluster of reporters had gathered. An officer waved the car on through. Just a few seconds later, Boyden pulled the car alongside a stretch of railroad track. There was the body, hanging from a power pole. Several uniformed policemen were standing a few yards away from it.

As Riley stepped out of the car, she recognized Chief Raymond Alford as he trotted toward her. He looked none too happy.

"I sure as hell hope you had a good reason for us keeping the body hanging here like this," he said. "We've had a nightmare on our hands. The mayor's threatening to take my badge."

Riley and Lucy followed him toward the body. In the late afternoon sunlight, it looked even weirder than it had in the photos Riley had viewed on her computer. The stainless steel chains sparkled in the light.

"I take it you've cordoned off the scene," Riley said to Alford.

"We've done it as best we could," Alford said. "We've got the area barricaded far enough away that nobody can see the body except from the river. We've rerouted the trains to go around the town. It's slowing them down and playing havoc with their schedule. That must be how the Albany news channels found out that something was going on. They sure didn't hear about it from my people."

As Alford spoke, his voice was drowned out by the TV helicopter as it hovered directly overhead. He gave up trying to say what he meant to say. Riley could read the profanities on his lips as he looked up at the aircraft. Without rising, the helicopter swung away in a circle. The pilot obviously intended to circle back this way.

Alford took out his cell phone. When he got someone on the line, he yelled, "I *told* you to keep your damned chopper away from the site. Now tell your pilot to take that thing up above five hundred feet. It's the law."

From Alford's expression, Riley suspected that the person on the other end was giving him some resistance.

Finally Alford said, "If you don't get that bird out of here right now, your reporters are going to be barred from the news conference I'll be giving this afternoon."

His face relaxed a little. He looked up and waited. Sure enough, after a few moments the helicopter rose to a more

239

reasonable height. The noise from its engine still filled the air with a loud and steady drone.

"God, I hope we don't get a lot more of this," Alford growled. "Maybe when we cut the body down, there'll be less here to attract them. Still, in the short run, I guess there's an upside. The hotels and B&Bs are getting some extra business. Restaurants too— reporters have got to eat. But in the long run? It's bad if tourists get scared off from Reedsport."

"You've done a good job keeping them away from the scene," Riley said.

"I guess that's something," Alford said. "Come on, let's get this over with."

Alford led Riley and Lucy nearer to the suspended body. The body was held in a makeshift chain harness that wrapped around and around it. The harness was tied to a heavy rope that looped through a steel pulley attached to a high crossbeam. The rest of the rope descended to the ground at a sharp angle.

Riley could see the woman's face now. Once again, her resemblance to Marie shot through her like an electric shock—the same silent pain and anguish that her friend's face had displayed after she'd hanged herself. The bulging eyes and the chain that gagged the mouth made the sight all the more disturbing.

Riley looked at her new partner to see how she was reacting. Somewhat to her surprise, she saw that Lucy was already taking notes.

"Is this your first murder scene?" Riley asked her.

Lucy simply nodded while she wrote and observed. Riley thought she was taking the sight of the corpse awfully well. A lot of rookies would be off vomiting in the bushes at this point.

By contrast, Alford looked decidedly queasy. Even after all these hours, he hadn't gotten used to it. For his sake, Riley hoped that he'd never need to.

"Not much of a smell yet," Alford said.

"Not yet," Riley said. "She's still in a state of autolysis, mostly just internal cell breakdown. It's not hot enough to speed the putrefaction process along. The body hasn't started melting down from the inside. That's when the smell would get really bad."

Alford looked more and more pale at this kind of talk.

"What about rigor mortis?" Lucy asked.

"She's in full rigor, I'm sure," Riley said. "She probably will be for another twelve hours."

Lucy still didn't look the least bit fazed. She just kept jotting down more notes.

"Have you figured out how the killer got her up there?" Lucy asked Alford.

"We've got a pretty good idea," Alford said. "He climbed up and tied the pulley in place. Then he hauled the body up. You can see how it's anchored."

Alford pointed to a bundle of iron weights lying next to the tracks. The rope was tied through holes in the weights, knotted carefully so that it wouldn't come loose. The weights were the kind that might be found in weight machines at a gym.

Lucy bent down and looked at the weights more closely.

"There's almost enough weight here to completely counterbalance the body," Lucy said. "Odd that he dragged all this heavy stuff with him. You'd think he'd have just tied the rope directly to the pole."

"What does that tell you?" Riley asked.

Lucy thought for a moment.

"He's small and not very strong," Lucy said. "The pulley didn't give him enough leverage by itself. He needed the weights to help him."

"Very good," Riley said. Then she pointed to the opposite side of the train tracks. For a brief stretch, a partial tire track veered off the nearby pavement onto to the dirt. "And you can see that he pulled his vehicle up very close. He had to. He couldn't drag the body very far on his own."

Riley examined the ground near the power pole and found sharp indentations in the earth.

"It looks like he used a ladder," she said.

"Yeah, and we found the ladder," Alford said. "Come on, I'll show you."

Alford led Riley and Lucy across the tracks to a weather-beaten warehouse made of corrugated steel. There was a broken lock hanging from the hasp of the door.

"You can see how he broke in here," Alford said. "It was easy enough to do. A pair of bolt cutters would have done the trick. This warehouse isn't used for much, just long-term storage, so it's not very secure."

Alford opened the door and switched on the fluorescent overhead lights. The place was, indeed, mostly empty, except for a few shipping crates swarming with cobwebs. Alford pointed to a tall ladder leaning against the wall next to the door.

"There's the ladder," he said. "We found fresh dirt on its feet. It probably belongs here, and the killer knew about it. He broke in, dragged it out, and climbed it to tie the pulley in place. Once he got the body where he wanted it, he dragged the ladder back here. Then he drove off."

"Maybe he got the pulley from inside the warehouse too," Lucy suggested.

"The front of this warehouse is lit up at night," Alford said. "So he's bold, and I'll bet he's pretty fast, even if he isn't very strong."

At that moment there came a sharp, loud crack outside.

"What the hell?" Alford yelled.

Riley knew immediately that it was a gunshot.

CHAPTER NINE

Alford drew his gun and charged out of the warehouse. Riley and Lucy followed with their hands on their own weapons. Outside, something was hovering in circles around the pole where the body was hanging. It made a steady buzzing sound.

Young Officer Boyden had his pistol drawn. He had just taken a shot at the small drone that was circling the body and was getting ready to take another.

"Boyden, put that damned gun away!" Alford shouted. He holstered his own weapon.

Boyden turned toward Alford with surprise. Just as he was putting away his weapon, the drone rose higher and flew away.

The chief was fuming.

"What the hell did you think you were doing, firing your weapon like that?" he snarled at Boyden.

"Protecting the scene," Boyden said. "It's probably some blogger taking pictures."

"Probably," Alford said. "And I don't like that any more than you do. But it's illegal to shoot those things down. Besides, this is a populated area. You ought to know better."

Boyden hung his head sheepishly.

"Sorry, sir," he said.

Alford turned toward Riley.

"Drones, hell!" he said. "I sure do hate the twenty-first century. Agent Paige, please tell me we can take that body down now."

"Have you got more pictures than the ones I saw?" Riley asked.

"Lots of them, showing every little detail," Alford said. "You can look at them in my office."

Riley nodded. "I've seen what I needed to see here. And you've done a good job keeping the scene under control. Go ahead and cut her down."

Alford said to Boyden, "Call the county coroner. Tell him he can stop waiting around twiddling his thumbs."

"Got it, Chief," Boyden said, taking out his cell phone.

"Come on," Alford said to Riley and Lucy. He led them to his police car. When they got in and were on their way, a cop waved the car past the barricade onto the main street.

Riley took careful note of the route. The killer would have brought his vehicle in and out along this same route that both Boyden and Alford used. There was no other way into the area between the warehouse and the train tracks. It seemed likely that someone would have seen the killer's vehicle, although they might not have thought it unusual.

The Reedsport Police Department was nothing more than a little brick storefront right on the town's main street. Alford, Riley, and Lucy went inside and sat down in the chief's office.

Alford placed a stack of folders on his desk.

"Here's everything we've got," he said. "The complete file on the old case from five years ago, and everything so far on last night's murder."

Riley and Lucy each took a folder and began to browse through it. Riley's attention was drawn to the photos of the first case.

The two women were similar in age. The first one worked in a prison, which put her at some degree of risk for possible victimization. But the second one would be considered a lower risk victim. And there was no indication that either of them frequented bars or other places that would make them especially vulnerable. In both cases, those who knew the women had described them as friendly, helpful, and conventional. And yet, there had to be some factor that drew the killer to these particular women.

"Did you make any headway on Marla Blainey's murder?" Riley asked Alford.

"It was under the jurisdiction of the Eubanks police. Captain Lawson. But I worked with him on it. We found out nothing useful. The chains were perfectly ordinary. The killer could have picked them up at any hardware store."

Lucy leaned toward Riley to look at the same pictures.

"Still, he did buy a lot of them," Lucy said. "You'd think some clerk would have noticed someone buying so many chains."

Alford nodded in agreement.

"Yeah, that's what we thought at the time. But we contacted hardware stores all around these parts. None of the clerks picked up on any unusual sales like that. He must have bought a few at a time, here and there, without attracting a lot of attention. By the time he got around to the murder, he had big pile of them handy. Maybe he still does."

Riley peered closely at the straitjacket the woman was wearing. It looked identical to the one used to bind last night's victim.

"What about the straitjacket?" Riley asked.

Alford shrugged. "You'd think something like that would be easy to track. But we got nothing. It's standard issue in psychiatric hospitals. We checked all the hospitals throughout the state, including one real close by. Nobody noticed any straitjackets missing or stolen."

A silence fell as Riley and Lucy continued looking at reports and photos. The bodies had been left within ten miles of each other. That indicated that the killer probably didn't live too far away. But the first woman's corpse had been dumped unceremoniously on a riverbank. Over the five years between murders, the killer's attitude had changed in some way.

"So what do you make of this guy?" Alford asked. "Why the straitjacket and all the chains? Doesn't that seem like overkill?"

Riley thought for a moment.

"Not in his mind," she said. "It's about power. He wants to restrict his victims not just physically but symbolically. It goes way beyond the practical. It's about taking away the victim's power. The killer wants to make a real point of that."

"But why women?" Lucy asked. "If he wants to disempower his victims, wouldn't it be more dramatic with men?"

"It's a good question," Riley replied. She thought back to the crime scene—how the body had been so carefully counterbalanced.

"But remember, he's not very strong," Riley said. "It might be partly a matter of choosing easier targets. Middle-aged women like these would probably put up less of a fight. But they also probably stand for something in his mind. They weren't selected as individuals, but as *women*—and whatever it is that women represent to him."

Alford let out a cynical growl.

"So you're saying it was nothing personal," he said. "It's not like these women *did* anything to get captured and killed. It's not like the killer even thought they especially deserved it."

"That's often how it goes," Riley said. "In my last case, the killer targeted women who bought dolls. He didn't care who they were. All that mattered is that he saw them buy a doll."

Another silence fell. Alford looked at his watch.

"I've got a press conference in about a half hour," he said. "Is there anything else we need to discuss before then?"

Riley said, "Well, the sooner Agent Vargas and I can interview the victim's immediate family, the better. This evening, if that's possible."

Alford knitted his brow with concern.

"I don't think so," he said. "Her husband died young, maybe fifteen years ago. All she's got is a couple of grown-up kids, a son and a daughter, both with families of their own. They live right in town. My people have been interviewing them all day. They're really worn out and distraught. Let's give them till tomorrow before we put them through any more of that."

Riley saw that Lucy was about to object, so she stopped her with a silent gesture. It was smart of Lucy to want to interview the family immediately. But Riley also knew better than to make waves with the local force, especially if they seemed to be as competent as Alford and his team.

"I understand," Riley said. "Let's try for tomorrow morning. What about the family of the first victim?"

"I think there might still be some relatives down in Eubanks," Alford said. "I'll check into it. Let's just not rush anything. The killer's in no hurry, after all. His last murder was five years ago, and he's not liable to act again soon. Let's take time to do things right."

Alford got up from his chair.

"I'd better get ready for the press conference," he said. "Do you two want to be part of it? Have you got any kind of statement to make?"

Riley mulled it over.

"No, I don't think so," she said. "It's best if the FBI keeps a low profile for the time being. We don't want the killer to feel like he's getting a lot of publicity. He might be more likely to show himself if he doesn't think he's getting the attention he deserves. Right now, it's better for you to be the face people see."

"Well then, you can get settled in," Alford said. "I've got a couple of rooms at a local B&B reserved for you. There's also a car out front you can use."

He slid the room reservation form and a set of car keys across his desk to Riley. She and Lucy left the station.

*

Later that evening, Riley sat on a bay window seat looking out over Reedsport's main street. Dusk had fallen, and streetlights were coming on. The night air was warm and pleasant and all was quiet, with no reporters in sight.

Alford had reserved two lovely second-story rooms in the

246

B&B for Riley and Lucy. The woman who owned the place had served a delicious supper. Then Riley and Lucy had spent an hour or so in the main room downstairs making plans for tomorrow.

Reedsport truly was a quaint and lovely town. Under different circumstances, it would be nice place for a vacation. But now that Riley was away from all talk of yesterday's murder, her mind turned toward more familiar concerns.

She hadn't thought about Peterson all day until now. He was out there, and she knew it, but nobody else believed it. Had she been wise to leave things like that? Should she have tried harder to convince somebody?

It gave her a chill to think that two murderers—Peterson and whoever had killed two women here—were at this very moment going about their lives however they pleased. How many more were out there, somewhere in the state, somewhere in the country? Why was our culture plagued with these warped human beings?

What might they be doing? Were they plotting somewhere in isolation, or were they comfortably passing their time with friends and family—unsuspecting, innocent people who had no idea of the evil in their midst?

At the moment, Riley had no way to know. But it was her job to find out.

She also found herself thinking anxiously about April. It hadn't felt right to simply leave her with her father. But what else was she to do? Riley knew that even if she had not taken this case, another one would come along soon. She was simply too involved in her work to deal with an unruly teenager. She wasn't home enough.

On an impulse, Riley took out her cell phone and sent a text message.

Hey April. How are U?

After a few seconds, the reply came.

I'm fine Mom. How are U? Have U solved it yet?

It took Riley a moment to realize that April meant the new case.

Not yet, she typed.

April replied, *U'll solve it soon.*

Riley smiled at what sounded almost like a vote of confidence. She typed, *Do U want to talk? I could call U now.*

She waited a few moments for April's reply.

Not right now. I'm good.

Riley didn't know exactly what that meant. Her heart sank a little.

OK, she typed. *Goodnight. Love U.*

She ended the chat and sat there, looking out into the deepening night. She smiled wistfully as she remembered April's question ...

"Have U solved it yet?"

"It" could mean any of a huge number of things in Riley's life. And she felt a long, long way from solving any of them.

Riley stared out into the night again. Looking down at the main street, she pictured the killer driving straight through town on the way to the railroad tracks. It had been a bold move. But not nearly as bold as taking the time to hang the body from a power pole where it would be visible in the light from the warehouse.

That part of his MO had changed drastically over the last five years, from sloppily dumping a body by the river to hanging this one up for the world to see. He didn't strike Riley as particularly organized, but he was becoming more obsessive. Something in his life must have changed. What was it?

Riley knew that this kind of boldness often represented an escalating desire for publicity, for fame. That was certainly true of the last killer she had tracked down. But it felt wrong for this case. Something told Riley that this killer was not only small and rather weak, but also self-effacing, even humble.

He didn't like to kill; Riley felt pretty sure of it. And it wasn't fame that spurred him to this new level of boldness. It was sheer despair. Perhaps even remorse, a half-conscious desire to get caught.

Riley knew from personal experience that killers were never more dangerous than when they started turning against themselves.

Riley thought about something Chief Alford had said earlier.

"The killer's in no hurry, after all."

Riley felt sure that the chief was wrong.

CHAPTER TEN

Riley felt sorry for the county coroner, a middle-aged and overweight man, as he spread out the photos on Chief Alford's desk. They displayed every gruesome detail of Rosemary Pickens's autopsy. The coroner, Ben Tooley, looked slightly ill. He was undoubtedly more accustomed to examining corpses of people who had died from strokes and heart attacks. He looked as he if he hadn't slept, and she realized he'd surely been up late last night. And Riley guessed that he hadn't slept soundly whenever he had gotten to bed.

It was morning, and Riley felt remarkably rested herself. Her bed had been soft and comfortable, and neither nightmares nor real intruders had disturbed her sleep. She had badly needed a night like that. Lucy and Chief Alford also looked alert—but the coroner was another story.

"This is as bad as Marla Blainey's murder five years ago," Tooley said. "Worse, maybe. Lord, after that one, I'd hoped we'd put this kind of awful thing behind us. No such luck."

Tooley showed the group a close-up of the back of the woman's head. A large, deep wound was visible, and the surrounding hair was matted with blood.

"She sustained a sharp blow to the left parietal bone," he said. "It was hard enough to crack the skull slightly. Probably caused concussion, maybe even a short interval of unconsciousness."

"What kind of object was used?" Riley asked.

"Judging from the pulled hair and scraping, I'd say it was a blow from a heavy chain. Marla Blainey had the same kind of wound in about the same place."

Alford shook his head. "This guy is all about chains," he said. "Reporters are already calling him the 'chain killer.'"

Lucy pointed to some tight close-ups of the woman's abdomen.

"Do you think she was beaten generally, over time?" she asked. "Those bruises look bad."

"They're bad, all right, but they're not from being beaten," Tooley said. "She's got contusions like that all over from being chained so tightly. Between the chains and how tight the straitjacket was, she spent a lot of time in severe pain. Same with

Marla Blainey."

The group fell silent for a moment, mulling over the significance of this information.

Finally Lucy said, "We know that he's small and not very strong—and we're assuming that it really is a 'he.' So it looks like he must've subdued each of the women with a single sharp blow to the head. When they were dazed or unconscious, he lugged them into a nearby vehicle."

Riley nodded with approval. It struck her as a good guess.

"So how was she treated during her captivity?" Alford asked.

Tooley shuffled the photos to reveal images of the dissected body.

"Pretty badly," he said. "I found almost no stomach contents. Not much in her intestines either. He must have kept her alive on water alone. But he probably wasn't trying to starve her to death. That would have taken much longer. Maybe he was just trying to weaken her. Again, it was the same with Marla Blainey. The slashed throats were the decisive and fatal blows."

Another silence fell. There was little left for anyone to say, but much to think about. Riley's head was abuzz with too many questions to ask. Why did the killer hold these women captive? The usual motives didn't apply here. He didn't torture or rape them. If he'd always intended to kill them, why had he taken his time about it? Did it take time for him to build up the will to do that?

Obviously, she thought, the killer was obsessed with rendering his victims helpless. That gave him some kind of satisfaction. He'd probably suffered similar helplessness himself, maybe in childhood. She also suspected that he'd starved the victims for other reasons than simply to weaken them. Had the killer been starved himself at one time or another?

Riley stifled a sigh. There were so many questions. There always were this early in a case. Meanwhile, there was a lot of work to do.

*

Two hours later, Riley was driving Alford's loaner car south along the Hudson River, with Lucy as a passenger. They were on their way to Eubanks, the town where Marla Blainey had lived and was murdered. They had just left Rosemary Pickens's house, where they had interviewed her two grown children.

Riley reviewed the meeting in her mind. It hadn't been very

productive, and the distraught brother and sister hadn't offered any solid information. They had no idea why their mother, always a kindly and helpful soul, would be targeted for such a brutal crime.

Still, Riley was now glad that she had left much of the questioning to Lucy. Again, she was impressed by her new partner's work—especially her ability to deal with people who were undergoing terrible shock and grief. Lucy had gently gotten the brother and sister to reminisce about their mother quite freely.

Courtesy of Lucy's sympathetic questions, a portrait of Rosemary Pickens was becoming clearer. She had been a loving, witty, and generous woman who would be badly missed by her family and everyone else in Reedsport. Riley knew how important it was to develop this kind of understanding of a murder victim. Lucy was definitely doing good work so far.

As Riley drove along the two-lane road that bordered the wide Hudson River, she realized that she still knew very little about the talented young agent who was sitting beside her. Right now Lucy appeared to be deep in thought, undoubtedly considering the meager facts they had so far.

"Tell me something about yourself, Lucy," Riley said.

"Like what?" Lucy asked, looking at Riley with surprise.

Riley shrugged. "Well, you're not married, I take it. Have you got a significant other?"

"Not at the moment," Lucy said.

"How about the future?"

Lucy thought quietly for a moment.

"I don't know, Riley," she said at last. "I guess I'm not one for long-term attachments. Whenever I try to imagine life with a husband and kids, my mind just goes blank. Believe me, that kind of attitude doesn't go down well with a Mexican-American family. Some of my brothers and sisters have already got kids. My parents expect the same from me. I'm afraid they're going to be disappointed. But what can I do?"

Lucy fell silent again. Then she said, "It's just that I already love this job so much. There's good work to be done. I want to give it everything I've got, make a real difference in the world. I don't see how I could make time for anything else—not even a relationship. Does that sound selfish?"

Riley smiled rather sadly.

"Not selfish at all," she said.

By contrast, Riley had to wonder about her own choices. She'd tried to have it all—a marriage, a family, a demanding job. Had that been selfish of her? If she'd started off with Lucy's

251

priorities, might things be better?

But then I wouldn't have April, she thought. *And April ... April is worth the extra effort.* She loved her daughter dearly and hoped that she hadn't botched the job of raising her to be a genuinely good adult.

A moment later they pulled into Eubanks. The town was larger than Reedsport, but it still wasn't hard to find the modest but pleasant two-story house. Two men were sitting a swing chair on the front porch. They rose to their feet when Riley and Lucy got out of the car and walked toward the house. A stocky, uniformed man of about Riley's age stepped forward to greet them.

"I'm Dwight Slater, officer in charge here in Eubanks," he said.

Riley and Lucy introduced themselves. The other man was tall with a strong, friendly face.

"This is Craig Blainey, Marla's widower," Slater said.

Blainey greeted Riley and Lucy with a handshake.

"Sit down, make yourselves comfortable," he said in a startlingly deep and pleasant voice. It occurred to Riley that he might make a good preacher.

Slater and Blainey sat back down on the swing chair, and Riley and Lucy sat in a pair of outdoor chairs facing it.

Riley began with the essentials.

"Mr. Blainey, it may seem strange for me to say so at this late date, but I'm very sorry for your loss. And I'm also sorry to have to dredge up what must be terrible memories. My partner and I will try to keep this short."

Blainey nodded.

"I appreciate that," he said. "But you should take as much time as you need. I understand there's been a new murder up in Reedsport. I'm very sorry to hear it. But if I can do or say anything to put a stop to this monster, it will do my heart good."

Riley took out a notepad and began to write. She noticed that Lucy did the same.

"What kind of work do you do, Mr. Blainey?" she asked.

"I own a hardware store. It's been in my family for a couple of generations. That tradition's coming to an end with me, though." His smile turned a bit melancholy. "My kids aren't interested in keeping the family business going. Not that I can complain, they're doing fine on their own. Jill's studying at the University of Buffalo and Alex is a radio announcer over on Long Island."

A note of pride had come into his voice.

Riley nodded to Lucy, a silent signal to go ahead and ask her own questions.

"Do you have any other family here in Eubanks?" Lucy asked.

"My brother and sister used to live here, and they've got kids of their own. But the whole thing with Marla …"

Blainey paused for a moment to control a surge of emotion.

"Well, this town was never the same for them after that. The memory was just too awful. They had to get away. Amy and her family resettled in Philadelphia, and Baxter and his family moved up to Maine."

Blainey shrugged and shook his head.

"Don't know why I didn't feel the same way. I just felt all the more rooted here, for some reason. But then, I'm the type to remember the good times more than the bad. And Marla and I had a lot of good times here."

Blainey looked off into space with a wistful expression, lost for a moment in memories. Lucy spoke gently to bring him back to the present.

"I understand that your wife was a corrections officer," she said.

"That's right. In the men's penitentiary across the river."

Riley could see that Lucy was thinking hard about how to pose her next question as delicately as possible.

"Mr. Blainey, being a prison guard's a tough job, even for a man," Lucy said. "For a woman, it can be brutal. And whether you're a man or a woman, it's pretty much impossible not to make enemies. Some of those enemies can be very bad people. And they don't stay in prison forever."

Blainey sighed and shook his head, still smiling sadly.

"I know what you're getting at," he said. "It was the same five years ago. The police from Albany wanted to know about enemies she'd made there. They were just sure the killer had to be a former inmate with a personal grudge."

Dwight Slater looked at Lucy and Riley earnestly.

"The thing is, I knew Marla Blainey really well," Slater said. "She and Craig here were like family to me. And believe me, Marla wasn't your stereotypical prison guard. You know the type I mean—sadistic, mean, corrupt. The truth is, a lot of people didn't know what to make of her."

Blainey nodded in agreement and rose from the chair.

"Come on inside," he said. "I'll show you a few things."

Riley, Lucy, and Slater all followed him into neat, comfortable living room. Blainey invited them to sit and make themselves comfortable. There were plenty of family pictures on

253

the wall—picnics, graduations, births, weddings, school pictures. It was easy to see that Craig Blainey truly had surrounded himself with the best of memories.

As Blainey opened a roll-top desk and shuffled through its contents, Riley's eyes fell upon a photograph of Marla Blainey in her correction officer's uniform. The woman was tall like her husband, with a similar strong, determined face. Even so, she had a smile that fairly lit up the living room even five years after her horrible death.

When Blainey found what he'd been looking for, he handed Riley and Lucy each a couple of handwritten letters. Just a glance at the letters was enough to surprise Riley.

They were thank-you messages from former inmates at the prison where Marla had worked. The men wrote to thank her for kindnesses she had showed them during their incarcerations—a word of encouragement, something to read, a bit of useful advice. The men had clearly put their criminal lives behind them. They felt that they owed at least a little of their success in the world outside to Marla.

Blainey talked while they read.

"I don't want to give the impression that Marla had an easy time with her job, or that everybody liked her. She was surrounded all day long by bad people—liars and manipulators, most of them. She didn't let herself get drawn into inappropriate friendships. She was a prison guard, and of course some of the prisoners had no use for her, actually hated her. Even so, I don't think she ever *made* any real enemies, even there."

While Blainey spoke, Dwight Slater looked around the room, enjoying his own share of memories. He said, "I talk to the warden from time to time, and he still says she probably did more genuine good there than the social workers on his staff. She was like that with everybody."

Riley looked at Lucy and saw that she shared her surprise. Who would have thought that a female prison guard would have been such a beloved character? And why on earth had someone chosen to take her life in such a hideous manner?

Blainey's hospitable smile widened.

"Well, I'm sure you've got more questions," he said. "Would you like something to drink? Maybe some iced tea? I brewed some fresh just a little while ago."

"That would be nice," Riley said.

"Yes, please," Lucy said.

Riley nodded in agreement, but her mind was already

elsewhere. She was beginning to feel familiar nudges just beneath her conscious awareness. She knew that her ability to get inside the mind of a murderer was rare, and she also knew that she was usually right about whatever came to her.

That meant there was something else she really needed to see.

Something important.

CHAPTER ELEVEN

A short time later, Riley and Lucy were in their car again, following along behind Slater. As always when approaching a crime scene, Riley felt her senses quicken into sharper alertness.

It hadn't been easy to persuade Slater to lead them there. As far as he was concerned, there was nothing at all to see—especially after all these years. Even so, Riley was anxious to get a look at the site where Marla Blainey's body had been left. She knew that photographs couldn't tell her what actual places sometimes could.

A short distance out of town, the two-lane road crossed the railroad tracks and continued along the edge of the river. Slater pulled onto the shoulder of the road. Riley pulled their car in behind him.

"I think this is where it was," Slater said, getting out of his car. "It's hard to remember after all these years."

"Let me look at those photos again," Riley said.

Slater handed her the folder full of photos of the Blainey crime scene. Riley peered through the trees at the side of the road. The bank sloped sharply down to the river's edge, which was only about fifteen feet away.

Riley compared the spot to a photo of the body that had been taken from the road. The underbrush had changed over the years, and for a moment it was hard to see any resemblance between the photo and the actual place.

In the photo, she saw that Marla's body, bound in chains and a straitjacket, lay in a heap against a fallen tree trunk. Riley stepped into the long grass beside the road. There it was, the same tree trunk down there next to the water's edge.

"You're right, this is the place," she told Slater. "How do you think he got the body down there?"

Slater shrugged. "There wasn't much to it," he said. "He pulled his vehicle about where we are right now. Then he just rolled the body down the bank. The grass and brush were mashed down all the way."

He pointed to the photo Riley was holding.

"You can see just the edge of a tire track right there on the shoulder," he said. "Probably a van, but we couldn't track down the vehicle. Nobody noticed the body for several days—not until someone saw buzzards circling."

As Riley compared the photo and the actual scene, she realized that she was standing on the exact spot where the killer had dumped the body. She gazed down the slope for a long moment, taking in the scene. She began to picture the chained and straitjacketed body rolling down the hill. Then she noticed that Lucy was staring at her intently. It struck her as odd. She returned Lucy's gaze with quizzical look.

"Oh, I'm sorry for staring," Lucy said, a bit embarrassed. "It's just that … well, I've heard you've got uncanny instincts when you're at a crime scene. They say it's like you get right into a killer's head, feel what he felt, see what he saw, understand exactly what he was thinking."

Riley didn't know what to say. She often did, indeed, become deeply absorbed in crime scenes. And her capacity to identify with a killer's perspective sometimes disturbed even her. It was just her way of doing things, but Lucy was making it sound like an almost legendary skill. It made Riley feel uncomfortable and self-conscious.

In any case, she wasn't getting any vibes from where she was standing, no sense of the killer's thoughts. She didn't know whether that was because the place was too nondescript or because of the other people watching.

"Hold this for a moment," she told Lucy, handing her the folder.

Then Riley scrambled down the slope, leaving Lucy and Slater watching in surprise.

"You be careful," Slater called after her.

"Do you want me to come too?" Lucy asked.

"No, I'm okay," Riley called back. "You stay there."

The slope was steep and more treacherous than it looked from the roadside. She stumbled down against brush and branches, scraping herself a good bit along the way. The sharp descent was also a stern reminder that she was still hurting from her recent injuries. Muscles that had just started to feel better suddenly began to ache again.

Finally, she reached the bottom of the slope. She stood beside the fallen log, only about a yard away from the water's edge. This was it—the place where Marla's body had fallen and stayed until it was discovered. The quiet was interrupted by the noise of a speedboat tearing down the river a short distance away. Its wake of gentle wavelets broke against the log, then died away into stillness.

Drawing upon the memory of the photo, Riley pictured

Marla's body lying at her feet. She could see it clearly. She also realized that, if not for the log, the body would probably have kept right on rolling into the river. It had only gotten caught here by accident. Working in the dark, the killer might not have even realized that the body hadn't gone all the way into the water.

Judging from the slope, Riley guessed that the water was deep right here. Weighted down with chains, the body might well have sunk without a trace. It might never have been found.

At last, she began to feel a tingle of understanding. This woman's body, like the place itself, had meant nothing to the killer by the time he dumped it here. It might be discovered or it might not be—it didn't matter to him one way or the other. The chains and the straitjacket had been solely a matter between him and his victim. They were used to torment the women, and they had some special meaning for the killer. They hadn't been for public display.

Something drastic had changed between the two killings. Now the killer wanted desperately for everyone to see the full horror of his deed. With the second victim, he was trying to communicate something that he hadn't cared about the first time.

Riley groaned under her breath. It was likely to mean that the killer was going to accelerate. Whatever was driving him was stronger now. Whatever he'd kept under control for five years was pushing harder at him to show the world his pain.

At that moment, her phone buzzed. She took it out of her pocket. She was surprised to see that it was a text from April.

Hey Mom, it said simply.

Riley felt deeply startled by the sheer incongruity. Here she was, standing exactly where a corpse had once been abandoned, receiving a text from her daughter who oftentimes wanted nothing to do with her. Should she explain that now was not a good time to exchange texts?

Hi April, she wrote back. *What's going on?*

The reply came quickly …

School ends tomorrow. I have my last exam in the morning.

Riley typed, *Are you ready?*

I dunno, April replied.

Riley sighed. Her conversation with her daughter had already become perfectly meaningless.

But then April typed:

I want to talk.

Riley's heart surged with unexpected emotion.

Me too, she typed. *Could you wait till I get back to my room?*

April's next text took her thoroughly by surprise.

Not on the phone. Right here. Come home and let's talk.

CHAPTER TWELVE

Riley came to a stop on the Amtrak platform. She still had doubts about what she was doing, even though she and Lucy had talked it through more than once. They both felt sure that nothing more was going to happen here in Reedsport. The chain killer had struck in two different towns, and whenever he killed again it was likely to be somewhere else.

"I still don't know about this, Lucy," Riley said. "I don't usually leave a case in progress."

"It's okay," Lucy replied with a hint of exasperation. "I know what to do. Interview everybody I can. Go to the funeral in case he's there. Check out who sends flowers."

At that moment, the conductor called out, "All aboard!"

Riley said, "If anything important happens, I'll come right back."

"Go," Lucy said firmly.

"Thanks," Riley replied.

The little BAU jet that had brought them to Reedsport had left almost immediately after their arrival, so it wasn't a travel option this time. Lucy had offered to drive Riley to Albany to catch a flight home, but Riley had chosen the train instead. It would take her right to Quantico, with just a change in New York City. The trip would give her a chance to go over her files and consider the mind of a killer.

She climbed up into the spacious business class car and took her seat. She had two big chairs to herself, giving her room to spread out as much as she wanted to. She looked out the window as the train started to pull out of the station. Lucy was nowhere in sight. Riley knew that she was headed straight back to work.

She tilted the chair into a reclining position and started to relax. The steady, friendly rumbling and soothing vibration of the train car helped Riley begin to process information with her customary mental skill. To begin with, there was the question of just why the killer had starved both victims. Of course he must have meant to weaken them. Riley also felt pretty sure that he had probably been starved earlier in his own life and felt compelled to inflict the same suffering on others.

But now something else occurred to her. Feeding the women

would have meant acknowledging their humanity. In doing that, he might run the risk of feeling sympathy for them. They were of use to him only as objects, as *symbols* of whatever had hurt or enraged him in the past.

Riley breathed deeply. Yes, she beginning to feel connected with him—much more than she had at either crime site.

He's human, she thought. *He's all too human.*

He was not some cold and unfeeling sociopath. He was likely to be capable of sympathy and even kindness. Those were the very qualities that he feared most about himself, because they might well be his undoing.

Riley closed her eyes. She could feel the staggering effort it took for him to suppress his human qualities. And weak as he was, how long he could handle the strain and effort of being a murderous animal? All he knew was that he had no choice.

Something else began to make more sense to her. The shocking staging of his most recent murder, with the body hanging where everyone could see it, was not just an attempt to shock the world. It was also for his own benefit. He had a need to convince everybody—including himself—that he was far more savage than he appeared to be.

As his desperation mounted, Riley knew, his crimes were likely to become ever more outrageously vicious. He couldn't allow himself to display the slightest telltale hint of mercy or humanity. He must do his best to become a monster beyond even his own imagining.

The steady click-clacking of train wheels was having a pleasantly hypnotic effect. Riley hadn't thought she was tired, but now she realized she'd been under considerable strain for the last couple of days. She closed her eyes.

As Riley huddled in the musty crawlspace, her cage door opened and a stream of flame broke through the pitch darkness. The white light blinded her for a moment. The flame of that propane torch was the only thing she ever saw in this awful place—aside from the glimpses it gave of Peterson himself.

Now her tormentor's face took form again as he taunted her with the hissing flame, forcing her to dodge its extreme heat. She couldn't quite see what he looked like, but his presence was becoming familiar all the same.

"Welcome home," Peterson said gleefully.

"This is not my home," Riley said.

"It's the only home you deserve."

261

Riley wished she could grab the torch away from him and turn it against him. But his motions were too deft and swift. All she could do was duck and dodge, trying to escape being burned.

"I'm going to kill you," she said, mustering a tone of defiance. "I want you to know that."

Peterson chuckled grimly.

"Welcome home," he said again.

Riley was awakened by the conductor's shout …

"Penn Station!"

It was time to change trains.

*

As she drove into Fredericksburg that evening, Riley kept repeating in her mind: *One monster at a time.*

The dream about Peterson had left her badly shaken, troubling her during the rest of her train trip to Quantico. Even so, she'd managed to get a fair amount of work done. She'd run searches on her laptop using the train's Wi-Fi service, and pored over her own copy of the case documents and photos. She had emailed a report directly to Brent Meredith. There was no pressing need to stop at the BAU, so she had decided to drive straight to Ryan's house where April was waiting for her.

Riley reminded herself that monsters took many forms. Right now, she wanted to focus on an altogether different monster—the monstrosity that her personal life had become. Perhaps there was hope of conquering this one, of reshaping it to a more agreeable form. After much grief and rebellion, April now wanted to talk to her. It was a positive sign. Riley wasn't going to let her daughter down, not this time.

Besides, Riley was well aware that she needed to make some serious changes in her life. There wasn't much point in waiting for a break between cases. There seldom seemed to be much of a break, and there probably wouldn't be one in the foreseeable future.

First, she figured that she had to move out of her little house. Peterson's break-in proved that it was much too isolated and vulnerable. When she'd first rented it, she and Ryan had just split, and she had felt financially insecure. The place outside of Fredericksburg had been all she could afford, and it had served to get her far away from her former life.

But the divorce would be final soon, and Ryan had agreed to

pay regular child support instead of the erratic contributions he was kicking in now. He'd actually become generous, which she recognized as his way of freeing himself from any other responsibilities toward their daughter.

That was fine with Riley. She would be happy to have full care of April, and she desperately wanted to be a good mother to her. She just had to figure out how to manage her own responsibilities better than she had in the recent past.

Looking out her car window, Riley saw that she was driving past rows of attractive townhouses. When her supplementary income became steady and predictable, she could seriously think about a new place to live, maybe even about buying something suitable in town. It would be good to have neighbors, and the location would be convenient for April's school. And Fredericksburg was big enough that she wouldn't have to worry about crossing paths with Ryan.

The prospect of raising April on her own brought up another issue that had been on her mind. Riley couldn't escape the fact that she spent a lot of time away from home. She needed someone to help take care of her daughter.

Gabriela was the obvious choice. She and April really liked each other, and April wouldn't object to their longtime housekeeper being around to keep tabs on her.

Might Gabriela agree to move in with them if she could have a room and bath of her own? Or at least stay over when Riley had to be away for days at a time? Riley made a mental note to talk it over with Gabriela as soon as she got the chance.

When Riley reached her destination, she drove her car up the driveway and under the carport alongside the house. When she got out of the car and walked to the front door, she rang the doorbell, as had become customary since she moved out. Gabriela answered with an anxious look on her face.

"Señora Riley!" she exclaimed. "Do you know where April is?"

CHAPTER THIRTEEN

Shock jolted Riley's entire body.

"Isn't April here?" she asked.

"She was, but not now," Gabriela said. "*Vente!* Come in!"

Riley stepped inside and Gabriela shut the door.

"She was here when I went out to the *tienda* for groceries," Gabriela explained. "When I came back she wasn't here. I told Señor Ryan, and he said not to worry. But still I worried. She said nothing about going out. I don't understand."

Riley's agitation mounted.

"Where's Ryan?" she asked.

"Having dinner."

Gabriela led Riley to the dining room. Ryan was seated at the table, simultaneously picking at his dinner and talking on his cell phone. Another place was set, but it had not been used. Gabriela nervously began clearing the table.

"That will be fine," Ryan said to whoever was on the phone— a client, Riley guessed. "I'll be there at nine. We'll take care of everything tonight."

He ended the call and looked up at Riley with surprise.

"I hadn't expected you here today," he said. "I thought you had a case in Upstate New York. How's it going?"

"Where is April?" Riley asked.

"How should I know?" Ryan replied with an annoyed shrug. "She's in one of her moods. She gets that from you, not me. Do you think she'd tell me anything?"

Riley ignored her ex-husband's accusatory tone.

"Where have you been today?" she asked.

"Not that I have to report my comings and goings," Ryan said. "But I've actually been upstairs all day, working in my home office. I haven't left the house since this morning. I've barely been out of the office. I've been busy."

"Did April come home from school?"

Ryan finished his meal and set his napkin down.

"Yeah, and we had a fight. Don't ask me what it was all about. I couldn't make any sense out of it. I sent her to her room, told her not to come out until she was ready to apologize. I thought she'd stayed there until Gabriela came to my office and told me she was gone."

Ryan got up from the table and started to walk away.

"Look, I've got to get ready to go meet a client," he said. "It's a lot more important than this, believe me—especially since you expect me to be so generous with my support payments. Honestly, I don't understand why you and Gabriela are in such a panic. The girl took off in a huff, and she'll come back when she feels like it."

Riley stepped in front of Ryan, blocking his exit.

"She did *not* take off in a huff," Riley said. "She said she wanted to talk to me, and I texted her that I was coming back. She was expecting me. She wouldn't have left the house."

"Well, that's exactly what she did, apparently," Ryan said. "She's probably at your house right now."

Riley felt a glimmer of hope. Was it possible that April had expected to meet Riley at her own house? Might her daughter be waiting there for her?

Riley pulled out her cell phone and dialed her own landline number. She listened to her recorded answering machine message, then after the beep she said, "April, if you're there, pick up. I came back to see you."

There was no response.

Then she tried April's cell phone number. When she got April's voice mail message, she couldn't stop herself from yelling. "April, if you're there, pick up. Where are you? You've got me scared to death. Call me right now."

Riley ended the call and stood staring at the phone in her hand.

"She'll call whenever she feels like it," Ryan said. "Now if you don't mind—"

He tried to push by Riley, but she wouldn't let him pass.

"You're not going anywhere," she said.

"I've got a client, Riley."

Riley's voice was shaking with barely restrained rage and fear.

"You've got a daughter too," she said.

Riley turned around and saw that Gabriela was standing in the kitchen doorway, looking stricken and horrified.

"Gabriela, what time did you go out for groceries?" Riley asked.

"About three, I think," Gabriela said. "April's bedroom door was open and she was there. When I got back, she was not in the house and I told Señor Ryan."

Riley turned toward Ryan again. His expression was still

unconcerned. She found it maddening that he couldn't see how serious the situation was.

"Did anyone come to the door this afternoon?" Riley asked.

"I don't know. Like I said, I've been in my office the whole day," Ryan said.

"Ryan, *think*. Did you hear the doorbell at all today?"

Ryan paused to think for a moment.

"Once, I think. In the afternoon. Yes, I did hear a car pull up and then the doorbell. It was after I'd sent April to her room. I'm sure Gabriela answered it."

Riley turned to the housekeeper.

"Gabriela, did you answer the door for anybody today?"

"I did not hear the doorbell ring all day."

Riley was now shaking with alarm and ager. She turned back to Ryan.

"Gabriela did *not* answer the door," she said to him fiercely. "She was out getting groceries. April answered the door, and she's been gone ever since. By now, she could have been missing for four hours. Gabriela told you, and you didn't care."

Ryan was starting to get flustered now.

"Look, you're making too much of this," he said. "It was probably her boyfriend. He probably drove up and she took off with him. When she gets back, I'm going to ground her but good. You should have done it long ago."

Riley's mind flashed back to catching April and her boyfriend smoking pot in her back yard.

"Have you even met her boyfriend?" Riley snapped. "His name is Brian, and he's fourteen or fifteen. He doesn't drive. It wasn't him, and it wasn't any of her friends. She doesn't have friends with cars. Jesus, Ryan, don't you know *anything* about your daughter?"

Riley didn't wait for a reply. She pushed past Ryan and headed straight up the stairs to April's room. Ryan and Gabriela followed her. As Gabriela had said, the door had been left open. The room was its typical mess.

Again Riley took out her phone and dialed April's number. This time, her heart dropped. She could have sworn she heard a buzzing from the bed.

She rushed over to the bed and pushed aside some clothes and her heart stopped.

It was right there.

Riley picked up the buzzing phone and stared at it in horror.

April didn't have her phone.

And that could only mean one thing.
She was taken.

CHAPTER FOURTEEN

April cringed at the sound of the man's footsteps overhead. He was pacing back and forth on the wooden deck less than a foot above her head, chuckling to himself, occasionally laughing out loud. She struggled to keep from screaming. He had told her he would shoot her if she screamed, and she was sure that he would.

She knew that the man walking on the deck was Peterson. It had to be him. Like everyone else, April had doubted her mom's conviction that Peterson was still alive. She had wanted to believe that the murderer who had once captured her mother was dead. But he was alive and now he had taken her.

She remembered with horror the little that Mom had said about this man, about how he had treated her as a captive. But April was even more terrified by what her mother *hadn't* told her. She was sure that her mother had held back the truth of her own suffering. She always did that to spare April, but now April dreaded finding out what horrors had been left unsaid.

Even after hours in captivity, April still didn't have any idea where she was. When Peterson had dragged her out of the car trunk, she'd glimpsed a small house with a large raised deck. But how long had she been in that trunk? How far away from home had they traveled?

When he'd pulled her from the trunk, he'd ripped the duct tape gag off her mouth, and she'd still been too scared to scream. Then he'd carried her over his shoulder to the house, shoved her under the deck, slapped a barrier in place, and just left her there, still bound hand and foot. She had writhed and twisted in panic but the plastic restraints held tight.

When she had been able to stop her body from shaking, she had looked around her prison. The base of the deck was enclosed with wooden lattice. He had removed one section to put her in this cage and the fastened it back in place. She thought that the lattice was made of fairly flimsy wood—but she didn't dare try to kick it out. Not now, with Peterson walking right overhead.

April squirmed around in the shallow space. She could sit up but she couldn't stand. She leaned back against the house foundation. It was dim under the deck, but it was still daylight outside. From what she could see through the square holes of the lattice, the house seemed isolated. The land all around was barren except for a few scattered trees. She could see no sign of other houses and she had no idea how far away the nearest human being might be.

The sound of his footsteps and laughter was becoming maddening.

How could I have been so stupid? she wondered. But she knew that her stupidity had started earlier than today. She had let him set her up to be easily captured. When he'd come to her father's front door, she'd recognized him right away. He'd been the driver that she and Brian had hitched a ride with a few days ago. Now she realized that he'd been targeting her all along.

The split second she'd seen the gun in his hand, she'd tried to push the front door shut. But he moved too quickly, grabbing her wrist and forcing it painfully behind her back. He kept her arm tight and the gun pressed against her back as he walked along the front sidewalk. For a moment she'd frozen in her tracks. It was from fear, not resistance. The man had been startled and he'd staggered, planting one foot in the flowerbed.

Will anyone see that footprint? April wondered. *Does anybody even know I'm missing?*

Maybe she could have seized that moment and … done what? Attacked the man? Tried to take his gun away? It was a joke to imagine she could have overpowered him.

She kept replaying the whole thing in her head. Peterson's car had been backed up under the portico at the side of her father's house. It was a newer, fancier car than the one he'd been driving when she and Brian had hitched with him. The trunk was already open when he walked April around to the back of it.

She shuddered as she remembered what he'd done next. Still holding her at gunpoint, he had forced her to gag her own mouth with duct tape and bind her own wrists with plastic restraints. The indignity had made the horror even worse.

She felt vaguely ashamed now.

I shouldn't have cooperated, she thought. *I was a coward.*

But what would have happened if she'd refused to bind and gag herself? He probably would have killed right then and there. Her father, so absorbed with his work in his office, so lost in his own little world, might not even hear the gunshot. It would be left to poor Gabriela to find her body when she got home from buying groceries.

She'd struggled in terror when he bound her ankles together in the trunk. After that she'd been completely helpless.

Now her whole body hurt from the bumpy ride in the trunk and from struggling against the restraints. She was hungry, too, and tired. She fought down the screams and sobs she could feel rising in her throat. She knew that Peterson would kill her if she did anything to attract attention. And she mustn't waste her energy. She had to stay alert, pay attention, not miss the slightest opportunity.

Suddenly something dawned on her—something almost like hope. Her mother was coming back from her job today. She might even be back in Fredericksburg already. If so, she surely she knew that April was missing.

He was laughing louder now, and the clomping of his feet sounded like he was dancing a jig. April couldn't keep quiet a moment longer.

"My mother's going to find me!" she shouted. "And when she does she'll kill you!"

The sounds overhead stopped. All was silent for a moment. Then came another quiet chuckle.

"Oh, she'll come looking for you, all right," he said. "I'm counting on it."

The sound of his footsteps changed. This time he was coming down the porch steps. She shivered deeply with fear. Then he pulled loose a piece of lattice and looked in through the opening. He climbed under the deck, leering at her, holding some kind of metal cylinder in his hand.

What was it? A fire extinguisher? What on earth would he be doing with a fire extinguisher?

Suddenly there was an eruption of hissing white flame. Now she knew what it was. It was a propane torch. Mom had mentioned the torch. But she hadn't told April just what he had done to her with it.

"Come here, pretty thing," he said over the rumble of the flame.

He crawled toward her, waving the flame in front of her. She backed more tightly against the house.

"Come right here and I'll melt those restraints right off of you," he said.

April couldn't move a muscle. She was paralyzed with fear.

"Scared of the flame?" he said. "So was your mother. Well. Just wait till you get good and hungry. Then maybe you'll be braver. We'll just have to see."

April pressed her mouth into her clenched fists to keep herself from screaming.

Peterson switched off the torch and crawled out from under the deck, closing the opening behind him. She heard him walk back up the steps and across the deck. She heard him enter the house and shut the door.

Should she scream now? No, it was too dangerous, and besides, she was sure that nobody would hear her.

She realized that it was just starting to get dark. What would it be like after the light was gone? What would he do to her then? She wondered if it was possible for her to be frightened to death.

Mom, she prayed silently. *I beg you. You're all I have in this world. Find me.*

CHAPTER FIFTEEN

Riley stared at the buzzing phone in her hand and knew that her worst fears had come true.

"So she forgot to take the phone with her," Ryan said weakly.

"She didn't forget. She never goes anywhere without it. She's practically glued to the damn thing."

Ryan stared at her blankly. Riley could see that he was starting to grasp the awful truth of the situation. She pushed past him again and headed back downstairs. As she strode toward the front door, she glanced around the living room, looking for anything unusual or out of place. Nothing caught her eye.

She rushed outside and walked around to the portico where her own car was parked. She saw that the garage behind the house was closed. No one could see that Ryan's car was inside. No one would assume that he was at home today.

A scenario was unfolding in Riley's head. When Gabriela went out for groceries, someone watching the house might well have thought that April was in the house alone. And the truth was, April might as well been have been alone, with Ryan so isolated in his office at the back of the house and so focused on his work.

So what might have happened if April had answered the door and found herself face to face with a stranger?

What if the stranger had a gun?

Riley retraced her steps back to toward the house. As she glanced back and forth, something new caught her eye. It was a boot print in the flowerbed, just off the edge of the sidewalk. It was too big to be from Ryan's foot, much less Gabriela's, and besides, it was extremely fresh.

Someone had been thrown off balance, stumbled, and left the print in the dirt.

Riley felt the air rush out of her lungs. She couldn't breathe for a moment. Whoever was here had possessed the sheer nerve to abduct a teenager in broad daylight. She knew who that someone must be.

Ryan and Gabriela were now standing on the front steps.

"Call 911," she yelled at Ryan. "Tell them our daughter has been kidnapped."

Ryan couldn't seem to speak. His face was glazed over with

mute shock.

"Do it!" Riley yelled.

Startled into alertness, Ryan nodded in agreement. He hurried back into the house, followed by Gabriela.

Riley took out her own cell phone, wondering who to call first. The BAU hotline was efficient for emergencies. Even so, Riley was wary about calling that number. By now the FBI was teeming with rumors about Riley's obsessive belief that Peterson was still alive—a belief that no one else shared. What if she couldn't get anyone to listen to her?

Instead, she called Brent Meredith's personal number. To her relief, he answered immediately.

"Riley?" he said. "Is something going on?"

"I need your help," she cried. "My daughter has been kidnapped."

"April?" Meredith replied, sounding stunned. "Are you sure?"

Riley moaned aloud. Meredith had always been her one true ally at the agency other than Bill. What would happen if he thought this was just a case of typical teen behavior?

"I'm sure," Riley said. "It's Peterson, sir. He's taken her. You've got to believe me."

A brief silence fell.

"I believe you, Agent Paige," Meredith finally said. "Where did this happen? When was she taken?"

Riley suddenly felt disoriented, confused by her sheer panic.

"It's—I'm—" she stammered. "I'm where I used to live, in Fredericksburg, my ex-husband's house. She was taken right here. Sometime this afternoon."

"Has anyone called 911?"

"Ryan did just now."

The sound of Meredith's voice was low and calming.

"Good. Stay put. Don't try to do anything just yet. I'll put together all the information we've got on Peterson. I'll get everything underway. I'll send some agents to you right away. Sit tight."

"I'll do that, sir," Riley said, stifling a sob. "Thank you."

The phone call ended, and Riley went back in the house. Ryan was standing by the fireplace, numbly staring into space. Poor Gabriela was sitting on the couch sobbing helplessly.

"*Es mi culpa, es mi culpa,*" Gabriela kept saying as she wept uncontrollably.

"No it's not, Gabriela," Riley said. She sat down beside her and patted her hand. "It's not your fault. You couldn't have known."

Ryan turned his gaze bitterly on Riley.

"This is your fault," he said.

Riley had to choke back her rage. She knew what she wanted to say.

"Damn right, this is my fault. It's my fault for thinking I could trust you with April. It's my fault for thinking you gave a shit about her or anyone else."

Riley kept such thoughts to herself. Now was no time for recriminations, however justified. Too much was at state to indulge her anger. Now was the time for cool, clear-headed action.

She paced the living room, wondering what Meredith was doing right now. Putting herself in his situation, she knew that one of the first things he'd want was a photo of Peterson. It would be necessary to get lots of copies of it out there. Police would need them to go door to door asking people if they had seen the man.

But Peterson was, after all, a shadowy figure whose past was all but unknown. The only existing picture of him that Riley knew of was a mug shot taken when he'd been arrested for a minor offense years ago. He'd started a fight in a convenience store.

She'd stored that photo in her own cell phone and still kept it there. It had actually helped Riley and Bill track Peterson down and get close on his trail once before. But would it be of any use now? Riley herself had barely been able to see him during her captivity, and she felt sure that he'd changed his appearance.

At that moment, she heard police sirens approaching. She knew they would check the neighborhood to find out if anyone had seen the man at Ryan's house, or had noticed his car. Although the houses weren't close together, several others had a line of sight to Ryan's front yard. There must be somebody out there who could help—an eyewitness who had actually seen him and could identify him.

Who could that be? Riley asked herself silently.

Suddenly, the answer came to her. She pulled April's phone out of her pocket. The number was in there, Riley was sure of it. It ought to be easy to find.

If only I could stop my hands from shaking, Riley thought.

CHAPTER SIXTEEN

Riley's hands were sweating when she knocked on the door. She hoped and prayed that she'd find out what she needed to know here.

Six minutes earlier, she'd frantically gone through the phone numbers in April's phone until she'd found the one she was looking for. It was Brian, the boy she'd caught smoking pot with April yesterday. She'd called him and told him she was coming right over. She hadn't bothered to explain why.

A tall, slender, well-kept woman answered the door. She looked like she went to a lot of trouble not to look old enough to have a teenage son.

Riley showed the woman her badge.

"I'm Agent Riley Paige," she said.

She wasn't sure what to say next. It was truly a bizarre situation—an FBI agent investigating the disappearance of her own daughter.

The woman saved Riley the trouble of explaining herself.

"Come on in," she said nervously. "I'm Carol, Brian's mother. Brian told me you were coming."

Riley followed the woman into a spacious and elegant living room where Brian was already waiting. As Riley took a seat nearby, she observed how small the skinny boy looked, stranded in a huge overstuffed armchair. He hardly looked like the same stoned but cocky kid she had found smoking pot with April that day.

He certainly did look scared. He undoubtedly thought that Riley had come here to report his pot smoking to his mother.

He ought to be scared, Riley thought. But her own fear was so searing that she had no desire to put anyone else through unnecessary trauma.

The boy's mother stood behind the chair. She also looked frightened.

"Is Brian in some kind of trouble?" she asked.

For a moment, Riley again found herself at a loss for what to say. Of course she knew that Brian had nothing to do with April's abduction. Even so, she had hitched that ride with him. And the truth was, Riley was angry about that. She sternly reminded herself to keep her feelings out of it. She took out her notepad.

"Brian," she said, looking him straight in the eye, "April has been kidnapped."

The boy's eyes widened and he grew pale. Riley understood why. Just a second ago, the worst thing he could imagine was getting in trouble for smoking pot. Now his fear had ratcheted up to a new level.

"Who is April?" Carol asked.

"She—she's my girlfriend," the boy stammered nervously.

"Oh," Carol said, sounding mystified.

"And she's my daughter," Riley added, knowing perfectly well how weird these words sounded under the circumstances.

For a second, the woman looked almost as if she might faint. She walked unsteadily to another chair and sat down.

"I'm so sorry," she blurted out. "How terrible."

Riley, too, felt a terrible surge of emotion. It was anger and fear all mixed together. For a moment, she was afraid that she'd go to pieces right there and then. Why had she let herself get into this situation? Why hadn't she waited until another agent was available to do this—someone whose nerves weren't raw and exposed?

She wished Bill were here. Or Lucy. Lucy would be exactly the kind of presence she needed right now—calm, intelligent, and compassionate. It really ought to be Lucy asking these questions, not Riley.

But there was nothing to be done about it now. And there was no time to lose. From her own experience, Riley could imagine all too well what April was going through. But what she didn't know was how long April might have to live.

Brian and his mother were both staring at her. After a moment Carol asked shakily, "But what does Brian … what does my son have to do with it?"

Riley swallowed hard and managed to speak in a steady voice.

"Brian, you and April hitched a ride to my house the other day. I think the man who drove you took April."

"Oh my God," the boy said with a gasp.

"I need for you to tell me everything you can about that day. What kind of car was it?"

Brian paused, trying to remember.

"It was a Ford, I think. Yeah, a Focus, kind of old, 2010 maybe."

"What color was it?"

"Gray. It was kind of beat-up. There was a big dent in the passenger door."

Riley breathed a little easier as she jotted down the information. Whatever she might think of the boy, it was clear that he wanted to help. But the most important question was coming next. She took out her cell phone and brought up Peterson's photo. She looked at it without showing it to him.

"What did the man look like?" she asked.

"He was a big guy. Not fat, but tall, and—wide, I guess."

Riley felt even more heartened. Although she hadn't gotten a very good look at Peterson during her captivity, she remembered him as being an imposing presence. The mug shot said that he was over six feet tall.

"That's good," Riley said. "Go on."

"He had kind of shaggy hair," Brian said. "And he had stubble on his chin. But it didn't look like he'd forgotten to shave. It was more like a fashion kind of thing."

Riley compared the boy's description to the photo. In it Peterson was shorthaired and cleanly shaved. She'd remembered him without stubble. She'd been right in assuming that Peterson's appearance had changed.

The boy was struggling now to remember more.

"What about the shape of his face?" Riley said.

"Oh, yeah, I remember. He had a pretty big square chin."

Riley remembered the man's jutting chin, how it protruded in the light from the propane torch. The same chin was clearly visible in the photo on her cell phone.

She thought fleetingly of showing Brian the photo to see if he recognized the man. She quickly decided against it. She no longer harbored the faintest doubt that the driver had been Peterson. But she also knew that she still had to persuade her colleagues at the BAU. For that, it would be best for Brian to describe the driver solely from memory. It mustn't look as though Riley had influenced him.

Riley turned toward the boy's mother.

"Carol, I need for you and Brian to come with me to the police station," she said.

The woman's lips were trembling and her voice was shaky.

"Do I need to call our lawyer?" she asked.

"It's nothing like that," Riley said. "Brian's not in any trouble. I just need him to give a description to a sketch artist. He's a very good observer and it will be helpful."

Carol looked relieved.

"Let's go, then," she said. "We'd be glad to help out however we can."

Riley was grateful for their willingness to help. She would get the boy started with a police artist and leave them there.

Then she would go to BAU and get what she needed to track Peterson down—and kill him.

CHAPTER SEVENTEEN

The FBI Behavioral Analysis Unit buzzed with activity as agents went about trying to locate April. Now they all knew that Riley had been right all along. Peterson was still alive, and as much of a threat as ever. The flyer had put any remaining skepticism to rest, and some of the agents looked as embarrassed as she thought they should be.

The mug shot of Peterson and the sketch that had been made from Brian's description were side by side on the flyer. Both showed an ordinary-looking man who might not stand out in a crowd except for his large size and prominent jaw. The resemblance between the sketch and the photo was unmistakable.

Riley wished she could feel vindicated. Instead, she felt utterly wretched.

Meredith stepped into her doorway, his craggy features knotted with sympathetic concern.

"How are you holding up?" he asked Riley.

Riley swallowed hard. She couldn't let herself cry. She had to hold herself together.

"I feel so guilty," she said. "Does that make sense?"

"No," Meredith replied. "But nothing does at a time like this."

Riley nodded. Meredith was absolutely right. She ought to know that as well as anybody. But after all her years as a field agent, she'd never been in this position. She'd been threatened, but she'd only observed this kind of terror from the outside. These emotions were new to her.

"Have you got any news?" Riley asked.

Meredith sighed wearily. "Not much," he said. "We've got cops going door to door in your husband's neighborhood with the flyer. Nobody recognizes Peterson so far."

"What about the car?" Riley asked.

"The Fredericksburg cops located the car the boy described. Peterson had stolen it. It was found abandoned not long after he gave the kids a ride. A neighbor across the street said that she noticed a black Cadillac backed up in your ex-husband's driveway. It was probably stolen too, and we're trying to find out about it. But the neighbor didn't see anything that happened."

Riley's heart hung on Meredith's every word, listening for

some reason to hope. She didn't hear much to encourage her.

Meredith gazed at Riley for a moment. Then he said, "There's nothing you can do here right now. I don't suppose I could talk you into going home and getting some sleep."

Riley shook her head.

"It's still early," she said.

Besides, she knew she wouldn't be able to sleep until April was found. She doubted that much of the BAU would sleep until then either.

"Okay," Meredith said. "I'll let you know when we know more."

He left her office. Riley stared at the flyer again. She picked apart Meredith's choice of words just now. He'd said "*when* we know more." He hadn't said *if*. Riley tried to take comfort in that. Of course she knew that Meredith had chosen his words carefully. Did he really hold out any hope that April would be found alive?

Right then she heard a familiar voice from her doorway.

"Riley."

She turned around and saw Bill standing there.

"I heard," he said.

His eyes were full of concern. They showed no trace of anger or resentment. Whatever bad blood had been between them recently, Riley knew that it had evaporated in the face of this tragedy.

Riley made one last vain attempt to keep her emotions under control. But then it hit her that she didn't need to. Her friend was back—a friend who understood her better than anybody in the world.

Tears burst from her eyes and she leaped to her feet. She threw herself into Bill's arms.

"Oh, Bill, you're here, you're here."

She sobbed uncontrollably as Bill rocked her gently in his arms.

*

Bill was driving the SUV they'd taken out at Quantico. In the passenger seat beside him Riley was loading four three-inch shells into a Remington 870 twelve-gauge shotgun that she cradled in her lap. She'd requested the gun at the BAU before they left for D.C.

"Remember, that thing's a SWAT weapon," Bill said. "We're just likely to be interviewing civilians for a while."

"I'll leave it in the SUV for now," Riley replied.

Bill knew that he'd been right to come with her. His best friend was emotionally raw and in need of his presence. Abandoning their partnership when she was in such dire straights would have been all wrong. He was aware that his taking off tonight could mark the end of his shaky marriage, but he couldn't let Riley go without him.

She was brilliant but she could be foolhardy. She had come so close to being killed when she'd struck out alone on their last case, and he couldn't let that happen again.

"Talk to me," Bill said. "About Peterson. Have you found out anything since we last hunted him down?"

"He's changing, Bill," Riley said.

"How?"

"It's hard to pin it down exactly."

After a brief silence, Bill nudged her thoughts again. "Riley, I hate to ask you to remember it all. But think back to things that he said to you when he was holding you. Does anything stick out in your mind?"

"He told me once, 'You're not my type,'" she said.

"Hmm, okay, you weren't his type," Bill mused. "Did he say anything else?"

"Yeah, he went on to say something like, 'But I like you anyway. You're opening my horizons.'"

"What do you think he meant?"

"There's so much we don't know about him," Riley said. "Nobody is sure just how many women he's tortured and killed. The only ones we know of are the four that were found in shallow graves. There are probably more out there that nobody has found."

"Right," Bill said. "And the women we found were all markedly well-off. The first was married to a psychiatrist. The second was a newspaper editor. The third was married to a real estate developer. The fourth was high up in the food chain of a big corporation. Finally, there was Marie, a Georgetown lawyer. Obviously, this started off as a class thing. He probably grew up poor. He resented it. He especially resented women who had money."

Riley nodded in agreement. "It made him feel emasculated," she said. "So he went on a spree of revenge, targeting women who represented everything he hated. They also happened to be women who weren't available to a guy of his social standing. Maybe his first victim was a wealthy woman who rejected his advances. He probably fantasized that he was some sort of one-man revolution. So his anger had a sexual component, even though rape was never part of his MO."

"You're getting at things we hadn't worked out before," Bill said. "Keep going."

"And he got to be very good at it," Riley continued. "Judging from the pictures we've got of him, he's probably the kind of guy who can blend in anywhere. And the last car he stole was a Cadillac. Just by taking the right clothes and props, he can probably pass himself off as rich. He might have socialized with the women, even dated or slept with some of them. What mattered was what they represented—the kind of wealth and privilege that he felt cheated out of."

Bill grunted—the sort of noise he made whenever an insight came to him.

"Riley, that's it," he said. "You're *not* his type—not a wealthy professional, not some society housewife, not the kind of trophy he'd been looking for till then. But he liked you anyway. That surprised him. He realized that the whole class thing didn't matter to him anymore. He wasn't some lone fighter for the oppressed. He was in it for the sheer sadism—the joy of inflicting pain and terror."

"You've nailed it perfectly, Bill," she said. "He's no ordinary serial. He can change. He's adaptable. That's why he's been so hard to catch."

"Let's hope that's about to change," Bill said.

Right then, they arrived at their destination—a desolate block of condemned row houses. It was dark in the ramshackle neighborhood, all the more so because some streetlights were out. All that was left of the house where Peterson had held Riley was an empty lot. The explosion had destroyed the house where Peterson had been squatting. The two empty houses on either side had been damaged so badly that they were promptly torn down.

Bill pulled the SUV to the curb and parked. He said. "Do you want to call in the D.C. police? They could cover a lot more ground, questioning people."

"No, Riley replied. "If the search becomes that obvious, he'll get spooked and disappear. Let's just go it on our own for a little while. We've got two car keys, so we can split up. You go east, and I'll go west."

"Okay," Bill said. "But you call me if anything happens—anything at all."

He watched as Riley walked onto the vacant lot where she had encountered Peterson before. He knew that she needed to confront her demons there.

Bill headed down the street, determined to find some lead, some answer to where Peterson was holding Riley's daughter. He knew that if he found the man first, he'd probably kill the monster himself.

CHAPTER EIGHTEEN

Riley watched Bill walk away. She looked back at the SUV longingly, feeling reluctant to leave the Remington behind. But carrying a shotgun around at this time of night would draw the wrong sort of attention. The plan for now was to search, not to destroy.

At least not yet, Riley thought.

Right now, she felt the need to reach back into a dark recess of her memory—a place where she'd come to know what little she knew about Peterson.

She walked out onto the barren lot. She'd returned here just once since her captivity and escape. It had been broad daylight then. But she had felt certain then that she'd found the place she'd been looking for. Now she retraced her steps the same way. Soon her instincts told her that she was there—standing in the very spot.

She breathed the night air deeply. Yes, this was it. There was no doubt about it. Below her feet was exactly where she'd found Marie in that dark and dismal crawlspace. It was where she'd been captured in the very act of setting Marie free. It was where she'd suffered days of pain, torture, and humiliation.

A feeling of rage rose up in her. It seemed to seep up from the ground, into her toes and feet, up her ankles and legs, all through her abdomen and arms, until her chest and head felt ready to burst with it. For a moment, the house itself seemed to be a real presence all around her.

If only it really was still here, she thought. *If only he were here.*

How gladly she'd do what she'd done before—beat the man nearly unconscious, open his propane tanks, throw a match inside, and watch the whole place erupt into a fiery explosion.

If only it could be her own life on the line again and not April's.

When she turned back toward the street, she spotted a vagrant who looked like he must be familiar with this part of town. She stopped the man and showed him the flyer.

"Have you seen this man?" she asked.

The vagrant answered without even a moment's hesitation.

"Yep, I've seen him several times. It's the guy in these pictures, all right—a tall guy with a big chin. He comes here almost every day. Early this morning was the most recent. I was across the street there, sitting on the curb. He came walking right along here, like he always does. He stood on the sidewalk about where we are now, just looking across this lot here. And then he walked over where you were, ma'am. He always does that. He stands there looking down at the ground, just like you did. He always says something too, but I'm never close enough to hear him."

Riley could barely contain her excitement.

"Does he come here in a car?" she asked.

The vagrant scratched his head. "Not so's I know about." He pointed west. "Today he went off that way. I always keep watching as he goes, because he strikes me as odd somehow. He always turns off onto one of the side streets. Maybe he keeps a car parked nearby, or maybe not. I don't know."

"Thank you—oh, thank you," Riley sputtered. She reached into her purse for her wallet. It was hardly professional procedure to give money to helpful witnesses, but she couldn't help herself. She handed the man a twenty-dollar bill.

"Much obliged," he said. Then he went rattling away with his shopping cart.

It was all Riley could do to keep from hyperventilating. She took a long, slow breath. He really was here. Maybe he was close by right now. Maybe he even lived near here. Maybe she was getting close to finding April right now.

*

After hours of walking, walking, walking, Riley still had found out nothing. Absolutely nothing. She'd prowled every street all the way to Georgetown, talking to everyone she met. Some people had recognized the man on the flyer, and two said they'd seen him recently driving a Cadillac. But nobody she talked to could to pin down where he might be.

She hoped that Bill was doing better, wherever he was right now. She doubted it.

Peterson has got me beat, she thought in despair, turning to head back to the SUV. *I'm doing everything wrong.*

To make matters worse, a light drizzle started to fall. Within seconds, it turned into a steady rain. She'd be soaked to the skin long before she got back to the vehicle. She was relieved to see that a bar up ahead was still open. She went inside and sat down on a barstool.

While the bartender was busy helping another customer, Riley wondered what to order. Anything alcoholic was out of the question. She'd stopped drinking altogether after that drunken call to Bill that had nearly destroyed their relationship. Now was no time to start again.

Or was it?

Riley's eyes scanned the rows of bottles lined up against the mirror behind the bar. Her gaze fell upon the bourbon bottles—especially the hundred-proof brands. It was so, so easy to imagine the rough, burning, comforting feeling of gulping down a shot. It was easy, too, to imagine gulping down another, and another, and another …

And why not, after all? She'd done all she could. The situation was hopeless, at least for now. Some whiskey was just what she needed to relax her, to give her shattered nerves some welcome relief.

The beefy bartender stepped toward her.

"What'll you have, lady?" he asked.

Riley didn't answer.

"Lady, last call is in five minutes," he said.

She thought about it. In five minutes, she could put away a lot of whiskey. Still, she struggled. April was out there, in a monster's clutches. What did she think she was doing, even *thinking* about having a drink?

A tall, rough-looking man leaned on the bar next to her. He was too close to her for her liking.

"Come on, little lady," he purred. "What'll you have? It's on me."

Riley's jaw clenched. The last thing she needed right now was some jerk coming on to her.

"I don't drink," she said in a tight voice.

She felt relieved at the sound of her own words. There, it was said, and she felt good about her decision.

The man chuckled. "Don't knock it if you ain't tried it," he said.

Riley smirked a little. Who did this guy think she was? Did he really think she'd never had a drink before? Maybe in the dim light of this place he couldn't see how old she was. Or maybe he was just too damn drunk to see straight.

"Give me a club soda," Riley said to the bartender.

"Naw, we'll have none of that," the man next to her said. "I

286

know just the drink you'd like." Looking up at the bartender, he said, "Clyde, mix this girl a strawberry daiquiri. Put it on my tab."

"Bring me a club soda," Riley insisted grimly.

The bartender shrugged at the man. "The lady says a club soda," he said. He opened the stainless steel refrigerator, pulled out a bottle, and snapped it open.

"Have it your way, bitch," the man said.

Riley's nerves quickened.

"What did you say?" she asked.

But the man was walking away from her toward the door. He called to a friend who was sitting alone at a table.

"C'mon, Red. It's closing time."

The friend got up and the two men left the bar.

Fighting down her anger, Riley paid for the club soda. She quickly drank it straight out of the bottle. She put some change on the bar for a tip.

"Thanks," she said to the bartender. The place had emptied out and she was the last to leave. When she walked out the door, she was relieved to see that the rain had stopped for now. The night was still damp and dark, and it would probably rain again soon.

As the bar door closed behind her, she felt a strong hand grip her arm—and she heard that familiar ugly voice.

"Hello, there, little lady."

Riley turned to face the leering man. She could feel anger rising in her gut.

"Sorry about that little tiff we had back there," he said. "What do you say we kiss and make up? Then we'll just see what happens next."

Riley stepped backward, but another arm reached around her neck from behind. The man's friend had been waiting out here too.

"Don't make a fuss and you won't get hurt too much," the man behind her said.

Riley's rage erupted through her whole body. It was sheer, mindless fury—fury against killers, kidnappers, and guys like these who thought they could take whatever they wanted.

She jabbed her elbow hard into solar plexus of the man behind her, and her knee went straight to the other guy's crotch. Both men buckled over in pain. She pulled out her Glock and waved it at them. But she didn't want to shoot them. She wanted to beat them both to a bloody pulp, just like she had with Peterson when she'd escaped his clutches.

She whipped the pistol across the face of the man who'd first accosted her. Then she whirled around and smashed the heel of her hand into the other guy's face. She felt and heard the bridge of his nose breaking.

After that, everything came automatically to her, a deeply satisfying sequence of kicks and punches, turns and slices. When she stopped, both men were lying on the sidewalk, groaning in pain.

Riley, unable to stop her flood of rage, her desire for revenge, bent over and lowered her Glock to the head of the first man. She pulled back the pin with a satisfying click.

The man looked up, eyes wide with terror, and suddenly peed his pants.

"Please," he whimpered. "Don't kill me."

He was pathetic.

Riley knew it was illegal, what she was doing, aiming a gun at an unarmed civilian; she knew it was immoral, too, despite what he had done. She was going too far.

Yet she couldn't stop herself. As she knelt there, she felt her hand trembling with rage, and for a moment felt she might really kill him. She tried to stop herself, but it was an epic battle within. There had been too many demons—and too few outlets.

Finally, Riley put her Glock back in its holster, feeling her fury draining away. Should she arrest these guys? No, it would take too much time and she had more important things to do.

"If I ever see your face again," she whispered, "I will kill you."

She stood and the men scurried to their feet and limped away, never once, in their terror, looking back.

CHAPTER NINETEEN

Riley was crouched in the dark again. She could smell the mold and mildew of the crawlspace, feel the dirt underneath her. But this time she was ready. She was gripping the Remington tightly. It was loaded and the safety was off.

"Show yourself, you son of a bitch," she growled.

It was so dark that she couldn't see anything, not even her weapon. But the second she saw the light of that flame, she meant to blast away at Peterson.

But then she heard the familiar low chuckle.

"You don't think I'm going to make it that easy, do you?"

She swiftly pointed the gun in the direction of the voice. But suddenly the sound came from a different direction.

"I'm hard to see without my torch, eh?"

She pointed the gun in the new direction, but now the voice came from directly behind her.

"Give it up," he said. "I'm getting better and better at this."

The voice was to her right now.

"And I'm having a great time."

Now it moved to her left.

"You'll never get to her on time."

She raised the gun and fired it.

Riley awoke to the sound of Bill's voice.

"Here's something to eat."

She opened her eyes, shuddering from her nightmare. She found herself lying down in the back of the SUV. Bill was sitting in the car door with a paper bag and two cups of steaming hot coffee.

Riley remembered now—the long futile search, asking questions that led nowhere, and the fight outside the bar. She'd come back to the SUV to lie down. She'd meant only to take a short nap.

"What time is it?" she asked.

"About four," Bill said.

Riley sat up and saw that the SUV was now in a small parking lot.

"Why did you let me sleep?"

Bill fished around for the contents of the bag.

"There was no one left to talk to—at least no one sober. Anyhow, you looked like you'd had enough activity for one night. I slept a little too. When I woke up, I drove to this little convenience store I checked on last night. It's always open."

He handed her a paper cup of coffee and a wrapped sandwich.

"Thanks," Riley said, grateful that he wasn't asking her any questions. She didn't want to talk about her temptation to have a drink, nor about how she'd pulverized those two guys. She unwrapped the sandwich. It was egg and sausage and she bit into it eagerly. She was very hungry.

"I've got some good news," Bill said. "The cashier at the diner changed since I first went by there. The new guy told me that he's seen Peterson. He thinks he works in a neighborhood grocery store near here."

Riley took a final gulp of coffee.

"What are we waiting for?"

Riley went into the store to use the restroom. When she came out, she and Bill walked the few blocks to the little grocery store. It looked like a family-owned business. Lights were on inside, but Riley's heart sank to see that the store wouldn't be open until nine. Then she looked through the wired-mesh glass panel in the door and spotted movement inside. Someone was bending over a box, pulling things out.

Riley knocked hard on the door. A small, dark-skinned woman stood up and glared at her, then continued putting merchandise on a shelf. It was probably the owner, stocking shelves during the store's off-hours. Riley banged on the door again, holding her badge up to the window. The woman came to the door and peered through it at the ID.

"FBI," Riley yelled. "Open up."

The woman unlocked the door, peered at Bill and Riley for a moment, and finally let them inside.

"What can I do for you?" she asked in an Asian accent, locking the door behind them.

"I'm Special Agent Riley Paige, and this is my partner, Special Agent Bill Jeffreys. We're looking for a murder suspect."

Bill showed her the flyer.

"Have you seen this man?" he asked.

"Why it looks like …" she began, peering at the pictures. She looked up at Riley. "I think it might be a man who worked here until a couple of weeks ago. But why are you looking for him?"

Riley said, "He's wanted for kidnapping and murder."

The woman looked shocked. "He was always perfectly pleasant around here," she said, smiling as if remembering something. "He could be quite charming."

Bill warned her, "This man is very dangerous. Don't ever let him near you again."

The woman got more serious. She pointed to the mug shot. "But this wasn't his name. It was Bruce. Let me see …"

She led Bill and Riley over to the counter and brought up some information on her computer. "Yes, it was Bruce Staunton."

The woman looked at Riley and Bill anxiously.

"And you say he is a murder suspect?"

"I'm afraid so," Riley said. "We need for you to tell us anything that might lead us to him. Do you have an address for him?"

The woman looked again at the computer screen.

"Yes, but it's out of date. He used to live near here. He said he'd just moved, and he wanted to work closer to home. That's why he quit."

Riley stifled a groan of disappointment.

"Did he leave any kind of forwarding address?" she asked.

"Or where he might be working next?" Bill asked.

"No, but he said it was in the Northeast. He said he planned to be close to the river."

Riley knew that Washington, D.C., was divided into four geographical quadrants. They were now in the Northwest, so the Northeast district the woman was talking about would be straight east from here. But it was a big area.

"What river?" Bill asked.

"The Anacostia. I've never been there but I know it's in that district."

The woman brought up a map on her computer.

"There," she said, pointing to where she thought the suspect might be. "From what he said, I'd say that's where he was probably going. Somewhere around there, in the Northeast and on the other side of the river."

Riley thanked the woman, who unlocked the door and let them outside.

"I might be wrong," the woman said. "It might not be the man in your picture."

"It was him, all right," Bill said. "Don't let him in if he returns here. Call the cops."

She shook her head and closed the door again.

Riley was already walking back to where they'd parked the

car. Bill caught up with her and said, "I'm going to run that name just in case anything comes up."

When they reached the SUV, Riley got into the driver's seat while Bill spent a few moments connecting to BAU. Soon he looked up at Riley with a surprised expression.

"A man named Bruce Staunton recently changed his mailing address," Bill said.

"Where's the new one?"

After a few more seconds, Bill told her, "It's right in the area that the grocery store woman just told us about."

"Then let's go." Riley started the car.

"Not so fast," Bill said. "There's something not right here. That was awfully easy. Peterson's a smart guy. He had to know we might come around here asking about him. Still, he told his employer where he was moving, and he even changed his mailing address so we could find it? What are we supposed to make of that?"

Riley didn't reply. She just put the SUV in reverse and backed it out of the parking space. Then she turned it facing the street.

"You direct, I'll drive."

Bill was right, and she knew it. Peterson had given the woman this information for one of two reasons. He was either trying to throw her off the scent, or he was drawing her into a trap.

Riley hoped he was drawing her into a trap. She would be more than ready for him.

CHAPTER TWENTY

"Turn left in fifty feet," the female GPS voice said.

As Bill switched on his turn signal, Riley felt oddly comforted by the voice. The sense that someone knew where they were going relieved her stomach-wrenching fear and dread just a little.

She'd tried figuring out the way with a map before they'd started driving. She was normally very good with maps, but her mind kept filling up with terrible images of April in captivity and Peterson taunting her with a propane torch. She couldn't think straight, couldn't figure out a feasible route. Bill had insisted on using the GPS and now the friendly voice was taking care of things.

Soon after the turn, the SUV crossed a bridge over the river. They were well into the Northwest now.

"We're getting close," Bill said.

But close to what? Riley wondered.

It was still very dark outside, and the rain was now heavy and steady. She had no idea how April was being held, but she knew that rescuing her wasn't going to be easy. She wondered yet again whether she and Bill shouldn't call in a SWAT team. They still didn't know if the address they'd gotten for so-called Bruce Staunton was correct. Besides, if it was, it was best not to have a small army storming the place. It might be the surest way to get April killed.

If she wasn't dead already.

The thought was unbearable. Riley had to put it out of her mind. It couldn't be true. She wouldn't let it be true.

"Turn right. You have reached your destination."

"Damn," Bill murmured.

Riley shared his discouragement. It wasn't a house at all, just an all-night convenience store. Its glaring interior light jarred against the rainy darkness. Bill parked the SUV. They both got out of the vehicle and opened umbrellas.

"I don't think it's a total fail," Riley said. "It's unlikely he'd give this random address if he'd never spent any time in the area. He's not here, I'm sure of it. But I also think he's been here. I think he's in the area. He likes to taunt, after all. He likes to let us know he's not afraid of us, and that he's smarter than us. Thus he would give an address that's not where he lives—but close to it."

Bill sighed.

"At least it's open," Bill said. "Let's go in and ask some questions."

"You go ahead," Riley said. "I want to look around a bit."

"Okay," Bill said. He went on inside the store.

Riley stood in the parking lot, surveying the area. She saw that they had arrived in a middle-class family neighborhood, with small houses bunched close together. Across the street, the block was comprised entirely of row houses. A couple of the homes were lighted even at this hour. Riley guessed that commuters were getting ready to drive to work.

Where and how could Peterson be holding April in such a densely populated area? A neighborhood where everybody probably knew everybody else?

This isn't right, she thought.

Still, her every instinct told her that Peterson hadn't misled them—not completely. Perhaps it was only wishful thinking, but Riley was sure that Peterson had set a trap for her, and that she was getting closer and closer to finding out where it was. A part of him, after all, wanted to confront her.

Bill came out of the store, splashing through rain puddles as he trotted toward Riley.

"The guy in there thinks he recognizes the face," he said. "He thinks he's seen him around a construction site near the river."

Riley felt encouraged.

"Let's check it out."

She and Bill climbed back into the SUV.

"The guy said this street takes you there," Bill added.

As they drove, Riley's alertness sharpened. The area seemed less populated and more promising. It ought to be easy to spot an abandoned house—someplace isolated, where no one could hear a woman's desperate cries for help.

When they reached the chain link fence surrounding the construction site, Riley said, "Stop here."

Bill stopped the car, and they got out, opening their umbrellas. A large sign on the fence announced the construction of a new apartment complex. There were only a few inhabited homes nearby. The area reminded Riley of the tenement where she had been held. She felt her heartbeat quicken.

"I think we're close," she said to Bill. "Look how much more isolated this is."

Bill shook his head. "I don't know, Riley. It seems that way at night, but look at all this equipment. By day these grounds are crawling with construction workers. Do you see any place where Peterson could be holed up?"

Riley looked all around. This part of the site was lighted, but she couldn't see anybody anywhere.

"There must be a night watchman around somewhere," Bill said. "Maybe he can tell us something." He pointed. "Let's go around to the other side of the site. We might find him there."

Just then, Riley heard what sounded like kids' voices. It was a startling sound at this hour, in the dark and the rain. She turned and saw a group of kids standing under an awning near the construction site.

"You go ahead," she said to Bill. "I'm going to talk to these kids."

Bill walked away, and Riley approached the group of teenagers. There were seven of them, a mixed bunch—black and white, male and female. They were trying their best to look like gangsters and thugs, dressed in the proper attire and smoking cigarettes. She also caught a whiff of pot.

Riley pulled the flyer with the pictures of Peterson out of her bag. She displayed it to the kids as she approached.

"Have any of you ever seen this man?" she asked.

One of the kids swaggered toward her. He looked like the oldest, and he seemed to fancy himself the group's leader. Riley noticed him give a silent signal to the biggest kid, who started to move around her. She knew that she needed to watch her back.

"What are you, some kind of cop lady?" the older kid asked.

Riley pulled out her badge.

"That's what I thought," the boy said with a sneer. "What makes you think we're gonna go talking to cops?"

"An innocent girl is missing," Riley said. "She's being held near here by a psychopath. She's probably being tortured. She's going to be killed soon if I don't find her."

She held the picture closer to the kid who had approached her.

"Have you seen him?" she asked.

The boy sneered again. "If I did, why would I tell you?"

"Better not do her that way, Mayshon," a younger black girl said. "She probably ain't here alone."

The boy laughed sourly.

"So what?" he said. "We ain't done nothing wrong."

Riley noticed the boy nod ever so slightly, and she knew it was a signal to the bigger kid who was now behind her.

Riley whipped around and caught the bigger kid by the wrist

as he raised a knife toward her. She grabbed his arm in a lock and twisted his arm sharply as she pulled it up behind his back. She knew she could easily break it.

And yet, despite how much he may have hurt her, she didn't want to hurt him. He was big and strong, but he was still just a kid.

He dropped the knife and groaned in agony, writhing, unable to get free.

The other kids stood there, wide-eyed, staring back in panic and surprise.

"I wasn't going to do nothin'!" the big kid called out. "Don't bust my arm!"

Riley was fuming. She imagined what this boy might have done to someone else who was not as capable as she.

"I could send you to jail for that," she hissed in his ear. "For a long, long time."

The boy whimpered, while the other kids shifted uncomfortably. A few of them turned and bolted.

"I'm sorry, lady!" he whimpered. "I'll never do it again."

Riley finally sighed sharply and released her grip. She had to remind herself that this was not the enemy she was after—and that sometimes, mercy is the greatest gift she could give someone. She had to give it out while she could; she did not know if she would have any left for the man who had her daughter.

As soon as she let go the boy turned and ran, and Riley reached down and picked up the knife. She stared back at the leader, the only boy left, who looked too scared to run.

"Get out of my sight," Riley sneered.

The boy finally bolted.

When Riley saw they were long gone, she folded the blade and pocketed it. She heard a noise and was surprised to see the girl who'd spoken had stayed behind. She emerged from the shadows and stared back at Riley with an awed expression.

"That was cool," she said. "I never seen a lady do nothing like that. Don't mind them, they're just assholes. Who is this girl you're talking about?"

"She's my daughter," Riley said. "She's fourteen."

Riley could tell her words got to her. She guessed that this girl was about April's age.

"I seen him—the man in the pictures," she said. "I think he lives near here."

She pointed.

"Over that way, past all this building stuff, almost at the river. It's not far. It's a little house, the only one over there. Last I saw, he drove a big Cadillac."

Riley's heart quickened. She started to walk in that direction.

"Come on," she said to the girl. "Show me."

But the girl hung back.

"Uh-uh," the girl said. "This is where I get off. Last time I got too close to that place, he pulled a gun on me."

Without another word, she broke into a trot toward the bus shelter. She stopped midway and turned back toward Riley.

"He's a mean son of a bitch," she yelled.

"I know," Riley whispered to herself.

She went back toward the SUV to get a flashlight. She also wanted to get the Remington. She was pretty sure she was going to need it.

CHAPTER TWENTY ONE

He might not even have to kill me, April thought. *Maybe I'll just die anyway.*

It was pitch dark under the wooden deck. Rain was beating against the floorboards above her and dripping between the cracks. It had been raining off and on for hours, and the ground beneath her had turned to mud. Even though it was a warm August night, she was soaked to the skin, and she shivered from the wetness. And she was very hungry and thirsty.

After night had set in, Peterson had crept under the deck with her several times, holding a plate of food while he waved the lighted propane torch to warn her away from it. He'd chuckled cruelly at her hopeless attempts to grab at the food with her two bound wrists.

So now she knew that this was exactly the kind of torture Mom had endured at his hands. But Mom had gotten away from him once. Could she do that too?

At least the rain was keeping him away for now. He had been in the house for a while and she hadn't heard a sound from him. Maybe he was asleep. Maybe now would be her chance to escape.

April's hands and feet had turned numb again from being bound by the plastic restraints. As she'd done many times before, she rubbed and twisted her ankles and wrists to get some circulation going. After a moment of sharp, icy tingling, she got some feeling back again.

She rolled through the mud toward the square of lattice that he always opened and closed. She couldn't see it in the dark, but she knew exactly where it was—at a corner of the deck away from the house.

She pushed against the lattice with her feet. It was no good. It was too solid in that spot. Peterson must have unlatched and relatched hooks or bolts whenever he came and went. She couldn't hope to open them from inside, not with her hands bound.

Still unable to see anything at all, she rolled back toward the house until she bumped against the cinderblock foundation. She thought the lattice might be weaker where it butted up against the house. She fingered its edges, finding out exactly where it was nailed to a thick wooden post next to the house. Then she stretched out and pushed against the upper corner with her feet.

She gasped when she felt the lattice budge a little. It was looser here!

She pushed again. It didn't move much, but she heard the sharp, noisy sound of wood cracking. She froze with fear. Could Peterson hear her in the house? How could he *not* hear her? In her fearful and exhausted state, the noise seemed to be almost deafening to her.

What would he do if he heard and found her trying to escape? Whatever it might be, it couldn't be much worse than what he planned to do to her anyway.

She held still and listened. She heard no footsteps. Maybe he hadn't heard.

Still, she had to do all this more quietly somehow. She pressed against that corner with the heels of her wrists, slowly and carefully, hoping to push out the nails little by little. She felt a slight budge with every push. Then a single nail came completely loose.

She kept pushing and the remaining nails loosened, little by little. They made alarming squeaking sounds with every push. There was simply no way to do this silently.

Finally, with a crackling sound, the whole square section of lattice gave way and fell to the ground. She could get out now—at least if he hadn't heard that last sharp burst of noise. But where would she go, and how?

Crawling through the mud like a caterpillar, bunching her knees and hands together and stretching out again and again, she made her way outside. She managed to get across the piece of lattice without being hurt by any nails. From there, her face rubbed into the ground with every motion, scraping against muddy grass. She guessed that her face was probably bleeding by now—and her wrists and ankles as well. But there was nothing she could do about it.

When she was completely clear of the deck, she sat up and looked around. It was still raining pretty hard. A single light shining from a window reflected off the chrome trim on the big dark car, parked some fifteen feet away. In the yard closer to her there were only a few scrubby bushes. She could make out the shadowy shapes of some trees farther away, but she saw nothing beyond the trees—no streetlights, no lighted windows. There was no sign of traffic in any direction.

A sob rose up in April's throat. She was alone, and she had no idea where the nearest helpful human might be found. She clenched her teeth and forced back a wail. She thought about her mother and tried to picture what she would do, but her imagination could find no easy answers.

But her mom wouldn't give up. That was the only thing she knew for sure. Her mom never gave up on a problem. In fact, the thought whispered through her mind that her mom had never given up on *her.*

April knew that she had to make her way far enough to find somebody, anybody, to help her. Someone who could call her mother, who would arrive with a SWAT team to destroy the monster in the house and set April free. For a moment she pictured the flare of many guns firing and solving the situation once and for all.

But there was no SWAT team on hand and she had to keep moving. It didn't matter where, as long as she could get away from the house, away from Peterson.

She decided that it was easier, faster, and less painful to roll than to bunch up and stretch out again and again. She lay down and started rolling.

But just then, a bright light pierced the darkness. She froze in place and saw that the light in front of the house had come on. The door opened and Peterson stepped out. April's heart was pounding horribly.

He heard me, she thought. But the man wasn't looking around as though in search of her.

She flattened on the ground, trying to make herself invisible. But how could he not see her, out in the open like this? There were only a few shrubs that might just partly shield her from his sight.

Still, the night was very dark, and it was still raining. She barely breathed as he stepped down the front steps.

To her surprise, he walked right past her, barely three feet away. He got into the car and turned on the headlights and started the engine. For a moment, April dared to hope. If he drove away, it might give her time to escape.

But then he opened the car door again and got out. He shut the door. April choked with fear. Maybe he'd seen her after all. No, he headed straight back toward the house. Apparently he had forgotten something.

April's mind buzzed with a new escape scheme. Peterson had left the car running.

If only she could steal it and drive away! But how could she possibly do that? She was bound hand and foot.

Still, she had to try. She rolled over and over until she reached the car. Then she pulled herself to her feet and opened the driver's door. She scrambled into the seat and sat staring through the rain-streaked windshield. Suddenly this seemed like a completely insane idea. Not only was she bound, she'd never driven a car in her life. She didn't even know how to turn on the windshield wipers.

But she had no choice. Peterson would surely come back at any second. She wasn't completely ignorant about cars.

"You can do this," she said out loud.

She managed to release the hand brake, then put the car into drive. To her alarm, it moved forward right away. She hit the brake with her two bound feet and the car lurched to a jarring stop.

How am I going to do this? she wondered.

She put her bound hands on top of the steering wheel, hoping she could see well enough to avoid any obstacles. Then she took her feet off the brake and pressed down on the accelerator. The car moved forward and kept right on going.

Through the rain, she could make out the shapes of trees coming up. Steering frantically, she managed to avoid them. She had no idea where she might be going.

In a few seconds, she was past the trees and bouncing across an open field. She kept pressing the accelerator to keep the car moving.

At one rough bump, the driver's door flew open. She hadn't shut it tightly enough, but she certainly couldn't reach out and pull it shut again. She wasn't harnessed in and was in danger of being thrown from the vehicle as it lurched across the rough earth.

One bounce made her push the accelerator too hard, and the car leaped forward. For a moment, the vehicle seemed to be airborne. Then it hit the ground again and reeled ahead. In the headlights, she saw a large tree coming up, but too late to shift her feet to the brake. As the car slammed against the tree, an airbag erupted in front of her, cushioning her from the sickening crash.

April was dazed for a moment, and she tasted blood on her lips. She realized that the car engine was no longer running and steam was gushing out from under the crunched-up hood. One headlight was still shining ahead. She climbed out of the car, but she fell, rolled down a weedy slope, and splashed into shallow water. She managed to sit up and look around.

In the glare of the headlight, she saw that she was in the edge of a river. Through the rain, she could dimly make out some lights on the opposite shore. It didn't look too far away, but how deep was the water?

*

Damn that girl! Peterson thought as he staggered through the rain. He clutched a flashlight in one hand and his pistol in the other.

The flashlight had caused the problem. Just a few moments ago, he had gotten in the car and was ready to drive away. It was high time, he'd thought, to abandon this vehicle somewhere and steal another one. Probably something less flashy. A rainy night like this was perfect for getting both things done without attracting attention.

And besides, he had figured, the girl was perfectly helpless, reduced to a wet puddle of shapeless fear under the deck.

But just before he'd put the car in gear, he'd remembered that he'd need a flashlight. He'd snapped the glove compartment open and saw that he hadn't left it there. It was still in the house. He'd cursed himself soundly. He liked to think of himself as better organized.

He'd hurried back to the house, still unworried—and unhurried, too, or so he'd thought. When he'd found the flashlight, he'd switched it on and realized that its batteries were shot. He'd had to scrounge through a kitchen drawer to find new batteries, and he'd barely gotten them in place when he heard the car drive away.

He'd charged out of the house just in time to see the car zigzagging off among the nearby trees and disappearing altogether into the darkness.

Now he could hardly believe what had happened. Shining the light around the back deck, he'd seen that a piece of lattice was broken off and lying in the mud. That's when he'd known that the girl was out and she had taken his car.

A lot like her mother, he thought. *Too much like her mother.*

But had the girl gotten loose from her plastic restraints? If so, did she know how to drive? She was too young for a license, he was sure, but perhaps she'd been learning. If so, she could have taken off for anywhere.

But as he followed the crazy trail of fresh, muddy tire tracks, he doubted it. Her driving had been wildly erratic, as if she'd had no real control over the vehicle. No, even if she did know how to drive, she was still bound. She couldn't have gotten far. She must have crashed the car pretty quickly. All he had to do was keep following the trail. He'd catch up with her soon.

He was angry and frustrated. She'd spoiled everything. Her mother was probably tracking him right now, and might get here soon. He'd been counting on it. He had hoped to make the girl's death painful and dramatic—a fitting punishment for the woman who had thwarted him. She'd be so sick with horror and guilt, she'd beg for him to kill her too. And he'd be glad to oblige.

But now the whole thing had turned sloppy and chaotic. He simply hated that.

When he saw the damaged car up ahead, he only hoped that the girl hadn't killed herself in the crash. He fingered the trigger of his pistol, just itching to use it.

No more games, he decided. *It's time just to kill her.*

CHAPTER TWENTY TWO

Standing outside the SUV, Riley removed the Remington 870 twelve-gauge shotgun from its case and slung the weapon over her shoulder. The heft of the Remington felt good. Then she took out her Glock, checked it, and holstered it again. She picked up a flashlight and put it in her jacket pocket. The street here was well-lighted, but she might need it soon.

Although it was still raining, she tossed her folded umbrella into the vehicle. She wanted to have both hands free for whatever was about to happen next. She didn't mind getting wet.

I'm ready, she thought, clenching her teeth and slamming the SUV door shut.

She looked around, but didn't see Bill anywhere. He'd gone around to the other side of the construction site hoping to run into a night watchman. She couldn't wait for anything or anybody now, but she had to let him know what was going on.

She pulled out her cell phone and texted.

"I know where he is. West beyond construction. Hurry."

Then she wondered just how quickly Bill would be able to catch up. He might not even read her message right away if he were talking to a watchman. She added another text.

"Isolated house near river."

She walked briskly through the rain and soon passed the rest of the construction site. The road dead-ended at a broad, open field with trees scattered here and there. She knew the river must be somewhere straight ahead, but she couldn't see it.

The only light came from a small house just off one side of the road. That was it. That was Peterson's lair. From what the girl had told her minutes ago, there was no doubt about it. She approached the house cautiously, Glock now in hand.

Normally, her next move would be to bang on the door and announce that she was FBI, but nothing was normal here. Peterson was holding April somewhere. Before Riley confronted him, she needed to find her daughter and free her.

She crept nearer the front of the house and checked its foundation. From her own experience, she expected Peterson to be holding his victim in a crawlspace under the house. But this was just a low cinderblock foundation and she saw no openings in it.

She thought that perhaps there might be access on another side.

Riley moved quietly around the house until she encountered a wooden deck.

She's got to be under there, Riley thought.

But then her eyes fell on a broken piece of lattice lying on the ground, leaving an opening under the deck. She bent down and used her flashlight to look inside. No one was there, although she could see where the muddy ground was gouged. Someone had been under there recently. It had to have been April.

But where was she? Had she gotten away, or had Peterson hauled her out, planning to do away with her?

Riley's pulse was pounding. No longer worrying about being heard or seen, she rushed up onto the lighted deck and to the window. She could see no one inside the house. Then she tried the door. It was locked. She smashed the window, reached inside, unlatched and opened it, and crawled through.

Her Glock ready, Riley explored the house. It didn't take long. After a quick sweep of a bedroom, a bathroom, a living room, and a kitchen, she knew that the place was empty. But with the lights on like this, it looked as though Peterson might have left hastily. Why?

She opened the back door and stepped back onto the deck. The rain was dying down. Shining her flashlight across the yard, she saw something new—deep tire tracks that zigzagged away from the house, toward the open field. Dashing toward the tracks, she saw deep boot prints on top of some of the tire marks. It looked as though someone—Peterson, probably—had followed the car on foot.

What does this mean? Riley asked herself. *What could have happened?*

But she couldn't just stand there trying to figure it out. She holstered her Glock and slung the shotgun off her shoulder, cradling it with her right arm. If she was about to confront Peterson, this was her weapon of choice. Even in the dark, if she had a clue where he was she'd be sure to hit him.

She hurried along the muddy trail of mixed tracks. They led across a field, winding wildly back and forth to miss the occasional trees.

At last, she saw a light up ahead. As she came nearer, she saw that it was the single remaining headlight of a Cadillac that had slammed against a tree. The driver's door was open, and there was no one inside.

The car headlight angled across a drop to dark water beyond.

She had reached the river. Down the bank ahead of her, someone was waving a flashlight around. She turned off her own flashlight and pocketed it.

Then she heard April's sobbing voice.

"Oh, please, please!"

"Too late, smartass," snapped a familiar male voice. "Stop your whining!"

"April!" Riley shouted.

The name was out before she could think. It was a mistake. She had just announced to Peterson that she had arrived. She'd lost the element of surprise.

Riley stepped forward and almost tumbled down a sharp slope that dropped away just beyond the tree. She caught herself and saw Peterson clearly in the light from the car. He was standing ankle-deep in the river. Just a few feet from him, April was half submerged in the water, bound by her hands and feet.

Riley realized that Peterson could see her too. Carrying the shotgun, she made her way cautiously down the slope toward him. He raised a pistol and pointed it at April.

She stood there, just feet away from the man who had haunted her dreams, and her heart slammed.

"Don't even think about it," Peterson called. "One move and it's over."

Riley's heart sank. If she so much as raised her shotgun, Peterson would kill April before she could fire.

"Put the gun down," he ordered.

Riley gulped hard. She didn't have any other course of action. April's life was at stake.

She stooped and put the shotgun on the ground at the edge of the water.

Then Peterson immediately swung his pistol toward her and pulled the trigger.

Riley braced for the impact.

Nothing happened. Peterson's gun was either jammed or empty.

Riley knew she had a fraction of a second to take action.

She reached into her pocket for the knife she'd taken from the street kid. She snapped it open and lunged, splashing through the shallow water toward him.

She aimed for his solar plexus—that soft spot where stabbing would be easiest. But she slipped in the muddy river, and the blade entered high between two ribs. It stuck there.

Peterson roared with pain and backed away. The knife stayed

in his chest, slipping from Riley's hands.

He suddenly hurled himself forward again, before she could regain her balance, and she slipped on the mud. She found herself falling backwards, onto her back, into the shallow water, shocked by how freezing it was.

And then a moment later, before she could reach up to stop him, she saw his big meaty hands wrapping around her throat—and felt her head being shoved underwater.

Riley felt her world go numb. No longer able to breathe, she writhed and kicked, feeling the life leaving her. How awful, she thought, to die here, in this shallow water, being strangled to death just a few feet from her daughter.

It was the thought of her daughter that brought her back. April. Riley couldn't allow herself to be killed here. Because her death would mean April's death.

Riley redoubled her efforts, thrashing like a wild fish, until finally she managed to raise one knee between his legs. It was a powerful enough blow to take out any other man.

But Peterson, to her surprise, did not budge. He loosened his grip for a moment as he bucked. But then he tightened again, squeezing twice as hard.

Riley knew then that she would die here. That was the best she'd had—and it wasn't enough to take out this monster.

Suddenly, Riley saw an image moving fast, high above; her vision was obscured from beneath the shallow, running water, and at first she wondered if it were an angel, coming to take her away.

But then she realized: it was April. She had found Riley's shotgun, and was holding it awkwardly between her bound wrists. Given her wrist-ties, all she could grab hold of was the barrel itself. Riley watched in amazement as April, feet bound, unable to walk, inched her way closer behind Peterson, her knees scraping stone. When she got close enough, she raised it high and swung it down.

There came a loud crack, audible even beneath the running water, as the stock of the shotgun smashed into Peterson's temple with a force that surprised even Riley.

And for the first time, Peterson loosened his demonic grip on her throat, stumbling backwards.

Riley immediately sat up, gasping for air in huge breaths. She wiped water from her eyes to see Peterson staggering back, clutching the side of his head, his expression one of mixed pain and fury as he dropped to one knee. April stood there, looking stunned at what she had done, and looking, in panic, at the shotgun on the riverbed. It must have slipped from her hands. And Riley watched in horror as the current caught it and it floated away.

Peterson let out the roar of a wounded animal as he charged April. He tackled her to the ground, spun her around, and grabbed the back of her hair. With both hands he shoved her down, face-first, underwater. She was unable to raise her head, and within moments, Riley knew, her daughter would be dead.

Overcoming her shock, Riley leapt to her feet, scanning the riverbed and grabbing a sharp rock as she did. She let out a primal roar herself as she lunged on top of Peterson, swinging the rock with all she had, with a mother's fury.

Riley felt the rock make a satisfying contact with his head. It hit hard enough to knock him off of April. Riley yanked her back, and April rolled over, gasping for air. She was, Riley was relieved to see, still alive.

Riley jumped into action; she could not give Peterson a chance to recover. She jumped on top of him before he could get up.

He spun over, with a fraction of the strength he had but moments ago, weak, eyes glazed, and looked up at her vacantly as she lay on top of him. She raised the rock high overhead with both hands and held it there, arms shaking. There he was, in the flesh, the demon who had plagued her all these nights.

He grinned back at her, a demonic grin.

"You won't do it," he said, blood trickling from his mouth. "If you do, we'll be bound forever."

Riley took a deep breath, and she remembered all the ways he had tortured her, had tortured all those other women, had tortured her daughter—and then she let it out and brought the stone down with everything she had. The sharpened point entering the center of his forehead, and she let it go. It was like letting go of her own personal demons, like letting go of the boulder on her back.

The river darkened with blood, and within moments Peterson lay there, eyes opened, lifeless, the only sound that of the trickling water over his face. This time, he was truly dead.

"Mom," came the voice.

Riley knelt there, atop Peterson, and she did not know how much time had passed. She turned and looked over to see April beside her. She was crying, holding out a shaking hand for her.

"Mom," she said. "He's dead."

Riley looked back down at Peterson, and could hardly believe it.

He's dead.

A moment later there came splashing in the river, and she looked up to see Bill. He slowed as he approached, slowly lowering his gun, staring down at the scene in disbelief and horror, clearly too stunned to speak.

Behind him, Riley saw the traces of orange in the sky. It was almost sunrise. It did not seem possible that the sun could rise again on this world.

And yet rise, it did.

CHAPTER TWENTY THREE

The funeral crowd was dispersing when Lucy spotted a short, slim young man who seemed markedly suspicious. He had just turned away from the gravesite and the expression on his face was not one of mourning. Head down, hands in his pockets, he seemed to actually be smiling.

That's him, Lucy thought, her nerve ends tingling. *That's got to be him.*

She stood still and watched him as he walked by her just a few feet away. That was definitely a grin on his face. This man was gloating, not grieving, Lucy was sure of it. She turned and started to follow him.

From behind, she could see his shoulders shaking a little—from laughter, not sobbing, there could be no doubt. She took longer strides to catch up with him, thinking carefully how to confront him. She thought it best to be straightforward—to identify herself as an FBI agent and demand to ask some questions. If he tried to run, he wouldn't get very far—not with the local police right here and on keen alert. She pulled out her badge and broke into a trot.

At that very moment, a middle-aged couple stepped toward the man.

"Hugh!" the older man said.

"How are you holding up?" the woman asked.

The younger man turned toward the couple, still smiling.

"I'm okay," he said. "I know it's odd, but I just keep thinking about how funny Aunt Rosemary could be. Do you remember how she used to ..."

His voice trailed off as he and the couple huddled closer together and began to move away from Lucy. Then Lucy could see hear all three of them chuckling sadly at whatever story he had told.

She put her badge away. It was a false alarm. The young man had been grinning over the kind of happy memory people often shared at funerals. She was grateful that she hadn't caused a scene and embarrassed herself.

"Go to the funeral," Riley had told her. *"This one might be the type who feels remorse. He might be there."* But if the

murderer had been here, she hadn't discovered him. She turned slowly in a circle, surveying the whole scene.

It was a pleasant, sunny morning. Rosemary Pickens's closest relatives were still clustered under the blue canvas tent by the graveside, accepting condolences from dozens of caring friends and relatives. Other people were wandering away in groups.

Lucy realized that she'd made a miscalculation. In such a small town, she'd expected a small, intimate funeral—and consequently, an easy time spotting someone who seemed odd and out of place. She'd been wrong. She hadn't realized how much of the population would come out for this. Reedsport was not only a place where everybody knew everybody else, but where everybody seemed to *care* about everybody else.

She walked back toward the tent, looking over the masses of flowers that covered and surrounded the coffin. Every single plant or bouquet would need to be accounted for in hopes of turning up the name of a stranger who might have murdered the woman.

Fortunately the local police would gather data on orders that were sent through the large commercial outfits. Lucy wanted to go to the local florists in person and ask about their deliveries. She was about to leave the gravesite when her attention was drawn to a young man who was standing beside the coffin—another short, slight man who appeared to be here alone. He was rather homely-looking, with a large nose and a rather heavy brow.

Could this be him? Lucy wondered. She edged toward him.

But when she got near enough, she saw that tears were streaming down the man's cheeks, and his face was knotted up in genuine grief. As he turned away from the coffin, he took a tissue out of his pocket, blew his nose, and wiped away some tears. When he looked up and saw Lucy, he managed to smile sympathetically. He waved to her weakly, then walked away. Lucy was sure that this couldn't be the one she was looking for. His grief was too unfeigned, too heartfelt.

She felt a surge of discouragement. She hadn't made any real progress since Riley left. The local townspeople had been eager to help, but none had given her any useful information. She'd followed up on details that people thought might be important—strangers in town, unknown vehicles, and the like—but they had all led nowhere.

She was sure Riley would say that eliminating suspects and possibilities was an important part of their work.

It just doesn't seem very exciting, Lucy thought.

Later in the morning, Lucy reached the last of town's three florist shops. At the first two, she had asked about any strangers buying flowers for the funeral, but she'd turned up no leads. The florists had known all of their customers.

When she went inside, this store looked very much like others she had visited—fairly gutted of blossoms and a little disorderly after such intense business. But in the previous places, Lucy had detected no satisfaction at the rush of sales. Those florists had known Rosemary Pickens and were grief-stricken about her loss.

An elderly woman was cleaning a now-empty refrigerated display case.

"Are you the store owner?" Lucy asked.

"Yes," the woman replied in a tired voice.

Lucy took out her badge.

"I'm Special Agent Lucy Vargas," she said. "I'm investigating Rosemary Pickens's murder. I'd like to ask you some questions."

"Of course," the woman said. "How can I help?"

"We're just trying to cover every possibility," Lucy said. "Do you remember anything odd about anybody who bought funeral flowers here? Anyone unfamiliar, for example."

The woman looked thoughtful.

"There was a young man I didn't recognize," she said. "And there was something odd. Let me think for a moment."

She rubbed her forehead with her hand.

"Such a sad day," she said. "It was so crowded this morning, and I was running out of everything. I probably wouldn't have noticed him at all, but he stood out because ... yes, I remember. He had a terrible stutter. He could barely speak at all."

The woman led Lucy over to the front counter.

"By the time he got here, there was hardly anything left in the store," she said. "He found it so hard to talk, he wrote something down. Here, I'll show you."

The woman handed Lucy one of the shop's business cards. On the back was written in neat, careful handwriting ...

"Please give me just a few daisies."

The woman said, "Luckily I had some daisies left. So I sold them to him."

Lucy got out her note pad to jot down information.

"Could you describe him for me?" she asked.

The woman knotted her brow again, thinking hard.

"Oh, no, not really," she said. "All I remember is that he was young and not very tall. And of course the stutter."

"Please try," Lucy said.

The woman thought some more.

"I'm sorry, but there was *such* a crush of customers today, and I just didn't pay much attention to him. And I'm no good with faces anyway. All I remember was that he simply couldn't say what he wanted to say, so I gave him a card and a pen to write with."

Lucy managed to hide her disappointment.

"I would like to take the card," she said. "It might provide some kind of evidence."

The florist handed over the card, apologizing for not being more helpful. Lucy thanked her and left the store, bagging the card as she walked away. She tucked it in her notebook and headed toward her car, which was parked a couple of blocks away.

She felt a bit encouraged now. It seemed likely that the buyer of the daisies might have been the murderer himself. The card might yield some fingerprints, and the handwriting might reveal something. And of course she now knew something else.

He stutters, she thought. *At least that's something to go on.*

She had parked her car a couple of blocks away. As she walked in that direction, she pulled out her phone. She wanted to call Riley, to give her an update and ask her advice.

When she reached the corner and turned to cross the street, she was startled to see a white van moving along slowly very close to her. Sun reflecting off the front window obscured the driver's face. Lucy stopped on the curb to let it go by.

Suddenly the van accelerated. It careened around a sharp right turn and sped away on the cross street.

Startled, Lucy held up her cell phone and snapped a picture.

What's wrong with him? she wondered. The van rounded another corner and was gone.

Lucy felt an urge to call the local police and report a reckless driver. But she told herself that the van hadn't done any damage. It might not even have been going all that fast. She'd just been startled by the sudden acceleration and turn.

When she crossed the street and reached her car, she sat down and put through the call to BAU.

"This is Special Agent Lucy Vargas," she said to the female operator. "I'm working the serial case in Reedsport, New York. Please connect me with Agent Riley Paige's office," she requested.

"Agent Paige isn't at BAU right now."

"That's okay," Lucy said. "I'll call her personal phone."

313

The woman's voice took on a fresh urgency.

"You mustn't do that, Agent Vargas," she said. "Agent Paige is not to be disturbed."

"What's wrong?" Lucy cried. "Has Riley been hurt?"

"I'm sorry, but that's all I'm authorized to say."

"We're working a case together. I have to know if she's all right,"

"Hold on a minute."

After a brief silence, Brent Meredith's voice came on the line.

"Agent Vargas?"

"Yes. Is Riley all right?"

"She's all right. Her daughter was kidnapped but it's all over now."

"April kidnapped? Oh my god!"

"They got her back. Agents Paige and Jeffreys are on their way here now with the girl."

Lucy was stunned. "All right," she sputtered. "Thank you for telling me."

"You'll be brought up to date later. Is there anything else?"

"I, uh…" Lucy tried to remember why she had called in the first place. "I do have something that might be evidence in this case."

"I'll connect you with the evidence lab."

"Thank you."

Lucy was distracted when she talked with the lab technician. "I have a business card with the suspect's handwriting," she said. "Possibly prints as well. I'm taking it to the local police right now. They'll dust it for prints and I'll send you anything they find."

"Anything else?" the technician asked.

"The suspect probably has a stutter," she said.

The lab technician said he'd make a note of that and they ended the call.

Lucy tucked her cell phone back into her handbag without giving another thought to the picture she had just taken.

CHAPTER TWENTY FOUR

As the van driver careened around the corner and sped away, the pile of chains in the passenger seat rattled loudly.

"Be quiet!" he told the chains.

But then came a bump in the road, and the chains rattled again. There was no doubt about it, the chains were calling for his attention. They were demanding that he exert mastery over them—or else they would prove their mastery over him, holding him captive as chains had when he was a child.

"Be patient," he pleaded.

He forced himself to slow the van down. It wouldn't do to get caught for a traffic violation now. He needed to make his way out of Reedsport without being noticed.

But he knew the chains were furious. They had expected him to take the FBI agent for them. They had thought he would strike her right there in the street where she was walking. But she had turned and seen him following her in his van. There was no opportunity to strike her by surprise, and he was sure that she had a gun.

"She wasn't right," he told them.

The road was bumpy and the chains rattled at him again.

"I know she is an authority," he argued. "I saw her FBI badge when she pulled it out at the funeral. But she wasn't wearing a uniform. We do like to see a uniform."

The rattle of the chains still sounded angry.

"She was too young," he explained. "She was really nothing like the women we chose before."

He drove very carefully the rest of the way out of town.

"It would have been foolish to take another woman in this small town," he told the chains. "We'll drive north, all the way to Albany. There are lots of uniforms there. Lots of women of the right age and type. I'll find someone you like."

The chains quieted down for a while and he thought he had made a convincing argument. As he drove up toward Albany he avoided the interstate and was careful not to exceed the speed limit. He explained to the chains that he didn't want to attract attention. Even so, they rattled softly from time to time, reminding him that they were there and they were not pleased with him.

He had lost his nerve back there in Reedsport, and he must not do that again.

"I'll find another one," he promised the chains again and again. "I'll find someone soon."

CHAPTER TWENTY FIVE

"I just read your report, Agent Paige," Special Agent Meredith said as Riley walked into his office. "Congratulations are in order." He shook her hand and added, "By the way, you look like hell."

Riley smiled weakly and sat down. Meredith was right on both counts. She deserved to be congratulated on taking down Peterson at long last. She also felt like hell, although she was trying not to show it. She'd spent the last couple of hours trying to pull herself together.

Bill had taken care of notifying BAU and the D.C. police about Peterson's death. He had wrapped the wet, muddy, and emotionally shaken Riley and April in blankets and driven them directly to Quantico. Riley and April had clung to each other during the whole ride, crying with desperate relief.

Riley had taken April to the BAU clinic to take care of her many scrapes and cuts, none of which were serious. They had both showered there in the building and put on clean clothes that young Agent Emily Creighton had been kind enough to round up for them. April had settled down in the break area, and Riley had spent a couple of hours writing up her final report on the Peterson case.

Agent Meredith thumbed through the written report.

"I'm impressed," Meredith said. "This was some pretty amazing work."

"Thanks, sir," Riley said. "But he had my daughter. No way was he going to get by with that." Then she added, "How soon can I get back to Upstate New York?"

Meredith chuckled. "Not so fast. You're not going anywhere."

Riley was surprised. "Why not, sir?"

"Have you looked at yourself in a mirror? You're exhausted—and with good reason. You need a rest. Besides, you're not needed up there. That case is going nowhere."

"No clues at all?" Riley asked.

Meredith shrugged. "Not enough to go on. Agent Vargas found a florist's card that might have the killer's handwriting. But aside from the florist's prints and Vargas's, there was only a partial print that we can't track down. Vargas is just spinning her wheels up there, and we'll probably bring her back soon."

Meredith leaned back in his chair.

"Besides," he said, "the locals are doing a good job, and if any new leads turn up in Reedsport they'll let us know. The killer is probably in a completely new area by now. Unfortunately, we might not know where until he strikes again."

Riley felt strangely deflated.

She began to protest. "But sir—"

"You're going on leave, Agent Paige. Consider it an order."

Meredith craned forward and looked at Riley with concern.

"You've got a daughter who needs all your attention right now," he said. "I saw her in the break room. That's where you should be."

Riley thanked Meredith again and left his office. She went straight to the break room, where she found April clutching a soft drink can and staring off into space. Riley's heart ached for her daughter.

She sat down next to April and took her hand.

"I'm so sorry," she said for what seemed like the thousandth time.

April swallowed hard and said, "He said I was a killer."

Riley squeezed April's hand tightly.

"*He* was the killer," she said firmly. "And we took him down. The both of us. You did good back there. Don't ever forget that."

A tear rolled down April's cheek.

"Just don't make me stay with Dad tonight," she said. "Don't make me stay there ever again."

Riley was startled that such a thing was on April's mind. But as she thought about it, it made sense. She had phoned Ryan when they'd gotten to Quantico. She'd told him what had happened, but not all the harrowing details. He'd sounded shocked, then relieved, then not terribly interested.

No, Ryan was not who April needed right now.

"Let's just go home," Riley said.

"No," April said with a gasp. "Not yet. Not there either."

Riley understood this reaction all too well. Their house was where Peterson had stalked both of them. Riley wasn't eager to rush back there either. She realized that it was a good time to talk about something that had been on her mind for a while.

"April, I've been thinking about moving," she said.

April looked up at her with sudden interest.

Riley continued, "I think I will be able afford to buy a townhouse in Fredericksburg. That way we wouldn't be so isolated. And you'd be closer to your school and your friends."

She could see April's whole body relax a little.

"And I've been thinking," Riley added, "that maybe Gabriela could move in with us. I haven't asked her yet."

April smiled. It seemed to Riley that she hadn't seen that smile in a long time.

"I'll ask her," April said. "She'll do it. I know she'll do it."

Riley squeezed her daughter's hand and smiled too. She felt a flood of relief that maybe she had a good solution to at least one longtime problem. And now she was on leave so she and April could have some time together. But where? They were both exhausted and they both needed a break.

Then a thought came to her.

"April," she blurted, "let's go to New York. Let's just enjoy ourselves for a few days."

April's face brightened even more.

"Really? New York City? Do you mean it?"

"Yes. Right now. Bill can drive us to the airport. There's no need to go back to the house. Let's just go."

"But what will I wear?" April cried, looking down at the jeans and shirt that Emily Creighton had loaned her.

Riley laughed with pleasure at the so-typical-teen question.

"Don't worry about clothes," she said. "We'll buy what we need right there. We'll splurge. Get a nice hotel room and catch a couple of shows."

"But can we really afford it?" April asked.

Riley shrugged. "No, but I'll charge it up to all the vacations we haven't taken. I'll hit the savings account hard. We deserve it."

April laughed aloud.

"That sounds just great, Mom!"

April's laughter was the sweetest sound that Riley could hope to hear.

*

Later that afternoon, Riley and April stepped out of a cab in front of their Manhattan hotel. April's expression was positively wonderstruck as she looked around at the bustling traffic, then up at the towering buildings. It did Riley's heart good to see that look on her daughter's face.

"Oh, Mom!" April said. "Where do we even start?"

Riley laughed. "First things first," she said. "I guess we need to do some serious clothes shopping. Do you want to check into our room first?"

"Can we go shopping right now?" April begged. "These things that Emily got for me are kind of embarrassing."

"Let me think," Riley said. "It's been a while since I've been here."

The hotel was just a few blocks south of Central Park. Riley led April along Seventh Avenue toward Times Square. She remembered a couple of shops in midtown that didn't have outrageous prices.

At their first stop, April bought ankle pants and a shirt. Riley picked out a pants suit that challenged her budget, but after all, she did have to wear something decent in the city. At their next stop, Riley had to catch her breath when she saw April in the dress she'd picked out. Her daughter was clearly becoming a young woman rather than a child.

"Please, Mom," April said. "I love it."

The dress actually was very pretty and suited April perfectly. They bought it, and they both topped off the shopping spree with shoes and handbags.

Finally, they made their way back to the hotel, laden with bags and laughing happily. They checked in and took the elevator up to their twelfth-floor room.

As they hung up the clothes, Riley could see that April was looking tired. It was no wonder, after all that she'd been through.

"I think we should stay in tonight," Riley told her. "Order dinner in the room and do our touristy stuff tomorrow."

"That would be good," April said. She went into the bathroom.

Riley stared out the hotel window. Their room had a fine view of the city skyline. She started running some plans through her head. Maybe they could catch a Broadway matinee tomorrow. She would check and see what might be available.

Riley sighed. When had she stopped taking her daughter on vacations? When had she forgotten how to enjoy one herself? When April was small, she and Ryan had taken her on vacations. They'd gone to Chincoteague to see the wild ponies and to resorts in the mountains.

But in more recent years? Not so much. Several years ago, she'd taken a few days off when April had been on summer break and Ryan had been too busy to go anywhere. So she and April had rented a condo at Virginia Beach. She'd done nothing like that since.

She knew that April had always dreamed of coming to New

York. But she wondered if this trip really would feel to April like a dream come true. Her daughter had been through so much. The excitement of being here and shopping was sure to drain away soon.

When April came out of the bathroom, she sat down on the edge of one of the beds. She had that distant, troubled look again.

"Mom," she said quietly, "I can't look in the mirror."

Riley sat down and put her arm around April.

"I know what that's like," she said.

She didn't need to ask April why she felt this way. The poor girl's face was still cut and bruised. Just looking at it was enough to bring back the horrible trauma she'd endured at Peterson's hands.

April leaned her head against Riley's shoulder.

"Tomorrow's my birthday," April said.

Riley's heart sank. She'd forgotten, of course.

"I'm sorry," she said.

"No, I don't want you to feel like that," April said. "You've just bought me lots of things. That's not why I'm telling you. The thing is, tomorrow's my birthday, and ..."

April heaved a single sob.

"And suddenly I don't even care," she said. "I don't care about anything."

"I know how you feel," Riley said.

"I know you do."

They sat there in silence for a few moments. How life had changed in just the last few days! One of Riley's greatest frustrations as a parent had always been trying to get April to understand her job—why she was so obsessed with it, how important it was, and how dangerous.

Now April understood it all perfectly. And Riley wished with all her heart that she didn't.

It was Riley's turn to go to the bathroom. But she hesitated. She remembered something that Meredith had said ...

"Have you looked at yourself in a mirror?"

Just like her daughter, Riley was apprehensive about looking into the mirror. She knew what she was likely to see there—the faces of countless victims and their tormentors. And in her own face, she'd see something that she really didn't want to see.

She'd see the face of a woman who had no business, no right, to hope for a normal, happy life, who was a fool to imagine that she could raise a daughter in this terrible world. There were still too many monsters out there.

321

At the core of her being, Riley always felt it imperative to stop them, whoever they were, wherever they were. And despite all that Meredith had said, she couldn't stop thinking about the monster who was still loose in Upstate New York.

CHAPTER TWENTY SIX

The man was nodding, almost asleep, when the chains in the passenger seat began to grumble again. His van was parked in a shopping center parking lot in Albany. The chains weren't actually rattling, but he could hear them grumbling even so. And he knew what they were complaining about. It was that FBI woman yesterday—the one he hadn't taken.

"How many times do I have to tell you she wasn't right?" he snapped. "If I'd taken her, you wouldn't be happy. You'd ask why she wasn't older, wasn't wearing a uniform, hadn't done what she was supposed to do. You'd only complain."

The chains quieted a little, but didn't stop their grumbling altogether. It didn't surprise him that he and the chains were especially at odds right now. They'd been cooped up together in the van for most of twenty-four hours. Naturally, they were getting on each other's nerves.

After the incident with the woman yesterday, he'd driven straight to Albany and made this parking lot his base. Sooner or later, he knew the right victim was sure to come by. But the rest of the day came and went without that happening. After the mall closed that night, he'd moved the van to a nearby side street and slept on its floor. He'd come back here first thing this morning.

Now it was getting dark, and he was wondering whether he was going to have to spend another night here. The chains would definitely get more and more irritable. He wasn't sure how much longer he could take that.

He, too, was tired and irritable. But patience and vigilance were essential. He took a candy bar out of his glove compartment and began to eat it. It wasn't much, but it would have to suffice for nutrition and energy. He couldn't get out of the van and go buy something to eat. The chains wouldn't allow it. And of course they were right. If he left his post even for a few moments, he might miss the perfect victim.

At this hour, more people were leaving the mall than entering it. They consisted mostly of young, childless couples and families with kids. He saw no one who came close to suiting what both he and the chains needed.

Even so, the candy bar lifted his spirits. He felt better about everything. Really, he had all that he needed in life. He was especially pleased with his van. It had brought him here years ago and served him well all this time. It was big enough that he could sleep in it when he needed to and also convenient for transporting the women. He had quickly realized that the women, too, could sleep here—the beginning of their final sleep.

And he had certainly never regretted leaving his former home. It had been the scene of too many childhood horrors. He'd been perfectly happy to drive away all alone until he'd finally decided on a new hometown and settled in.

He'd been eighteen then. He'd liked his new home from the start, and the people there were kind to him. For several years he'd lived quietly and hadn't caused anybody any harm. That had changed five years ago when he took his first victim.

Nibbling the last of the candy bar, he wondered what had gone wrong. He never wanted to hurt or kill anybody. He still didn't.

Perhaps he shouldn't have stolen those straitjackets when he was released from the mental hospital. It's just that he had an irresistible feeling that someday he was going to need them. And the chains that he accumulated little by little over the years insisted that he keep them.

But what was going to happen now? If he didn't claim another woman, he knew that the chains would overpower him, bind him up, fasten his door so he couldn't get out, render him as helpless as he'd been as a child. He needed to find a third victim, and quickly.

Suddenly, the chains murmured, telling him to look sharp. Sure enough, two women were coming out of the mall—both of them wearing nurse's uniforms. One was slender and much too young. But the other was stout and middle-aged, exactly the woman he was looking for.

He watched as the two walked to a car in the next parking lane. The woman he needed was going to drive. He started the van and drove along after the car.

As he followed the car into a suburban neighborhood, he knew that something was wrong. Even if he could catch the stout woman, he still wouldn't be able to take her. The problem was simple.

I didn't choose the others. They chose me.

The first time, five years ago, that poor woman in Eubanks had provoked him when he'd picked up some change that she'd dropped in a store.

"Such a sweet boy!" she'd said.

Those words and that tone—so condescending, as if he were

retarded. It stung him unbearably, reminding him of his mother and the nuns.

It was the same with the woman in Reedsport.

"What a good boy!" she'd said when he helped her with her groceries.

Both women had sealed their fates with those well-intentioned words. But this woman had said nothing to him at all. Without such an impetus, such a provocation, he was helpless to act.

And if he didn't act, he'd be at the mercy of the chains.

The car he was following stopped in front of a house. The younger woman got out, waved goodnight to the driver, and went into the house. The other woman started driving again, and he kept on following her. He still had no idea what to do next.

But now the chains were chattering to him, explaining everything. Somehow, he was going to have to provoke *her* into provoking *him*. And the chains had their own ideas about how to do that. It was going to require perfect timing, and the chains weren't at all sure that he was up to the task. He decided to prove them wrong.

Now he was following the woman on a road that wound through a park. He saw nobody anywhere. It seemed like the perfect place to act.

"Here?" he asked the chains.

The chains chattered in agreement.

Up ahead, at the edge of the park, was a traffic light. The light was green, but the chains assured him that it was just ready to change. He carefully passed the woman's car and drove directly in front of her. The light turned yellow, and he sped up a little, as if he were meant to make it through the intersection before it turned red.

Then he hit the brakes good and hard. Sure enough, the woman's car struck the rear end of the van with a sharp bump. The collision wasn't hard enough to cause much damage, but it served his purposes.

He shifted into park, put on the parking brake, and got out of the car. The woman backed her own car away from the van a few feet, then got out, looking very concerned. He walked to the back of the van and surveyed the minor damage to both cars. As the woman approached, he tried to explain to her what had happened—and to apologize.

"I—I—I—" he stuttered.

The woman's face was suddenly full of sympathy.

"Oh, you poor thing!" she said. "It was my fault, of course.

I'll go get my insurance information."

She got back in the car and opened her glove compartment.

He felt exactly the surge of aggression and anger he needed.

"Oh, you poor thing!" she'd said.

What did she think he was, a baby?

He opened the back of his van and took out a heavy bundle of chains. Then he stood there waiting, holding the chains behind his back with one hand. When the woman came out again, he pointed again to his back bumper, as if trying to draw her attention to some further damage.

"What is it?" she asked.

When she bent over a little for a closer look, he brought the chains crashing against the back of her head. She collapsed perfectly, falling head first into the bed of the van, completely unconscious. All he had to do was lift her legs into the van and shut the back doors.

As he drove away, the chains were silent. He understood why. They were slightly awestruck. They hadn't expected him to accomplish this so boldly and deftly. They had underestimated him. He had proven himself their master—at least for now.

*

He arrived at his house about an hour later. He pulled the van beside the house and backed it around to the basement door. Then he got out, walked to the back of the van, and opened the doors.

There she was, lying completely still, a pool of blood around her head. He bent over to make sure she was still breathing. Fortunately, she was. The chains wanted her to be alive, at least for now.

He'd stopped along the road outside of Albany put her into the straitjacket. Sooner or later, she'd regain consciousness, and the chains had thought it best to put her in the straitjacket right away.

Now came the difficult task of getting her into the basement. The woman was slightly heavier than the others had been, and he was none too strong. He tugged and pulled until she fell out of the van, then tugged and pulled some more until he got her to the basement door. He opened the door and pushed her on inside.

As he rolled her across the concrete floor, she emitted a loud groan, then fell silent again. He had the cot ready. Clumsily, he pulled the woman's upper body up on it, then wrestled her legs onto it as well.

From that point on, things were much easier. He began to

wrap the chains around and around her, binding her tightly to the cot. The chains laughed with delight. They were well-pleased with his work.

When he finished wrapping, he heard her speak.

"Where am I?" she said, just starting to regain consciousness. "Oh, God, where am I? What's going on?"

He shushed her loudly. If he could only talk, he'd explain to her that she mustn't say a word. In this place, only the chains were allowed to speak.

But his shushing didn't do any good.

"Where am I?" she said in a slurred voice, her terror rising. "Somebody help me."

He stuffed a rag into the woman's mouth, then gagged her by wrapping a chain all the way around her head. She continued to writhe and groan. Her wide-eyed gaze was fixed across the room. He followed the gaze and saw that she was staring at the little altar he had made.

A bulletin board rested atop a table pushed against the wall. On the table he had respectfully placed shoes, a prison guard's badge, a nurse's uniform and nametag, a few buttons, and other items belonging to the other two women. On the bulletin board were pinned obituaries, funeral handouts, and pictures he had taken of the flowers he had left at the gravesites.

He was glad she was looking there. It ought to give her some comfort. Surely she understood that she, too, would be memorialized there when the time came. A tear came to his eye and he thought about how he had mourned those two women—and how he would mourn this one.

But the woman groaned sharply against the gag. She didn't understand. It was infuriating. This whole thing was going to play out the same way it had before. He'd loosen the chains and remove the rag to give her a drink of water, and she'd scream uncontrollably.

Maybe he could make this one understand. He took his straight-edged razor out of his pocket, opened it, and held it close to the woman's throat, shushing again. Surely she'd understand that he didn't want to slit her throat, and that the choice was hers. All she had to do was keep quiet.

Her groaning quieted a little. Even so, he still saw a trace of defiance in her eyes. It was no good. Sooner or later, this one, too, was going to scream, and he'd have no choice but to kill her.

And like last time, he would hang her up for all to see. The warning was absolutely necessary. The world had to know. The world had to understand. The world must be told to leave him alone. He didn't yet know how and where he would display her. The chains would tell him what to do.

This was how it always went. Killing the women was never his intention. But sooner or later the chains would give him no other choice. It was just a fact of life, and he'd never be able to change it.

CHAPTER TWENTY SEVEN

The message came on their third day in New York, while Riley and April were sitting in the food court of the Museum Natural of History. They were eating hot dogs loaded with a variety of toppings. Riley was startled to see that her buzzing cell phone showed a text from Lucy.

"Sorry to bother U on vacation. Call if U can."

Riley's interest was piqued.

"What is it, Mom?" April asked Riley.

"It's Lucy—I mean Agent Vargas. You met her the night we had the break-in."

April looked intrigued. Riley hadn't seen that look of honest interest on April's face since they'd arrived in the city.

They'd been doing all the obligatory tourist things—visiting the Statue of Liberty, going to the top of the Empire State Building, and taking in a Broadway matinee. Still shaken from her ordeal, April's earlier enthusiasm had faded.

Riley couldn't blame her. The truth was, she was thinking that this trip might have been a bad idea from the beginning.

"What does she want?" April asked.

"She wants me to call," Riley said. "It can wait."

"Why wait?" April asked with a shrug.

It was a good question. It wasn't as if Lucy was likely to spoil anything. Riley punched the number.

"Riley!" Lucy almost shouted when she answered. "Am I glad to talk to you!"

"What's going on?"

"We've got another victim," Lucy said.

Riley's nerves quickened. She'd had a hunch that the killer was going to strike again sooner rather than later. Sometimes she didn't like being right.

"I'm in Albany," Lucy explained. "A woman here disappeared from her car. She was a nurse. In uniform, like the last one."

Riley's interest grew. That confirmed a definite pattern—a prison guard and now two nurses, all women in uniform.

"Are you sure it's our guy?" Riley asked.

"Yeah, our field office agents are sure too. The police found a small length of chain on the pavement. They knew about the chain killer, so they made a report to the FBI field office and the agents contacted me in Reedsport. Of course, the chain could just be a coincidence, but … "

"But chains sure point to our psychopath," Riley said, taking a long deep breath. Then she noticed that April was watching her and listening apprehensively.

"Why did you want to talk to me?" Riley asked.

A silence fell. Riley sensed that Lucy was getting ready to ask for a favor.

"Riley, I called it in to Quantico," the junior agent said. "Agent Meredith said they'd send somebody up to partner with me. I don't know who yet. And of course I'm already working with the field office here, but …"

Lucy's voice trailed off.

"Naw, it's crazy," she said. "You're on vacation. I shouldn't have bothered you. I'll let you go."

"Tell me," Riley said.

There was another pause.

"Look, whoever they send up, I'm probably going to be lead investigator, because I'm on this case already. I'm not sure I'm ready for that. I'm already feeling out of my depth. I was wondering if you could come up and …"

Lucy stopped again, but she didn't need to finish her sentence. Riley understood perfectly that Lucy wanted her to take charge again.

"I don't know about this, Lucy," Riley said. "Meredith has got me under pretty strict orders to stay on leave."

"I understand," Lucy said. "I knew it was crazy. Sorry to bother you."

"No, wait, don't hang up," Riley said.

Another silence fell. Riley wavered as to what to say.

"Let me get back to you," she finally said.

"Okay," Lucy replied.

They ended the call.

"What was that about?" April asked.

"There's been another abduction in Upstate New York," Riley said. "Lucy wants me to come up and work on it."

April's eyes widened.

"So what are you going to do?" she asked.

"I'm thinking maybe I should go," Riley said. "I'd have to get the next train to Albany."

April looked alarmed.

"Oh, no, Mom," she said. "Don't even think of it. You're not sending me back to stay with Dad. I'm just not going there."

Riley sighed. April had a point. But what were the alternatives?

Then April said, "Why don't I come with you?"

She was smiling. Riley found it nice to see her smile again.

"Maybe I could help," April added.

"Absolutely not," Riley said. "If you come, you're staying put in our hotel room. And I don't want to hear any complaints about it."

April pouted just a little.

"Okay," she said. "But the hotel had better have a pool. And I'll have to buy a bathing suit. I'm still on vacation, even if you're not." April fell silent for a moment, then added, "I promise to let you do your job. I'll stay out of the way."

"It's a deal," Riley said. She dialed up Lucy to tell her that she was on her way.

*

About four hours later, Riley was in Albany, riding in a car with Lucy driving. They had just left April in a nice room that Lucy had reserved. It connected directly to another room where Lucy was staying. Riley and April had been able to buy a bathing suit right there in the hotel, and she had left her daughter happily splashing in the pool. It felt good to know that April was in a safe place.

Lucy drove them into a park and stopped near a taped-off lane where an empty car still sat on the road. A couple of Albany police officers were nearby. That portion of the surrounding park was also cordoned off from the public with crime scene tape.

"Here we are," Lucy said. "I asked them to leave everything in place until you got here."

They got out and went to inspect the scene. Riley could see that the front end of the abandoned car was dented, but not severely. It obviously had not been a high-speed crash. The driver's door was still open.

"Her name is Carla Liston," Lucy said. "She was on her way home after finishing her shift at the hospital and doing some shopping with a friend. That was Myra Cortese, another nurse. Liston had dropped Cortese off before she got to this point."

Lucy pointed to the pavement in front of the car.

"Here's just the trace of a skid mark," she said. "And some glass shards on the road, but that's from her headlight."

331

Riley bent over and inspected the dent in the front of the car. "Have these white marks analyzed," she said. "They're sure to be from the killer's vehicle and they'll identify the make. That also means that it has a dented back bumper."

Lucy said, "The abductor's vehicle must have stopped suddenly at the light. My guess is that he deliberately tricked her into rear-ending him. He attacked her when she got out of her car to inspect the damage."

Riley nodded in agreement.

"And we're pretty sure he's small and non-threatening," Riley added. "So she wasn't scared of him when she saw him. Have you got anything new in the way of a profile?"

"Yeah," Lucy said. "I think he stutters. I got that from a florist who remembered a stranger who couldn't tell her what he wanted to buy for the funeral."

"Good work," Riley said. "That could be an important lead."

She looked more closely at the front of the woman's car.

"The damage is higher up than you'd expect from a regular-sized car. That means probably a van or truck. We'd already guessed that he probably uses a van. What about the chain you said the cops found?"

Lucy took a color photograph out of a folder and handed it to Riley. The picture had been taken while the chain was still laying the pavement. It was a short, small brass chain, the kind that might be used to latch a door.

"It's not the kind of chain he used to bind up the victims," Lucy said. "Do you think he left it as some kind of a message?"

"I don't think so," Riley said. "He makes his statement when he hangs up the victim. My guess is that this just fell out of the back of his van without his noticing it. He probably drives around with all kinds of chains in the van."

"But why?" Lucy asked. "I mean, aside from to attack his victims?"

Riley didn't reply. It was a good question, and an important one. Whatever was driving this killer wasn't coming clear to her. She wanted another opinion.

"I'm going to make a phone call," Riley said.

She walked over to a park bench and sat down, then dialed Mike Nevins's number on her cell phone. Her forensic psychiatrist friend had a wide range of experience with various kinds of murderers and other criminals. The FBI often called him in as consultant on difficult cases.

When she got him on the line, Riley said, "Mike, I need your input. I'm up in Albany working on the chain killer case. He's abducted another woman."

"I thought you were on leave," Mike said.

Riley sighed. She really didn't want to get into this with Mike. He wouldn't approve of her defying Meredith's orders.

"Well, I was, but now I'm not. Don't ask a lot of questions about it, okay? I take it you're familiar with the case."

"Yes, I've been keeping up. He's committed two murders. Both times the victims were found in straitjackets and wrapped with chains."

"That's right," Riley said. "And they're wrapped with far more chains than needed to hold anybody. He even wraps them across the victim's mouth. It looks like he's just obsessed with chains of all kinds. He must collect them wherever he goes. God knows how many he's got at home. It's like chains are some kind of fetish."

Riley got up and began to pace.

"The thing is, I don't get it," she said. "Why chains? Why not something else? And why are they even needed on top of a straitjacket? That why I need your take on it."

A long silence fell.

Finally, Mike said, "I can think of possible reasons, but at this point it would all just be speculation. I do know somebody you should talk to—but you'll have to visit him in Sing Sing."

CHAPTER TWENTY EIGHT

A guard escorted Riley into a small room with cream-colored walls and a barred window. On one wall was a framed mirror that was obviously an observation window for anyone watching from the other side. The guard looked at Riley inquiringly and she said, "It's okay." He left and closed the door behind him.

The prisoner, clad in a dark green jumpsuit, was already sitting at the table waiting. He was smiling at her.

Riley wasn't yet sure what to make of that smile. It was, after all, the smile of a cold-blooded killer who was serving a life sentence. She sat down in the vacant chair on the other side of the table, facing him.

Shane Hatcher was a sturdily built African-American. Mike Nevins had told Riley that he was fifty-five years old, but he looked younger. Riley guessed that he took good care of himself and made use of Sing Sing's exercise equipment.

"So you must be Agent Riley Paige," Hatcher said. "Mike Nevins has told me things about you."

"Good things, I hope," Riley said.

Hatcher didn't reply, and his smile got just a bit more inscrutable.

He was wearing small reading glasses that were perched low on the bridge of his nose. They didn't make him look bookish, though. His face was too imposing for that.

Yesterday, Mike had told Riley she should talk to Hatcher, and she had promptly set up the visit for this morning. She'd made the two two-hour drive from Albany to Sing Sing Correctional Facility alone, because Lucy was waiting at the FBI field office in Albany for her new partner to arrive.

"I like ol' Mike," Hatcher said. "He contacted me after he read one of my articles. I've published in a few magazines, you know. I've done a lot of studying here on the inside. Criminology, mostly. I've gotten to be kind of an expert. Earned some respect in the field. I figure maybe if I can share some insights with the world, it's some kind of atonement."

He leaned toward her and added with a note of confidentiality, "I've changed a lot. I'm not like the kid that came in here." After a brief silence, he added, "But then nobody stays the same for long

334

in here."

Riley sensed that this was true, but she wasn't sure in what way. This man had been in Sing Sing for a long time. Was he rehabilitated, ready to return to free society? No parole board had thought so in several long decades. No, there was a reason Shane Hatcher was still behind bars. There was also a reason why he had survived. He might be a better human being than the kid who came in here, but he was also more cunning—perhaps more devious. That could actually be more dangerous.

He looked at Riley closely, apparently sizing her up.

"So why should I talk to you?" he asked. "I mean, what am I going to get out of the deal?"

It wasn't an entirely unexpected question. Before coming here, Riley had wondered whether she should bring a little contraband—a pack of cigarettes or a small bottle of whiskey. Prisoners always wanted something from visitors. Hatcher was going to be no exception.

"What do you have in mind?" Riley asked cautiously.

Hatcher drummed his fingers on the table.

"Well, I'll tell you what you want to know—as long as *you* tell me something in return when we're done. Something that you don't want people to know. Something you wouldn't want anybody else to know."

Riley tried to conceal her unease. This could be tricky. He very likely was hoping that she'd tell him something that he could use as leverage or even blackmail.

But what really surprised her was that he wasn't asking for this favor up front, before he'd even talked to her. Riley could renege, of course.

Or could she? Did he have her correctly pegged as someone whose word could be trusted?

"It's a deal," she said.

"Then let's get started," Hatcher said.

Riley decided to get right to the point.

"Mike tells me that you know a lot about chains," she said.

Hatcher's smile turned a bit darker.

"Yeah, I was called 'Shane the Chain' when I was gangbanger back in the day. I did a lot of fighting with chains, sort of as a trademark. That made me one scary bro, so I rose up in the ranks real fast. And I killed a few people with those chains. Never mind how many. I was a street warrior, after all."

His face took on a faraway look as he slipped into memory.

"There was a beat cop who especially had it in for me," he

said. "Swore he'd take me down, and I swore that I'd kill him if he tried. Well, that day came, and I pulverized him with a set of tire chains. There wasn't much left of him by the time I was through. It was a closed casket funeral."

His eyes narrowed.

"Oh, I should mention that I dumped his body on his front porch for his wife and kids to find. That's when I got caught. And that's how I got here. Why I'm still here."

Riley was startled by how calmly he said this, as if he were talking about somebody else. She studied his expression for some trace of regret, but she couldn't detect very much of that. His story made it clear why he had not been paroled.

Hatcher continued, "Mike told me about the serial you're after. How he binds up women with chains, tortures them, leaves their bodies all chained up. In straitjackets, too."

"Right," Riley said. "He's obsessed with chains. He seems to collect them, all kinds of them."

"I can see why," Hatcher said. "Chains give you a feeling of power. For me, they started out as a gimmick, a way to intimidate. I never expected to kill anybody. But they got to be an addiction. I really got to love them. And the killing, well, it felt just great, and I never wanted to stop. Those chains pushed me right over the edge, from a screwed-up kid into a bloodthirsty monster."

Hatcher scratched his chin thoughtfully.

"What kind of physical evidence have you got?" he asked. "I mean, aside from his interest in chains and straitjackets?"

Riley thought for a moment.

"My partner found a business card that might have a sample of his handwriting," she said. She pulled an enlarged image of the card out of her folder and passed it across the table. Hatcher picked it up and looked at it, pushing the reading glasses up the bridge of his nose.

"I take it that it's been checked for fingerprints," he said.

"Yeah, we only got a partial and couldn't match it."

Hatcher adjusted his glasses for a better look.

"What have the BAU handwriting experts said about it?" he asked.

"We haven't heard back from them yet."

Hatcher seemed to be more and more fascinated by the card.

He said slowly and tentatively, "There's something about that handwriting. I'm not sure just what …"

Then he snapped his fingers.

"Yeah, I know what it is. It looks just like David Berkowitz's handwriting. You've heard of the 'Son of Sam,' haven't you?"

"I sure have," Riley said.

She'd studied about David Berkowitz at the academy. He was a psychotic serial killer who murdered six people and injured seven others during the mid-1970s. Before he was caught, he'd left behind letters signed "Son of Sam." The name had stuck ever since.

Riley also knew that Berkowitz had done some time at Sing Sing. She wondered if Hatcher had gotten to know him. It would have been a fascinating relationship.

Hatcher pointed to details in the writing.

"It's the same vertical letters," he said. "It also looks tense and tight, like Berkowitz's. I'll bet your guy has a lot in common with him."

"For example?" Riley asked.

Hatcher leaned back in his chair.

"Well, Berkowitz was given up for adoption as a baby. He grew up feeling abandoned. Had a real 'mommy problem.'"

Hatcher thought some more.

"It starts to make sense," he said. "Berkowitz wasn't into chains, but I've known a few others who are. I've talked to them about it. One thing most of the chain fanciers have got in common is childhood trauma, maybe abandonment. They were mistreated with chains as kids, beaten with them, restrained with them. They were powerless, so they look to chains for power."

Hatcher was growing more animated. He obviously enjoyed having someone to talk to, especially someone he could educate.

He continued, "Of course the chains won't ever *give* them that sense of power, because chains were what made them feel helpless in the first place. But I'm sure you've heard Einstein's definition of insanity."

Riley nodded. "He called it doing something over and over again and expecting a different result."

"Now, that's not *my* profile, because I'm no psychopath," Hatcher said. "But if you're talking about a true serial killer, well …"

Hatcher looked Riley straight in the eye.

He said, "I think you'd better check out orphanages and the like. Look for somebody who's been both abandoned and restrained. Someone who's been tortured."

He rapped his knuckles against the table.

"Is there anything else I can help you with?" he asked.

Riley felt more than satisfied.

337

"No, that should do it," she said.

"So what is it you don't want people to know about you?" he asked.

Riley said nothing for a moment. She wavered. Now was the time when she could simply get up from the table and walk away, breaking her part of the bargain. The man posed no threat to her, after all. He was never getting out of this place.

But his eyes were still locked on hers. His will was extremely strong. And he understood her in a most discomforting way. He knew that she wouldn't break her word. Even if she didn't know why, she couldn't do that.

But what could she tell him that wouldn't give him more power over her than he already had?

"I'm a lousy mother," she said.

Hatcher shook his head and chuckled sourly.

"You're going to have to do better than that," he said. "I'm not looking to hear something that everybody who knows you knows already. Even I had that figured out."

Riley felt a chill. He probably really had figured out that much about her. She thought in silence for another moment.

Finally she said, "You told me that it felt great to kill with chains. I know that feeling."

"Is that so?" he asked, sounding intrigued.

"The other day I killed a man with a sharpened rock," she said. "I smashed his head in, again and again. And the thing is, I didn't regret it, one bit. In fact, I wish I could do it again."

He smiled broadly, apparently enjoying her answer.

"And now, if you don't mind, I'd like to go," she said.

As soon as the words were out of her mouth, she asked herself, *Why am I asking his permission?*

He really did have tremendous force of will.

"Just one more thing," Hatcher said. "I'd like an honest answer to a simple question. Do you think a man like me is worth keeping alive?"

Riley felt a smile form on her own face.

"No," she said.

Hatcher chuckled darkly and rose from his chair.

"Come back and see me any time," he said. Then with a shrug and a wink, he added, "I'll be here."

*

After her talk with Hatcher, Riley returned to the FBI vehicle for her drive back to Albany. Before she started the car, she called Lucy at the field office there. She told her what Hatcher had said and asked Lucy to get the BAU team looking into orphanages, foster homes, and adoption services and cross-reference for speech impediments, especially a stutter.

"You mean checking for places that have been charged with using excessive restraint?" Lucy asked.

"Yes, but they should look at it the other way too, for records on kids who have been restrained. Especially with chains. They should cross-reference all of that with what we've projected as the probable age and build of the chain killer. We still don't know exactly what we're looking for, but it will be a start."

"Okay, anything else?"

"They should actually cross-reference for anything to do with chains."

Lucy agreed and hung up. Riley hoped that the BAU search would be more helpful than the interviews they'd done with the kidnap victim's family and co-workers. The woman's family was emotionally devastated and in serious denial. They refused to believe that she had been kidnapped. Maybe she'd been hurt in the accident, they insisted, and was wandering around in a state of confusion. Still, they were anxious for the police and the FBI to take care of everything. To find her and return her home.

The nurse who had been dropped off by the victim had tried hard to be helpful. She had described everything they'd done at the mall after work, but she'd often stopped and corrected her story, putting events in a different order.

"I'm so sorry," she had wailed. "I know I should remember more. We were just having a good time shopping after work. Everything was so normal."

Riley had asked the distraught woman to call if she thought of anything else, even a small detail. But that prospect didn't seem likely.

Riley was feeling grim as she drove back to Albany. But she hoped that the BAU would bring up something useful by the time she arrived.

*

Less than two hours later, Riley walked into the front office of the FBI field office. When she saw who was there with Lucy, she stopped dead in her tracks. The man signing in was Bill Jeffreys. He turned away from the desk just in time to see Riley.

"What are you doing here?" he asked.

"What are *you* doing here?" Riley replied.

"Meredith sent me to help Agent Vargas," he said. "I know he didn't send you. You're supposed to be on leave. He told me it was an order."

Lucy looked mortified.

"Oh, no," she said. "This is all my fault."

"No, it's not, Lucy," Riley said wearily. "It was my decision."

Bill looked as though he could hardly believe his eyes.

"Riley, what do you think you're doing? You got fired once. Do you want to get fired again? And after everything you went through with your daughter, do you think you're in any state of mind to go back to work?"

"There's nothing wrong with my state of mind," Riley said.

Bill shook his head. "And what about April?" he asked. "Where is she right now?"

"She's right here in Albany," Riley said. "She's safe, Bill, and she's going to stay that way."

Lucy tried to step between Riley and Bill. She said, "Agent Jeffreys, I take full responsibility. I asked her to come."

Before Bill could reply, there came a tentative voice from nearby.

"Um, Agent Paige …"

Riley and her companions turned around. A shy, nerdish young technician had just come into the area.

"I think we've got some leads," he said.

CHAPTER TWENTY NINE

Things weren't at all comfortable in the field office meeting room. Bill was clearly not pleased by Riley's presence in Albany. He and Lucy sat at one side of the table, going over the list of possible suspects. Seated directly across from them, Riley made sure that she got a look at every item under scrutiny.

Paul Nooney, the rather mousy technician who had called them in from the front office, sat nearby, sorting through his folder of possible suspects. His laptop was open, and he was intermittently running searches.

"What about this one?" Bill asked, passing Lucy a sheet of paper.

"I don't think so," Lucy said. "This guy resisted arrest, and it took three cops to subdue him. We're not looking for somebody that strong."

Riley reached out and slid the paper where she could see it. She just nodded.

"Hey, here's somebody," Nooney said. "His name is Wayne Turner, and he lives up in Walcott. He's twenty-eight years old, five foot six, weighs a hundred and fifteen pounds. According to his sheet, he's got a slight stutter. He was an orphan and spent some time in an orphanage before he was adopted. Seven months ago, he was arrested for attacking a woman outside a movie theater. That's his only offense, but still ..."

Riley's interest was piqued.

"Can you find anything else about him?" she asked.

Nooney ran a search on his laptop. "He recently got a job with a hardware wholesale company," he said. Looking up at the others, he added, "That means he'll have access to lots of chains. It also means he'll be traveling up and down the river valley a lot. Maybe he already is."

Bill looked at Lucy and said, "Sounds like someone we should pay a visit to."

Lucy nodded, and she and Bill stood up. Riley stood up too.

"Not you," Bill said to Riley. "You're not assigned to this case. Just go back to your hotel and spend some time with April. She needs your attention."

Riley felt stymied. She heard the implied "and we don't" at

the end of his sentence. She knew that Bill had a point. April had been doing just fine but she would probably appreciate some company.

Then Lucy said, "I'll go back to the hotel. I can do some work there and also check in on April."

Riley and Bill both looked at Lucy with surprise.

Lucy shrugged and said, "Look, I don't understand all that's going on between you two, but you've got to sort it out. And I'll only get in the way. Go. Do your job."

Bill leveled his gaze at Riley. Then he growled, "Okay, let's go."

*

During the half-hour drive from Albany to Walcott, Riley tried to make conversation with Bill a few times. It didn't go very well. She ventured once or twice to apologize for coming to Albany against Meredith's orders. She'd also suggested that maybe they needed to discuss some sources of the tension between them, including her drunken phone call.

But Bill really didn't want to talk about any of it. That worried Riley. His taciturn attitude didn't bode well for interviewing a potential suspect.

Bill parked the FBI car in front of a small, white house—an ordinary-looking little home in an ordinary little town. But Riley thought that it was, in fact, just the sort of place where the chain killer might live.

They walked to the door and knocked. A startlingly baby-faced individual answered the door. He was short and extremely thin.

For a second, Riley almost asked, "Is your father at home?" But she stopped herself.

"Are you Wayne Turner," she asked.

"Y-yeah, w-why?" the man stuttered nervously.

Bill took out his badge and said, "We're Agents Jeffreys and Paige, FBI. We'd like to come in and ask you a few questions."

"I-I d-don't understand."

"We'll explain everything," Bill said. "Just let us come in."

Wayne Turner led them into a tidy, modestly decorated living room. With a wordless gesture, he invited Bill and Riley to sit down.

Turner took a long breath to bring his speech under control. Then he said, very slowly but smoothly, "I'm sorry about the stutter. It happens when I'm nervous. I've had a lot of therapy for it. Usually I can control it."

Bill said, "Can you tell us where you were last Wednesday night, between dusk and midnight?"

Turner looked uneasy, but managed to control his speech. "I was driving. Between here and Dudley. I was visiting my parents there."

"Can anybody confirm your whereabouts during that time?" Bill asked.

"N-not between the hours you're t-talking about," Turner said, his anxiety mounting. "I-I left my parents' house about eight. I d-didn't get home until almost midnight. It-it's a long drive."

Bill's expression showed increasing suspicion.

He asked, "What about Sunday night? Between eight and ten?"

Turner's eyes darted back and forth.

"Sunday? I-I was at h-h-home," he said.

"Alone?" Bill asked.

"Y-yes."

Riley could see that Turner was starting to panic. But that didn't necessarily mean that he was the man they were looking for. Riley had seen perfectly innocent people get spooked by questions like these. She knew that this interview would go better if she and Bill didn't put him on the defensive. She decided she'd better ask the questions herself.

"We heard that you got a new job," Riley said, not unpleasantly. "Congratulations. Could you tell us about it?"

Turner looked confused, but also a bit flattered. He was able to speak more calmly now.

"I just started working for Decatur Brothers Hardware. A wholesaler. I'm a sales representative. I'll be traveling a lot. I like that. I like to get around."

"And before you got this job?" Riley asked.

Turner lowered his head. She could see she'd touched on a topic that bothered him.

"I-I had trouble getting work for a while," he said. "It's n-not easy when you've g-got a problem talking. It can h-happen at the wrong time."

"I hope this new job works out for you," Riley said.

"Thanks."

Bill put in, "We hear that you got arrested a few months back. Could you tell us about that?"

From Turner's reaction, Riley saw that Bill had touched on an even more difficult subject than employment difficulties. She hoped it wouldn't scuttle the interview altogether.

"Oh, th-that," Turner said, looking quite ashamed. "A woman c-cut in f-front of me in a m-movie line. I c-complained. She m-made fun of me for my st-stutter."

He shook his head.

"I d-don't know what g-got into me," he said. "I h-hit her. I've never d-done anything else like that."

Riley studied his expression. He might be telling the truth, or he might not be. She couldn't be sure.

She said, "Mr. Turner, I hope you don't mind my asking about this. You were adopted, weren't you?"

Turner nodded.

"You said you that you visit your parents in Dudley," Riley said.

Turner took careful control over his voice. "I go there every week," he said.

"So you're on good terms with your parents?" Riley asked.

"Oh, yes," he said. "They've always been good to me."

Riley paused, then said, "You were in an orphanage before you were adopted, weren't you?"

Turner nodded again.

In the gentlest voice possible, Riley asked, "Were you ever mistreated there?"

Turner looked directly into her eyes and spoke with remarkable calm.

"I didn't like it there," he said. "I'd rather not discuss it."

Riley was slightly startled by his sudden composure.

Then Turner asked, "Am I a suspect in some sort of a crime?"

"We're investigating two murders and an abduction," Bill said.

Riley stifled a sigh. Bill's answer wasn't the least bit graceful. Even so, Turner seemed remarkably unperturbed.

"I haven't killed or hurt or abducted anyone," Turner said. "Now if you don't mind, I'm through answering questions. If you need to ask anything else, I'll want my lawyer present."

Bill was about to say something more. Riley silenced him with a gesture.

Turner got up from his chair and walked to his desk. He searched through some cards, then picked one and handed it to Riley.

"Here's my lawyer's card," he said. "Please contact him if you've got any more questions."

Riley smiled politely and said, "We understand, Mr. Turner. Thank you for your time."

Bill and Riley left the house and got into the car.

As Bill started to drive, he said, "Did you hear how his speech changed? He hardly stuttered at all toward the end. What do you make of that?"

Riley didn't reply. The truth was, she wasn't sure what to make of it. The change in Turner's demeanor could well be characteristic of a cold-blooded psychopath. On the other hand, a man who went through life with Turner's speech problem had surely developed more than his share of coping strategies. Perhaps what they'd seen and heard just now showed how strong he was deep down.

As Riley mulled it over, she fingered the card that Turner had given her. Suddenly, something dawned on her.

"Bill, he's not our man," Riley said.

"Why not?"

"Do you remember the business card Lucy told you about? The one the florist gave her?"

Bill nodded. "Yeah, the one that probably has the killer's handwriting."

"It was how he ordered the flowers," Riley said. "He wrote it out by hand. Wayne Turner wouldn't have done that. He'd have talked to the florist, even if it was hard to do. It would be a matter of pride for him. The man we're looking for isn't like that. He can barely talk at all, according to the florist. Some people might actually think that he's mute. Or mentally challenged."

Bill nodded and added, "And he wouldn't be able to get a job as a salesman."

At that moment, Riley's cell phone buzzed. The call was from Lucy.

"Riley, are you making any progress there?"

"No," Riley said. "This wasn't the right guy. We're coming back."

"Oh good," Lucy said, sounding excited. "You'd better get back to Albany as soon as you can."

Riley felt a surge of panic.

"Has something happened with April?" she asked.

"Oh, no, April's fine," Lucy said. "I'm at the field office. I asked one of the hotel cleaning ladies to keep an eye on her. Gave her a pretty big tip for it. April will be okay with this lady."

Riley breathed a sigh of relief. Lucy had probably found a Hispanic woman, someone who would remind April of Gabriela. It was a smart move.

"So what's going on?" Riley asked.

"Myra Cortese is coming in to the field office," Lucy said. "She's the other nurse who had been with the kidnap victim. She says she's remembering some things."

CHAPTER THIRTY

Maybe at last we'll get a break, Riley thought. Maybe the nurse had remembered something that would give them some direction, some idea of where to begin looking for Carla Liston. Maybe they would find this very strange chain killer before he murdered the woman he was holding.

When she and Bill got back to the field office, Lucy and Myra Cortese were already waiting for them in a meeting room. The slender, dark-haired woman was not in her nurse's uniform right now. She looked tired. Doubtless she hadn't gotten much sleep since her friend had disappeared. But she also looked eager to help.

"I'm sorry I couldn't tell you anything more when you talked to me last time," Myra said when Bill and Riley sat down at the table. "I was just such a wreck. I was in shock. I couldn't think clearly about anything. I think I can remember more now. At least, some bits and pieces have started coming back to me."

"We appreciate your help, Ms. Cortese," Bill said. "Anything you can remember will be a great help."

Riley could see that Bill was ready to start asking questions. Riley shook her head at him and gestured subtly toward Lucy. Riley preferred that Lucy bring her sensitivity and skill to this interview. Bill understood the message, nodded, and said nothing.

"I'm not sure where to start," Myra said. "I'm remembering details, but I don't know which ones matter. I just thought I should come in and try again."

"That's all right," Lucy said. "We'll talk you through it. Let's start back at the mall. You and Carla were shopping after work, and …"

"Actually, that's not quite right," Myra explained. "We weren't really shopping. There's a little cafe in the mall that we like. We go there most days after we close up the clinic. We just stopped in for some cappuccinos and conversation about anything but work."

Riley felt heartened. She could tell by Myra's tone of voice that she was in a much better frame of mind than she had been during the previous interview.

"Very good, Ms. Cortese," Lucy said. "I hope you don't mind

347

if we ask some of the same questions we asked you before."

"Not at all."

Lucy looked at her with a patient, pleasant expression.

"In the cafe, did you notice anything odd?" Lucy asked. "Any people that stood out? An employee or a customer?"

Myra stopped to think.

"No," she said. "Jenna was the barista as usual. Otherwise, there weren't a lot of people in the cafe. There was an elderly couple at a nearby table. And a woman Carla and I both knew was at another table, a good friend. A young couple ... a group of girls ... I don't think there was anyone else."

"What time did you leave?" Lucy asked.

"Oh, close to nine, I guess," Myra said. "We walked straight through the mall on the way to the parking lot. It wasn't very far."

Lucy patted the woman's hand.

"On the way through the mall, do you remember anyone who sticks out in your mind?" Lucy asked.

Myra closed her eyes.

"There was a man," she said. "He was tall, heavy, red-haired, had a beard. He made eye contact with me. I think maybe he was leering. I didn't like it."

Riley found all this detail very encouraging. The man she mentioned didn't fit their profile, of course. But if she *had* gotten a good look at the killer, she might remember him and be able to describe him.

"Very good," Lucy said. "And when you went outside?"

"There were just—people, most of them headed toward their cars, like us. There was a bunch of teenagers. Nobody stood out."

The woman's eyes were still closed. Lucy didn't press her with any more questions for a few seconds. Riley understood why. It was best to allow the woman to let her memories float to the surface.

"What about vehicles?" Lucy finally asked. "Just name any that you can remember."

"Well, we were parked next to some kind of low-slung sports car." She paused again, then said, "There was a pickup truck in front of Carla's car. It had a small camper on it. I think there was a big SUV on the other side of us."

Riley started to jot down notes. It wasn't impossible that the killer drove either an SUV or a camper.

Then Myra said, "Oh, and I remember a white van. It backed out just when we did. It was a delivery van, the kind without windows on the sides."

Lucy drew her hand back. She looked shocked.

"Oh my God," Lucy cried.

Riley was startled at Lucy's sudden loss of composure. Myra opened her eyes, surprised as well.

"Is that important?" she asked. "You know, I think that I actually saw a white van again when Carla stopped to let me off. I don't know if it was the same one."

Lucy was searching her cell phone. Then she showed an image to Myra.

"Did it look like this?" she asked.

"Why yes it did," Myra said. "I'm pretty sure the one at the mall looked exactly like that."

Lucy went pale and she trembled a little.

"Myra, you're being a great help," she said, her voice shaky. "Could you wait here a minute while I talk to my colleagues alone?"

"Of course," Myra said.

Lucy got up from her chair. Riley and Bill followed her out of the room.

"Oh my God," Lucy said. "I'm afraid I really screwed up."

"What is it?" Riley said.

Lucy paced back and forth.

"Back in Reedsport, after Rosemary Pickens's funeral, I was walking along and a white van pulled up close to me. Too close, I thought right then."

She showed Bill and Riley the picture on her cell phone.

"Then it sped up and drove away, and I snapped this picture. It was kind of automatic, but you can see I didn't get the license number. I didn't give it another thought—until just now. It must have been him. I missed him. I let him get away."

Riley felt a surge of disappointment. It was the first really foolish thing she'd known Lucy to do. But Bill didn't seem to feel that way.

"Take it easy," he said to Lucy. "We're still not sure the van you saw is the one Myra remembered. There are lots of white vans out there. It could be just a coincidence."

Riley doubted that very much. Judging from her anguished expression, so did Lucy.

"I've got to fix this," Lucy said. "I've got to make this right. I have to go talk to Paul, the technician. He can contact the mall, check their security photos."

*

A little while after they had thanked Myra Cortese for being helpful and let her go home, Riley, Bill, and Lucy were in the lab, waiting to see what Paul Nooney could turn up. Right away he had told them that the van in Lucy's photograph was a Ford, about ten years old. It had no letters on the side or any other identification, although the paint was definitely scratched.

Now the computer tech was searching mall security camera images for a match.

"Got it," Paul said. "Have a look."

Riley huddled with Bill and Lucy behind Paul. Sure enough, the camera had caught the back of a white Ford delivery van pulling out of the mall parking lot.

"How can we be sure it's the same vehicle?" Bill asked.

Lucy held the picture on her cell phone next to the image on the computer.

"Right there—you can see where the paint is scratched in the same place. It's the same van, all right. I really did screw up. But at least we've got a clear shot of the plate. It's a Pennsylvania plate. Paul, how fast do you think you can track down the owner?"

"Give me just a minute," Paul said. He got back to work.

Riley took Bill by the elbow and led him a short distance away from Lucy.

"I'm so disappointed in her, Bill," Riley said quietly so that Lucy couldn't hear. "I thought she was better than this."

"Come on, Riley," Bill said. "Don't try to tell me you didn't make your own share of screw-ups when you were a rookie. I sure as hell did. And even if she dropped the ball at first, she didn't forget completely. She came through in the end."

Riley knew that Bill was right. He almost always was, and sometimes that pissed her off. She turned and saw that Lucy was looking miserable.

Riley walked over to the young agent and said, "It's okay."

"No, it's not," Lucy said.

Just then Paul called out.

"Here it is. Come here and let me show you."

They all gathered behind Paul and looked over his shoulder. The security photo was still on the screen, next to some DMV documents.

"The registration is way out of date," he said. "It's been expired for years. The date sticker in the photo looks current, but I suspect it's a phony. The name and address on the registration also turns up in driver's licenses. He's still at the same location. His name is Walter Sattler, and he still lives in Hoxeyville, Pennsylvania. That's just over the state line, only a couple of hours from here."

The driver's license photo showed a thin, boyish face. The man was five feet seven inches tall. He was thirty-three.

"That's got to be him," Bill said. "Let's get a warrant and go."

Riley nodded.

"We might still have time to save Carla."

CHAPTER THIRTY ONE

Riley thought that maybe this long day would end in success after all. Starting with the trip to Sing Sing, the bits and pieces that had come together pointed to this address in Hoxeyville, Pennsylvania. She and Bill approached the house cautiously.

It had taken longer than they'd expected to get a search warrant and the drive had been a couple of hours, so it was now very late and very dark. The modest working-class neighborhood seemed pleasant and peaceful. Although no lights were on inside or outside the house, the street was well lighted. Riley could see that the house had basement windows—just the place where someone might be held captive. Although no vehicle was parked near the house there was a closed-up garage. The van was probably in there.

"Weapons?" Riley asked quietly, getting ready to pull her Glock. They had decided that the captive might stand a better chance of survival if they didn't storm the place with a SWAT team.

"Not yet," Bill said. "With luck we won't need them. He's not a shooter and not very strong."

As they stepped up onto the front porch, Riley hoped he was right. Still, she hadn't dealt with many cold-blooded murderers who hadn't put up some resistance. And most of them were armed.

Bill pushed the doorbell and also knocked sharply on the front door. No reply came for a few moments. Bill knocked again.

"FBI," Bill called out. "Is this the residence of Walter Sattler? We've got a warrant."

Again there was no reply, but Riley thought that she heard movement behind the door. Instinctively, she drew her pistol in spite of Bill's reluctance to use guns.

Suddenly the door swung open. A smallish man wearing pajamas stood inside, pointing a shotgun at them. Riley leveled her Glock at his face.

"Put the weapon down," Bill barked, drawing his own pistol.

"Easy," the man said, swinging the gun barrel back and forth between Riley and Bill. "Take it easy. I don't want any trouble. I just want to see badges."

With their free hands, Bill and Riley displayed their badges.

The man lowered his weapon.

"Put the gun down," Bill said again.

"Okay. Jesus." The man stooped down and put the weapon on the floor. Riley picked it up.

"Hands on your head," Bill said.

The man complied. "I'm cooperating," he said. "What's this all about?"

Riley's heart sank.

He can talk just fine, she thought. The man sounded as nervous as anyone might be in this situation, but there was no trace of a stutter.

Still, she recognized the man whose picture they'd seen on the driver's license. This was definitely Walter Sattler. There had to be a reason the evidence had led to him.

Could they be dealing with two perpetrators working as a team?

But no, that didn't fit.

Riley was getting ready to holster her weapon when a woman's voice snapped her back to attention.

"Walter, what's going on? Should I call 911?"

The woman was standing at the top of the stairs in her nightgown. She had curlers in her hair.

"No, you don't have to do that, Peg," Walter Sattler said. "It's the FBI. I don't know what they want. Just check and make sure the kids aren't scared. Go back to bed. I'll handle this."

The woman went back upstairs. Sattler was still holding his hands where they could be clearly seen.

Bill quickly patted him down for other possible weapons. Finding nothing, he holstered his pistol, but Riley kept hers drawn.

"We've got a warrant to search the place," Bill said, producing the document.

"What if I don't want you to?" Sattler said.

Riley said, "You can take that up with your lawyer later on." Turning to Bill, she said, "The basement seems the most likely."

Bill walked back through the house and disappeared.

"What's all this about?" Sattler asked Riley. "What are you looking for, anyhow?"

"Do you own a white Ford delivery van?"

Sattler looked completely taken aback.

"What? No! We've got a Nissan station wagon. It's back in the garage. Why, I haven't had a Ford since ..."

His voice trailed off. He seemed to be remembering something. Bill came back into the room.

"Nothing suspicious in the basement," Bill said. "Should I check the attic?"

"No," Riley said. "Hold off a few minutes."

With a wife and kid upstairs, she knew that it wasn't likely that the missing woman was a prisoner here. It seemed pretty obvious by now that Sattler wasn't keeping anyone captive, at least not in this house.

Sattler's demeanor was much more docile than before.

"Look, there's been a misunderstanding," he said. "Sit down. I think maybe we can sort this out."

Riley and Bill sat down with him in the living room.

"Tell me more about this Ford van you're talking about," Sattler said.

"I'll show it to you," Riley said.

On her cell phone, she brought up the photo that Lucy had taken, alongside the security photo. She showed it to Sattler.

"Damn it," Sattler growled. "I thought I'd seen the last of that van."

"Please explain this to us, Mr. Sattler," Riley said.

Sattler took a long, slow breath.

"Look, the guy you're looking for isn't me," he said. "You're looking for my cousin, Eugene Fisk. I haven't seen him for years. What has he done?"

"He's a suspect in two murders and an abduction," Bill said.

Sattler's mouth dropped open with shock.

Riley asked, "How did he wind up with your van?"

"I gave it to him nine years ago," Sattler said. "I wanted him gone so badly, I didn't bother to transfer the ownership. I just handed him the keys and said, 'Drive away from here and don't let me ever see or hear from you again.' That's what he did."

Sattler hung his head guiltily.

"I know it wasn't the right thing to do," he said. "I've had second thoughts about it ever since. But if you knew Eugene … Well, I just wanted him out of my life for good."

Sattler stared across the room with an expression of shame and regret.

"What can you tell us about him?" Riley asked.

"Eugene was my mother's sister's kid," Sattler said. "Her name was Sherry Fisk. I never really knew her. The whole family—my parents included—thought she was just trailer trash. Folks also said she was crazy."

Sattler paused for a moment.

"Nobody knew who Eugene's father was," he said. "And I

354

never really got to know Eugene—at least not as a kid. His mother was murdered when I a teenager. Eugene was ten, I think. I never heard the details, how it happened. It was one of those family secrets nobody wanted to talk about. They never caught the killer."

Riley was taking notes.

"What happened to Eugene after his mother was killed?" she asked.

"I think he was in a foster home," Sattler said. "He got into some kind of trouble, and he wound up institutionalized for mental problems."

Sattler paused again.

"They let him out when he was eighteen. I was in my twenties, married, getting a pretty good start in life. Like I said, I never really knew him when we were kids. But now suddenly he acted like we'd always been close. And he was ..."

Sattler shook his head.

"Well, he was weird, that's all. He could barely talk at all. It was so bad he'd sometimes write notes to you instead of saying anything. And he was needy. He was always hitting me up for money, hanging around for meals. It wasn't just awkward. It was scary. It was almost like stalking. I just had this feeling when he was around ..."

His voice trailed off again.

"Anyway," he said, "that was when I gave him the van. And told him never to come back."

Riley took a moment to mull over what she'd just learned. Maybe there was someone in Hoxeyville who might be able to tell them more about Eugene Fisk.

"Are your parents alive?" she asked Sattler.

"No, I'm the last of the family. Except for Eugene."

"Where was Eugene institutionalized?"

"It was at the Hoxeyville Psychiatric Center, right here in town."

Riley figured that would be their next stop. Surely they'd be able to learn more there. But maybe she could get one other thing from Sattler.

"Do you have any pictures of your cousin?" she asked.

"None that would show how he looks now," Sattler said. "But I think I've got an old one ..."

He got up from his chair and opened a drawer. He rummaged around inside until he found a snapshot. He handed it to Riley.

"This one was taken when we were just kids," he said. "I kept it because it was pretty unusual for us to get together."

While Bill asked a few final questions, Riley stared at the photo. It showed two young boys. The taller one was recognizably Sattler. The shorter one was an odd-looking child, his features somewhat exaggerated.

Even so, Riley couldn't help thinking ...

What a sweet smile he has!

She couldn't imagine what had turned that smiling little boy into a serial killer.

CHAPTER THIRTY TWO

Carla had no idea how long she'd been chained on the cot in this basement. The windows high up on the cinderblock walls were covered with cardboard, sealing out every trace of outdoor light. Whenever the overhead light was off, which it was right now, she was in complete darkness.

She did know that she was hungry, soiled, and in terrible pain. She'd had nothing to eat during the whole time she'd been here. Sometimes the monstrous little man would loosen the chain gag from her mouth and give her a sip of water, and that was all.

She'd long since stopped being bothered by her own stench. Her dignity no longer mattered to her. Her survival did.

But so far, escape had eluded her.

He'd cudgeled her with a chain when he first took her back in Albany. Now that the delirium from her concussion had passed, she was dazed and bewildered from pain and hunger. She'd sleep or pass out from time to time, then wake up with no idea where she was or what had happened.

But she always managed to bring herself back to her horrible present reality. Clear-headedness was essential. There was a way out, she was sure of it. She thrashed a little in the darkness, rolling her body back and forth. She'd been doing that all along, whenever he wasn't here. He'd wrapped the chains around her and the cot, but they apparently weren't really fastened. Little by little, she had felt them loosening.

Right now she guessed that they hung loosely enough for her to try to slip out of them. The straitjacket was yet another problem, but she'd deal with that afterward.

Starting with her shoulders, she wiggled and squirmed so that the chains began to slip.

But then she heard his footsteps. He was probably on his way down here. Now was no time to struggle with the chains. She let her exhausted body go limp.

She heard the door open at the top of the flight of stairs that led from the house down into the basement. Then she was blinded by the overhead light. She shut her eyes, pretending to be asleep. She listened to the sound of his footsteps coming down the stairs.

In a moment, she could hear his breathing as he leaned over

her. She could feel that he was fingering the chains. As he often did, he started whispering to them—whispering so quietly that she couldn't make out his words. It was as if she weren't here at all, and the chains were the only living things in the basement.

As a nurse, she'd dealt in the past with psychotic patients. This man was seriously mentally ill, and she knew it. He'd often go over to his worktable and stretch out other chains that he kept there. He'd carry on long conversations with them, sometimes pleading with them, sometimes swearing his loyalty to them, sometimes assuring them that everything was going as they wished.

When he tried to say anything to her, he was always wracked by a hopeless stammer. But he could always talk perfectly to the chains.

She breathed slowly and regularly, as if asleep. After a while, she heard his footsteps going back up the stairs and through the house. She heard the front door open and close. She opened her eyes. It was pitch dark again.

She listened closely. She couldn't hear any more footsteps above her. That must mean that he had left. Sometimes he went away completely for hours at a time, and that's what she was hoping for now.

Her whole body screamed with pain as she began to wriggle and writhe again. Like a moth struggling to emerge from a cocoon, she managed to make the coil of chains slip down along her abdomen. Soon she was free of them all the way down to her waist.

Struggling against the straitjacket, she managed to sit up. For a moment she was seized by dizziness and she nearly fainted. But she recovered and shook and wiggled her legs until the chains slipped down to her ankles. She tucked up her knees and pulled her feet free.

She was sitting on the edge of the cot, still bound by the straitjacket. Now it was time to deal with that problem. She'd been thinking about how to get out of it for as long as she'd been down here. She'd been unconscious when he'd put it on her, but he must to have done it in a hurry because he hadn't pulled it very tight.

She remembered seeing an escape artist on television demonstrating how to get out of a straitjacket. In her mind, she carefully went over the steps he'd used.

I can do that, she thought. *I will do it.*

First she relaxed and exhaled, making her body as small as possible. The straitjacket felt looser. Then she swung her outer arm toward the opposite shoulder. From that position, it wasn't hard to lift the arm up and pull the restraining strap over her head and to the front of her body. She raised the buckle on her sleeve to her face, then opened it with her teeth. Then she did the same with the other arm.

Now her hands were completely free. It was easy to unfasten the remaining buckles, stand up, and slip out of the straitjacket altogether.

But free as she was, the pain was greater than ever, and she dropped back down onto the cot. Muscles that hadn't been used in days were now in agony, and parts of her body were numb from the lack of blood flow.

She shook herself all over, then mustered up all her willpower and forced herself to stand again. She knew that there was a basement door that led outside. There was also a stairway up into the house. The man who held her had come in and out both ways.

Groping with feet and hands, she found her way to the back door. She fumbled around until she found the doorknob. She turned the lock on the doorknob and twisted it. The door didn't come open. She felt around above the doorknob and realized that she couldn't open it without a key.

For a few long moments, Carla felt like giving up. To get out of the basement, she would have to go up through the house. She finally mustered up her courage to do that. She really had no other option.

Dark as the basement was, she had a fair idea of how to get to the stairs. She staggered around until she found the banister and the bottom step. Step by step, she moved upward as silently as she could. When she reached the door at the top, it wasn't locked.

Carla pushed the door open and stepped out into the killer's house. The cramped and dingy living area was silent. The killer must not be there.

Carla's weakness almost caught up with her then. She hadn't eaten for days and dizziness nearly overcame her. But she gathered her resolve and moved across the little living room to the front door.

When she opened the door, she looked outside into the dim light of day. She couldn't tell whether it was early morning or evening. A white van was in the driveway—the same van the man had used to capture her. Beyond that, she saw another house just a short way down the road that ran by the house.

That's where I have to go, she told herself.

But just as she moved in that direction, the nightmarish little man appeared from the other side of the van. He must have been puttering around back there, and now he stepped out just in time to see her. He was holding a bundle of heavy chains in one hand when their eyes met. She opened her mouth and tried to scream, but nothing came out.

She turned back into the house and tried to slam the door to shut the man out, but he was too fast. He pushed his way inside.

Carla called on all her resources now. Despite her pain or dizziness, she seized on whatever she could find to throw at him. She overturned a small table in his path. He dodged the table and came relentlessly toward her.

She backed into the tiny kitchen and snatched up a heavy pan from a countertop. She swung it hard into the side of his head, and he dropped to his knees.

She looked at him and sized him up, and she realized with a shock that she was more stout than he was. He was practically puny.

Carla had never hurt anyone in her life, but now a primal instinct kicked in. She found her body flooded with rage, and she leapt atop her would-be killer. She tackled him to the ground, and was amazed to find herself stronger than he was. She landed on top of him and raised her fists and punched him in the face, again and again.

The killer tried to fight back, but he couldn't overpower her. Instead, he whimpered like a little boy.

Finally, his face a bloody mess, he stopped moving.

Carla looked down, stunned. She also felt the room spin, and as she reeled herself, she realized how weak and dizzy she was.

She jumped off him, not wanting to touch him or be anywhere near him. She spit down on his face, stepped over him, and walked for the open door with a rush of relief.

Suddenly, Carla couldn't breathe. She couldn't understand what was happening, until she heard him behind her and she reached up and felt a length of chain wrapped around her throat. She struggled and kicked, but this time, he was too strong.

And in another few seconds, the world went completely dark.

*

Eugene dragged the woman by the neck back to the basement door. She was unconscious and heavy, and she fell down the steps. When he followed her down and looked closely, he realized that she was dead. He had broken her neck by dragging her that way.

360

"Oh, no," he gasped.

Tears of grief and panic sprung to his eyes. This wasn't the way it was supposed to happen. He'd expected to keep her alive another week at least.

He opened the back door, switched on the basement light, and pushed the body down the stairs. He saw where the chains that had bound the woman lay all around the cot. They were angry with him. He knew it. He had let them down.

He thought maybe he could mollify them with a familiar gesture—by doing what he'd done to kill the other women. So he picked up his straight-edged razor and slit her lifeless throat. But it was no good. He couldn't pretend that he'd done what the chains demanded.

Now he would have to take her back to where he'd captured her, displaying her for the world to see. After that he needed to find a new victim, and quickly. The chains would make his life hell until he did.

CHAPTER THIRTY THREE

Checking into the motel had been rather tense.

"Do you want separate rooms?" the woman at the desk had asked.

Bill had actually turned to Riley, as if waiting for her response. She hadn't reacted at all, so he'd told the woman, *"Yes."*

It was morning now, and they were on the road. Riley was wondering what would have happened if she'd nodded her approval at that critical moment. What might last night have been like?

This morning they weren't discussing that question or much of anything else. They'd barely even said a word to each other over breakfast back at the motel. They'd scarcely talked at all on the drive to the Hoxeyville Psychiatric Center where Eugene Fisk had spent a large part of his life.

Riley had called the hospital earlier this morning. She'd been surprised that Eugene's supervising physician seemed perfectly happy to meet with them. Physicians normally balked at this kind of interview because of physician-patient privilege. For some reason, Dr. Joseph Lombard didn't seem concerned about that, and she was eager to find out why.

Steady, she thought as the hospital building came into view. *This is no time to think about last night.*

After all, Bill was desperately trying to patch things up with Maggie, and Riley had a swarm of personal issues to deal with. They also had work to do, and their formerly solid rapport was shaky already.

Still, she couldn't help wondering about that drunken suggestion she'd made to Bill over the phone, the one that had all but ruined their friendship. Had he really been offended by it, or had he been scared instead? Scared that something was almost sure to happen between them sooner or later? Was the possibility still in the air?

She glanced sideways at Bill. He looked every bit the well-disciplined FBI agent that he was, with his dark hair carefully combed. In fact, he'd made a greater effort than usual to look professional. He didn't always wear a suit and a tie. At the moment, he seemed to be completely focused on his driving, but she couldn't help but wonder if he was asking himself questions similar to hers. His strong face gave her no clue.

Riley put all such thoughts aside as Bill parked in the visitors' lot. They walked into the hospital, checked in, and were escorted directly to Dr. Lombard's office.

The doctor, a tall man of about sixty, rose from his desk to meet them.

"Agents Paige and Jeffreys, I presume," he said. "Please sit down."

Bill and Riley sat down in the chairs in front of the doctor's desk. For a moment the doctor stood looking at them with an anxious expression.

"You said that you want to talk to me about Eugene Fisk," he said. "He was in our care about ten years back."

The doctor sat down and continued. "When you called you mentioned that you were in Pennsylvania searching for information about a murderer over in New York. You mentioned chains, straitjackets, slit throats. And you said that there's another captive? Horrible."

He paused for a moment.

"Am I correct in understanding that Mr. Fisk is a suspect?" he asked.

"He's our only suspect," Bill said.

Dr. Lombard didn't reply, but his expression was one of deep concern.

Riley said, "Dr. Lombard, as I stressed to you, information is urgent. We appreciate your willingness to talk to us about Mr. Fisk without a warrant."

"Yes, I'm sure that's unusual," Lombard replied. "But Pennsylvania law is quite specific about the matter. I'm only forbidden to exchange medical information that 'blackens' my patient's character."

Dr. Lombard gazed significantly at Riley, then at Bill.

"I'll make sure not to cross that line," he said.

Riley understood. The doctor was eager to cooperate. But this was not going to be a typical interview. What went unsaid was likely to be as important as what was said. Riley knew that she had to be alert to unspoken clues.

The doctor opened a file.

"I've got his records right here," he said, glancing over its contents. "He was admitted here sixteen years ago. He was eleven years old. He was an orphan, and he'd been living in a group foster home that had just burned down. He was … deeply traumatized afterwards."

The doctor stopped. Riley detected that he was leaving a great deal unsaid.

She said, "We understand that he stayed under your care until he was eighteen."

"That's right," Lombard said. "When he first came here, he was barely communicative at all. He stayed huddled up and ignored anyone who tried to talk to him. But little by little, he improved. He came out of his shell."

The doctor knitted his brow, remembering.

"He had a terrible speech problem," he said. "Never got rid of it, even after he started getting better. I'm sure that he'd had it from early childhood. He could talk to *me* just a little. But often he'd write down what he wanted to say instead of trying to speak."

Lombard leaned back in his chair.

"He made slow but excellent progress," he said. "Or so I'd thought. He learned a lot while he was here. He learned to garden, how to use a computer, took some classes. He was extremely good-natured, generous, kind. He was never the least bit aggressive. Everybody liked him—other patients, the personnel. I liked him."

He pulled a photograph from the file and passed it over to them. The teenager had a warm smile, but Riley thought his eyes looked rather blank.

The doctor continued, but a tone of regret was starting to creep into his voice.

"He seemed more than ready to go out into the world. We released him. We tried to keep track of his whereabouts and activities. But soon he disappeared completely. I worried about that. It was nine years ago."

The doctor's voice trailed off. Riley knew that she was going to have to coax more information out of him.

She said, "Dr. Lombard, we're going to ask you a few questions. If you can legally answer them, please do so. If you can't, you don't have to say anything. Does that sound okay with you?"

"That sounds fine," the doctor said.

Riley glanced at Bill. He nodded. Riley could see that he understood this tactic and was ready to join in.

"Dr. Lombard," Riley said, "when Eugene's foster home burned down, was arson ever suspected?"

The doctor stared ahead fixedly and said nothing.

Bill put in, "Did anybody die in the incident?"

Again, the doctor said nothing.

Riley asked, "Was somebody murdered?"

The doctor looked at her without saying a word.

Finally he said, "I think that's all I can tell you."

Bill said, "Maybe you could help with one more thing. Has the foster home been rebuilt? Is it operating now?"

"It is," Lombard said. "I'll give you the address."

Lombard wrote down the address and handed it to Bill.

Riley looked again at the photograph of Eugene Fisk. "Could you give us a copy of this?" she asked.

"You can keep that one. I'll print another for the file."

Bill and Riley both thanked him for his help and left his office.

"That was informative," Bill said as they headed for the car. "Let's head right over to that foster home."

Riley said, "While you drive, I'll call Sam Flores back in Quantico. I'll get him to look for news stories about what happened at the orphanage."

*

The St. Genesius Children's Home was located in Bowerbank, Pennsylvania, about a half hour from Hoxeyville. While Bill was driving, Riley received a newspaper article from Sam Flores. What she read chilled her to the bone.

Sixteen years ago, the group foster home was burned to the ground. Arson was suspected. The body of a twelve-year-old boy, Ethan Holbrook, had been found in the ruins. The article didn't specify the cause of death.

"That poor kid could have been Eugene's first victim," Riley said after she'd finished reading the article to Bill.

"Jesus," Bill murmured. "He started as a pre-teen? What kind of monster are we dealing with?"

Riley remembered Dr. Lombard's stony silence when she'd asked him if someone had been murdered. She thought about the smiling young child she'd seen in the photograph at Walter Sattler's house. How soon had that child been turned into a killer?

When Bill parked the car, Riley observed that the group home was housed in a clean, modern building. Outside in front was a playground with colorful equipment. There were dozens of kids playing happily.

Two gray-clad, smiling nuns were watching over them. Riley and Bill approached the closest one.

"Excuse me, Sister," Riley said. "Could you take us to this facility's director?"

"That would be me," the nun said pleasantly. "Sister Cecilia Berry. What can I do for you?"

Riley was surprised at how young she looked. It didn't seem likely that she'd been in charge of this place all those years ago. Riley wondered what they could hope to learn from her.

Riley and Bill both took out their badges.

"We're Agents Jeffreys and Paige, FBI," Bill said. "We'd like to ask you a few questions."

Sister Cecilia's smile dropped away. She turned pale. She looked around, as if to make sure that nobody was watching.

"Please come with me," she said. She called to another nun to take over the playground supervision.

Riley and Bill walked with her into the building. On their way to nun's office, Riley noticed that the building was organized like a dormitory. Down one hall, she saw rows of rooms, many with their doors open. A couple of kindly-looking nuns were checking in on the kids, stopping to talk with them as they went. Music, conversation, and laughter could be heard.

From what Riley could see, the St. Genesius Children's Home was a warm, welcoming place.

So why is this woman so uneasy? Riley wondered.

Riley and Bill sat down in Sister Cecilia's office. But the sister didn't sit down. She paced with agitation.

"I don't know why you're here," she said. "We've had no complaints since this new facility opened. We have lawyers to deal with the old cases. If you've checked with the DHS, they'll tell you that we pass every inspection with a perfect score. I'll show you the latest report."

She started to open a file drawer.

"Sister Cecilia, I don't think you understand the nature of our visit," Bill said.

Riley added, "We're here to ask about a child who was here sixteen years ago. Eugene Fisk. We're trying to find him. He's the subject of a murder investigation."

"Oh," the sister said with surprise. She sat behind her desk.

"Please excuse my mistake," she said. "We're trying to put our history behind us. I'm sure you can understand."

The truth was, Riley didn't understand, and she was sure that Bill didn't either.

"What can you tell us about Eugene Fisk?" Riley asked.

Sister Cecilia looked wary.

"What do you know already?" she asked.

Bill said, "We know that he was transferred to a psychiatric hospital after your old facility burned down. A boy died in that fire—Ethan Holbrook. We're here to find out more about what happened."

"It was before my time, of course," Sister Cecilia said, getting up from her desk and going back to the file cabinet. "But I know Eugene's story well."

She opened a drawer, took out a file, and sat down again.

"It was a terrible story," she said, opening the file and scanning its contents. "Most of the nuns thought Eugene had started the fire. They even thought he might have killed Ethan. Nothing was ever proven."

"Why would he have killed another child?" Riley asked.

Referring to the old file, Sister Cecilia explained, "It seemed that Ethan Holbrook was an awful bully. He was particularly ugly toward Eugene. Eugene was small, weak, and awkward. And he had a terrible speech impediment. Ethan tormented and mocked him about it."

"Why didn't the nuns put a stop to the bullying?" Riley asked.

Sister Cecilia fell silent.

"I get the impression there's something you don't want to tell us," Riley said.

Slowly and reluctantly, the sister said, "There's quite a lot I'd rather not tell you, actually. It's not exactly a secret. It's not a secret at all. You can find court records about it, and old news stories. It's just so awful to have to dredge up the past. And I'd hate to have it all in the news again. With the Lord's help, we've tried to put it all behind us. We do nothing but good work here now. We really do."

"We're sure that's true," Riley said. "But it would help if you'd tell us."

Sister Cecilia said nothing for a moment. Then she continued, "After the fire, when the home was just starting to be rebuilt, the truth began to come out. The director back then was Sister Veronica Orlando. She'd run the place for more than a decade. She and her nuns were merciless. They encouraged the kids to bully each other. And she and the nuns would punish kids horribly for the smallest things—like sneezing or wetting the bed."

Riley was struck by the sister's sad expression. She could see that Sister Cecilia was doing her best to redeem the home from its awful history. Even so, the poor woman couldn't help but be haunted by a past for which she had no responsibility.

"Sister Cecilia," Riley asked in a gentle tone, "did any of these punishments involve chains?"

"If you're asking whether the kids themselves were chained up, no," she said. "But Sister Veronica and her nuns did sometimes lock them up by putting chains on the doors."

Sister Cecilia tilted her head inquisitively.

"But it's interesting you should ask about chains," she said, checking the record again. "Eugene came here when he was ten years old. He'd been found with a shackle on one ankle, chained to a post in his house. He was starving, and he couldn't talk at all."

"Where was his mother?" Bill asked.

"She'd been murdered. Her body was found right there in the house, right in front of the child where he would have seen the whole thing. The killer was never caught."

"How was she killed?" Riley asked.

"Her throat was slit," Sister Cecilia said. "The straight razor that killed her was found there too, thrown down on the floor near her. But they didn't find any prints on it."

Then the nun looked out the window, still with that haunted expression.

"The newspapers didn't say it," she said, "but that was how Ethan Holbrook died, too."

CHAPTER THIRTY FOUR

Riley was awakened by Lucy charging through the door between their adjoining hotel rooms.

"Turn on your TV!" Lucy cried.

Riley yanked herself to a sitting position. "What?" she asked. She saw that it was morning. She and Bill had gotten back to Albany last night. In the other bed, April growled sleepily, "What's going on?"

"I'll get it," Lucy said. She found the clicker and turned the television on herself. The first words Riley heard were those of a news announcer.

"We must warn our viewers that some of the images you're about to see are graphic."

Riley immediately saw that the announcer really meant it. The first image was of a chain-bound body dangling from a tree branch. Mercifully, the body was facing away from the camera.

The announcer continued, "A woman was brutally murdered last night, her body left in Albany's Curtis Park. This seems to be the latest in a series of 'chain murders' that have terrorized the Hudson River area over the last five years. The victim's identity is being withheld pending notification of her family ..."

"No," Riley muttered. "It can't be. Not yet."

The tree branch overhung a road, and it looked like the same park where Carla Liston had been abducted. The hanging body surely must be that of Carla Liston. But it was too soon. He'd only taken her a few days ago.

As the announcer continued, the camera panned to show that a small crowd of gawkers had clustered just outside the area that the cops had taped off. The whole situation was an investigator's nightmare.

Now the on-the-scene reporter was talking to the man who had discovered the body a couple of hours earlier.

"I was just driving through the park on my way to work," the man said. "When I saw it, I almost wrecked my car. Then I thought maybe it was a dummy hung up by some sick pranksters. But when you look you can tell ..."

At that moment came a sharp knock on the hotel room door. While Riley stared at the TV screen, Lucy went to the door and let

Bill in.

He said, "I just got a call from Harvey Dewhurst, the head of the Albany field office. He's going out of his mind. That guy you see on camera there called the media before he called the police."

Riley shook her head wearily. "Well, he's sure getting his fifteen minutes of fame," she said.

Bill continued, "As soon as the police heard about it, they knew it was our case and called the field office. But by the time Dewhurst and his people got there, the media was all over the scene. And the sightseers had also started to arrive."

"We have to get over there," Lucy said.

Riley was already out of bed, scrounging around for clothes. She carried her things into the bathroom and got dressed in a hurry. No time for breakfast, she knew. Maybe they could grab some coffee when they went by the motel breakfast room.

When she came out, Bill and Lucy were waiting by the door.

"We've got to go, April," Riley said to her daughter. "All of us. You stay put right here."

"It's your job," April said. "Go. I'll be fine."

*

During the drive to Curtis Park, Riley was still trying to get her mind around what had happened.

"I don't get what's going on," she said. "He's breaking his own MO. He's supposed to hold his victims captive for a longer time. For weeks. Why did he kill her so fast?"

A wave of discouragement swept over her.

"I thought we had more time to find Carla Liston," she added sadly.

"We did everything we could," Lucy said from the back seat.

But Bill said nothing as he drove. Riley knew that he felt exactly the same as she did. After all their years doing this job, they'd never gotten used to losing a victim. It was especially hard when they felt that they were closing in on the killer.

When they arrived at the park, Riley saw that television crew vans were mingled with police vehicles. The crowd outside the taped-off area had gotten larger, and people were snapping pictures with their cell phones. She and Lucy followed Bill as he pushed his way through to the police tape. They showed their badges to a pair of cops who were doing their best to control the area.

Then the three of them walked up the road toward where the body was still hanging in plain view. Riley could now see that the victim was clad in a straitjacket, just the same as the earlier victims. And like Rosemary Pickens in Reedsport, she'd been hauled up on a rope that ran through a pulley.

Riley stopped and stared, shaken by the sheer audacity of the display. Eugene Fisk must have stopped his van here before dawn, climbed up onto the overhanging limb, fastened the pulley in place, then climbed back down and hoisted Carla Liston's body.

And all without being seen, Riley thought. He'd been more than daring, but he'd also been lucky.

This wasn't some abandoned warehouse by a railroad track, but a well-used road through a city park. With any other serial killer, Riley would assume that he was becoming more brazen, thumbing his nose at the authorities. But she knew that Eugene Fisk was a different sort of creature. This was more likely to be a gesture of sheer desperation. Again she wondered what was going on with the maniacal killer.

Special Agent Harvey Dewhurst trotted toward them. He was overweight and middle-aged, and at the moment he was anxious, red-faced, and sweating. He was also as angry as hell.

"I hate it when this kind of shit happens," Dewhurst said. "You guys are the Quantico experts. You tell me what we can do for damage control."

"First of all, you'd better get her down," Bill said.

Riley agreed. She had asked Chief Alford to leave Rosemary Pickens's body hanging until she could get to the scene, but this was a different matter. The Reedsport police had been in better control of the crime scene. Here, too many pictures had been taken of this corpse already. And she and the rest of the FBI on site had already looked everything over.

Dewhurst turned to the local cop in charge.

"Tell your people to bring her down," he said. "And tell the coroner to get right to work on the body." He looked around and added, "And clear those onlookers out of here. Move the tape back where they can't take pictures and open up some room for the coroner to get his wagon in."

The cop hurried away to carry out Dewhurst's orders.

"What next?" Dewhurst asked.

Riley thought for a moment.

"We might as well take advantage of the media," she said. "Have the local TV stations alert the public that we're looking for a white Ford delivery van. A dented rear bumper, no other known markings, a Pennsylvania license plate. Agent Vargas can give you a photo that she took of it. Make sure the public sees it."

Then Riley reached into her bag and pulled out the photo of Eugene that the psychiatrist had given her.

"This picture shows the suspect as a teenager," Riley explained. "He's now twenty-seven years old. Take this back to the field office and run it through the age progression program. We should be able to get a good image of what he probably looks like now. Then make sure it gets on TV and the Internet."

She thought another moment and said, "Don't mention that the perp has a stutter. That will help filter the calls."

At that moment the coroner called out to Dewhurst, "You'd better have a look at something over here." He was crouched over the body that had been lowered carefully to the ground.

Riley, Bill, and Lucy all followed Dewhurst to see what the coroner was indicating. The woman's eyes were wide open, and she still wore a terrified expression on her face. The coroner pointed to her throat.

"Her throat was slit," he said, "and it's my understanding that's how he finished off the other victims. But look here. There wasn't much bleeding at all."

He turned and looked at them. "It wasn't the cause of death. This time, her neck was broken first."

Bill looked at Riley with surprise.

"Another change from his MO," he said to her. "What's going on with this guy?"

"I don't know why he's changing so fast," Riley said. "He doesn't seem like the type who would change at all. But I do know who we should ask about it."

CHAPTER THIRTY FIVE

Riley was once again inside Sing Sing Correctional Facility. She hoped this turned out to be a good idea. Bill was with her, although he had joined her only reluctantly, insisting it was a detour from their investigation. But deep in her gut, Riley felt that Shane Hatcher would still have valuable insights to share.

"I sure hope you're right about this," Bill grumbled as the guard led them into the visiting room—the same cream-colored room where Riley had met with Shane Hatcher two days ago.

As soon as they sat down at the table, Hatcher was escorted into the room by a pair of guards. He sat down across from them, and for a long moment he stared over the top of his reading glasses at Bill. Then he turned to Riley.

"I see you brought a friend with you," he told her.

"This is Special Agent Bill Jeffreys, from Quantico," Riley said. "He's come to Albany to join in the investigation."

Hatcher sat there with that now-familiar inscrutable smile on his hardened face. Again, he looked Bill over the way he'd looked at Riley the last time—sizing him up, figuring out what made him tick.

Riley knew that in spite of—or perhaps because of—being locked up for a long time, Hatcher was a cunning observer of human nature. She wondered what kinds of observations he was making about Bill right now.

"You don't need to tell me why you're here," Hatcher said. "I saw it all on TV. Quite a scene. I figured you'd be back."

He shook his head with disapproval.

"All those vultures out there—reporters, gawkers, TV executives crazed for ratings. Doesn't it make you crazy? One thing about this place, you don't have to deal with that kind of barbarity. Sure, we've got our own various kinds of barbarity, but really, I prefer it. It's like I tell everybody here, freedom is overrated. Do they believe me? Never."

Riley heard Bill's derisive snort. She found it a bit weird herself to hear this kind of moralizing from a multiple murderer. But she reminded herself that Shane Hatcher was no ordinary monster. She thought that even if she were to talk to him every single day for years on end, he'd always be able to surprise her—

and probably also to scare her.

"You were right about everything," Riley said. "The perpetrator was tormented as a kid. His mother chained him up, he was bullied in an orphanage—bullied by other kids, and also by the nuns who were supposed to take care of him."

"What else have you found out?" Hatcher asked.

"He's been killing since he was a kid," Riley said. "He slit his own mother's throat when he was ten. A year later, he slit another kid's throat and burned down the orphanage. He was institutionalized for years, but he convinced everybody he was fine, including his doctor. That's why he's free now."

Hatcher nodded knowingly.

"Something's different now, isn't it?" he said. "He's changed his *modus operandi*. That's why you want to talk to me."

Riley could see that Bill was leaning forward and paying close attention now. Her partner could be disdainful, but he never had a problem appreciating whatever sources of information turned out to be valuable.

"This guy is moving faster now," Bill said. "He's not keeping his victims alive for as long."

Riley added, "And he didn't kill this latest victim the same way as the others. He did cut her throat, but not until after she was already dead."

"What was the cause of death?" Hatcher asked.

"Her neck was broken," Bill said.

Hatcher squinted his eyes with interest.

"I can tell you for sure, he didn't mean to do that. It was an accident. The throat-slitting—it's part of his ritual, he can't change it, not deliberately. So he did it afterwards, but that didn't work for him. He's losing control. He's going to move even faster now, trying to get his equilibrium back. But he can't. Nothing will work for him. Nothing will go right. He'll make mistakes."

Hatcher paused and thought for a moment.

"Don't underestimate the power of his psychosis. What he does isn't about trying to get any advantage, like money or status. It isn't about taking revenge. And he definitely doesn't do it for thrills. This guy is absolutely driven by something he doesn't understand. He may not even want to do what he's doing."

Riley realized she'd been thinking much the same thing all along.

"He's remorseful," she said.

"That's right. He feels guilty as hell. And the only way he can think of to absolve himself of all that guilt is …"

374

Hatcher gestured to Riley to finish his thought.

"To keep right on killing," she said. "To appease the demons driving him."

Hatcher nodded and smiled. "Smart girl. It doesn't make sense, but that's the way he is. His desperation is mounting and that might give you an advantage. He won't just disappear, go into hiding. Not for long."

Hatcher drummed his fingers and added with a slight smirk, "Whether you can catch him before he kills somebody else—well, that's up to you. Glad that's your job, not mine. That's another thing that's no part of life here in the Big House. "

Suddenly Hatcher called out, "Guard, I think we're through here."

Riley was startled. She'd expected to be able to ask a few more questions. Hatcher obviously had different ideas, and she knew better than to argue with him about it. Besides, he'd told them a lot in very short order.

Hatcher leaned across the table toward Bill and Riley.

"One more thing," he said quietly. "I can feel all the fighting going on between you two. Get over it. I'm not saying you're good for each other. You're probably bad as hell for each other. But you get good things done when you're together. That matters more in the long run than all the other stuff."

He gazed closely at Bill, then pointed to the wedding band on his finger and said, "And forget about trying to fix things with your wife. It can't be done. She'll never understand the kind of life you've chosen. Or that has chosen you."

Riley could see Bill's jaw drop with shock.

Then Hatcher turned to her and said, "And you. Stop fighting it."

Riley was on the verge of asking, *"Fighting what?"*

But no, she had to draw the line at taking personal advice from a cold-blooded murderer. That couldn't be healthy.

Not even if he's right, she thought. *And he probably is.*

"Oh, and something else," Hatcher said. "You two are just like all the cops and investigators I've ever met. You psych yourselves into thinking you're immortal, even if you know better. Don't let yourselves do that with this guy."

Hatcher's voice took on an added urgency.

"He's wounded where it hurts most—in his soul. There's nothing more dangerous than a wounded animal. Watch out. Don't get as sloppy as he's getting."

Hatcher rose from his chair and smirked again.

"He's liable to kill one of you before he's done."

CHAPTER THIRTY SIX

The next morning, Hatcher's words kept rattling through Riley's mind.

He's liable to kill one of you before he's done.

Before that, she hadn't been thinking about the chain killer as a direct threat to her or other agents. The victims he sought out, took, and murdered were of a specific type. But she knew better than to ignore Hatcher's warning. The man had uncanny insight, apparently born of years of focusing on human behavior from his special perspective in a high-security prison

Even here, in the ultra-secure Albany FBI field office, considering those words created an irrational but palpable sense of danger. It seemed almost as if Eugene Fisk was among them right here and now, unseen but poised and ready to snatch one of these agents from a desk. It didn't make sense, but there it was.

Riley was walking through the open area where agents at desks were taking phone calls, collecting tips and leads. The air was filled with phone chatter. Riley was moving from desk to desk, asking about everybody's progress—or lack of it.

At one desk, a young male agent was just ending a phone call.

"What was it about?" she asked.

The agent shook his head wearily.

"A teenaged girl over in Searcy was sure that her Uncle Joe was our guy," he said. "He fit the description. But too many details don't fit. I asked about a stutter, and he talks just fine. If what she told me is true, though, Uncle Joe is definitely a perv who ought to be behind bars. I referred her to Family Services."

"Keep at it," she said, patting him on the shoulder. "We'll get something soon."

She looked across the room at all the focused and dedicated faces, doing their best to find Eugene Fisk. As expected, hundreds of people had called the hotline number, many of them suspicious of a neighbor or relative.

Since no mention had been made to the media about a stutter, asking callers about that was a quick way to find out that the lead was false. Callers often said something like, "Well, no, he doesn't stutter, but he's a mean creep."

And of course, countless people had spotted white Ford vans

up and down the Hudson River Valley. Those tips were harder to sort through, but the agents were doing their best to filter the information. Lucy was also working there in the room, helping the field agents sort out plausible leads from the loads of useless chatter. They were passing any credible tips along to Bill, who had been assigned as the lead agent on the case.

Deciding that it was time to see how he was doing, Riley made her way to the temporary office Bill had been given. When she opened the door and peered inside, he gestured for her to come in.

"Anything new?" Riley asked as she walked in and sat down.

"Not a damn thing," Bill growled. "We've had five confessions so far—guys who turned themselves in in different towns. Nothing but your garden-variety attention whores."

Riley sighed with discouragement. At her best, she could get into the mind of a true serial killer. But the mind of a wannabe psychopath remained an impenetrable mystery to her. What on earth could these guys be thinking?

Just then, Lucy poked her head in the door. Her face was set with determination.

"We've got something," she said, coming into the office. "I'm afraid it's sort of a good news, bad news situation."

She gave Riley and Bill copies of a printout.

"These are transcriptions of three recorded calls," Lucy explained. "They're all from people in Talmadge, a town about halfway between here and Reedsport. Each one of these people called about a guy who calls himself Eugene Ossinger. He fits the description perfectly, right down to the stutter."

Riley skimmed the transcripts.

"I see that he drives a white Ford van," she said.

"Right," Lucy said. "It didn't occur to any of our callers to write down the license number before our bulletins got out. The van's not there now. But two of them remembered it as having Pennsylvania plates."

"Sounds like him all right," Bill said. "What's the bad news?"

Lucy sat down beside his desk.

"We also got a call directly from the Talmadge police department," she said. "One of these people had called them first. The local cops have been to the scene already, and a SWAT team too. Eugene Ossinger's not there anymore. Nobody knows where he's gone."

Riley refused to be discouraged.

"It's a start," she said. "Let's get over there right away."

*

About a half an hour later, Bill, Lucy, and Riley arrived in Talmadge, a little town on the west bank of the Hudson. When Bill pulled the car into the address they'd been given, the place was already taped off and surrounded by local cops and members of a SWAT team. A few neighbors were gathered nearby. Everybody seemed to be just waiting around for the FBI agents they knew were on the way.

The three agents got out of the car and strode toward the house. Bill introduced himself and his companions to the cop in charge.

"He must have known he'd been spotted," one cop told them. "He was gone before we could get here."

"Let's have a look at the premises," Riley said. They walked through the front door into a very small living room. The rest of the house included a single bedroom, a rudimentary bathroom, and a mini-kitchen. The old and worn furniture looked like it had been used by many renters.

As Riley and Lucy poked around, Bill nodded and said, "I'll go look in the basement."

Riley noticed a few signs of a recent struggle, including a broken lamp. Otherwise, everything in the house was reasonably neat and clean. The place struck Riley as a sensible choice for someone with a minuscule income. She figured that Eugene patched together a living by doing odd jobs of one kind or another. The bedroom closet held a few ragged clothes. Riley guessed that he had taken whatever he could with him, although he probably didn't have much to his name.

She heard Lucy call out from the kitchen, "There's just a little food in the refrigerator. Nothing unusual."

Riley stepped out of the bedroom just in time to see Bill come back from the basement.

"This is his place, all right," Bill said. "Come have a look."

Riley and Lucy followed Bill down a short flight of wooden steps to a bare, concrete floor.

A bloodstained cot was in the middle of the small, cell-like space. There could be no doubt about it. That was where he'd kept and tormented his victims, probably enchained and straitjacketed all during their captivity.

A strange calm settled over Riley. She was here at last, in the very heart of the killer's world. She was exactly where she needed to be.

"Give me a minute alone," she said to Bill.

Bill nodded. Of course, he understood exactly what she meant. So did Lucy by now. They both went back upstairs and shut the door behind them.

Riley took in the scene. A single overhead light was already on, probably switched on by the local police. She saw that the windows were tightly covered, so if that light was off, the room would be completely dark.

God only knew how many hours of total darkness the three women had endured in Eugene Fisk's clutches. But what the women had felt mattered little to Riley at the moment. This was her chance to learn something about what Eugene himself felt and thought, how his sick mind worked.

Riley found herself looking at a bulletin board atop a beat-up wooden table against one wall. This seemed to be a shrine of sorts. Neatly arranged on the tabletop were various items that had no doubt belonged to the women he brought here—shoes, a badge, a nametag, some buttons. Fastened to the bulletin board were all kinds of mementoes—obituaries, news stories, photos that he himself had taken of the gravesites.

Riley took a deep breath, reaching for the thoughts of the fiend who had haunted this dismal place. An insight began to take shape in inside her.

This is more than a shrine, she thought. *It's a sacred altar.*

As long as he'd held them captive, the women had been quivering, moaning, starving masses of flesh, blood, and bone. They had been under his uneasy, precarious control. But upon leaving the world, they had become avenging spirits, like the Furies of Greek legend.

Whatever items he left to appease them, whatever tears of regret he shed over this table, were all in vain. He could never, ever make amends for the suffering he had caused them.

On the opposite side of the room Riley saw another table. A rusted steel vise was fastened to the side, a vestige of long ago when it had been used as a worktable. A pegboard on the wall behind the table had once been filled with tools, but was now empty.

Riley sensed that this table, too, had a story. She went over to it and looked closely at its surface, studying strange patterns of scratches in the worn top. What were those patterns? What did they spell or mean?

A vision of chains filled her mind. These were the marks left by chains. He'd kept piles of them here, sometimes coiled neatly and other times stretched out the full length of the table. He'd always handled them with the utmost reverence.

For the chains, too, were deities of a sort. Chains had ruled over him since childhood, when his mother had chained him in his own home, and again at the children's home, where the nuns had chained the door to his room shut.

He couldn't help but gather up more and more of them throughout his life. And here, right here, was where they'd called out to him, commanding him, instructing him. But like the spirits of the women, they were always unappeasable, no matter how devotedly he served them.

Riley looked back and forth between the two tables. These were both altars, and they were the twin polestars that steered his life—one an axis of guilt, shame, and repentance, and the other of impotent futility, always mocking the helpless child that he still truly was.

But unlike the table with the pictures and the mementoes, the table that had harbored the chains was now empty. What did that mean?

Riley breathed deeply, in and out, allowing herself to empathize with what Eugene was going through right now.

He'd taken the chains with him, of course. He couldn't leave them here. Without them, he'd have no purpose in life. However much he might hate what they made him do, they provided the only meaning he could cling to.

She also sensed how uprooted and lost he must feel, exiled from his sacred altars. He was alone and more desperate than ever, and the chains were doubtless furious with him. He must be frantic right now, struggling to regain some footing.

Just then she was hit by a realization. She dashed up the stairs and opened the door. Bill and Lucy were upstairs waiting for her to finish her private vigil.

"I know where we can find him," Riley said.

CHAPTER THIRTY SEVEN

The cemetery was silent and dark. Here, away from the drive that ran through the property, the only light came from the bright moon in the sky.

But moonlight will be enough, Riley thought. Her confidence was high.

She was looking out from behind a large marble angel with widespread wings. The sculpture stood on the hillside above a group of graves below. One of those graves was fresh. Carla Liston had been buried there that morning.

In the moonlight, Riley could easily see the walkway and the cluster of headstones below. When she and Bill had come out here a little while ago, she'd noticed a group of graves off to the right that were enclosed by a metal fence with sharp pickets. The angel she was hiding behind overlooked them all.

Riley hadn't attended the funeral that morning. She'd felt certain that Eugene wouldn't be there—not with all the media attention he'd gotten. Bill and Lucy had gone, checking out the crowd just in case, scanning for anyone resembling the computer-aged photo. Myra Cortese and several other nurses had kept watch as well. But Riley had been right, the killer wasn't there.

Instead of going to the funeral, Riley had spent her morning at the hotel with April. They were getting along well right now. Riley felt their relationship growing stronger, and she believed that this time it might last. At least, she thought, the bond felt sturdy enough to survive the rest of the teenage tumult that was certain to come.

Riley had saved her own keen watchfulness for tonight. And now here she was. Bill was also keeping watch, hidden in a grove of trees off to one side of Carla Liston's grave.

After her moment of realization in Eugene's basement, there wasn't a doubt in Riley's mind that the chain killer would show up here. She knew that those two sacred altars had given him the only meaning he had in life. The one he'd left behind made his appearance here a certainty. He simply had to find an outlet for his terrible remorse.

But the stakeout had to be conducted discreetly. Riley and Bill had decided to come here alone, taking care to remain almost invisible. Eugene would be especially vigilant right now. Even a few cops and agents stationed at the graveyard entrances would be sure to catch his attention.

Even so, the Albany office knew what Bill and Riley were up to. There were plenty of agents at strategic locations nearby, all on the lookout for Eugene or his white van. Lucy was with them, helping to coordinate their efforts. Riley was sure that she and Bill would spot Eugene—and she was equally sure that he couldn't get away.

Suddenly she heard hushed voices nearby. She whirled around and saw a young couple laughing and giggling as they approached along a path. It looked like a pair of teenagers who thought they'd found a great place to make out.

Riley stepped out from behind the marble angel and stopped them. She held out her badge in the moonlight, and put her forefinger to her lips to silence them.

The boy and the girl looked thoroughly startled. Did they realize that Riley was here looking for a killer? Riley didn't care as long as they went away. Sure enough, that's exactly what they did, turning around and quietly disappearing among the trees in the direction they'd come from.

Riley returned to her hiding place behind the angel and leaned her forehead on its wing, peering out beneath the marble feathers. The night was quiet for a long time after that.

Again, she remembered Hatcher's words …

"He's wounded where it hurts most—in his soul. There's nothing more dangerous than a wounded animal."

She also thought of something else that the Sing Sing inmate had said to her …

"Stop fighting it."

He might have meant a whole host of things—her obsession with work or her attraction to Bill, just for starters. She'd probably never know what he'd had in mind. Maybe it was just as well. And anyway, this was not the time or place to be wondering about it.

Just then she saw a movement down among the gravestones. The figure of a smallish-looking man crept stealthily along, occasionally turning on a flashlight. She drew her gun and stepped silently out from behind the angel.

The man walked up to Carla Liston's grave. He shined the flashlight on the stone, clearly checking the name. He dropped some flowers on the grave—daisies, she could see in the beam from the flashlight.

Adrenaline shot through Riley's body. The chain killer had

left daisies at the grave in Reedsport. This was definitely him. Eugene Fisk had come to show his remorse to the woman he had murdered.

His face was angled away, and Riley moved down the hillside toward him as quietly as she could. Even so, he must have heard her. He turned and looked in her direction, then whirled around and ran.

Riley took off after him. She resisted the urge to call out to Bill. She was sure that Bill had seen what was going on and was already on the move.

Riley followed the killer, weaving through the maze of headstones and statues. She was surprised by his sudden display of catlike agility. She'd long guessed that Eugene Fisk wasn't very strong, and she was probably right. But she hadn't anticipated that he was so nimble and fast. She wondered if he could even see in the dark better than she could.

She was gaining on him when she tripped over a small headstone. She staggered and almost fell flat. By the time she regained her balance, she couldn't see the killer anywhere. She stood completely still, watching and listening.

She heard movement off to one side. When she turned, she saw that it was Bill, who had been running close behind her. He, too, seemed to have lost track of the man. He stopped in his tracks.

Both Riley and Bill stood motionless, scanning the whole area. Soon there came a flicker of light that briefly revealed a figure ahead of him. The man had turned a flashlight quickly on and off to help see the path.

Riley and Bill both broke into a run toward where the light had appeared. As she ran, an image came into Riley's mind. As a little girl she'd been out catching fireflies, following the flashes in the dark. She remembered the sheer impossibility of catching an airborne firefly after seeing it flash.

Then she heard Bill cursing. He had run into the spiky metal fence that surrounded a set of graves. Riley managed to stop just before she hit the spikes herself. She cut to one side to get around the fence, and Bill headed in the other direction.

But when they got to the far side of the fenced graves, the figure they were chasing was nowhere to be seen. There was no sound or motion other than their own.

"Damn it," Riley heard Bill murmur just a few feet away from her.

He took out his cell phone and called Lucy to alert the surrounding agents that the suspect was on the move. Meanwhile,

Riley kept searching, shining her flashlight everywhere. When Bill finished talking, he also took up the search again.

Riley looked everywhere she could—behind trees, statues, some of the larger headstones, and the doorway of a mausoleum. Finally, her path converged with Bill's at a parking lot that was empty of cars. His hand was bleeding from his collision with the fence.

"Son of a bitch," he growled. "Well, he won't get far—not with so many agents all over town."

But Riley had a sinking feeling down in her gut. Their quarry's agility and swiftness had taken her completely by surprise. She also felt sure that he was too smart to have parked his van anywhere nearby. Again, she remembered how hard it was to trap a firefly in the darkness.

"No," she said to Bill, catching her breath. "We've lost him."

CHAPTER THIRTY EIGHT

It was dawn, and the chains were grumbling. Eugene had passed the second night huddled in the passenger seat of his van, afraid to sleep in the back where the chains might overcome him. They were angry.

"I keep telling you," he said sleepily, "there was nothing else to do."

But the muttering continued. Eugene knew that there was no point in trying to explain things all over again—that he'd been identified, and that the police would soon come to his house, and that he had to flee and take all the chains with him. Otherwise they'd be alone there. And what would happen to them when they were discovered?

Eugene twisted around, trying to get the kinks out of his weary body. After his hairbreadth escape from the graveyard last night, he ached all over. He'd had no idea that he could run so fast or so far. And he'd covered a vast obstacle course—through back yards and over fences until he could reach the van. He'd taken care not to park it near the graveyard.

He'd driven cautiously out of Albany, winding through the smallest streets and alleys, aware that cops must be on the lookout for him. He'd breathed a huge sigh of relief when he left the city on a small, southbound road and finally pulled off into a thickly wooded area to get some sleep.

Now Eugene knew he would have to go out on the road again and he had no idea where it would take him. And even though he'd disguised the van, he was still nervous about that. Years ago, realizing that a day like this might come, he'd stolen New York license plates and ordered magnetic decorations. With big colorful flowers on each side and small signs on the doors naming an imaginary business, he hoped it would pass as a florist's delivery vehicle.

He reached into the bag of food he'd brought along when he left his house. Only a single stale donut was left. He munched on it slowly.

"Where can I go?" he asked the chains.

But their murmuring was all confused, with some irritable voices saying to drive north, others to drive south, and still others telling him to head west into the Catskills. He'd never known the chains to be so quarrelsome among themselves. They'd been like this ever since he'd bungled the killing of the last woman, breaking her neck instead of slitting her throat.

He knew that it was all his fault. Everything was his fault.

Still, he had to drive somewhere. He started the van and began to pull out from among the trees. As the van rocked over the bumpy ground, the chains rattled noisily. He turned back toward them.

"What do you want now?" he demanded.

Then came a loud screeching of tires and the blare of a car horn. He braked hard and brought the van to a stop. Because of the chains' distracting rattle, he'd pulled out onto the road in front of an approaching car.

Now the driver was staring at him in shocked and angry surprise. Eugene swerved his van into the far lane and continued on his way.

Forcing himself to pay attention, he drove slowly past a few houses, a restaurant, and a post office. He hoped that nobody in the little village would notice him. When the road was again lined by trees, he relaxed a little.

But the chains were agitated again. They wanted something. They always wanted something.

In a few moments, he saw a woman walking toward him along the side of the road. She was wearing white. He thought it looked like a waitress uniform. She wasn't a nurse or a guard like the others, but still …

"Her?" he asked the chains.

He heard them murmur with approval.

He pulled onto the shoulder and stopped his van, but left the motor running. He got out, went around to the back and opened the doors. He picked up a heavy handful of chains.

By that time, the woman was walking past him on the edge of the road.

"Do you have some sort of problem?" she asked, stepping toward him with a polite smile. "There's a repair shop …"

But then her expression froze with horror. She recognized him. Just as she turned to run, Eugene smashed the chains into the side of her head. She fell to her knees with a cry, and he hit her again. He caught the unconscious woman beneath her arms. Fortunately she was small enough and light enough for him to handle. He dragged her into the van and scrambled back into the driver's seat.

"I hope you'll be happier now," he said to the chains.

But as he drove, a new wave of despair began to sweep over him. How could he possibly deal with this woman in a manner that would fully quell the chains? For one thing, he had no place to keep her. He'd have to kill her much too quickly. And where could he even do it? Where could he take her now?

The road still wound among trees. After a time it bent to the right, led across railroad tracks, and ended at an old marina. There was a ramshackle pier with a couple of old fishing boats tied to it. A massive rusted steel structure loomed over the pier.

When he realized what the structure was, Eugene laughed aloud. He could hardly believe his luck. It was an old boat crane, used to lift small yachts and place them in the water. It didn't look like it had been used for a long time, but there was still a pulley up there on its arm. A cable ran through the pulley and dangled to the ground. It would be easy to hang the woman up here, where she could be found by her family and neighbors.

It would require outrageous daring, to do all this in the daylight.

So much the better, he thought.

Maybe the chains would be impressed.

To be sure that no watchers were nearby, he walked out onto the pier. He had to move carefully because some of the boards were missing and others were obviously weak. When he reached the end, he turned and surveyed the shore.

No one was in sight. He looked out over the water. A few boats were out there on the Hudson, but most were too far away to notice him. Someone on the craft nearest him did wave in a friendly manner. Eugene waved back and watched the boat move away. Letters on the side spelled *Suzy.*

The Suzy, he thought. *What would it be like to be out there on a boat called the* Suzy?

Standing on the pier's end, Eugene was seized by a strange craving. If he had a boat and could go out on the water, could the chains follow him? How could they?

Out there he might be free. He couldn't remember what it felt like to be free.

Two old boats were tied up at the pier. They were both floating and seaworthy. Could he get one of the engines going and sail away from here forever?

But then he heard a loud groan from the van. The woman was starting to regain consciousness. He had to go subdue her and put her into a straitjacket and chains. Then he had to go through with the rest of his horrible task. The chains gave him no choice. They never would give him a choice.

CHAPTER THIRTY NINE

Riley knew in her gut that something was about to break. She didn't know why she felt that way. They'd chosen their route on the basis of some pretty scanty information. Bill was driving, and the three of them were headed south from Albany.

After Eugene Fisk's escape from the graveyard yesterday, the public was responding to bulletins with more calls than ever. Field agents had spread out in all directions trying to follow up on anything that seemed at least remotely plausible. There had been a cluster of sightings reported on the highways south of Albany, and Bill, Riley, and Lucy had decided to head out in that direction.

"How far we from Callaway?" Lucy asked from the back seat.

Riley turned and saw that Lucy was looking at a text message. It was probably an update from the Albany office.

"We just passed a turnoff for Callaway," Bill said.

"We need to go back and take it," Lucy said.

Without asking any questions, Bill slowed the vehicle and turned it around. As he drove, Lucy explained the tip she had received.

"A man in Callaway said some crazy guy pulled out from nowhere on the road in front of his car. It was a white delivery van for a business called June's Flowers. The man got a good look at the driver. He swears it's our man, and that he was headed toward an old marina. Everybody in the town has been notified to stay away from there."

Riley's heart quickened. Yes, this was it. She was sure of it. The business name came as no surprise at all. Everyone at Albany's HQ knew perfectly well that Eugene Fisk had probably disguised his van by now.

"Lucy, send a return message that we're on our way," Bill said, making the turn that he'd passed by a few moments before. "We're liable to need backup. Riley, check the GPS to see what we're driving into."

Riley brought up the map on her cell phone. She was heartened by what she saw.

"We're on the right road," she said. "It goes through Callaway, then straight to the marina. It ends in a cull-de-sac. If Eugene Fisk went there, this road is his only way out."

Bill put his foot on the accelerator as the siren blared.

He slowed down when they crossed the town line into Callaway. A few anxious-looking residents stood on the sidewalk watching them go by. On the far side of the village, local police had set up a roadblock. Bill held up his FBI badge and they waved him on through. He sped up again and in a matter of minutes, the marina came in sight.

Bill brought the car to a stop and turned off the siren.

Riley's heart pumped faster. There it was, parked beside a rusted crane-like structure—a white van decorated with flowers and the business name June's Flowers. The three agents jumped out of the car and headed for the van. Bill got there first and yanked the rear door open.

A woman was huddled on the floor, bound with a straitjacket and chains. Her eyes opened and she moaned aloud through the chain that had been wrapped around her face to gag her.

She's alive, Riley thought with relief. They had gotten here in time.

But there was no sign of Eugene Fisk.

"Lucy, take care of the woman," Riley said. "Bill and I will find him."

Riley headed around the van to search the shoreline, but she stopped at the sound of Bill's voice.

"Riley!"

She turned and looked at him. His eyes met Riley's with a determined and yet sympathetic expression.

"This guy is not Peterson," Bill said.

For a second, Riley couldn't understand what he meant.

"What?" she said.

Bill narrowed his eyes and said much more slowly, "He's not Peterson."

In a moment of clarity, Riley understood exactly what he meant. Her use of deadly force against Peterson had bordered on vengefulness. But the Bureau hadn't raised questions about it—not after all she'd suffered at Peterson's hands. This situation was different. They should be able to bring in Eugene Fisk alive.

This kind of instantaneous communication was one thing she treasured most about working with Bill. She'd missed it during their estrangement.

"I understand," she told him.

Guns in hand, Riley and Bill moved around the van. There was a drop to the water. Along the high ground, clusters of trees could easily hide the killer. Riley was sure they were close to him now. She moved carefully toward the trees on the left. Bill moved off to the right.

Riley had realized that the killer wasn't where she was searching when she heard Lucy's voice call out, "I see him!"

Riley turned and saw that Lucy was headed away from the van. She had drawn her weapon and was running toward the pier. The horrible little man was a few yards out on the old structure.

"Stop right there!" Lucy called out to him, her weapon raised. "Hands where I can see them!"

Eugene stopped and turned, his hands raised above his head. In one hand he was clutching a bundle of chains.

Riley drew her own weapon and walked toward them. She felt a flood of relief. This was going to end easily and without violence. What had happened with Peterson was not going to happen here.

Lucy stepped out onto the pier, focused intently on Eugene. But after a few steps, a rotting board broke out from under her, and she fell into a tangle.

"Damn it!" Lucy cried out.

Eugene moved with the same dexterity and speed that he'd shown at the graveyard. In an instant, he grabbed and held Lucy from behind. He wrapped the chain around her neck with one hand. With the other had he took a straight-edged razor out of his pocket. He flipped open the blade and held it at Lucy's throat. Her face was contorted with pain.

Eugene was trying desperately to talk.

"Drop—drop—"

Riley knew that he was trying to tell her to drop her weapon. She wasn't ready to do that.

Lucy let out a scream of pain as Eugene pulled her loose from the broken board. He forced her forward along the pier back toward the shore. It looked like her ankle was broken.

"Let—let me—"

Riley understood. The chain killer wanted to take Lucy back to his van as a hostage and drive out of here undisturbed.

She heard Bill's voice from nearby.

"Easy, easy," he was saying to Eugene. "You can't get out of here. You know that."

But Riley saw that neither she nor Bill had a feasible shot. Lucy's body formed too effective a shield.

"Let—let me—" Eugene said again. He was on the shore now and backing toward the van with his hostage.

Bill was standing beside Riley, his Glock raised.

Riley's thoughts clicked away as she tried to assess the situation. She knew one thing for certain. Eugene Fisk wasn't bluffing with the razor. He'd slit women's throats before, and he'd do it again in an instant if either Riley or Bill made the wrong move.

Shane Hatcher had been exactly right.

He's liable to kill one of you before he's done.

Riley glanced over at Bill.

"Stand down, Bill," she said.

Bill looked at her with surprise. But then he lowered his weapon.

Riley stooped and placed her weapon on the ground.

"I'm putting down my gun, Eugene," she said. "You can let her go. We can end this peacefully."

But Eugene was shaking his head.

"N—no," he stammered. He was still determined to make his escape with Lucy as a hostage. He continued dragging Lucy toward the van.

Riley looked directly into his eyes. He stared back, unable to break their gaze, as if hypnotized. His eyes were small and beady, but Riley saw terrible worlds in them—worlds of childhood suffering and adult humiliation, of pain both physical and emotional, and of almost unfathomable self-loathing.

"He's not Peterson," Bill had said just a few minutes ago.

Riley now knew that Bill had been more right than he'd realized.

Eugene Fisk was the most pitiable monster she'd ever encountered. And she could turn that insight to her advantage.

As Eugene waddled backwards dragging Lucy along, Riley moved slowly in the same direction.

"I know about the chains, Eugene," Riley said in a sympathetic voice. "I hear them too. You're not alone. You're not the only person who hears them. I do too."

Eugene stopped in his tracks. He looked positively stricken now. Riley was getting to him. She knew it.

She remembered something else that Shane Hatcher had said.

"He's wounded where it hurts most—in his soul."

And I'm probing that wound, Riley realized.

"Don't you hear what they're saying now, Eugene—the chains?" Riley went on. "They're saying it's over. You've uprooted them, you've failed them for the last time, and they're through with you. It's really over. The chains are saying so. I hear them. You do too."

Those small eyes were getting larger now. They glistened with tears.

"The chains don't want you to take this woman," Riley said. "She isn't what they need."

Eugene nodded with understanding.

"You know what the chains want you to do instead," Riley said.

Eugene nodded again.

Then he drew the blade across his own throat and sliced it deeply, all the way across.

Riley heard herself scream.

Eugene fell to the ground, clutching his throat, gurgling and coughing. Lucy was drenched in his spurting blood, but she was free of him now. She fell too, but rolled away from the wounded killer.

Riley threw herself upon Eugene as he twitched and writhed. Her hands fumbled around his throat, trying to staunch the bleeding, to plug up the rapidly escaping breath. It was no good. There was nothing she could do. His eyes were wide open, fearful and fading. In a matter of seconds, he lay motionless. She knew that he was dead.

Bill was standing at her side. He reached down and tried to help her to her feet.

"Come on," he said. "We've got to take care of the woman."

But Riley found that she couldn't stand.

"I killed him," she said.

"You did what you had to do," Bill said.

"No," Riley said. "I killed him."

She broke down and sobbed as the sound of approaching sirens filled the air.

CHAPTER FORTY

As she looked around her new townhouse, Riley felt freer, luckier, and richer than she ever had, even in the elegant house she used to share with Ryan. This home, after all, was hers.

Even so, something was troubling her deep down.

What is it? she wondered.

She couldn't put her finger on it.

Without a doubt, this place was better than Riley had dreamed of. The main floor of the house was open, with the living and dining area flowing together and a large deck at the back. The kitchen was fabulous, more than Riley thought she would ever need, but Gabriela loved it.

And it had been Gabriela's room that had really sold the house to Riley. The basement room that opened to the little back yard had been converted into what the real estate agent called an "in-law suite." It was a big carpeted room with a gas fireplace and a private bathroom.

Gabriela was down there now, unpacking and organizing her things.

April came wandering out of the kitchen, munching on a sandwich.

"How are you coming with getting your room organized?" Riley asked.

"It's so big!" she said, beaming. "It's like twice the size of what I had! And so is the closet!"

Riley smiled, feeling happy for the first time in a long time. Feeling like a real mom.

"So is it ready for me to see yet?" Riley asked.

"Not yet. Just a few more things to put away. Then I'll need your help hanging some things on the wall."

"Just let me know when."

April swallowed the last of her sandwich. Then she said, "Mom."

"Yes."

"Mom, I love it! I love this house. I love my room."

"And I love you," Riley said, giving her daughter a hug.

April hugged her back and then scampered away upstairs.

Riley drew a deep breath of relief. Not only did her daughter love the new house, but she was once again the bubbly teenager who had been missing for months now.

She had been lucky to find the house on a tip from a co-worker before it actually went on the market. The drive to Quantico would only take her thirty minutes, and April would be able to get around by public transportation—no more hitchhiking ever. And she wouldn't have to change schools.

It certainly marked a new beginning, the start of a different life. She felt confident that it would be a better life for both April and herself. Her divorce was final, and Ryan was paying the support that he had promised. Riley and April both understood that their contact with Ryan would most likely be civil but infrequent. Riley thought that would probably be best for all of them.

Ryan had already moved on to a more suitable liaison, a divorced D.C. society woman who could support him in every way. Riley wouldn't be surprised if he moved closer to Washington sometime soon.

Yes, Riley thought, *this will suit all of us fine—April, Gabriela, and me.*

Still, some nagging discord kept whispering through her brain. She decided to ignore it. She looked around, thinking about where she would need to fill in with a new piece of furniture here and there.

Her thoughts were interrupted by the front doorbell. When she answered the door, Bill was standing outside.

"Just thought I'd stop by and see your new place," he said.

Riley could tell by his forced smile and his ragged, tired look that he was here for more than that.

"What's wrong?" she asked.

"Can I come in?" Bill said.

"Of course."

Bill came inside and the two of them sat down on the couch.

"Maggie is filing for divorce," Bill said. "I've already moved out, into an apartment near the BAU."

"I'm sorry," Riley said.

Bill shook his head with confusion and dismay.

"It's just that I've tried so damn hard for so many years," he said. "It's weird to think that it's really all over. Maggie and I have been strangers for a long time. But the kids … I don't want to be a stranger to my boys."

Riley patted his hand.

"You won't be," she said.

"You don't know that," he said.

Riley sighed. Bill was right. She didn't know anything of the kind. There were far too many things in life that she didn't know.

Bill seemed eager to change the subject.

"That last case," he began, then shook his head and sighed. She could see that it was still haunting him, too. In some ways it was comforting to see she was not the only one who was haunted. "Have we ever dealt with one that twisted?"

Riley thought for a moment.

"Twisted? No, that's not exactly right. He was the most damaged, though."

"Damaged, twisted, take your pick," Bill said, shaking his head. "Chains and straitjackets and a straight razor—it's a new combination for me."

Riley remembered her experience of the chain killer's mind.

"Eugene was the most reluctant killer I've known," she said. "But he would never have stopped if we hadn't caught up with him."

"And we did stop him," Bill said. "We're good at that. Together, we're very good."

*

After a short while, Bill left. He'd said he didn't want to bother Riley when things were going so well for her. She'd protested that he was no bother, that he was never a bother and never would be, but he went away anyhow.

As she watched him drive off, she thought about what a deeply decent man he was. She was lucky to have him as a partner and a friend. Whatever happened between them in the days ahead, she hoped their friendship wouldn't be ruined. They'd come too close to losing it already.

Then she walked through her house and out onto the back deck. Several houses down, children were playing in the yard. Riley had longed for exactly this—a bustling neighborhood where people went about normal lives in an ordinary way.

What was missing? What was wrong?

Then she remembered—she still had trouble looking into a mirror. The faces of all those victims and monsters kept looking back. And now there was Eugene's face also, his beady eyes full of hurt, guilt, and self-hatred. She'd understood what had gone on behind those eyes only too well. And as horrible a man as he was, his fate still haunted her.

She had merely fought with Peterson and killed him in a

primal way, in a blur of self preservation, for herself and for her daughter.

With Eugene, she had used her powers of empathy and understanding.

With Eugene, she had used deadly force.

And not a person in the world could understand that except Riley.

She knew that more monsters lurked out there in the world, probably in more variations that even she had yet imagined. It was her job to stop them. But what would she do the next time she faced those who tormented and destroyed?

She remembered what Hatcher had told her.

"Stop fighting it."

She still didn't know what "it" was—but she was starting to think that it was something huge, maybe as big as her whole life. And what did it mean that a multiple murderer understood something about her that she didn't know herself?

Her cell phone interrupted her questions. She saw that the call was from Brent Meredith. She knew he wasn't calling just to find out how the move was going.

Her heart beat faster. He was calling about a new case.

She stood there and looked at her buzzing cell phone. She turned and looked away, looked out the window, down the block, at her new house—anywhere but at the phone.

Yet still, it kept consistently buzzing. It was like her life, like the flood of cases that never ended, always buzzing at her.

Stop fighting it.

Had he meant fighting the urge to take on a case? Or had he meant something else? Fighting having a life? Living life for the first time?

Riley watched her phone buzz, again and again.

This time, she was not so quick to answer it.

And she did not know if she would again.

ONCE CRAVED
(A Riley Paige Mystery—Book #3)

When prostitutes turn up dead in Phoenix, not much attention is paid. But when a pattern of disturbing murders is discovered, the local police soon realize a serial killer is on a rampage and they are in way over their heads. Given the unique nature of the crimes, the FBI, called in, knows they will need their most brilliant mind to crack the case: Special Agent Riley Paige.

Riley, recovering from her last case and trying to pick up the pieces of her life, is at first reluctant. But when she learns of the grievous nature of the crimes and realizes the killer will soon strike again, she is compelled. She begins her hunt for the elusive killer and her obsessive nature takes her too far—perhaps too far, this time, to pull herself back from the brink.

Riley's search leads her into the unsettling world of prostitutes, of broken homes, and shattered dreams. She learns that, even amongst these women, there are glimpses of hope, hope being robbed by a violent psychopath. When a teenage girl is abducted, Riley, in a frantic race against time, struggles to probe the depths of the killer's mind. But what she discovers leads her to a twist that is too shocking for even her to imagine.

A dark psychological thriller with heart-pounding suspense, ONCE CRAVED is book #3 in a riveting new series—with a beloved new character—that will leave you turning pages late into the night.

Book #4 in the Riley Paige series is also now available!

Blake Pierce

Blake Pierce is author of the bestselling RILEY PAGE mystery series, which includes eleven books (and counting). Blake Pierce is also the author of the MACKENZIE WHITE mystery series, comprising seven books (and counting); of the AVERY BLACK mystery series, comprising six books; and of the new KERI LOCKE mystery series, comprising four books (and counting).

An avid reader and lifelong fan of the mystery and thriller genres, Blake loves to hear from you, so please feel free to visit www.blakepierceauthor.com to learn more and stay in touch.

BOOKS BY BLAKE PIERCE

RILEY PAIGE MYSTERY SERIES
ONCE GONE (Book #1)
ONCE TAKEN (Book #2)
ONCE CRAVED (Book #3)
ONCE LURED (Book #4)
ONCE HUNTED (Book #5)
ONCE PINED (Book #6)
ONCE FORSAKEN (Book #7)
ONCE COLD (Book #8)
ONCE STALKED (Book #9)
ONCE LOST (Book #10)
ONCE BURIED (Book #11)
ONCE BOUND (Book #12)

MACKENZIE WHITE MYSTERY SERIES
BEFORE HE KILLS (Book #1)
BEFORE HE SEES (Book #2)
BEFORE HE COVETS (Book #3)
BEFORE HE TAKES (Book #4)
BEFORE HE NEEDS (Book #5)
BEFORE HE FEELS (Book #6)
BEFORE HE SINS (Book #7)
BEFORE HE HUNTS (Book #8)

AVERY BLACK MYSTERY SERIES
CAUSE TO KILL (Book #1)
CAUSE TO RUN (Book #2)
CAUSE TO HIDE (Book #3)
CAUSE TO FEAR (Book #4)
CAUSE TO SAVE (Book #5)
CAUSE TO DREAD (Book #6)

KERI LOCKE MYSTERY SERIES
A TRACE OF DEATH (Book #1)
A TRACE OF MUDER (Book #2)
A TRACE OF VICE (Book #3)
A TRACE OF CRIME (Book #4)
A TRACE OF HOPE (Book #5)